"What we have, at large on Oerlikon, is a human who can initiate severe and extreme bodily changes, major structural modifications, without burning itself up in metabolic stress. This bespeaks fine control of an area we can't control ourselves. Plus its apparent immortality. For these reasons alone we would wish to examine it. But there is something more . . . that we defend ourselves from it."

"If it unravels who it was and why she was on Oerlikon in the condition she was in, we can expect a visitor, here on Heliarcos, perhaps other places:

"An immortal assassin who can change identity."

M.A. FOSTER
has written:

THE WARRIORS OF DAWN

THE GAMEPLAYERS OF ZAN

THE DAY OF THE KLESH

WAVES

THE MORPHODITE

TRANSFORMER

TRANSFORMER

M. A. FOSTER

D A W B o o k s , I n c .
Donald A. Wollheim, Publisher
1633 Broadway, New York, N.Y. 10019

(For color prints of Michael Whelan paintings, please contact:
Glass Onion Graphics, 172 Candlewood Lake Rd., Brookfield, CT 06804.)

FIRST PRINTING, APRIL 1983

1   2   3   4   5   6   7   8   9

DAW TRADEMARK REGISTERED
U.S. PAT. OFF. MARCA
REGISTRADA. HECHO EN U.S.A.

PRINTED IN U.S.A.

For Don and Elsie

. . . who put up with my erratic schedule and surprise packages with great good humor.

And for Betsy, with whom I proposed bizarre covers for this story at the '78 Worldcon, Phoenix.

1

"Civilization is not technology, as those who rely too heavily on technology find out. This is an error of both perception and judgment, which normally leads to conclusions which are dire, if not fatal."
—H. C., *Atropine*

Cesar Kham waited for the arrival of the Regents, occupying the time by reminding himself who he was now and where he was. To mistake one mutable identity for another, here, now, could have unpleasant consequences, not only for himself, but for many others. He began by denying the name, and the identity that went with it, an identity cultivated for almost two decades of standard years on Oerlikon. *I am not, here, Cesar Kham. If these people know that name at all, it is only as an obscure footnote to a datascan. That means nothing here. Here, on Heliarcos, I am Czermak Pentrel'k, which is who I was a long time ago.* The name was strange, seemed not to fit. He had come to think of himself as Cesar Kham, as had most of the long-timers in the Oerlikon Project. That was why so many of them retired there, still in the possession of their clandestine secrets. As many had been the flaws of Oerlikon, one got used to it, to its verities that changed, if at all, so slowly that the rate was imperceptible.

Some things remained the same, here as well. But one had to be observant, cautious. He forced himself to *observe* the chamber in which he waited, not just receive impressions: Bare, sparse, functional. There were some plain desks, for administrative aides, behind him, now empty. There was a podium at the place where he would stand, surrounded by a simple wooden rail on three sides. Before him, a long table covered by a metallic cloth. There were backless chairs, stools, behind that table. The ceiling was high and illuminated from the sides; the walls were hung with heavy draperies. As far as he could determine from where he stood, a point precisely located at the spot which divided the length of the room into the Golden Ratio, the room was a perfect cube.

Pentrel'k had chosen to wear the clothing of a service techni-

7

cian. This was a simple tunic top with a Roman collar, and pants of plain cut, both a uniform gray. In this clothing, he made a statement to those who would come here—that he considered himself a simple workman, of no pretensions. He had only done the duty that had been required of him by extraordinary circumstances. He had, formally, the right to wear the academic gown and the badges of excellence he had earned long ago, but he had left them behind. Arunda Palude would be doing the same, by common consent. Arunda? No longer. Here, she was Morelat Eickarinst.

They would see here not a professed member of their own exclusive circles, but a technician, a workman, a fixer. Pentrel'k was of less than average height, stocky of build, bald, with a slightly sallow complexion. His face was notable for a heavy, lumpy nose, deep-set brown eyes, a mouth which was harsh and sensual at the same time. His beard, shaven (even here) and not depilated, showed as a faint steel-blue sheen along the lines of his jaw.

Behind him, he heard the door open, and a rustling began, unbroken by conversation. He did not look around. Presently the Regents filed to the front of the hearing room and in line took their places, remaining standing until all were in place, whereupon they all sat, like a single organism. There were seven, and in this room, in this conclave, they held something more than the power of Life and Death.

They all wore dark gowns which concealed their bodies, and hoods. The gowns were ornamented only with small colored diamonds on the sleeves, right, left, or both. The one in the center wore two such diamonds, white, on the left. This one opened a bound document, without rattling it, and began immediately, without ceremony, "You are Czermak Pentrel'k."

"That is correct."

The central member continued, "You maintained on the world Oerlikon the identity Cesar Kham." The remarks were not intoned as questions, but as statements.

"I was so assigned."

"What were your duties there?"

Kham-Pentrel'k began, "I was Senior Field Evaluator."

"Explain in some detail, please."

"My function was to maintain security of the mission, and to evaluate all expressions of change, such as revolutionary movements, as well as activities on the part of the local government authorities. I spent the majority of my time in the city Marula, in the province Clisp, and in selected locations from which government power was exercised.''

A Regent, second left from center asked, ''Did you act independently or with permission?''

''Normally, with coordination and direction from Mission Central. There were circumstances when I could act voluntarily, but this was not required until the last events.''

The central Regent now asked, ''What did you do then, and why?''

Pentrel'k began slowly, as if trying to recall with exactitude, ''I was in Clisp, evaluating an odd incident, and making normal reports through our mnemonicist, Arunda Palude. I came to understand that I was, for unknown reasons, suddenly cut off from Central. Simultaneously, seemingly out of the ground, a series of rapid changes began happening. The situation in Clisp rapidly changed, and the locals there took control of their own affairs, seeing that the government was preoccupied. They were not challenged. I made my way back to Central, to report in person, and by the time I got there, disintegration of the central authority, that is, for the locals, was well advanced, and a low-grade civil war was on. Also the Head of Mission was absent, reportedly mad, and wandering somewhere. The Second Head of Mission was acting in an incompetent manner. Palude and I took command of the mission and salvaged what we could. Those who wished to leave Oerlikon were given a fair chance at it, and most made it. I turned Porfirio Charodei over to the authorties here when we arrived.''

''We have discussed events on Oerlikon with Charodei. You need not inquire his real identity.''

Pentrel'k made no comment.

The central Regent continued, ''Charodei has made some statements about events on Oerlikon which are difficult to credit.''

''I have heard some of these. At first, I did not believe them, but later I met the Lisak who claimed to have set the events off, and his story matched exactly with Charodei's. I worked with this individual for some time, and grew to distrust him greatly. He most urgently wished to come here. I suspected a devious plot on his part, revenge, whatnot, and had him ejected into space.''

The second on the left said, ''We understand the pressure of events was demanding; on the whole you did extremely well.

Yet, one can question the judgment involved in the execution of Luto Pternam. His organization had succeeded in an area of research we have not mastered to that degree yet, and his knowledge would have been invaluable.''

Pentrel'k said, ''I accept the criticism; yet also I say that I had the weight of decision; and Pternam had created a force that was out of control, and was wrecking his . . .''

''Yes?''

''I was going to say 'country,' but it was rather more than that. He held us responsible for the ruin of his world, and I felt certain his eagerness to come here was to unleash another such creature on us, and see us in the same ruin as his people.''

''That is most irrational. We did not ruin his country. He did.''

Pentrel'k paused, and said, ''I had the testimony of Pternam, and also that of Charodei. There were others whom we were able to interrogate. Given the equipment and time, he could probably do it again. On Oerlikon, whatever the creature did was limited to that world. I did not feel secure in bringing him here, but to secure his cooperation, I agreed to allow him to board the lighter.''

The Second said, ''You assumed we would let him operate unsupervised?''

''He found a way to do it there, which I would not have thought possible. We had evaluated Lisagor as being impermeable to ambitious plots. Yet Pternam made such an attempt. He failed only because his creation was *too* successful.''

''You believe that Pternam actually made up some sort of . . . assassin?''

''More than that! Some kind of changeling, and reportedly possessed of an ability to see into the heart of a society and bring it down.''

''We know. We heard it all, of Charodei. And something else we heard of Charodei: immortal.''

''I heard that and discounted it.''

''Charodei didn't. Given what we have on the changeling, it may be possible. That is why we have such high regrets that you left both Pternam and his creature behind.''

Pentrel'k did not flinch. He said, ''I remind you I had my hands full with recovering our people out of there. It could have turned against us and there'd have been one hell of a massacre. We lived minute by minute. As it was, we got out clean, and those who stayed were not endangered. As for Pternam, you have my reasons. I was there: I saw what happened to Lisagor.''

"We cannot fault the empiricism of your knowledge, nor the accomplishments you performed under stress. So now we wish to know what happened to the creature—what you know of it.''

"I know little, and that through Charodei and others. They thought they had it trapped after it changed, and then it vanished. There was a report that a woman Azart vanished during a raid in Marula, where she was. It was widely assumed by those who knew about the changeling that it was killed then, by accident.''

The Regents looked at one another, up and down the line. At last the one in the center spoke, "But this was not confirmed.''

"No. If I may add, I can say that Pternam had access to these reports and doubted them. He was obsessed with the idea that the creature would come after him and would live through anything to do so. I saw no evidence to support this objectively and devoted the time to the primary mission.''

"Charodei claimed that this creature was trained in survival attitudes and methodology in addition to its . . . other talents. And he also said that when acting in his role as member of the revolutionaries, he had operatives in contact with the creature, and that Pternam insisted on killing it.''

"I heard that, of Pternam. I did not hear that they were successful.''

"Indeed. We have a report from another informant that the operative assigned to the creature was found dead.''

"In the raid on Marula. . . .''

"No. Not in the raid. An accident. Witnesses said he had been playing in a game, and was injured. There had been a woman with him. She disappeared.''

Pentrel'k said nothing.

The central member said, "The prime computation is that the creature Pternam made changed identity and survived.''

Again, Pentrel'k said nothing.

"Let me explore this a little for you. . . . What we have, at large on Oerlikon, is a human who can initiate severe and extreme bodily changes, major structural modifications, without burning itself up in metabolic stress. This bespeaks fine control of an area we can't control ourselves. Plus its apparent immortality. For these reasons alone we would wish to examine it. But there is something more.''

Pentrel'k ventured, "What more could you want of it?''

"Not what we want of it, but that we defend ourselves from it?"

Pentrel'k said, hesitating, "Ah . . . what I heard of it was that it was highly oriented to its own world; I could see no reason then, on Oerlikon, to worry about its having an offworld target. I still see none."

The outermost member on the right said, "Did you hear in your contacts who this creature was originally?"

"I heard that it originally had been an elderly woman, a person of no consequence who was picked up by Pternam's goons."

"Does the name Jedily Tulilly mean anything to you?"

"No. That was, I believe, the name of the subject Pternam started with. The name has no significance to me."

The Regents now stopped and glanced at each other, all up and down the line, with a slow, measured cadence, the stuff of nightmares. Now Pentrel'k knew for certain that they were playing with him. Now they would reel the line in closer.

The central member said, "Charodei also knew nothing about that name, even though he has so reported it. We know that in the initial training and changes Pternam caused the creature to undergo, it forgot much; who could blame it? It knows the name, and that's an Oerlikon name, at that, but as far as we know, that is all it has of the identity. Yet if it survived, would it not come to want to know who it had been? Wouldn't you, had such an event happened to you?"

"I would want to know, yes. Sooner or later."

"This must not happen."

"Your pardon, Regent?"

"Pternam did not know what he had taken, the woman who called herself Jedily Tulilly in Lisagor on Oerlikon. You do not know. Charodei did not know. Palude did not know. We know. She was not a native of that world, and. . . ."

"Yes?"

". . . if that creature, assumed alive and well-hidden, starts looking for who he was, and finds anything, that would not be desirable."

"Continue."

"If it unravels who Jedily Tulilly was and why she was on Oerlikon in the condition she was in, we can expect a visitor . . . here, on Heliarcos, perhaps other places. An immortal assassin who can change identity."

Pentrel'k interrupted, "Surely you don't think that that creature can get off Oerlikon, with no more connection than that place has with the rest of the worlds, and find its way successfully here, or anywhere else. . . . ."

"If it remembers, or if it can deduce it out, it will have the necessary motivation. And we don't know who we are looking for. Do you see some of the problem?"

"Quarantine Oerlikon. That's simple enough."

"It's already broken. We cannot impose embargo without revealing the reason why we wish it imposed."

Pentrel'k suddenly felt more confidence. He was still in piercing danger, but they still had use for him. He said, "Somebody did something to Tulilly . . . something secret."

The central Regent said, "It is not important that you know what that was; or who Tulilly was in reality, or what she did. A heinous punishment for a heinous crime, that's the word. You also need not know who pronounced the sentence. You do very much need to comprehend the magnitude of this problem."

"Knowing no more than I do, it is difficult, but I do see that you do not wish to have this creature perambulating about."

"Exactly! We would like to have it here, for study, since we have lost Pternam and his files; but under control. Under iron control, and from Charodei's testimony, we are not sure we can control it. He reported Pternam feared it and took extraordinary security precautions. Failing that, we want it eradicated."

Pentrel'k said, "I see your desires clearly; but as the former Cesar Kham, a field operative, I would doubt the wisdom of trying to do both."

"Not both. One or the other. Known and demonstrable security, or elimination."

"Who will accomplish this mission?" He asked, but he already knew most of the answer.

"As you say, Cesar Kham is a field operative, a specialist in security."

"Cesar Kham is no specialist in murder and kidnapping."

"You secured the net; you took actions, where required."

"Cesar Kham made decisions; technicians, specialists, carried those decisions out."

Again, the mutual glancing back and forth. At last, the central Regent said, reflectively, "This may not be germane. Yet you and Palude are the ranking survivors of the mission on Oerlikon, and you are certainly more knowledgeable about conditions there than anyone else. You yourself we know to be a sensitive investigator.''

''All else aside, I appreciate your confidence. But if you have followed my career as closely as I assume you have, you also know that I did not unravel the last events in Clisp in time. Had I done so, perhaps I could have averted. . . .''

The central Regent said, ''No. You couldn't have. You wouldn't have suspected this kind of penetration. But now of course you can.''

Pentrel'k nodded. ''Yes. I suppose so. Damned difficult, though. You understand the difficulties?''

''We have some measure of it. You will have to be extremely cautious, and not alert it, because if it thinks you are hunting it, it has, apparently, ways to perceive your approach. So you won't get but one chance. And. . . .''

''And? Yes?''

''Don't miss. We can't send backup to Oerlikon, and once it gets loose in space, we cannot predict what it will do.''

''I think I understand what you have in mind. I assume all the necessary arrangements have been made.''

''Correct. We knew you would not refuse.''

''What choices do I have?''

''None.''

''May I speak with Charodei? He knows things about this I didn't have time to cover in more than cursory detail. . . .''

''Denied. A full report text will be made available to you. Many more than Charodei were interrogated, and the results have been synthesized. Charodei . . . is unavailable.''

''I see. When do I get to consult with Palude?''

''Immediately. She is waiting outside. She has the report. She also has the names you must contact there. That is all.''

It was dismissal. Yet he waited, before turning from the examination dock. ''What fault will you have against me if I kill it?''

''None. Assess proper risk and do what you must. There will be no censure. You have that under seal.''

''At the risk of the charge of impertinence, may I ask if I will be enlightened as to the ultimate causes of your concern?''

The central Regent smiled a most unpleasant smile. ''In the normal course of events, after your return from the field, permanently, you might well reach the Board of Regents; possession of this data pertaining to the Tulilly case is an integral part of the process of acceptance of the responsibility of office. Possession and acquiescence with, in full.''

"Then there is something I would have to agree to.''

"You might say that.''

"Are there those who refuse to . . . acquiesce?''

"There have been some.''

"What happens in these cases?''

"They share Tulilly's portion. Are there any further questions? Then you have leave to depart. Palude waits outside, and has the details.'' The Regents stood, abruptly, folding their hands in their voluminous sleeves, in the formal manner of their tradition. The interview was over.

2

―――――――――

"Individuals attain the power, the Mana, to create something merely by asking for it; Institutions, at vast and great labor, obtain finally the power to obstruct."
―*H. C., Atropine*

This time, they would wait for him to leave the hearing room, after which the Regents would leave in their own good time. Pentrel'k stepped out of the auditor's podium, and walked briskly across the room to the tall, narrow doors, which opened as he reached them. He passed through without looking back, or to either side. Once outside the hearing room, he turned right and walked down a long corridor, his footfalls echoing. On either side were closed doors at regular intervals: examination rooms, similar to the one he had just left. The only lighting came from translucent skylights high overhead, and suspended from the distant peaked roof, long, severe chandeliers dimly illuminated from within. At the end of the building was an immense stained-glass window stretching from floor to ceiling.

As he walked, he reflected that in his long years on Oerlikon, he had forgotten how different Heliarcos was: On Oerlikon, in Lisagor, the buildings were large, firmly founded, plain, enduring. The crowds flowed among them like children, most of them content to let the higher-ups worry about things, amusing themselves with the anarchy of Dragon, their only game. The streets were level, more or less, gently curving, filled with the constant hum of the soft tyres of the velocipedes. But on Heliarcos. . . .

There was considerable use of stone on Heliarcos, mostly granite, and since the inhabited lands were hilly, or mountainous, there were abrupt changes of level. The streets were dark cobblestones, the buildings gray granite, built in a spiky, abrupt style the archaicists called neo-gothic. Most of the traffic was on foot, mixed with three-wheeled teardrop-shaped metal cars on the broader ways, that went by silently, their windows opaqued. Here, you could hear the wind in the groves of conifers, the spatter of runoff from the downspouts . . . little else. Passing footsteps.

Pentrel'k stopped only when he reached the foyer of the examination building, and from a dim little cloakroom off the entrance, retrieved one of the basic garments of this part of Heliarcos: a long raincoat with a hood, which he put on hurriedly, and pulled the hood up. Then he stepped outside.

The front of the examination building was a broad plaza, joined to the streets by long stairs, which were flanked with enormous granite pots, each housing ornamental junipers of ancient aspect, oversize bonsai. Palude was waiting beside the first of these, in the rain. At the sight of the trees and Palude, Pentrel'k glanced at the leaden sky, now beginning to darken into a pale blue dusk of a rainy day. It was late.

He walked directly to the woman, and said, "Well, I am here, as you can see."

Palude nodded. "So I see. And so you also agreed to go back?"

"Yes. I assume they offered you the same choices they offered me . . . none."

She said, "Yes. You understand we are fortunate in that regard. Very few of the returnees got anything. They might conceivably have been better off to have stayed on Oerlikon."

Pentrel'k said, softly, "They thought along the same lines I did, as you did: that we'd all have some reward for getting as much out as we did." He daydreamed, aloud, "We'd all come back here, go back into the Instructional Branches, do research . . . I would have taught a series of courses on Tactical Theory . . . I suppose we were all a bit naïve."

Palude nodded again, "Yes. I don't know what happened to

most. The ones I do know of . . . well, it's not so good. A lot of those got the stoneworks.''

"And Charodei?''

She shrugged. "To interrogation. Wise not to ask too closely beyond that.''

"I quite agree; it was close in there. They said nothing, mind you—it was what they didn't say. There was no need for them to. And so here we are, standing in the rain like a couple of bedraggled bosels! Shall we wind on down the hill and find a dry place in which to compare notes and plan strategies?''

"Yes.'' Palude glanced up at the rapidly darkening clouds. "We can go down in the lower city. The student taverns will be enough for us. No one will notice us there. And we should do so without delay: I have booked passage already.''

"How did you know I would come?''

"I didn't. They told me it would be me and one other. Presumably they had a replacement if you failed to meet their expectations.''

Pentrel'k snorted as he started off down the stairs, "Hmff! They couldn't replace us and they knew it.''

Palude joined him. "Not both. But either one they could have replaced.''

"When do we leave?''

"Tomorrow.''

Heliarcos was a small planet at the outer section of its primary's life zone; its warmest climatic zone was decidedly cool by human standards. Both poles were under permanent ice caps. With considerable axial tilt, and a fast rotation, it had changeable, stormy weather. Its parent star was a relatively young F8 type of an odd color between oyster and the palest of yellows, and when it did shine through the clouds, it seemed both brighter and larger than the sun of Earth, despite the greater distance.

The surface was highly mineralized with heavy elements, and the life-forms few in type and rather unspecialized. Its discoverers had pronounced it "a mountainous Permian,'' and rated it for the mineral concessions. The habitable land surface was simply too small, and the climate too severe, for large-scale human habitation.

One well-known account described it: "Fogs and mists, and when none of those, rain, snow, hail, at any season, often mixed in the same storm, or all at once. The vegetation is all dull green, and no flowers break the monotony. The animal life either placidly munches conifers, or else, almost as placidly, munches other animals. The animals are silent—they issue forth no challenges, mating calls, or expressions of well-being. One might wait years to hear even a serious grunt of exertion. Their reproductive methodology is efficient and uninspiring, their forms generalized and lumplike, a committee's-eye view of an evolutionary scheme. They stalk or repulse attacks with stolid persistence.'' In the end, the explorer had begged to be relieved of his post, resorting to the final damnation in French: *''J'ai le Cafard!''* This was boredom, L'Ennui, beyond hope.

Heliarcos had one advantage, however: it had a priceless location close by busy and populous systems, and because of its mineral deposits, rapidly became self-supporting. Several academic groups, seeing its possibilities for a convenient retreat, early established institutions of higher learning. Certain religious groups also moved onto the planet to make retreats and monastic communities. These, with the mining concessions, became the dominant form of human inhabitation there, and in a relatively short time, the three types of organization grew to resemble one another, and finally became indistinguishable. In this last phase, off-planet governments and industrial concerns set up research groups, which fit in without a ripple. The process had been completed.

The history of Heliarcos was utterly unlike any other planet's; there were no kings, presidents, statesmen, conquerors or revolutionaries—likewise there had been no countries, empires, states, principalities or interregnums. The larger habitable continent was parcelled out more or less equitably to the various groups, and the smaller one, by common consent, left wild and uninhabited by humans. Supported by offplanet organizations and the specialty mineral trade, there had never been an opportunity for nationalism to develop. And in effect, the planet had no central government, nor even its own currency. It became a place devoted exclusively to the cultivation of the mind, whose predominant cultural form was an institute of learning surrounded by the support activities necessary to a functioning human community.

Heliarcos, then, became a place whose unique product was the distillation of human learning: a university whose scale and diversity had never been attempted before in a single location. To this harsh little world came the best of all the worlds, to undergo courses of instruction, to receive professional finishing and polish, and to sharpen the muscles of the mind. Through its contacts with the other worlds, it carried an influence far greater than could have been obtained through armies or political power, and was agreed by all to be neutral ground—whatever the factional issue. It became, in its own way, immensely powerful, and men and women who were high in the society of Heliarcos had few equals elsewhere and were indebted to fewer. The governments who ruled unruly men had their locations elsewhere, but the influence of the Regents and Proctors of Heliarcos reached out through an intricate network onto all worlds, even some that knew of Heliarcos only by the dimmest of rumors.

The organization to which Cesar Kham and Arunda Palude belonged had originally been founded as a study institute whose purpose was to examine the ways humans adapted to new environments, or invented new cultural forms for newly opened planets. This had rapidly grown into several specialized areas, which had in turn given birth to even more specializations. Major areas included language, sociology, anthropology, political science, history, literature, as well as what were politely known as "support disciplines," such as computer science, mathematics, and physics, although these latter were not pursued with the singleminded devotion they knew at institutes where they were studied as the primary arts.

The Oerlikon Project, as it had been known, had been a joint field project supported by several major departments, and coordinated by its own semi-independent operations staff, which had of course grown in time and gradually assumed its own inertia. This situation could have endured indefinitely, until either the Opstaff changed, or until a revolution occurred on Oerlikon. Neither had been considered likely. Now, of course, all had been changed. The flow of students and field operatives onto Oerlikon had stopped, and those people who had escaped from Oerlikon had to be placed somewhere, as well as the now-unnecessary Opstaff members. It had been a trying time, a demanding time, and in a changing situation, it was natural that many expectations could not be fulfilled, which was a delicate way of putting it.

This particular inhabited area was called Pompitus Hall, from a once-prominent building which housed, originally, a small mathematics faculty. The Oerlikon operations staff had taken up two rooms of the original hall. But as the complexity of the operation had grown, it had gradually taken over the whole building, spread into several annexes, which had been consolidated back into newer buildings and rebuildings, and in turn sprouted further annexes. The Upper town was devoted to the faculty buildings proper, while lower down the slopes the Lower town filled a narrow river valley.

Kham and Palude made their way through the rapidly falling darkness and rain down the hill, through the housing areas into the town proper. The streets were still narrow and paved with granite cobblestones, but the buildings became smaller and somewhat more erratic in design. Here, the streets were busy, and windows were lighted. Crowds passed along the streets in easy confusion, and commercial places, hardly noticed during the day, now came to life. After some searching, they settled on a modest place calling itself The Armonela Inn, which had a large lower public room fronting on the river and warmed by several fireplaces. This was quiet, and frequented by students who appeared to wish to finish some studying away from the faculty buildings; the room was modestly lit, and free of heavy drinking and noise. Despite the quiet, however, it was well-filled, and they had to wait for one of the more secluded booths.

Pentrel'k and Morelat Eickarinst ordered a simple meal of braised fowl and dumplings, assigning the cost to the accounts of the Bursar of the Faculty, a procedure that was accepted without question. After a short delay, the meal was served and they set to it without ceremony or talk; for both of them the day had been both long and trying, and in fact they had both gone without lunch. They had serious matters to settle, and it could not be covered well by small talk between bites, for they were neither on a party nor an evening's pleasant games; this was serious business.

After dinner, however, over steaming mugs of the astringent tea which was the specialty of the house, flavored heavily with resin and some other acidic flavor which neither of them could identify, they began exploring the subject at hand. By this time the crowd had thinned a little, and they would be left alone.

Pentrel'k opened the discussion. "Well, as of tomorrow we will assume our identities of old. I will be Cesar Kham, and you Arunda Palude. We may as well resume tonight."

Palude raised her mug in a slight salute. "Indeed. Of course, being a mnemonicist, I never forgot Morelat, but I did put it off a bit. I never knew you, anyway, as Czermak."

"Of course not. We were of different classes. I had been on Oerlikon for some time when you came."

"I know. You did not matriculate here, did you?"

"No. Calomark. In the south. But enough of that, I suppose; we will have time to fill this in as we go." Here Kham betrayed a facet of his character that few ever saw. Secretive and careful to the point of willful paranoia within the guise of his assignment, he was abrupt and tactless with relationships in reality. He continued, "I assume you have had some access to the debriefings they have worked up."

"Yes—indeed, they let me see all of it, as soon as it was set in that I would be going back."

"Conclusions that they saw?"

"None. I read, I studied, I reflected. I made no report. But it would be less than accurate to say that I saw in the reports what they did."

Kham observed, "I should think they would see *more*. I mean, they are here, supervising, while we in the field. . . ."

"Not necessarily so! In fact, I early on came to understand that the people in the field were much more. . . . What's that old student slang word we used to use? *Dapt*. That's what we used to say. Meaning adept, able. And besides, Mnemonicism-Integration is a difficult discipline, one you have to work at. I am sure that none of these I've seen here can match my level without artificial aids."

"Well, whatever else we may say and do, I like your cynical candor. You kept it veiled on Oerlikon."

"Womancraft, Cesar. It is a part of discretion that a woman never reveals her true self casually, be that selfness ability of mind, strength of desire to achieve, or sexual desire. It's a legacy of old oppressions that are not yet entirely vanished. All subordinate peoples learn to dissemble, to walk clothed."

"Aha! Then what is it you show me?"

"One layer down. Not necessarily the reality."

"Well-said!"

"You did rather well at this, yourself . . . Glist, on the other hand, always let down too easily."

"Glist was not, in my opinion, a good choice for coordinator."

"One gets what one gets."

"Just so." He sighed. "What kind of particulars have you managed to build?"

She looked down at her mug, which was empty, now. Palude raised it on high, for a moment, and presently a waiter appeared, with a fresh pot. She shook her head. "I now know things I missed there in the heat of the fray. Things I overlooked, or didn't see at all. It is considerably more difficult than they make it out to be."

"I had an instinct for this and felt the same, although I could not justify it."

"That's the tactician talking. It feels wrong. And you know the old tactical motto: 'If it feels good, do it. Until it feels bad. Then quit.' This feels bad now, and won't get any better; still, what choices do we have?"

"None. Well, go on. What are we to face?"

"First: We will have to determine if the subject is alive. Positive identification and hard evidence. We do not in fact know now if it survived the tumults of Marula. If it died or was killed, then the task is simple. We return an report."

"We'll have to see if Pternam left any records, notes, bring those—or what survives of them."

"Or destroy them there."

"How so?"

"You saw yourself what that creature, that thing could do. There, in that time, it was limited in scope. It carried out its maker's instruction, and then pursued its own survival. But Oerlikon was then a severely limited environment—virtually encapsulated. It is not now. Also this: suppose we bring back enough textual material to enable them to reach for the Morphodite again, here? This world is not isolated, but interwoven with the whole human community. If it goes rogue, we are not talking about one continent on one world, but thousands."

"You believe, then, that such a creature could do it?"

"Absolutely. Now then—let's follow the other track. It lives. Very well. It will have to now be a male, because no trace of the woman Damistofia Azart has ever been found. Up to a point they trace her to a specific date and time. Then nothing. No corpse, and no further movement."

"Some held that it died."

"The evidence I have suggests that it changed successfully and escaped, and went somewhere to hide. It probably intended to do that anyway, because it knew that too many people knew it as Damistofia, for her to follow any kind of normal life.''

''Well, hellation and damnanimity! It could have made more than one change!''

''No. Only one. If it lived. The process is a horror to endure. It's like experiencing death, directly. No. It won't change for casual reasons.''

''That still doesn't help us. All we have done is eliminated half the population!''

''More than half—51.89 percent, to be exact. And we know something else about it.''

''What?''

''That it's young. Probable mid-twenties, standard. And such a person won't have any past. Also we know where to start looking. Clisp. Because Damistofia was in Marula, and she had no contacts except what she could make on her own, so she wouldn't be likely to leave Lisagor proper. And she wouldn't walk back into Crule—that's where his/her enemies were. The only place she could go and vanish would be a large city, like Marisol, in Clisp. It's the only logical place.''

''Aha! I see your drift. . . .''

''And you know Clisp and Marisol. . . .''

''Indeed I do. But it has some kind of ability to see what's going on around it.''

''Yes. But that has limitations.''

''It's nice to know that.''

''No need to be sarcastic. The creature has profound gifts, some given it by Pternam, some of those inadvertently, and a lot of what it developed of its own accord. But remember this: its weakness is that its system isn't passive, and. . . .''

''Explain.''

''It has a method of seeing conditions around it; but it has to 'ask,' as it were. It has to *look*, and the process isn't easy. So it doesn't spend all its time searching . . .''

''So we have to move without alarming it, or becoming visible to its powers . . . but. . . .'' He stopped, puzzling over an impossible contradiction. Then he continued, ''I understand that the creature has the ability to see distant events and circumstances that bear on it. If it looks, now, it can see that we are coming!''

''Now, let me explain what I think I know about what it does.

This will help. It isn't all-powerful. It has limits. I will describe what I believe to be its limits, and you, the tactician, with an understanding of the territory, can then conceive an attack.''

"You say that with some finality.''

"I don't want it brought here under any circumstances. *Any*.''

"Well, they don't either, unless it can be controlled.''

"It can't be controlled. Once alerted, it can find the place and time when it can escape, or make a move that will bring the house down around us. They underestimate it. I don't.''

"Proceed.''

"Its ability to find the pivot of a society and change that is a by-product of the system it uses to perceive events around it. Embedded in that theory, a pseudotheory as Pternam thought it; but the way it really is, is that the creature developed the perceptive system first, in secret. Or it saw in Pternam's idea a germ of a greater truth.''

"All right. How does it do it?''

"Are you familiar with the *I Ching*?''

"The *Book of Changes*? Somewhat. I never studied it deeply.''

"Basically, it is a binary code of two-to-the-sixth-power states, with selected elements being changeable according to specific rules. Sixty-four 'states' cover all human events.''

"Go on.''

"What is your opinion of that?''

"Mysticism, farrago, nonsense, occultism, fortune-telling. All other objections aside, I believe in the influences of the application of Will and Desire, and of course, it would seem that sixty-four conditions are much too shallow a reading.''

"Well. The *I Ching*, in the hands of an adept, has some remarkable powers that defy rational explanation, as we define rationality. It is outside the bounds of what we understand as causality. But throughout human history, it has never been given up. Even now, we could go out to the street of the booksellers and buy a copy. I would almost recommend it.'' Arunda Palude smiled at this, as if the idea were too much to bear. "But however that is . . . have you heard of the Tarot?''

"Distantly. More fortune-telling.''

"Instead of 64 basic states, it has 22.''

"That's less. So I would say it lacks subtlety.''

"But in the use of either system, the states interact. In an *I Ching* consultation, if all lines are changeable, then you double the possibilities to 128. With Tarot, it's larger, because you consider 22 values in a sequence of ten. Not 22 to the tenth power, but 22 partial factorial: Still an enormous number. And so *that* is very subtle indeed. And both of those two systems are founded on a base of some very shrewd observations. Nevertheless all of the bases are arbitrary value judgments, however well they approximate. You follow this?''

"Yes, I think so. It's a good guess, but not scientific, so so speak.''

"So. Imagine a system with a base larger than Tarot, but worked out in practice rather like the *I Ching*, with some 'lines' changeable. We didn't recover his bases, or what he calls them, but we do know that there are 55 values in the base sequence, and that the 'word' length is variable. And now imagine that the values in the base sequence are not developed empirically, but by ruthless scientific experimentation.''

"I can imagine such a concept, but it would be hard to remember it in practice.''

"It consults by knowing the base values, and then performing specific operations. There is some peculiar mathematics involved, as well. At any rate, that is what it does. And the system is, as far as we can determine, and for all practical purposes, absolute.''

"You have this data as factual?''

"Observations melded for commonality, from observers, remarks, things people heard it say, or heard repeated.''

"You have done a remarkable job of getting that much.''

"That's about all I have. That's how it perceives. Now consider it received the most intense training in the use of weapons, and of martial arts. Reputedly, it can kill with bare hands, or build a nuclear weapon from scratch, or set up total conversion objects. Whatever it needs to do the job.''

"Then this is much worse than I thought.''

"Agreed. Much, much worse. Our only chance will be in surprise.''

Kham asked, "Then you don't think we could capture it.''

"No. I don't think so.''

"We have a third choice.''

"Which is?''

"We could help it escape.''

"Why ever would you say that?''

"If we could contact it and persuade it to go away, somewhere. . . .''

"You heard the Regents: it must not know who Jedily Tulilly was. It can, theoretically, determine that from any place, if it becomes motivated to. Then we have no idea what might happen."

"Then it would seem that a surprise attack from space, total sterilization of Oerlikon, might work."

"Conceivably. If we knew it was on Oerlikon. And besides that, that option has been ruled out." Palude stopped now and considered Cesar Kham across the table from her. Bald, stocky, a powerful man who emitted absolute confidence in himself, but with limits. And these limits were easy to seek, easy to find. A superb tactician who thrived on emergencies, he totally lacked the long view, the powerful sense of consequences, of *karma*, which the mnemonicist could never escape. It was useless to try to provoke something out of him which did not exist.

Kham said, "I understand that: it would show the hand that guides."

Palude nodded. "That would bring much out into the open. You see, in a way, the Regents who set all this in motion. . . ."

Kham interrupted her. ". . . The ones who set this in motion are long since removed from retribution."

"True. But the ones who inherited, they feel limited, boxed in by these circumstances. If they act, they reveal. If they don't act, they get Jedily Tulilly back, but they don't know when. So they try to find the middle."

"Hmf. A difficult path, this. You understand we could die of this?"

"Cesar, I understand that; and that there are worse things than personal extinction."

"Oh, yes, there I agree. I know that sense well. Many times. Now you speak my language. So in that language, I ask you: why does this creature, who has demonstrable powers, not attack immediately?"

Palude looked off into the crowd. No one seemed to be observing them. If they had been taken for anything, it would be as members of the faculty, out on an evening's slumming, among the students. She leaned forward and said quietly, "We have grown so used to illusory pseudopower, in human history, that we read the real thing wrongly. One who *thinks* he has power—there's the one who attacks, but the one who has the real thing, that one lies low, seeks the unwatched space, the quiet time. It is the truthful confirmation, that we have this strong suspicion that the creature yet lives, and yet it does nothing."

"Then, if I follow you aright, the Morphodite does not seek to apply his powers, to rule, to revenge."

Palude said, emphatically, "That is my analysis."

Kham continued. "Then, paradoxically, there is little to fear from it, even if it uncovers Jedily."

Palude smiled. "Exactly."

"Did you make this point?"

"I made it. It wasn't accepted."

Kham pressed, "Then they don't want it known, even if nothing happens. . . ."

"Correct."

"Did they suggest anything to you?"

"About Tulilly? No. They guard it well. I can follow the thread myself up to a point, and then blank. There's a logic to it. She was dumped, so to speak, on Oerlikon, for some reason. I've tried conjecture: nothing fits."

Kham now nodded, slowly. "Yes, I see. So . . . we get to go and fix things up. Very well. I vote for murder. No reason to mince words."

"As odious as it is, that seems to be the only course. I could not in good conscience consider allying myself with that creature, when I have no idea of his aims. This is devil's work. I know it clear-eyed, but all the same, it's out of devils I know well enough."

Kham smiled, a rictus Palude had not seen in his face before. It was an expression of vast, calculating cynicism. He said, "Aye, you and I know them, don't we, but we don't know why they dumped Tulilly, or even where she came from, and there's devils of another Aleph ordinal, as we used to say."

Palude changed the subject. "There were dependable operatives left behind when we left Oerlikon?"

"Yes. I imagine a good many of them can be rounded up for a little quiet work. In addition we had sleepers controlling natives in a number of places, and these can be activated as well, although I don't think we'll rouse all of them, that follows. But we designed considerable redundancy into our systems there, so I am sure a few days' work will suffice to open something up."

"Good. You think we can determine something, then?"

"From here, a guess? Probable. I can say more when we get back. How do we re-enter Lisagor, or whatever it's called now?"

"We're going by courier *Frigate*. There's an inbound freighter

we'll match with and transfer to, to actually land. The landing
will be in Tartary, but reports have it there's trade now and we
can get a place. The plan is that we try to get a ship for a
Tilanque port, rather than Karshiyaka. This is supposed to be
feasible, according to the sources they still have active.''

"They are still reporting?''

"Sporadically, from Lisagor. Tartary station never went down.''

Kham mused, "Tartary station wasn't under us, as I'm sure
you recall.''

"True. But they weren't hostile to offworlders there, either.
Just indifferent. But it will be early, so I suggest we retire
without revel or carouse.''

Now Kham looked closely at Arunda Palude. By all accounts,
a distant, cool woman, who, although no longer young, still
maintained handsome good looks. Kham had heard no tales
about her, as he had heard about the others posted to Lisagor,
who took advantage of the native concern with footloose sex
to have a good time on the sly. Palude was tall, with a modest,
but well-shaped figure. She had a strong, clear face, formed
by the intense concentration of her profession, and loose,
flowing hair the color of walnut wood. Kham made an internal
adjustment, evaluating Arunda as probably not one prone to
dalliance. But sharp, and direct. And if on Oerlikon before,
she had followed his lead in organizing the chaos, it did not
bother him now to accept her lead in setting the long-range
goals. That kind of flexibility also fitted with the dancer's
poise of the tactician. He thought: *A shame we can't do
more, but we'll probably work well together. That will have
to do*. He said, "Yes. Where are you staying, and where
do I meet you?''

"At the Ozalide Inn. Come there at the fifth hour.''

"Very well. Good evening.'' He arose and made a courteous
gesture. Then added, "You understand that a lot will be different
this time.''

Palude nodded. "Yes. Very different.''

"We may have to move about quickly, alone, without the
support network. You'll need to move with me.''

"Why . . .? I thought you would . . .''

"You have a weapon to help us. You mentioned the *I
Ching*; you know about it, yes? Get a copy of the book. You're
going to use it. Ours may not be as subtle as his, but a

map's a map, no matter how crudely drawn, and Lisagor only has one shape. And so I will pull the trigger, but you will be doing some aiming." And with that request Cesar Kham turned away and departed for his own lodgings.

3

"Even paranoids sometimes have real enemies."
—*Remark attributed to Spiro T. Agnew*

"Paranoia is most definitely a survival trait."
—*H. C., Atropine*

The southern and western parts of Clisp were, geologically, a continuation of the ranges that made up the rugged spine of the isthmus which the inhabitants of Lisagor called The Serpentine, the narrow neck joining Lisagor with its subcontinent. But the peaks that marched across the southern horizon from east to west did more than provide the inhabitants of Marisol with a spectacular skyline; they blocked Clisp off from the influences of the southwestern ocean airs, and let the cool winds in from the northwest. Clisp was cool and somewhat arid, with frequent fogs along the northern seaboard, sometimes creeping as far inland as Marisol.

The northern part of Clisp was a low plain descending gently to the sea, traced and eroded by small ravines. Rain fell often in the mountains, and this runoff kept the water level up. Several of these streams had been diverted into feeder canals and shifted to the site of Marisol, where, through an easy descent of locks, the open sea could be contacted through a canal.

Marisol, then, partook of several natures at once, neither dominating: it was the administrative seat of government for a large and frequently turbulent province; inland commercial center for the province, which outside Marisol was largely agricultural; and it was a seaport, with canals linking many parts of the city. Lastly, it was the last place on Oerlikon where rebels against the stultifying sameness of Lisagor might gather and have a moment's respite, if not their way. Consequently, Marisol was

a large city of mostly low buildings, without monumental edi-
fices, but equally lacking slums and squatter camps. The air,
save during the fogs, was clear and transparent, and the wind
made merry, sliding across the plains out of the northwest. And
in the south, under the slow passages of the primary of Oerlikon,
Gysa, the bold mountains marched across the face of the world,
and played with towers of cloud and lightning. It was a place in
which one had to strive to retain a bad feeling. There was always
something in the wind.

Phaedrus and Meliosme had come to Marisol for the bottom-
less obscurity he sought, and she accepted, knowing peace within
herself from her long days in the wild. And for a long time their
lives settled into routine and stability; known things, not hard
decisions. Phaedrus worked as a landscaper and Meliosme took
on the weight of making the lives of the urchins and orphans
they had collected along the way whole again. There were more
of these than they had planned for; they had gained some on the
long road up from Zolotane, along the edge, the sea on one side,
and chaos on the other, people fleeing, order disturbed. Phaedrus
took them in without question. He remembered, he knew. He
had wrought this. He accepted the terrified children without
rancor, bearing them as a light burden he knew he owed and
could never fill.

He told Meliosme that because of the changes wrought in him,
he could sire no children, so the runaways and strays became
their own children. They, in turn, brought more in, and in time
the family of Phaedrus and Meliosme grew large. Since they
needed help in meeting the expense of feeding them, Phaedrus
had gone to the public audiences which the heridatary ruler of
Clisp was wont to give from time to time, and plainly asked for
aid. Pressed for details by Pompeo's clerks, he had revealed his
connection with events in Zolotane, and Pompeo had made the
necessary connection. The prince, a middle-aged man with a
balding head and a visible paunch, who stood on little ceremony,
asked Phaedrus to attend him in his private chambers.

There, Pompeo sat in a plain armchair and had spoken directly, "You are the fellow we heard about some time ago. I had
reports. One of my men met you. Salkim."

"Yes. I remember him. He is well?"

Pompeo shook his head. "Dead. Led a raiding party ashore in
the Far Pilontaries. Good man. Bit of a dandy, but nonetheless

true. Better than most. But his command won the day and returned. I read their reports.''

"You do not fault me that I did not take up his offer?''

"No. I wish you had, but no matter. And so you come to Clisp anyway.''

"Yes. Almost directly. As a fact, I got here rather sooner than if I'd left with Salkim.''

"That's so . . . Well, you haven't been invisible here, either. We keep an eye on things here, just like other places, but with an eye to helping the good instead of punishing the evil. Why bother? The evil will harm themselves.''

"You knew it was me . . .?''

"Not necessarily. We knew someone was taking in orphans and strays and runaways and setting them straight. Rest easy. We can help you do that easily enough. See Patroclo, the Bursar. Use discretion, which I know you will.''

"I will do my best.''

Pompeo stroked his jowls with his middle finger and thumb, looking downward, thoughtful. Then he had said, gruffly and directly, "But all things are, in Clisp, desirous of balance.''

Phaedrus had said, "Yes, m'Lord.''

"You are held in regard as being clearheaded, now a rarity. It pleases me to help you in your work. I request that you help me in mine.''

"How so?''

"Attend me here. About once every four weeks, or as I call on you. Then we will speak of values, ethics, the right choices. I have many advisers, out to succeed at Court. I have not seen your application, nor do you bow and scrape.''

Phaedrus breathed in relief, silently. "I will do so with pleasure, if it pleases you.''

"I do not know how you order your life, or those whose lives touch yours. But I have heard well of you. We try to reward excellence here . . . but these have been difficult times, more so than for most of my predecessors. There is the sense of great Change in the air; a new age for Oerlikon. I have my successor, a son, Amadeo, but I wish to set things on a certain course . . .''

"I understand. I am, however, neither a sage, nor a thaumaturge; I do not heal the sick, raise the dead, nor make the little girls talk out of their head.''

Pompeo smiled, in great good humor. "Of course not.'' And

the Prince stood, indicating that Phaedrus should leave. "About four weeks. Come as you will; I will see they come and get me."

And with no more formality than that, Phaedrus undertook to fill the part of one of Pompeo's many advisers and confidants. The meetings occurred as scheduled, but while Phaedrus was relieved that his secret was safe, there was a curious disjointed air to the talks he had with Pompeo. They never seemed to broach a subject openly, indeed, if there was any subject at all. Pompeo clearly wanted something from him, but at the same time seemed satisfied with the little he got.

Finally, Phaedrus asked him what he was gaining out of their meetings. Pompeo looked off through the careful landscaping of the palace grounds, to the far mountains, and said, reflectively, "I am trying to learn your sense of effortless composure. It would seem that virtually everyone would wish to be more than he is. You do not. True, I am Prince here, and should I wish to exercise it, have in fact considerable power to order things. I use it seldom. But because you do not seek more, I have little hold on you."

Phaedrus said cautiously, "There were times before Zolotane, before Clisp. I once chased the illusions as well. At least, let us condense it to that. I saw once that we have all the scope we can handle immediately before us—we do not need to look far afield."

"You do not seek esteem, regard, repute."

"There is never enough of that. No matter how much you get, it always needs more. I must step out of that cycle and *act*, here, now, in front of me. There is always much to be done."

"And what more would a prince want?"

"To be free of the weight of his obligations; one could not remain a prince and be unconscious of them."

"Exactly so! Do you read minds?"

"Not at all."

"And so you do what needs to be done. How do you know it?"

"Everyone knows it. They just don't want to do it. They keep putting it off, for one more try, one more chance. It was in knowing the waste of the old way that I looked and asked, 'is there value in the other way—obscurity, nobodyness?'"

"Are you succeeding?"

"It is difficult at times. But I remind myself of what I know of the other way, and then dig a little deeper."

"You know we tried to trace you, but the trail fades out in the hills between Crule the Swale and Zolotane. You were something before."

"Many things."

"You have no vendettas, no revenges?"

"None. Those things will never be that way again. We have *now*."

"You would not reveal them."

"I would prefer not to."

"Is there anything you would ask, now, for yourself?"

"Meliosme misses the hoots and calls of bosels. You have none in Clisp. We would go back to the east when things are settled down and folk can move about freely again."

"The one thing I can't grant. The breakup left many areas cut off, forced to operate as smaller units. Things are quieter, now, much more so, yet the old days of unity, however bad it might have been, are gone. Movements are restricted. No longer can one wander the length and breadth of Karshiyaka. Here in the West, we have gathered in as much as we can comfortably handle: Zefaa, The Serpentine, Zolotane. That is as far as Greater Clisp goes. There are other countries back there, now. Foreign lands, as hard to reach as Tartary."

For a moment, Pompeo looked off again, and then said, off-handedly, "If you were to speak your mind to me, advising me plainly, what would you have me do? A great time came upon my days, and I know I have not altogether done what I could have. The work of repacification is far from finished."

Phaedrus breathed deeply. Then, "You have done much. You let Clisp expand to its natural limits, when it was time for it to. Now let it go."

"Let go?"

"You have your successor; turn it over to him."

"And then what should I do? All my life I lived in secret, waiting for a restoration we were sure would never come. Then the great changes; and so here we are. But it's unfinished. . . ."

"It will never be finished. You have done well. You were there, but do not stay to mar it. Be content with your acts."

"Exactly as I have thought. You know, only a few more years and this would have missed me. Amadeo. . . . He's capable enough for these times, but I often wonder how it would have gone if this change had come in his time."

"You will never know that. Leave it now, while you can still smile about it."

"Very well, but what should I do, then?"

"We always have room for another guide . . ."

Pompeo laughed aloud and stood up. He said, expansively, "It will be as you recommend! But in my own time. In my own time." And with that note they parted.

For some time, Phaedrus heard no more from Pompeo. Once or twice he stopped by, but did not find the Prince in either time. And shortly after that, there was a brief public announcement to the effect that Pompeo had retired in favor of the new Prince, Amadeo II, who would now assume the proper executive functions. There was no great ceremony, no parades, nor did anyone think them necessary. Continuity had been assured. Things continued with no visible interruption. More significantly, the financial assistance he and Meliosme received, as well as certain administrative favors, continued without interruption.

The change of seasons in Clisp was more notable than the parts of old Lisagor Phaedrus could remember. The autumn was marked by a notable increase in night fogs, swept away by storms that blew in from the northwest. In these days, few ventured out at night. One such night, while the outside was muffled and supernaturally quiet, Phaedrus and Meliosme were preparing for bed, when they heard outside the faint noise of a motorcar, one of the rare electrics Clispish dignitaries favored. Presently there was a soft knock at the door. Phaedrus went to the door, and opening it, met a silent, elderly gentleman wearing the very plain clothing preferred by the inside servitors of the Ruling House. He said, "I am Phaedrus."

The chauffeur nodded, and said, "Pompeo requires a service of you, in accordance with your agreement."

"Now?"

"Now."

Phaedrus looked about uncertainly at Meliosme. Then back at the unsmiling chauffeur. "In Marisol?"

The chauffeur shook his head. "At the family estates. Cape Forever."

"That's in the farthest west of Clisp. And it's dense fog out there."

The man was undisturbed. He said, in his undertaker's voice, "No matter. I know the way well. We will be there by morning. You will be back tomorrow evening."

Phaedrus, still hesitating, asked, "Is there haste?"

"Not if you leave now," was all that was said.

Phaedrus gathered up his old night-cloak and threw it over his shoulders, glancing at Meliosme. She made a small gesture to him with her hand. "It's all right. Go on." He nodded, and stepped out into the night. The chauffeur followed, closing the door behind him, and opening the door to the passenger compartment for Phaedrus.

Inside was another man, almost invisible in the shadows, save for soft highlights reflected from the dimmed streetlamps. This person was tall, rangy, bald and carried a weapon, some sort of gun which Phaedrus could not identify. The chauffeur got in after him, settling himself in his own compartment, and spoke through a mesh connecting the two cabins. "This is Olin, a trusted retainer and man-at-arms. Trust him as you trust me. We are the personal staff of the Prince Emeritus. You do not walk in harm's way while under our guidance."

Phaedrus asked, "Is the Prince well? Why do we need such secrecy?"

The chauffeur turned to his motorcar and started it off through the damp, foggy, leaf-spattered streets, shiny with moisture. Olin answered, "The Prince is not well. He will explain everything. It will go as Bautisto has said: you should be back tomorrow evening."

Olin settled back, and Phaedrus, uneasy, nevertheless made an attempt to find a comfortable position among the overstuffed seats. The car whirred off into the fog.

Bautisto indeed seemed to know where he was going with supernatural accuracy. Although the fog was dense, thicker than usual for the season, he navigated through the silent and nearly empty streets of Marisol without any hesitation, and at a considerable speed. Phaedrus, who knew little of the city except the main streets and boulevards and the immediate area of his own house, was soon lost, but as near as he could tell, they were proceeding west in the night, and after a time, the few lights of Marisol grew even less, then rare, and at last there were no lights, save the running lights of the car, and an occasional isolated post along the road. Neither Bautisto nor Olin seemed to relax, but maintained an almost palpable sense of animal awareness which Phaedrus found profoundly disturbing, for all that they had said.

Notwithstanding his sense of foreboding, after a time the motion of the car and the sense of confidence Bautisto expressed in his driving over the empty roads of Clisp relaxed Phaedrus, and he dozed off. Once or twice, he awoke briefly, as they stopped to have the power cells recharged, at bare little stations where a single overhead lamp made a bright, furry cone out of the darkness that began just beyond the windows.

Phaedrus felt the road change, from the smooth gritty friction of the public roads to something more uneven. He opened his eyes to fog-shrouded daylight, broken by darker patches when they passed under enormous trees, of which he could see no detail except shredded, fibrous bark. He said, "Where are we?"

Olin grunted, "Cape Forever Plantation."

"I felt the road change."

"Um. Still a little ways."

Phaedrus settled back, and Bautisto drove on, following a double path seemingly going nowhere through the forest. He could feel in the wheels the changing surface they rolled upon; sometimes sandy, sometimes silent, as if they were rolling on fine leaf-dust. Other times, rocky spurs. The estate road was passable, but not well kept up. And although the road went mostly level, there were now a lot of gentle curves, and there was the sense of having left level ground long ago.

Finally, with almost no warning, they passed through an enormous stucco gate with a circular entrance, and only a low wall dividing the inside from the forest. The inside looked no different. They founded a sharp curve and stopped before what looked like a rough stone wall, irregular, higher than a man. Bautisto nodded, turning to speak through the mesh, "Toward the direction the car is pointing, you will find an entry. The door is unlocked. Go in. You are expected."

"Just walk in?"

"That is correct. This is not Court, but the house of one who wishes you well. Accept it. They pick their friends with care."

Phaedrus opened the door and hesitantly stepped out into the damp air. As soon as he closed the door, the car started rolling, and in a moment it was gone, vanishing into the morning fog almost as if it had never been there. For a moment, Phaedrus stood, trying to sense the place, capture something of its suchness. He smelled a dry, resinous odor from the forest, and a sharp overtone from something else. He listened. No wind, but a soft, burry muttering as from far off, or perhaps the other side of the wall. Something familiar in that; the sea? He began walking along the wall. Presently he came to a rather plain doorway, well-done, intentionally rustic, but by no means grand. Not exactly the front door of a Prince. He turned the iron handle, worn almost to a shapeless lump, and went in.

He was in a long foyer, which led directly ahead, the walls similar to the outside. Phaedrus walked along the hall until he came to a raised porchlike area, opening onto a large, but comfortable room, the far wall of which was glass, still opening onto the silvery blankness of the fog. The light was gray and weak. Inside, lamos and chandeliers banished some of the gloom. The floor was flagstones, covered by carpets in intricate and subtle patterns. At the far end, off to his right, there was a fireplace with a fire going, and several couches. And Pompeo, sitting in a chair by the fire, wrapped in a dark shawl and looking much older. Frail, thin, not at all the robust man of mature years Phaedrus remembered. Phaedrus walked across the flagstones without hesitation until he was standing before the fireplace, which gave off a dull warmth. Only then did Pompeo look up.

He pursed his mouth, as if collecting his words. After a moment, the Prince began, hesitantly, "Forgive me if I stumble. Drugs, medicines."

"You are ill." It was a statement, not a question.

"Yes. Man's last enemy, save himself. Cancer. Sometimes it seems almost gone, but it always comes back."

"Is there anything I can do?"

"You always seemed supernaturally wise, but always veiled, something you did not choose to show, or exploit. Tell me something."

Phaedrus understood, he thought. *Make this worthwhile*. He said, "I imagine the Moral Guides have counselled you."

Pompeo nodded. "Just so. But they do not *know*. I sense it. They repeat credo, verse and line, but there is no certainty. I am, in a word, dissatisfied."

"Each one of us endures initiations through life, which become steadily more challenging, more difficult. Free childhood, when innocence first reaches out into the imagination. Puberty, the learning and mastery of desire. Adulthood. Birth. Courtship. The family. Setting the children free. All these are tests. But they are all training, nothing more, for the final test of a person's innermost selfness, when he faces the eternity that is within each of us. Review what you have done, and see this as the final test for excellence."

Pompeo listened, nodding a bit, and when Phaedrus had finished, he said softly, "You cite no authorities, no verse and line, but you *know*."

Phaedrus shook his head. "I can't even claim that. Say that I have suspicions."

"You speak like a man who has looked death in the eye."

"I have."

"I will not ask. Keep your secret."

"More than once I have come within a hair's-breadth of telling you."

"No. Keep it."

"That is why I almost did. That you do not ask."

"Excellent! As always, you can manage, with a few simple words, to energize me. Would I could have persuaded you earlier. Were it not for other matters, I would urge you to stand by me now, but the little is sufficient, at least for the while. I may falter later. But I did not summon you here in secrecy for selfish reasons. You have only said what was in my heart anyway, which is wisdom enough, is it not?"

"There is another matter, m'lord?"

"Yes. To the point: Late in my reign, we uncovered some odd traces of trafficking between persons high up in my regime and parties elsewhere. At first, we thought of the usual sort of spies, such as we read of in the old tales, and some that we know direct from the days of the Rectification. It was exquisitely done, subtle, but we followed it out, tracing every loop and line, stitch and draw. In essense we found a careful line between Patroclo, the Bursar, to parties in such places as Tartary. More recently, to different locations in Old Lisagor. The subject was not state secrets, but you."

Phaedrus stood very still, and he felt an emotion he had never known and for which he had no name. *But it was an icy certainty that this was an absolutely unique moment.* He selected a sofa and sat down, saying nothing.

After a pause, Pompeo continued, "The nature of the thing

was as if a passive unit were activated, at first with a vague and general search pattern, later, which focused on you." Pompeo sighed. "That was curious, you know? I thought spies would be interested in the disposition of soldiers, of ships. Of orders-of-battle. Perhaps on the vices of Amadeo, who is fond to excess of pretty women. But no. Of all Clisp could divulge to foreign devils, they were most interested in you, and they pursued you with incredible subtlety and secrecy."

"Do you know who *they* are?"

"No. We have conjectures, but no confirmations."

"Patroclo. May I speak with him?"

"I fear it is no longer possible. He took poison when we confronted him. He had associates, but they also elected to step into the darkness. A few may have escaped us, but it does not appear so."

"Who do you think it is?"

"Olin thinks offworlders."

Phaedrus thought, *The bastards! Why bring it all back? They would know I would have stayed here forever. I had no mission in the stars. Or did I?* A suspicion struck him, but for now, he dismissed it. He said, "You thought I was in danger."

"We let it go on too long, trying to understand it. Time grew valuable. You needed to be told this, so you can take whatever measures you are able to. They seemed to regard you as capable of anything, indeed, they seem to fear you more than they do Clisp."

"They are more correct than you know, in that."

"What can you do?"

"I have . . . certain defenses. Ways of perception. Techniques."

"But you need to be out in the open, and aware."

"Yes."

"You need mobility, to move if need be, beyond the borders of Clisp. . . ."

"Maybe farther."

"Beyond Old Lisagor. Tartary. Perhaps even off Oerlikon."

"How can I do that? The offworlders have gone."

"They still maintain contact in Tartary, openly, as traders."

"Then there is some traffic yet?"

"Yes. And so I know you have little. You could survive in the wild, and presumably you have means to conceal yourself . . . we gathered that information. But you would find it hard to get offworld without funds.'' Here, Pompeo made an almost-invisible gesture, to which a servant responded, entering the vast room, bearing a small tray. Pompeo continued, ''I have put something modest at your disposal. I valued what you gave me, and I would not have a quiet person hunted like a bosel by foreign devils, no matter what he was in past life.''

Phaedrus said, ''I fear they do not come for my past, but to prevent a future I do not even know, now.''

''Then that is even more reason.'' Pompeo took a small object from the tray, a small medallion on a chain. The medallion was shaped like an ancient Egyptian cartouche, and bore stylized emblems on its surface. It was metal, similar to a dull stainless steel, but when Pompeo handed it to him, it was uncharacteristically heavy. He said, ''Platinum. This is an authenticator seal. They have been on Oerlikon since my ancestors first came here.''

''What do the symbols mean?''

''We do not know. There are theories, conjectures, but no knowledge. Remember, in a land that pursues the sameness of the eternal present, historians are in no great demand, nor are students of ancient languages. But from the beginning, the Family has used them as authentications for the most secret matters. Including offworld. Use it. Where you need to go, identify yourself as an agent of Clisp and have the charges invoiced to the palace. It will be accepted without question—or knowledge of who has it. Apparently it cannot be counterfeited. Trace elements.''

''This is a powerful amulet; surely you do not give such a teasure away?''

''Do what you must. Then return, and serve Clisp as you will, doing your best to insure that we are not overrun by evil and fear and ignorance.''

''You did not mention greed and lust.''

''They are self-limiting. But the others partake of the endless dark I will soon meet.''

''I am moved, and will do as you ask.''

''Even though I will not be here to see it, I believe you will.'' Pompeo made another gesture, and other servants entered, bringing trays of food. ''Breakfast. I assume Bautisto did not stop along the way?''

''He did not. He and Olin seemed iron men.''

"We had to move when you were not watched. We knew that at that particular time you were not."

"That suggests something I do not care for."

"So we thought. So, let us eat. Enjoy the view. Stay as long as you will. Leave as you must."

Pompeo and Phaedrus breakfasted alone, uninterrupted by even the silent and subtle servants of the retired prince. Both men elected, for the moment, to keep their silences to themselves. After breakfast, Pompeo indicated that it was time for one of his treatments, and he excused himself, indicating that Phaedrus should consider himself free to wander about, or rest, as he felt. The light falling through the window-wall was much brighter now, and the fog was gone, so he could see across an old-fashioned walled garden.

After a moment's search, Phaedrus found the door leading out into the garden and went out. He did not feel like resting at the moment; the information Pompeo had imparted to him was disturbing.

For a time he wandered aimlessly about the garden, admiring the sense of restraint the landscapers had held in mind when they had done the planting, and in maintaining it through the years, for it was obviously not a new garden. After a time, he found a narrow gate, almost hidden away in an acute corner. He made his way to it, and stepped through. Before him was the blue expanse of the northern ocean.

Immediately before him was a rocky shingle beach which curved off into misty distances far to the right, to the east, fading into the horizon and the line of sea-spray. To the left, the land became rockier, then mostly outcrops of brown stone, and at last a headland jutting into the ocean, crowned by a thin group of wind-contorted trees, their limbs distorted by the sea-wind into strange, histrionic shapes. Beneath the trees, a lone fisherman was casting a circular net into the blue water, pausing, withdrawing it, timeless motions that had passed unchanged since the dawn of history.

Phaedrus walked slowly out to the point, savoring the ripe sense of suchness of this scene: the clear northern sky, the open sea, a limitless deep indigo color. He felt a sudden urge to sail off into those distances, although he knew very well that for all practical purposes there was nothing out there, all the way around the world, except Tartary on the other side.

Drawing near to the fisherman, he saw it to be Olin, who was not catching much. This seemed to have no perceptible effect on the man, who continued casting his net, pausing, and withdrawing it; his catch was scanty, small fishes and strange creatures Phaedrus did not know, living things combining features of mollusk and insect in equal measures.

At one of the pauses, he ventured, ''I see they are not cooperating this morning.''

Olin withdrew the net, nodding. He said, ''True.''

Phaedrus said, ''I am not a fisherman, but I would imagine you do not do this entirely with the catch alone in mind.''

Olin folded the net up, carefully. ''No. One could use a huge dragline and scoop it all up, or plant blurt along the bottom and blow them to the top. But what then?''

''There would be no more.''

Olin sorted through his catch, placed perhaps a dozen in his basket, and threw the rest back into the cold water. ''Exactly.''

For a time, neither said anything, then Olin said, ''Now you know. What are your plans?''

''I thought to return to Marisol, but that seems unwise. At the least, I should arrange some way to get Meliosme out of there.''

''Your woman.''

''Yes.''

''I agree.''

''Are you aware of the situation?''

''That someone was having you watched? Of course.''

''Who interrogated Patroclo?''

''Bautisto. And few escape the old bustard, too. But that one got away, he did.''

''The prince told me; but what is your own evaluation?'' Phaedrus felt an instant trust, an instinctive regard, for the redoubtable Olin, whom Pompeo apparently trusted without question.

Olin looked off at the sea distances for a moment, and then said, as if musing to himself, ''I would have said something out of Old Crule. You know, all the diehards and lifers ran there after Symbarupol fell to the rebels. But their reporting nets didn't fit that pattern. There was contact with Tilanque, Karshiyaka, and Tartary. A lot of moving about on the far end. Decision was made to collect you because the usual spy networks stopped abruptly. We assumed they were close enough to use more ordinary methods. All the signs pointed to that.''

"You mean the people they were reporting to . . . were in Clisp."

"Perhaps not that close. But close enough to get here in a day."

Phaedrus didn't say anything. Olin added, "Rumor has it you did something vile in Lisagor."

"Yes, one might say that."

"Well, it's none of my affair. You've done well here, and Pompeo is satisfied with that. So are we. But I've orders to assist you, and so I will. What would you do? Pull out and go into the wild? There isn't much of it left, you know."

"If they found me in Clisp. . . ."

"Yah. They can probably follow you anywhere on Oerlikon. Do you know who and what they are? Perhaps we can eliminate some of them. . . ."

"If this is truly offworld, then there are more behind this than we can reach . . ." He let it trail off, thinking, *But I can reach into places Olin can't see.* Still, he would have to move, and he would have to have some data. He doubted he could derive an accurate answer with the limited amount and values he had. Assumptions. They could be oracles, better than gods, and they could be fools, worse than charlatans. . . ." But at any rate, I should get Meliosme out. Some of the hardier kids."

"No worry there. We would take over what was left. Your place was well-known, and needs keeping. We have people we can put to that."

"Have you rested?"

"Enough. Bautisto went home, so I'd have to round up a couple of worthy lads. No matter, that. We have plenty about."

"We should leave, and go to a place near Marisol, where we can arrange to have Meliosme contacted."

Olin picked up his catch, and the net, and set off, as if glad to have something decided. "I'll go get the car. It's charged up now and ready to go. We'll get the lads along the way. Go back through the house, tell the factotum. I'll meet you in front."

Phaedrus nodded, and set off toward the garden wall, but before he stepped through it, he looked back, once, at the limitless blue horizon, the darkness of the sea, the depths of the sky. He thought to himself, *I was shown paradise, but only to demonstrate that I can't have it. Someday.* . . . And he thought that it would be a good idea, after they had picked up Meliosme, for them to go off into the wild lands of Southern Clisp, among the mountains, for a while.

The fog had cleared inland as well as along the coast when they set out, leaving the estate behind, and Cape Forever. Phaedrus had come up this same road before, but it had been at night, in dense fog, and he remembered no landmarks. Now, with the sun in the south near noon, he saw a smooth road made of compacted yellow gravel, very fine and even-surfaced, that ran straight between cultivated fields. In the far distances on both sides could be seen the low, spreading turf roofs and sturdy stucco walls of houses and outbuildings, and in the south, farther still, the mountains of Clisp rose up, tier on tier, layer on layer, each level becoming lighter in tone until the last one, flecked and spotted with snow, nearly matched the pearlescent color of the southern horizon.

The car moved along the road eastward now, easily, silently. No one took notice of them as they passed. The road, although dry, left no dust trail behind them. Olin sat in the back, as before, with Phaedrus, apparently catnapping, but remaining wary as an animal. The two "boys" Olin had brought with him looked like hardened veterans of border wars.

Olin noted, out of the corner of his eye, that Phaedrus was watching the two in front closely. He said, quietly, "Not by tradition alone, nor by good manners, was the House of Clisp maintained during the cycle of darkness. We were quiet, we kept our own counsels, but now and again muscle was needed. These are representative of that class."

Phaedrus nodded. "They appear capable and loyal."

"Whatever comes, you are among friends and comrades. His word suffices." Olin nodded back over his shoulder toward the west, a curt, chopped motion. "I don't doubt we're dealing with planted agents and buried sleepers in the government, back in Marisol. You simply can't be sure of that many people. But these are our own."

Phaedrus saw the one on the passenger side bend over and work with the communicator, speaking at length. He could not make out what was being discussed. The man used a single earphone, and spoke so quietly nothing could be made of it. After a few moments, he replaced the earphone and turned, gesturing to Olin. Olin leaned forward in his seat, and carried on a close, whispered conversation, none of which, judging by the grim expressions on their faces, bore anything good. At last, Olin, finished, hesitated and turned to Phaedrus.

Phaedrus said, "Something not good. . . ."

Olin said, in a careful monotone, "Early this morning, unknown parties attacked your place. We were out of range until we passed that last milepost, and so could not be informed. There were other problems as well. They delayed until now to attempt contact. They would have to insure they had no plants, as well."

Phaedrus sat back, his face very still. "Go on."

"It was hit and run, very fast job. Apparently they wanted to catch you by surprise, so they did not waste time identifying victims. They came in shooting, scattered incendiaries all over, fired the place and left. By the time the police and guards responded, it was too late. The number of dead is very high. Some got out, helped the youngest ones, but Meliosme was not one of them. They haven't finished counting and finding the bodies yet, and the identifications. . . . They will have to figure backwards from the survivors."

The car rolled on, an almost inaudible hum coming from the electric motors. The two in front looked stolidly ahead, more alertly than before. Phaedrus nodded, reflectively, very still, seeing only the clear air, the mountains, with an impossible clarity. Finally, he said, "I see."

Olin sat back for a long moment, and said, "None of them were caught, and there were few witnesses, and what they report will have to be carefully sifted. It's a long chase, friend. We will do what we can."

Phaedrus said, dully, "They will have at least a day headstart on us."

Olin nodded, vigorously. "Exactly. Not that we can't pick up the trail, but by the time we do get on it, several more days will have gone."

Phaedrus mused, out loud, "I owe your organization a debt. Those who wished me harm came thinking I was there. Sure of it. So sure they didn't stop to even see who they were shooting. I owe you, not you me. Your group was proof against their penetration."

"Luck, in a way, Phaedrus. We moved fast, according to orders. But another day and you'd have been in there, too."

"Yes."

"You seemed to know something. Do you know where we should start?"

Phaedrus said, slowly, "I don't doubt what I can see of this. The ones who came on the raid, they were tools, they were order-takers, not originators. The orders came from somewhere else."

Olin agreed. "Exactly."

"I think offworld. But I don't know who, or why. Or from where. 'Offworld' is just a word, a symbol, but it takes in more than we know here, in Clisp, on Oerlikon. The people turned their backs on the places they came from, and so we really don't know what is out there."

Olin said, "True. A long way for Clisp to reach."

Phaedrus rubbed his chin thoughtfully. He thought, *Revenge, of course. But I've been caught by surprise, and blind reactions will accomplish nothing. In fact, if I rushed blind into that, they might be waiting for something like that. No. It will have to be measured, considered, planned, read out.* He turned to Olin, and asked, "Do you carry any rations in the car?"

"Rations? Like survival gear? Yes. Two packs, in the luggage compartment. We used to have to have them. We went the long way through the lower mountains."

"They have food?"

"Food, simple hand weapons, a shelter. Not much."

"Do you need them?"

"No."

"Could we combine the food from both into one?"

"Hm. Would be hard, but I think we could. Could throw some of the other stuff out. What have you in mind?"

"I have to disappear. That is all I can say to you, even in trust. You will never see me again."

"There is something you can do alone that we can't?" His tone was practical and faintly scornful, but not hostile.

"There is something I must do alone. . . . How isolated are the mountains?"

"Scattered steads along the lower hills facing north. Nothing, in the high mountains. On the south slope, wild folk and isolated fishermen. Are you going south? There are no roads and no passes to the south side of Clisp; in fact, but for the name, it's another country. . . ."

"Where can you let me off?"

"You are serious?"

"Yes."

Olin leaned forward and spoke briefly to the driver, then leaned back. "Not far, there's a side road. We can cut across to the old foothill track. Does it matter where?"

"Where? Ah, no. No matter. I could start from right here. There are the mountains." He gestured to the south. "I would proceed until I got there."

"No need. We'll take you to a suitable place. As a fact, back in the old days, I made a couple of stops there myself. Are you sure you don't want someone along? All of us, while fat and content now, were not always so. Once, we slunk in the dark through those empty mountains, while lobotomized cretins marched in ranks up and down the roads of the plain."

"You, yourself?"

"Myself, or Bucephalo, or Pandolfo. If you have desperate and evil deeds in mind, there are none better. As a fact, we'd do so without obligation. Peace, and the rule restored, now they're good things, but all the same, it is a clarity to the mind to have an outright enemy—no subtle stuff, no justice and mercy, just simple revenge. Our enemies are fallen of their own plots. Let, let us. . . . borrow yours."

Phaedrus managed a weak smile on a face that had become separated from the soul that animated it. "You say it truly. But all the same, let me go alone. Now will come a part of cunning and stealth—much later the night of the knives, or worse. Later will come in a far place—I know it not, now—and you would be far from your best loyalties, your own nature. I thank you, but I must go alone. I am stranger than you or the Prince imagine."

Olin sat back, as the car proceeded now south, with the mountains ahead of them, already looming higher than the windscreen. Neither Olin nor Phaedrus said more.

The land soon began to roll and pitch, forming swells and rises, and the road sometimes dipped down into narrow little draws shaded by low, wide-spreading trees. The farmhouses and outbuildings did not increase in number, but they did draw closer to the road, sleepy places in the waning afternoon light, seemingly untenanted except for an indefinable air about them, an order one could sense without being aware of it. *Someone lived there, even if you couldn't see them in front of you.*

The road narrowed, became rougher, and Pandolfo, who was driving, turned the car into a narrow lane heading back to the west. He made the turn, and drove along the farm track, with the easy assurance of one who had driven along that very road many times before. This road did not run straight for long, but turned up into the foothills, now beginning to be in shadow; it passed through cuts, ran across sudden flats covered with erect, spiky trees, switched back and forth, and forded shallow, rocky streams tumbling down from the heights. At last, in a dense grove of the low, spreading trees he had seen earlier, the car stopped.

Phaedrus got out, and stood very still, listening, looking, trying to absorb the place and time. There was no wind, and the forest was silent, save for the mutter of a nearby creek, over the rocks. Olin and the other two busied themselves making up the one pack as Phaedrus had asked. Finally Olin came around the corner of the car, carrying the pack, looking a bit fuller than it had been designed to be.

He said, "Here it is. We had to leave a lot of the stuff out, but there're rations in plenty, if you can stand them. All stuff you add water to. Don't stint on their use. Eat as much as you can stand; it's high-protein concentrate. If you pace yourself, you can go far. I suppose it's useless to ask. . . ."

Phaedrus took the pack, and shouldered it. It was surprisingly heavy, but he would manage it. "If I told you, you wouldn't believe me, and if you did, I could not be sure of your loyalty. No, I can't say where I'm going. But I have one last request."

"Say it. By the Prince and his House, we'll do it."

"Have them announce to the public that I was killed in the raid. And make sure that no one else ever learns that I wasn't."

"To the first, consider it done. We will have that set this night. From then on, you are deceased. As for the rest, I see no problem . . . but we will be as sure as possible. Very few saw you, and we know them all."

"Then good-bye. Tell the Prince I will never forget his generosity, and that in days to come, one whom his house does not know, will come here and repay the debt he conferred on me. And that where I walk, I will conduct myself to bring credit to Clisp, as if I were a native."

"That I will also do. Phaedrus . . .?"

"Yes?"

"We'll see to the remaining children. And that there will be a place for others."

"Good." And he turned away, and started walking. It didn't matter really which direction he set off in, just to be moving.

He had walked on for a good ways, out of sight of the car, when he heard it start up, just barely, and then heard the noise of its passage back the way they had come, fading rapidly, and then nothing. The road ahead of him dipped down sharply and forded a shallow stream, which had worked its way down from the mountains. When he reached it, he stopped and drank deeply, and looked up. He couldn't see much, because of the forest growth, but he knew the stream came down from the snows far above. *As good à place as any.* It was only after he had gotten well into the climb that he stopped and allowed the grief and anger and regret to flow through him. He let it run free, let it possess him; and when he could think clearly again, the light of day was gone and the forest and the stream were dark and still. Only far overhead was there light, a luminous blue sky, traced with a lacy fretwork of cirrus clouds, tinted pink by the setting sun.

4

"The wise man anticipates; the food grapples with what happened; the shaman determines events by deciding, defining the environment in which things 'happen.' "
—H. C., *Atropine*

Phaedrus did not stop for the night, but kept on walking, using the weight of the pack as a goad, a whip. He followed dim trails that led up, or south, or both, paths that narrowed rapidly down to hardly more than animal passages, or were perhaps only random arrangements of the way things grew. Tier by tier, ridge by ridge, he trudged steadily ahead, walking through the long night of Oerlikon. Now and again, he would look up, to the highest ridge above him, to see if it seemed any lower. It didn't, so after a time he ignored it, and watched the ground, only looking about to gauge the best way forward.

In Clisp, the mountains were left mostly alone. Phaedrus met no wayfarers, saw no signs of habitation. The land was dark and empty, and there was nothing but the night sky overhead, with its random and meaningless assembly of faint stars.

He stopped to catch his breath, looked up, and thought, *There. One of those points, or better, one I can't even see. One of those points has a world circling it, and on that world, men gave orders. They spent much, they came back, to track me down and put a cruel and drastic plan into operation. Strike quick, without warning, almost randomly. Only something like that would get me. But for the concern of Pompeo and his men, there would I have been, too.*

But for what reason? Revenge I want, now, and revenge I will have, but if I do not unravel why this occurred, I will be striking at gaseous bubbles while the real enemy stalks again unseen.

He saw without effort that punishment for what he had done to Lisagor would not explain the viciousness of the attack. Indeed, it would be foolish to punish him at all—he was the tool of a deeper conspiracy, and one does not govern a complex civilization spread across many planets by punishing tools, or performing other absurdities of like nature. *Punishment is not their aim.*

Those star-folk; they came here, stayed here, manipulated Lisagor to their liking, cleverly. And when it started to fall, coordinated with marvelous swiftness and decisiveness, and pulled out. These are not people who do foolish things. They plan, they think, and they act. They undertook a seemingly reckless act, one of potential high cost, to get me. The answer stood before him as obvious as the darkness of the night sky: *They attack, to prevent me from doing something.*

He reflected that it wouldn't be hard to understand how they knew of him. Several knew about the plan, back in Symbarupol. If they had been captured, or gone over voluntarily, then they would have known. But surely it was obvious he had no aims beyond his original task—and that once that was done, he would try only to regain some sort of normal life. He tried, as Damistofiya, but the old group tried to kill her. Again, as Phaedrus, he had tried, been as low as water, learned ambitiouslessness. No matter. Still they came. But this last attack—that had been the work of offworlders, not renegade Lisaks, however it looked. But there was the curious part, the part that wouldn't fit, no matter how he tried to move it about: if they knew what he was, then it followed that they knew he had no interest whatsoever in the offworlders. He could be no threat to them . . . unless they knew something about him that he didn't know himself. Phaedrus arrived at that point, and decided to walk on for a bit, and concentrate on the pack: that thought opened up more speculations than he wanted to explore right at the moment.

Crossing a watershed line whose gentle slope concealed its height, Phaedrus stopped and looked back along the way he had come; behind and below was darkness absolute, but beyond that, far off toward the horizon, he could make out the open lands of the plains in the dim starlight—a lighter tone of purple darkness, dotted with an occasional light. Ahead of him were a few more ridges, interrupted with startling lone peaks, rather more to the east than near him. Another group far off in the west. The night was clear, and far to the northeast a soft glow suggested the probable location of Marisol. And south, beyond the ridges, only the sky, dim and dark near the horizon. He couldn't see the ocean yet.

Differing emotions strove within him, each one wanting the mastery, each one clamoring for the decisive position. In one set, he berated himself for failing to protect the people who depended upon him—Meliosme, the children they had taken in. In this mode, he accused, *Fool! You scamped your responsibilities! You should have been sharpening your knife!* But the answer was clearer than the accusation. *But we went the rightest way. And for me to have given over to paranoid fantasies of self-importance would have set the crucial tone of the world wrong. Had he leered and plied his whetstone and blade, while the keystone, so would it have been throughout. And who knows how far that could have reached.* And he wondered if he was still in the position. He had only looked once.

Another voice clamored, *Revenge, that's the stuff! Get even! You have the power to see to the uttermost point, and fling bolts of doom like Zeus!* That much was true, he ruefully admitted, although he doubted he had enough data to get anything but a very dim picture of the offworlders, and his aim would be correspondingly bad—and bad aim demands high Circular Error Probable strikes—the main reason for the existence of nuclear weapons in the far past. But there was a more important counter to this. Revenge in any measurable degree of equality would involve suffering of innocents far beyond any compensation for what had been done to him. And even after that, Meliosme wouldn't be back. *No. Pure revenge is idiotic, nonproductive, and entropic. A reaction. No, at best we need to look at this as an exercise in solving a problem. But formulating the problem, that's the rub! What was the problem here? It could not be defined as crime, nor even as terrorism, but the area it lay within was vague and ill-defined.*

But a third voice, sliding up like a sleazy solicitor, offered something that, despite it's tone, seemed the most promising of all. This one said, *Ask yourself why often enough and maybe it'll dawn on you. Go ahead, do it!* And the answer was not hidden at all, but rather something that he'd hoped he'd not have to go into. *It's something to do with Jedily. . . . What she was. How Pternam got her as his subject for the one successful try to attain the Morphodite.* Phaedrus walked on, now briefly downhill, and looked at that one plainly. *That's either a circular answer, leading me back where I started—or else it's a rug to sweep everything under.* He couldn't remember Jedily, so she was a blank tablet—he could write all sorts of virtues and vices there—but writing them was no proof they had ever been there in reality. And this was reality—people don't spend large amounts of money and travel immense distances between the stars to murder for trivial reasons. But he could see a third possibility, *if Jedily had once been, not an Oerlikonian Lisak native, but an offworlder herself . . . perhaps one of the manipulators herself, once. But something changed, if this was true, and . . .*

IF. A big dependant to hang a future on, and he could feel the shakiness of that branch. And he could not read and get an answer clean. But there was a test he would have to make before he could go further. Yes. But what was the right question? Who was Jedily Tulilly? If she was what he had been told—an indigent scrubwoman turned over to the Mask Factory, very well. But if she had been something else. . . . They would possibly not wish him to find out who she was, had been, did, or said, or claimed, or could do. . . . Yes. Possible. Phaedrus felt his head clear a little. He increased his pace, driving deeper and deeper into the mountains of Clisp, into the deepest recess of the night. *Yes. We'll need to start at Symbarupol, take up the trail there. They think I'll track agents of fortune, but what I'll do is track myself—back into the past, and I'll bet the paths intersect. They'll think they got away clean, and as they think it, I'll step from behind a tree and say, 'Ahem. Good Evening!'*

And with that he settled a little better into place, and he increased his speed. It was not that he had to hurry to get where he was going, but that he could go there and meet what was coming with more confidence, instead of fear and loathing. Yes.

Phaedrus had to meet someone, a woman by night. And Phaedrus wouldn't be, anymore. He glanced at the sky. *But not tonight. No. We have to find a place where we won't be seen, and also where we can do some, uh, calculations. This time we're going to try to control it a bit. What of it we can control.*

By the slow light of dawn he found a high place that looked isolated enough, with a good view all around down along the slants of the ridges falling away. Far off, on the very horizon, was the line of the ocean, south.

It was a mossy alpine meadow, slanting gently down from a small scree flaking off a rock face. There were no thornbushes or large rocks. Nor were there steep slopes he could roll down. Not so far away a tiny stream bubbled in the rocks. Water. He'd need a lot of water.

The day he spent sleeping, arranging the packs, and eating on one of the packages of concentrate. And trying to empty his mind; all thoughts, all striving, were to be laid aside. Phaedrus sat up and stared long into the blue distances, and watched the star Gysa wheel across the sky in its measured pace.

When the sun got close enough to the horizon not to cast shadows anymore, he sat up, and began to focus on the task at hand. All day, he had thought of nothing but the methods of his unique art of *seeing*, of *reading*. Now he assembled those rules of the game and laid out the lines of it the way he knew how. First he cast for the identity of who he would be after Change.

He knew it would be female. As the exercise progressed, the lineaments began filling in, one by one, in odd, fragmented groups that seemed to occur deliberately so as to prevent anticipation. That was the way of it: recursive. You had to play out every step: no shortcuts. When the image began to come in, it was not precisely seeing, but feeling who you yourself were. A kind of self-image. This one did not sit well.

A long body and longer limbs, probably taller at full adult size than Rael had been, but now hopelessly oversized and uncoordinated. That was the age-regression of Change, too. He wondered if he could slow that. What he had to do would be hard on a girl just past childhood.

Large eyes, a large, full mouth. He shook his head. He had never been one to complain about appearances. Rael had been no prize, with his morose and saturnine countenance. Still, this didn't feel right at all. He erased his marks on the flat rock he had made and started over from the beginning, taking extra verification steps.

If anything changed, it was the clarity of the image. It was clearer. She would be attractive, would catch eyes. He examined that more closely. Could that conceal as well? Could he become that role? Could he slow the reversal process? This was a separate question.

The answer was hard, and took up most of the faint daylight that was left. Yes, but there were limits. He saw them clearly. The girl would have to make do with the end of adolescence. He couldn't tamper with the process Pternam had ingrained into him beyond certain limits. If everything went right, he might be able to get her up to twenty standard years, and he had no time to do the computation for another look at what she'd be *then*. Hopefully she'd have outgrown the worst of the childishness still in the image he had of her.

Phaedrus looked around himself. *One last time, I'll see this scene as me-now. It'll be different, then. Probably daylight by the time I come around.* He lay back and began relaxing, one muscle at a time, floating backward, away from consciousness, seeking the internal state of balance and self-awareness by which he could initiate the process of Change. He did not consider the pain and terror at all. Of what use was worrying about it? This had to be. Phaedrus had done what was proper for Phaedrus to do. Now it was another's turn. He drifted further within, reflecting with some wry humor that he hadn't even bothered to name this one. The outrageous awkward limbs suggested something preposterous: Beumadine. Hephzibah. Euwayla. No. Maybe it wouldn't be like that, at all. Let it go. He was sinking fast. He had to steer this, or else now fall into a sleep from which he would be too far in to awaken. Already outside sensation was gone. And deeper, he could begin to sense the glow of that center he was seeking, the core, where bright threads crawled and writhed in an impossible dance that never ended. Now they were clear, moving at blurred speeds, enlarging, multiplying, filling the universe, immense. In danger of being lost in that, he pushed back, almost losing the state. *Now, maintain orientation and slow them down.* This was the hardest one yet. But by great effort of will, the bright threads slowed, became visible, slowed still more, moving closer. Now. Dead stop. *This one.* He changed it. *And this one* for the control of age regression, and he saw with sad resignation why there were limits on this, but he could not have explained it in words. There weren't any. *And what else are these?* All his pasts were in there, encoded, reduced to a single set of rules which would set a recursive sequence in motion and expand to the whole: There was Phaedrus. Inside himself, he saw the reduction of what he had been. And there: Damistofiya. And Rael. That one was odd, not like the others. There were gaps in it. And one more . . . That one, that would have to be Jedily. And it was badly damaged. Shorter than the others, as if hacked off, but there were parts of it intact. He looked further, feeling once again the pressure of Time; he could not hold this stasis indefinitely. How could he recover that part, the only thing left of the original. *Yes*. There, make that one change and splice that Jedily section onto the template now ready to form for her who was to be. A name came into his mind from nowhere: Nazarine. He made the final change, and let go, and saw the core whirl away angrily, as if he had tampered too much. He felt a great fear, rising back up through the levels of consciousness and finally opening his eyes.

There was nothing but the night. In fact, there was still a glow on the far horizon. He sat up. He shook his head, expecting some symptom, some feeling. Nausea, lightheadedness. That one had been rough. This Change might well be a real ride. But there was nothing. He smelled clean air, the smell of moss and grasses, his own scent, more than a little tired and sweaty. He laughed, aloud. *No worry now about cleanliness! In an hour I'll have layers of every sort of nastiness.* He heard the wind, far off, moving lazily around the peaks and defiles. He tried to organize what he had seen into some pattern of order; what part of Jedily had he recovered. Now he could consider it. It was not any of her substance, or of her continuous memory. That was gone forever. Pternam had burned that out. *No. Wait.* He struggled to remember it as it had been. There were two levels of damage to the Jedily segment. One was clearly done by Pternam, reaching for The Morphodite. Jedily had forgotten all that under the stress she had somehow endured. Mindless in the end, personalityless. But there was an earlier set of damages to the "tape" and those were clear and methodical, not at all like the accidental erasures and smears of the last damages. That part had been done to Jedily before Pternam ever got her.

Phaedrus felt the ground move under him, a faint, seesaw motion, a jellylike trembling on the edge of perception. Earthquake? It went on a bit, and then subsided. *Of course!* He wanted to go back within, and examine it again, but he knew he couldn't; inside him a time bomb was running, and Change would start any moment. *Besides,* he thought, *I spliced the Jedily section onto Nazarine, because these isn't any structure or memory per se on it. Whatever's on that section will add onto Nazarine. It's fragments of some kind of knowledge, and she'll know it, without knowing how. And Jedily will be truly gone, then. It will transfer and vanish. If I ever go within again, there will be no Jedily tape there.* In the end, he himself had been the last assassin who struck the final blow. Whatever Jedily was, he would have to learn by conventional methods. That part of him was gone.

He felt the ground motion again, start up, shaking, growing stronger. *Oh, shit, I have to change in the middle of an Earthquake!* He lay back flat on the moss, and watched a small stone sitting atop another. The motion became more violent, but the rocks didn't move. Nor did grass-stems wave. But they had to move. The ground was shuddering like an animal in pain! He sat up and looked around, at everything he could see, the moss, the talus pile, rocks around him. Nothing was moving, falling over. He started to stand up, but the shaking was so intense he couldn't, and instead got on his knees, as if he were going to crawl. There was a loud buzzing in his ear, a piercing high tone, growing louder, painful, and he looked in desperation to the ocean horizon, the black line forty kilometers away, south. Steady, but then yellow glowing lava crawled down his forehead and slid over his eyes, and he was buried, covered, still in the crawling position. *Roasting! Some geologist will find me and wonder how the hell* . . . And then Phaedrus didn't have any more thoughts to think.

In the uninhabited wilds of the mountains of Clisp, a creature underwent terrible changes. It grovelled, made tentative crawling motions, fell back, moved its limbs uncertainly. From time to time, sudden and drastic alterations would take place: fluids erupted from every orifice in shuddering heaves and convulsions. Pungent and sickening odors vented off it, and patches of its body produced copious flows of loathsome substances. It made sounds, but they resembled nothing intelligible. Parts of its body steamed and smoked in the cool night air, and the rocky ground on which it lay was stained with secretions that left phosphorescent runnels for a time. For a long time it continued its random movements, but as the night progressed, these slowed and by daylight the thing was still, although clearly some reactions were still taking place.

Daylight revealed what to a casual observer might resemble a plague victim who had been burned badly and extensively. All the hair of the head and limbs was gone; the head and face were a shapeless lump. It did not move, and appeared dead, but there was a pulse, and if one could have looked very close, there was breathing, although almost imperceptible. The clothing it had worn was stained and soaked, unrecognizable now. And there was a very curious thing about the clothing: it was singularly ill-fitting. The hands, bony claws, protruded from the sleeves, and the feet, similarly, stuck out awkwardly from the bottoms of its pants, and the general appearance was that of a person tall and bony, with swollen, enlarged joints.

During the long Oerlikonian day, the creature did not move, or if it did, it was so slowly that the motion was unobservable. The starlight of Gysa shone down on it indifferently, and the shadows around it moved, following the sun. Dusk came, and then the night. In the first darkness, some of the stains around it on the rocks glowed faintly, a pale yellowish light like cave fungi, but after a time, this faded.

It was dark when consciousness returned to him, and he thought it was the same night. He remembered almost nothing; all he could experience was pain unrelenting. Skin like roasting meat, bones and joints like dislocations on the rack, muscles tearing, over and over again. He could move a little; his shoes hurt and cramped, and somehow he managed to kick them off, although the effort was almost beyond him, both from lack of strength and lack of coordination. Patches of flesh went with the shoes. He also managed to loosen some of the clothing, but could not get any of it off, and after a time faded out again, but this time, he was prey to numerous hallucinations, which he encouraged as an interested observer. Within themselves, they were perfectly coherent, but they did not connect with anything, or make any sense; he could not interpret them.

He awoke later, sometime; the stars were different, although it was yet dark, without a hint of dawn in the east. The pain was still with him, and he felt the delirious giddyness of high fever, but this at least seemed orderly. He could barely move. Now he remembered some things, and could begin to place some order on his perceptions. Odd fragments of scenes drifted before his eyes, sometimes obscuring what his senses reported, but at least he could understand that these were temporary lapses, not realities. He lay on the rocks for a long time, until a soft rosy glow begin to appear in parts of the east, and then he slept. But this time, it was sleep, not unconsciousness.

He awoke again, and his head was clearer. He remembered that he was Phaedrus, and that he had initiated Change, and that something had happened. The sun was far in the west, and shadows were long, but it was yet daylight. His body sent him conflicting messages: an incredible thirst and hunger, an emptiness such as he could not ever recall knowing, and simultaneously a nausea so powerful he dared not move for fear of making it worse. He reasoned carefully, like a drunk, that part of the reason for the nausea was the incredible stench that assaulted his sense of smell. With halting motions, he dragged himself to the little rivulet bubbling over the rocks. He remembered it had been nearby. Now it seemed as far away as the planets of the offworlders. He spent the rest of the daylight crawling to that water; and much of the dusk he spent arguing with himself whether to drink first or start washing. Thirst won. At the first, he could not keep the water down, but after several tries, he managed to retain some. He shivered violently with bone-chilling cold, and understood that the sensation was part of a fever that yet raged within his body. Still, slowly, interspersed with short flights of sleep, or fever hallucinations, he struggled out of his clothing, and began washing the worst off, feeling the sting of the cold water ten times over. And by the dawn of the next day, he understood that he wasn't Phaedrus any longer. By the light of dawn, he laboriously crept to the place where he had cached his survival pack, and dug out some thin blankets. Among the oddments of gear in the bag he found a signaling mirror, and looked in it curiously, seeing in the image distorted by the shaking of his hand a person he did not know, a clown's face with only a dark shadow where the hair would be, puffy eyes, a pulpy mouth of no recognizable shape, rubbery lips. He shook his head. He examined the body tentatively. Female. But she wasn't very much to look at. The frame was wasted and cadaverous, with bones showing everywhere. It did not resemble the image he had procured within of Nazarine, but whatever she was, she was long of limb, as long as Rael had been, maybe longer, and where the skin had settled down to just being skin, it was a sallow olive color. She put the mirror back in the bottom of the pack. Now to begin trying to eat something, and put some shape on this body. And she thought, *That Change was the worst I can remember. Is this the way of it? Does it get worse each time? Is this worth it?* For now, she admitted the answer was probably no, but she also knew that as her strength returned, it would assume more worth. Even so, she knew that it would be a long time before she could face Change again. Decades, perhaps. And that put limitations on her, what she would have to do. She had shed Phaedrus and become Nazarine, but Nazarine would have to be careful. Starting here. Now.

She had difficulty keeping solid food down, and was weak, for a long time unable to stand. It was ten days before she was able to walk any distance, and was still thin as a labor camp inmate. Nevertheless, Nazarine decided that it was time to start the long slopes back toward Marisol. She would have to build herself up as she went. There was a problem: the food concentrate in the survival packs was almost gone.

As she walked, she worked her arms, trying to loosen up. All her limbs felt stiff, overstrained. And she thought, *And until I can make use of the amulet Pompeo gave Phaedrus, I am going to look a sight*. She looked down at the long body she now possessed. Her feet stuck out of Phaedrus' old, serviceable pants, and already her chest filled his old shirt. She laughed, even though it hurt terribly around the ribs: *I look like a tramp!* The shoes had proven impossible to adapt, so she went barefooted, which made progress slow.

Two days later, the last of the food gave out. But she had come a long way down from the high mountains, and at night could see outlying settlements below her on the plains. She had also stopped one day at noon, and *read* for the pivot of the World. It was no longer herself. Who it was, she didn't *read*. Only that it wasn't her. She was free.

She walked on, concentrating on one step at a time, finally reaching the flat alluvial plains of Clisp. It was cool, but she still had the survival blanket, and wrapped it around herself. She walked along a dusty road for a day and a night, stopping only short periods to rest, and then going on. But finally her strength, none too sure to start with, began giving out, and the rests became longer. At dusk, she stopped under a huge spreading tree and leaned against its trunk wearily. She would just close her eyes for a moment. . . .

. . . She woke up and it was late afternoon: the sun was far off over the western peaks, and shadows were long. It was disorienting—waking up before one went to sleep. Impossible. Her stomach growled. How long had she been here? *A whole day*.

She felt a small motion at her neck, and brushed, as if pushing an insect away. It came back. She brushed again. Nothing. Then something touched her hair. She grasped at it, and her fingers closed on a hand, which was quickly snatched out of her grip, accompanied by a grunting giggle: "Hunh-hunh-hunh-hunh." She turned painfully to look, and saw an enormous cretin, grinning and reaching for her. She tried to get up, but sprawled out on the side of the road. Weak. She looked again. The creature was an overgrown boy with an expression of constant beaming mirth on his face, but larger than most men. Easily twice her weight, and in her present condition, much stronger. She doubted she had the ordination of those long, thin limbs. She shook his head, reprovingly, and came forward, kneeling down beside her. "Woman," he breathed. Then he reached, as if reaching for an overripe fruit, and grasped her left breast. It was still filling out and was sore and tender. She pulled away, freeing her legs, and shaking her head. The cretin nodded. He said, "Uh-huh. Woman." He leaned forward, clumsily, to touch her again.

Nazarine rolled a little back and kicked hard at the cretin's solar plexus, and to her surprise, it connected. It felt like she had kicked a tree trunk. What with normal strength would have disabled him, and left him gasping for breath in the middle of the road, now only rolled him off balance and made him mad. "Uh." He grunted. "Hurt." He surged to his feet like a tiger and stood over her with an altogether unearthly expression on his now red face. Nazarine tried to recall everything she could, desperately. He reached, suddenly, before she could counter it, picked her up and pummeled her viciously. It was like being dismembered by a whirlwind. Clumsy, he succeeded from sheer strength. She found herself lying in the road on her back with the cretin sitting on her stomach, pinning her arms with his tremendous knees, her head swimming. She heard something off to the side somewhere, to which the cretin responded, looking up suddenly. He shouted, sidelong, not speaking directly, "Colly find, Colly keep. This one not run away."

The voice hardened a bit, and said, now a lot closer, "No, Colly. Get up and let her be. Or we'll put the sparker on you."

Colly shook his head. "No sparker."

The unseen voice, thin and with an edge in it, repeated, "No, Colly. Not yours. Off!" She sensed motion, and there was a vicious crackling, like electricity, and with a sudden thrust in his knees, Colly abruptly stood up, moving to the side, making odd, tentative motions with his hands, held low, and shaking his head like an angry and baffled animal.

There was someone standing in the road, in the shadows of the tree, holding a thick metal tube longer than his arm, which had four stubby projections at the end of it. This he waved, back and forth in measured time. He said, "Get gone and don't come back—or I'll hot-wire your fundament to the house generator." This was not said in heat, but coolly, matter-of-factly, almost as if an idle comment. But Colly apparently understood the rod and the words well, for he turned and loped off, heading toward the west.

Nazarine slowly sat up, rolling over on her knees first, and tried to stand. Her legs felt like water. The figure stepped out of the shadows and offered her his hand. She took it, a little uncertain, but it was firm and she stood, shakily, but on her own feet.

She could see more clearly now. In the road stood a man of indeterminate age, rather thin, with sharp, crisp features, and the evidence of a hard life on the lines of his face. His eyes, however, were large, deep set, and alert. He looked at her carefully.

He said, "Sorry you had to find Colly. Or he find you. He's only dangerous if you let him slip up on you."

"What is he?"

"Colly is Colly. He's always been like that. Not all there." He shrugged, and made a motion with his forefinger to his temple as if he were screwing a bolt into place. Then he tapped it. "Like that. He does odd and heavy jobs around the farms, sleeps in odd corners of barns. . . . He's always looking for a woman, but of course no one would have him. He doesn't really know what to do, should he find one. The local topers once took him to a happy-house and threw a lot of money in the door after him. Thought it would calm him down."

"Did it?" She asked coolly.

"No. He's quite incompetent. The trouble is, he's strong enough to give someone a bad lick, if by nothing else than accident, and if you tried to fight him . . ." He shook his head. "Bad move, that."

"If things were normal, I could have handled him."

He nodded. "I see they are not. You appear to have had an adventure."

She said, "It is a longish story I would as soon leave. I walked over the mountains from the South Coast."

He shifted position, relaxing a little. "From the coast. Ah, now. You are not Clispish; I heard it in your speech."

"That is so. However, I was and am in the employ of the Prince."

"Present?"

"Not Amadeo. Pompeo."

"Well, good. We thought well of him, even though he was no hero. Things come to one in their own time, do they not? And so for Pompeo the great days came at the end of his reign, most of which was illegal, as you know. Still and all he wore them well. But of course Amadeo now holds the purse strings. Will you work for him as well?" There was a subtle undertone in his question, a subtle probing.

"I did not work for the government, but for the Prince himself. One of his servants. A courier."

"He still uses some?"

"A few. There are things he wishes to know, to do."

"Good, there. You will find Amadeo very different."

"So I have heard."

"Well. You were on your way from the South Coast to somewhere; would you return to Cape Forever?"

"No. I am for Marisol. But I need to stop for a while. I don't think I can make it as I am."

"Your mission continues, then?"

"My mission has just started."

"Allow me to further the work of the old Prince, then. I see you need some clothing, rest, food. These I can share, although they are plain enough. Come along." He turned and started off along the road, soon ducking under a low branch, and following a faint path across the side ditch into the fields. He looked back. "Are you coming?"

She nodded weakly, and started after him, slowly.

5

"The virtue of the Tarot, the I Ching, and the Sabean Symbols, and acts of divination using these schemata, is not that they reveal a future which was hidden from us, but that they remind us of the understandings we already possessed, but did not openly acknowledge."

—H. C., *Atropine*

While the people of Old Lisagor were in appearance an undistinguished group that could have walked anywhere among the civilized worlds without notice, the inhabitants of the other continent of Oerlikon, Tartary, would have been noticeable in almost any crowd. Tall and gaunt, with horselike faces and flapping black robes, each one lived essentially alone in a rude stone castle, preferably reared by their own hands, and each one was a law unto themselves. There was no government and no law in Tartary, save the complicated etiquette by which the makhaks lubricated those rare occasions of social intercourse they tolerated.

With indifference they allowed the offworlders to establish an enclave on a small embayment in the south, which was hardly less harsh a climate than the north. Those foreigners who could cope with the incessant winds, the complicated, arcane manners which all were expected to master without instruction, were welcome to visit; most stayed only long enough to transact a piece of business, and then left, eager to be away from the gaunt natives who asked no quarter and gave none. Nevertheless, among a few of the holds near the Enclave, offworlders were tolerated for somewhat longer periods and cynically pumped for everything they knew.

Master Amew Madraz maintained a freehold on Dankmoss Moor, an open, and to offworld eyes, curiously undefined patch of land a daywalk* north of the Enclave. Master Madraz seemed

*All distances within Tartary were spoken of relatively, rather than absolutely.

uncommonly well-off for a makhak, having half-a-dozen men-at-
arms and retainers quartered within his hold, bound to him by
the stiff and blood-curdling formulae by which makhaks defined
relationships involving personal services. And for some time,
Madraz had kept as guests an offworld man and woman, an
unheard of thing, who had chosen to rent a section of one of the
eccentric towers reared by a previous tenant. To these at various
times came other visitors, as well as an occasional Lisak. They
claimed that they had business which would not bear airing
within the close confines of the Enclave, where everyone knew
everyone else, and anyone's business was soon the property of
all.

The visitors were a curious lot: They had come on one arrival
of the offworlders' scheduled liner, missed another arrival, and
were now apparently awaiting the next, their business finished.
They were more self-contained than most, and evidenced no
curiosity at all toward the makhak custom, or the land itself.
Intense and disciplined, those were the words! Moreover, they
acted as much like makhaks as their own custom allowed, a fact
which left Madraz considerably at ease; they did not interact
much with himself, or with his bondsmen. Curious. Yet they
would shortly be gone, a minor incident of little importance.

Cesar Kham and Arunda Palude occupied a tower which had
been part of an earlier part of Schloss Madraz, and which they
had repaired with their own hands, correcting the worst of its
drafty and cold habitats. Still, it was cold and drafty enough.
They wore extra clothing, and exercised when it became too
much to bear. The stony, flat expanses of Tartary, grim and
hopeless under its virtually perpetual overcast, offered little in
the way of trees for firewood, and there were no grazing animals
to provide inflammable dung chips, either. There were peat
bogs, but their use was carefully guarded, and no makhak would
have thought twice about using fuel merely for personal comfort.
The very concept was impossible to frame in their language
without a circuitous series of euphemisms, typical of such a grim
folk.

Their sole heat source came from candles, made, it was said,
by certain makhaks of the north coasts who meticulously wove
gossamer nets and strained from the frigid northern seas tiny
crustaceans whose bodies were filled with wax. The candles
emitted a dense, oily yellow light and left behind them a distinct

marine odor. They spent much of their considerable idle time playing intricate games, complicated and overcomplicated to serve the purpose of passing time. Now and again, they would have a visit from one or another of their agents, and then spend days considering every aspect of the agent's report.

Their last visitor had left before dark, and now, over the thin gruel and swampberry hash the makhaks subsisted on, they considered his findings.

Kham ventured, "We'll have a few more reports before we leave, of course, but from all indications it seems that the job has been done successfully. There are no traces of that creature whatsoever."

Palude, her face pinched and prematurely aging from the constant cold, sniffled contemptuously and answered, "Yes, they are all certain, aren't they?"

"You don't think so?" He raised his almost invisible eyebrows, and, grimacing at the dank, smoky flavor, swallowed another spoonful of crushed swampberries.

"Well, you know they won't have to live with the consequences if they made a mistake. From what we know of that thing, it will probably be able to figure out where such an attack came from. If it didn't have any motivation before, it certainly will now."

"You've heard the same data I have."

"Yes, and I'm an integrator by trade. And there are some things missing. No positive identification, for one thing. And for lack of anything else, it just doesn't feel right. We did similar things back in the old days, and I tell you there is something slipshod—is that the proper word?—about all this."

"You have been practicing with those fortune-telling systems; what sort of answers do they give?"

"Ambiguous and haunting. Or openly disastrous."

Kham made a peculiar grimace in which he pressed his thin lips together so that his mouth became an almost-invisible line. "For example?"

Palude reached into her traveling bag and produced a small metal tube, shaking it. A dry rattling came from within. "Hei are the yarrow stalks. They cost me even more than the book did—the *I Ching*. I have been studying it closely, learning its ways, which are somewhat opposed to the way we look at things. We believe in causality; it explains coincidence and change. It is disturbing."

"Go on."

"When they sent the message that the attack had been done, I threw the stalks, asking the question, 'Did it succeed?' I got this answer: #44, Kou, 'Coming to Meet.' The maiden is powerful; one should not marry. There were changeable lines in positions one, two, four and six, leading to #63, Chi Chi, 'After Completion.' That one says, 'At the beginning, good fortune; at the end, disorder.' There is a lot more to it, and of course in some cases such a reading could imply a favorable course, but I found it not so good, considering what we were dealing with. So disturbing was this that I then asked, 'Specify the outcome of this event.' I got #49, Ko, 'Molting or Revolution,' changing lines one, three, four, five and six to become #23, Po, 'Splitting Apart.' "

Kham chuckled. "I thought one did not question oracles."

Palude shook her head. "One does not doubt. But it is permitted to ask for further explanation."

"Your interpretation?"

"We assumed that the Morphodite would be a young man, if it had survived; most likely in Clisp, hiding. We found, after, what we believed to be such a person, who seemed to have no origin, and who was leading a quiet and a charitable life. If he survived the attack, the elimination operation, he would change as an act of self-preservation, becoming a woman again. 'The maiden is powerful.' Then, 'At the end, disorder.' That appears to be his unique power, to institute Change at a fundamental level, a stage of disorder leading to another stable configuration."

"And the rest?"

"I should say it needs little reading-into. Assuming we read it specifically from our point of view, that reading means that change is due, will be caused, and that people opposed to our way of thinking will come to predominate."

Kham hunched forward in his seat, more attentive and not smiling. "If you believe that, than we have done worse than simple failure. We have stirred up something dire and evil."

"Cesar, you left out the best part of this."

"Eh? What's that?"

"We don't know who we're looking for, now."

"Hm. That's so, just so. *If* it's as you say, there. How about the rest? Let me hear an integrator speak."

"We got a body count. No identities, save that of his woman. There were four more adult-sized bodies in there; any one could have been him, or might not have. There is no confirmation."

"What report from the agents?"

"Official mourning. Righteous anger, and the dispatch of Clispish agents to various parts to see what they can turn up. The actions look proper, but there's a shakiness to them that doesn't quite look right . . . There is too much attention to it. It looks like a stage-act, with very few people knowing the truth, but this course does not reveal motives."

"Then he had help we didn't know about!"

"Not necessarily. The reports indicate no knowledge of his true abilities. That would have surfaced if it had been known. But he may have had some help without this knowledge. High up."

"Can we look into this? We have time to confirm something of this, surely, before the next ship departs."

Palude said, "I have already set that in motion, and we should soon be getting reports. I have instructed our plants to concentrate in two areas—accidental case, and help from very high. I expect nothing from the first, but we might get something from the second."

Kham nodded. "You were emphatic?"

"Rather. I told them, in fact, to take some chances and not be overly concerned about having to bolt and run. We need confirmation of success or failure before we go back."

Kham mused, "Well, if success, contrary to your oracle, we should have no worry."

Palude sat still in the dimness of the stone tower room, and then said, softly, "And if failure, there isn't anything we can do about it."

Nazarine had little reserve left after the long walk, and the exertion with the cretinous Colly, and when she finally arrived at the house, she did little for the next several days except sleep. Sometimes she woke for a time, and ate. Someone was there; at least, someone seemed to know when she'd need food. The meals were uniform, bland, and to her surprise, nourishing. She still retained a tremendous desire to sleep, and stayed awake only long enough to take minimal care of her body, but after an uncertain passage of time she noticed that she felt better, and her sleep was lighter. More significantly, her body was filling out.

She learned a little, but not much, about her host, who apparently was called Marcian. There was also a ghostly-quiet small girl-child, Cerulara, who came and went, saying nothing, and vanishing immediately. Both were quiet, busy with their own affairs. They gave her a place to recover, and left her alone.

Recovering more of her strength, Nazarine began to explore the house, and some of the grounds around it. It seemed to be nothing more than a farm, although it was very neatly kept. Marcian spent much of the day either out in the fields, or working silently and intently in one of the small outbuildings, repairing some piece of machinery, while the little girl seemed to keep the household chores at bay. Nazarine estimated the girl's age at no more than ten no matter what, but she suspected younger.

They were so strange and silent. She could have easily read the answer, but she sensed something private about their ghostly movements, about their grim silences, and she left it alone. Whatever it was, it did not concern her. It was curiously like the routines people adopt to put grief off, except that the original object had long since withered away, leaving them with a routine which they still adhered to. And what was their relationship? Father and daughter? She thought so, and yet there was something missing there as well. And if so, then where was the mother? Dead? She probed their movements and habits, sensing rather than doing a reading; there were none of the essential markers of a death in the family.

She approached Cerulara about repairing and refitting her clothing, which the child acknowledged with the fewest words possible, but also as if Nazarine had asked her an impossible question. The girl hurried off to find Marcian, for whatever he could add. Nazarine shook her head in confusion. But later that day, in the afternoon, late, when the shadows were falling down from the mountains into the glades of the dooryard, Cerulara came out into the yard, where Nazarine was sitting, with an armload of clothing, all of which seemed to have been stored away. Together, they went through it, piece by piece, selecting the suitable, returning the obviously unsuitable. Nazarine picked things that were serviceable and plain, and left aside the rest. She wanted now merely something to wear besides the ancient bathrobe Marcian had given her. Cerulara made several trips in and out of the old wooden house.

Cerulara fixed supper as the sun, Gysa, was sinking behind the ranges far off in the southwest, layers of blue and violet lightening as they approached the sky to a color not greatly different from the pale blue wash of the sky itself. Marcian always washed outside, in a homemade shower room he had built behind one of the outbuildings. Nazarine met him, wearing some of the things: a pair of loose brown pants, a soft beige blouse, and a vest over that. The nights were cool now, as fall deepened.

She said, "I am well enough to walk about."

"I know. You have done very well. You recover fast."

She added, "Carulara brought me some old clothes . . ."

"I see. Well, they seem to fit you well enough."

"I only need to borrow them for a while. . . ." He nodded, absentmindedly, going on into the house. Nazarine turned and asked, "Can I take my meals with you two now? I am well enough? Certainly not an invalid."

"Certainly. Although you may find it hard to make breakfast with us. We arise early."

"Get me up. And if you wish, I can help. I would like to repay some of your kindness."

"I know. We saw you had nothing but that cartouche. That's a powerful talisman. You don't need anything else. But of course you have to be somewhere where they can credit it back. At the moment, you're as poor as the rest of us." He seemed to be making some calculation back in his mind, weighing her. "You don't look much like a field hand, and that's what I need. No offense, but you've got a city woman's body."

"Perhaps. I am only what I am. However, I need exercise and motion."

He nodded assent, slowly. "Very well. You'll be leaving soon, then?"

Nazarine looked at Marcian closely. There was no barb in his question, but under it, there was a curious tone of sad resignation. "No. I'm in no hurry. I owe you something . . . for pulling me in off the road, and of course Colly."

"I hope you weren't planning to walk to Marisol in the condition you were in."

"I had nowhere else to go."

"You can stay as long as you want, and go when you want." It was incredibly generous, and yet there was an icy aloofness in it, too. She saw something else in him, too: a deep, intense appreciation of her body, but one he kept under strong control. *How did she know that?* Damistofia had hardly interacted with normal men, and Nazarine now recalled her responses as clumsy and rude approximations at best. *But now she knew, instinctive-*

ly. How? Then she remembered *Change*, and those torn fragments of the Jedily section. Jedily had lived a woman all her life, from youth to age, and apparently knew men well. There was no memory of anything. *That* was as blank as before. But there was something else present in her now. An established pattern of identity. And she appreciated Marcian seeing her that way, even if nothing ever came of it. All this went through her mind in a flash, and when the thought was gone, she looked back, returning at least the gesture-acknowledgment of his attention, from which he looked away abruptly. He said, "Ruli will set supper out."

Supper was an occasion which was no more animated than the rest of the routines they lived through. Cerulara cooked and set supper out, but at the end, everyone set to cleaning things up, and as soon as Cerulara saw that things were proceeding as they should, vanished into whatever part of the house was hers, presumably to bed. Marcian puttered about for a moment, and then found what he was looking for, a jar of some herb, with which Nazarine's nose wasn't familiar, from which he steeped up a fragrant herb tea. He offered Nazarine some. "It's the only luxury I allow myself."

"What is it?"

"Wintergall. Muscle relaxant." After a moment, he added, "You sleep without dreams you remember."

She took the cup and sat down. "The clothes are very nice Thank you."

"No need. There's no one else to wear them, and they'd probably dry-rot before Ruli grows enough to fill them out. Take what you need."

"Is Cerulara your daughter?"

"Yes."

"Is the lady of the house dead?"

"Not as far as I know."

"But she's not coming back?"

"No. Have no fears on that score. She won't be back." And he tossed off the cup of tea and began making ready to leave the room. He started to turn the light off, but saw that she wasn't finished, and so left it on. For a time, Nazarine sat in the silent kitchen and thought aimless things, hearing Marcian make small noises elsewhere in the house, until they, too, stopped. She finished the tea, turned out the lights, and returned to her own small room behind the kitchen.

And so it became that Nazarine entered into yet another routine of nothing more complicated than Basic Life, with all its attendant compromises and nagging problems whose solutions were never final. Weeding, harvesting, cleaning and repairing machinery. And as before, when she had been Phaedrus, seemingly in another geologic era, she found something deep and satisfying in it. And at the time, terrifying: all these people confronted nothingness daily, insignificance, nobodyhood, oblivion. Wherever they had originally come from, now they were stranded on a piece of star-stuff—and the starry stuff was no different from a clot of earth. But their every action expressed their basic drive to attain some kind of meaning to their lives.

She was particularly sensitive to this, having started her present consciousness from Rael, who had been placed at the very center of significance and, through her serial personality, had been running from that ever since. Yes. All people wanted to defy time, have power, make changes, leave something permanent, but to have such a power was worse: one walked with warlocks and evil wizards, perverse gods and terrifying demons. When people attained that power, they invariably went bad as they grasped at it.

And she felt the pressure now to re-enter that stream again, for many reasons, and yet she also sensed a deep-seated repugnance and disgust. Once back on that path, it would never end. There would never be an end to the uses she could put Rael's system to, and with potential immortality, there was no end-check on it. Yes. Phaedrus had been right to leave that.

But as she worked, she also knew that somewhere, something was hunting her, with a will that did not flag; some malevolent aim that was passed on from hand to hand. They would suspect, eventually, that they had missed Phaedrus, and then the apparatus would be activated again. She could hide here, certainly, in the back-country of Clisp, but who could say what further crimes could be done against, say, Marcian, or even Cerulara, should she remain here. She glanced across the rows to where Marcian was untangling some tangleweed from the tines of a harvester, and thought, *This cannot be again.*

At first, they tolerated her, as a well-meaning, but hopelessly inexperienced city-bred idiot who had no feel for the unending drudgery of keeping a farm up—or appreciating its rare moments when everything, for a moment, was done, and one could laze the day away. Rare, rare. But gradually, she kept at it, and the toleration slowly mutated into acceptance. But one thing did not change: the grim silence and the locked emotions that both Marcian and Cerulara kept. And yet they both responded more openly to her. More than once she had caught a small shred of affection from Cerulara, and also more than once, she had caught hints of Marcian's appreciation of her body, and unlike the boyish and subtle Damistofia, as Nazarine she had developed a full, ripe figure, distributed on a tall, loose frame. There was no leer in his glance, but simple desire, and something, probably from Jedily, also caught herself wondering how it would be to have love with such a one. For the moment, she let the question go unanswered, even in speculation.

As the autumn wore on into the gates of winter, the cooler air began to bite a little at night, and the work, at the same time, slowed, and they all had considerably more leisure time. She went on several trips with Marcian and Cerulara, to visit brokers, or to buy supplies for the house, and Nazarine found herself becoming attached to the simple life she had fallen into, the open air, the direct experience, the sunburned hands. To be sure, she remembered vividly the composite pasts of her former selves, the intrigue, and its brother, fear. Constantly. And she also remembered a thirsty enemy and the riddle she had not yet tried to answer—who had Jedily been. She was sitting in the open power-wagon Marcian used for all his errands, looking at the brightly dressed crowds milling about among the benches and stalls, with Cerulara behind her. She caught sight of Marcian making his way through the crowd, and when he saw her, his stern, angular face brightened. Fractionally, but enough. It was time to go.

That night, back at the farm, after supper there was more animation than she had seen since coming there, and as they were clearing everything away afterward, once Marcian briefly put his hand on her shoulder, affectionately.

Late, very late, after the house had long become quiet, Nazarine made up a packet of the most serviceable clothing, and after a quick, silent tour of the house, slipped out into the soft anonymous night of Oerlikon, with its random weak stars. She drew a deep breath of the cold night air, sighed, and set off down the road, away from the mountains behind her, and toward the northeast, where dimly one could barely make out the lights of something, perhaps a city, glowing faintly in the haze above the city proper. More than once she stopped and looked back. Twice, she stopped, hesitated, and then went on. Once she turned back, but she only went a few steps before resuming her old course.

She had left a short note, explaining why she had left, and promising to send some money from Marisol to help pay for her upkeep while she had been with them. She knew it wouldn't be sufficient. But it was better for them, and sometimes, she knew, one had to leave the things one wanted. (An image in her mind of Marcian, walking across the evening light in the yard, half-dressed, the muscles visible along his taut, slim frame. The harsh planes of his face, and the softness behind them. She hoped he would find someone to replace the woman who had left him, and the girl.)

The farm had receded out of sight, and the mountains seemed lower, smaller, less significant, and she was walking at a steady pace, which would cover a good part of the way to Marisol before tomorrow sunset. She felt confident, right, on the way at last, to whatever her search might bring. She did not feel any fatigue.

It was then that she noticed that she was being followed by someone along the dim, pale road behind her. Someone who did not bother to conceal himself, a large figure with a lumpy, heavy, rolling motion to his walk. Colly, no doubt, out prowling in the night. Nazarine stepped up the pace, thinking that he'd tire of it and leave off. But when she looked back, he was still there, puffing and blowing, but making an effort to catch up. She looked back toward the farm. It was gone into the darkness under the mountains in the starlight. Colly was a long way from his own area, and if he'd followed her this far, he'd follow her all the way to Marisol.

She stopped, and when he came puffing up, she looked about the empty fields and called out, "Go home! Leave me alone!"

Colly didn't even slow down, but he said, between breaths, "No sparker, no Marcian. Just pretty woman."

"I don't want to hurt you," she warned, calling up images in her mind from Rael, from Damistofia, and she felt her limbs settle into a posture someone in her knew well, deceptively relaxed in appearance. Colly stepped inside her circle, and reached for her, and grasping his wrist, falling back, she threw him across the road, and he landed tumbling, fetching up smartly against a fencepost. Rubbing his head, he lumbered to his feet and came at her with arms wide, to catch her if she tried to duck off either way. That was far from her mind: instead, she stepped inside the wide-flung arms, and making a flattened fist with her right hand, she drove a deep stroke into the man's solar plexus. He stopped with a surprised, driven exhalation, but his mass pushed him forward, as if stumbling. She chopped his ear with the other forearm and he went down like a felled tree, grunting as he hit the hard dirt of the road. For a second, he seemed stunned, but he bounded to his feet with terrifying speed for his bulk, reaching instinctively sideways. His arm brushed her leg, and it nearly threw her. Now she released the full sequence that she knew.

According to the training Rael had been put through, the martial arts blows and throws she now used without restraint were designed to maim and kill, but Colly, through some innate lack of ability to feel pain, or some deep force within him, kept coming, although he was accepting terrible injuries. She couldn't seem to hit a spot that would stop him. This rapidly became a nightmare. Even after she had broken both kneecaps, several ribs, he continued to come on, crawling when he could no longer walk, and finally she had to kill him with a blow to the temple, followed by pressure on the carotid arteries. He finally stopped moving, and the night became quiet; Nazarine listened closely. There was no breathing. She stood up, getting off the bulky body, lightheaded, dizzy, and walked a short distance away. She looked back at the still bulk, lying in the road in the starlight, and suddenly she turned and was violently sick in the ditch by the side of the road, her stomach heaving and knotting.

After a time, the cramps ceased, and she regained her senses, filled with disgust and a sense of waste. And after a long time, she gathered up her things that had fallen, and started off along the road again. There was no one there to see it, but as she walked, for a long time tears dribbled out of the corners of her eyes, streaking her face.

6

"Time: the infinite past, the infinite future, and between them the infinitely small zero-dimensional present, which moreover moves constantly, changing one into the other, a veritable nothingness. But all of the future and all of the past is contained within the present."
—H. C., Atropine

It is a commendable thing to require work of subordinates, but a fully functioning spy net is one thing, and a remnant tattered by revolution and restoration, and ripped to shreds by desperate actions is another matter entirely. In Tartary, Cesar Kham and Arunda Palude shortly found that their line of command into Clisp was both precarious and tenuous. What reports they did receive shed no more light on the subject, and Palude's early apparent successes with the oracles apparently failed her, and the answers became contradictory gibberish.

She had told Kham, "In Tarot, you can often feel the flow in it, the internal consistency. But the readings I am getting make no sense whatsoever!"

Kham and Palude had been walking outside in the bitter Tartarean airs. He had shrugged, and said, "Maybe you're not asking the right questions; that seems to have a lot to do with it. Or the card you use to identify the problem. That book you have puts a great deal of stress on choosing that symbol carefully."

"Perhaps. At any rate, the flow is gone."

Kham asked, half-jokingly, "Can one exhaust the oracle?"

"Supposedly not. I have never heard of that. But. . . ."

"What have you been asking?"

"The usual sort. Success of our venture, allegiance of subjects; that sort of thing."

"Ask it if the Morphodite lives."

"I . . . I don't really know what symbol I'd use. I tried that once, using *The Devil* as significator, but I got gibberish."

"Try it with another card. Now."

* * *

And so they returned to the tower, and after some reflection, Palude shuffled the cards carefully, three times as prescribed by rote, using #1, *The Magus*. The result was inconclusive. Kham picked up the pack and looked through the strange, enigmatic emblems of the deck. This one was so done to show ancient medieval scenes, most of which were only barely comprehensible in themselves. He snorted in derision a couple of times, and then pulled a card out of the deck, handing it to Palude. "Use this one."

Palude took the card. It was #14, *Temperance, or Art*. The figure depicted upon its face was that of an androgyne, hard at work in the laboratory of an alchemist. Kham added, "Ask if it's alive; what it intends."

Palude shuffled again, and then laid out an eleven-card reading. The cards read:

1. Self/Definition: *The High Priestess*.
2. Opposes: *Page of Swords*, reversed.
3. Ideal, or best expected: *Justice or Balance*.
4. Foundation: *Death*.
5. Behind: *Knight of Wands*.
6. Before: *Strength*.
7. Self, moving: *The Magus*.
8. Environment: *Nine of Wands*.
9. Hope or fears: *Ace of Wands*.
10. Summation to come: *The Hanged Man*.
11. Explanation: *The Star*.

Palude sat and stared at the layout for a long time, and then began writing in a commonplace notebook of crude paper, a local product. After a moment, she said, "Seven of the cards are Trumps Major, an arrangement you seldom see. That in itself is indicative of great forces moving. . . ."

Kham observed, "I see you drew a Death card."

"It's in the wrong place, and there's no card of violence associated with it. Note that it moves *from* Death, not toward it. Hmm, and here, of the four lesser cards, they are all Wands except one, a Sword. That one means espionage, surveillance. The first card is fairly obvious, as is the third. No mystery there. Behind it is Flight, Departure. Before it, Strength. It is a formidable antagonist; And its hopes are for a starting point, a begin-

ning. To come are trials and sacrifice, because of . . . Truth.
That's a strong ending.''

"Sum it up.''

"It's alive. It's a woman. It's not moving yet toward us. But
it will. But this doesn't suggest what it is going to actually do.
There's no real suggestion of violence, which I would expect to
see. . . .''

"Do you believe *that*?''

"It has the internal consistency.''

"Can we get any more juice out of the agents there?''

"I doubt it.''

"Then one of us is going to have to go to Clisp. You don't
know the area. I do.''

"I agree.''

"I hope this isn't a wild-goose chase?''

"I hope you can find what you're looking for. There are
probably a lot of young women in Clisp.''

"Doubtless. But this one won't have any roots. And. . . .''

"Yes?''

"That suggests it's still in Clisp.''

"Yes. So it does.''

And so Cesar Kham took the long journey back into Lisagor,
across the ocean; Tilanque; across the broad valley of Puropaigne,
through Symbarupol, now only a back-country junction town for
the beamline, half wrecked by war, half abandoned, with only
parts of it coming back to life. A melancholy place, filled with
the ghosts of the past, victories and defeats. Then across the
northern reaches of Crule the Swale, the silvery-buff grass flowing in the wind, and dour, silent locals watching the beamliner
pass with intolerance in their rigid erect postures. Then the
barren, rocky mountains of The Serpentine, harrowing suspen-
sions across dry gulches that fell abruptly to the sea, never far
away in this narrow land. And at last into Clisp.

Marisol was a city which managed to retain a decently
cosmopolitan air without the overwhelming presence of vice and
depravity which usually went hand in glove with such cities.
Even in the old days, Marisol had always been substantially freer
than the other cities of the Changeless Land. Kham felt somewhat at sea now, in Marisol. Except for the plain wood-and-
stucco facades, it almost seemed like a mainstream city, anywhere
else in the universe. An overgrown college town, perhaps, or

some pleasant backwater. Something was gone. He grimaced
with the pungent irony of his reflection; that Marisol, which had
never gone to the full rigor of Changelessness, but had always
tolerated more than other places in Lisagor, now had suffered the
least change from the revolution, while Symbarupol, a pharaonic
bastion of stability and eternity, had vanished as an entity. The
junction would remain; but in time, that city would be forgotten.
Marula had simply collapsed into itself and had been abandoned.
It would come back, but not as it had been.

He had little difficulty unearthing his prime agents in Marisol.
They were safely burrowed into the woodwork like little mice.
But after several days of following blind leads, they were unable
to unearth anything. If the Morphodite lived, they had lost him.
Or her. Or whatever the damned thing was. No trace. It was both
frustrating and thankless work, for the surviving members of the
net in Clisp remained certain that the person known as Phaedrus
had vanished without a trace, and no one had evidenced any
further interest in it. The terrorists responsible for the deed had
vanished back into the wilder country eastward; the prevailing
rumors seemed to place them somewhere in Crule. At any rate,
out of reach. None had remained behind.

Reluctantly, Kham disengaged himself from the net and began
his journey back. If Phaedrus had survived and now walked this
earth as a woman, she had left no traces, and possibly had not
even come to Marisol. Doubts gnawed at him like termites in a
rotten log, but there was nothing he could grasp. Silence.

The trip back across Lisagor was distressingly the same as the
way he had come. Few got on, or off, the beamliner, which was
allowed to pass the frontier between Clispish lands and Crule
without any more than glares from the border guards, while other
traffic was held up for hours, sometimes days. In fact, the only
notable point on the whole journey back occurred in Symbarupol,
where an attractive young woman boarded the beamliner coach
he was riding in. Unlike the locals, who now invariably wore
clothing that was simultaneously old, dark, and rather in ill
repair, this woman (or girl; Kham could not make a precise
definition—she looked young, but she carried herself with the
confidence of someone much more adult) was tall and graceful,
long-legged, with a ripe figure. She had a rather round face,
accented by brown hair which seemed to fall naturally into soft,
loose curls, and wore clothing that seemed almost modern: loose,

flowing pants, soft but serviceable shoes of plain design, a tunic of the same gray color as the pants, and a darker cloak.

Packing her small luggage away, she turned once, catching his attention out of the corner of her eye, and directed toward him one of those enigmatic glances women always directed toward strangers: as if asking, "Well, what is it you want?" She turned her back and settled in the wooden seat, but not before something flickered in her eyes, in an instant, something Kham could not identify, but which chilled any ardor her appearance might have incited. He looked away as well, out the window across the sad ruins of Symbarupol, softening in the long twilight of early winter. He shook his head. *Not that one, this time. But curious, all the same. What was she, with that much poise, dressed that well, in this ruinous city?* He gave it up, thinking that he would not be able to derive that answer any better than he had been able to find the Morphodite. As night drew on after the slow passage of time on Oerlikon, the coach dimmed, and the lighting system, never completely trustworthy, refused to work at all. The coach grew dark. Kham nodded, settled into a better position, and slept, knowing he would reach the shores of the ocean tomorrow morning.

When the coach lurched, passing under an uneven switch point, Kham awoke, stiff from sleeping sitting up on a wooden bench seat all night. It was daylight, and his land journey was almost over. He was now moving into Thurso's Landing, the small port that served the scant commerce that still trickled across from Tartary. He stood up to stretch. And noticed that the attractive girl was gone. Gone? Not in the coach. Where had she gotten off? And for what? There was essentially nothing between Symbarupol and the coast except farms. If she had been an enigma boarding the beamliner in Symbarupol, getting off in the middle of nowhere was even more mystifying. He moved to the place where she had sat. No luggage, no trace. She had vanished into the night. But this occupied his attention only for a moment, and presently, engaged in getting off the beamliner, and making his way to the shipping offices where he spent the day booking passage for Tartary, he soon forgot about the tall, slender girl he had seen on the beamliner. It was no matter. Kham had seen a lot of pretty girls pass, and they had vanished as easily as they had appeared. The only troubling thing was that as he aged, there seemed to be more of them as time went on.

* * *

Nazarine had reached Marisol without further incident, and now using the cartouche of Pompeo, secured lodgings temporarily in a small pension located rather far from the center of the city on the banks of the Grand Canal. Here she rested, made short forays into town for new clothing, a few pieces of modern, durable things for travel, and during the late hours of night began slowly casting her oracular net.

The problem with oracles is that the questions have to be maddeningly specific. The looser the questions, the looser the answer. If one asked any oracle if one was in danger, the answer would certainly be affirmative, for danger was an inherent condition of life, but some events had a higher probability than others; and in the loose casting, the calculation, as she preferred to call it, there was no discrimination. So she had to take one piece at the time, and unravel that one strand.

She quickly disposed of the question of Marcian. Totally uninvolved with any plot, by intent or accident, the only thing she could pick up about him was that he had been falling in love with her, and she already knew that. As a fact, she had begun to find the idea interesting herself. She had liked his grim reserve, his taut slimness, the intense, focused personality, the lean, hard body. And curiously, also the fact that he had obviously been emotionally injured sometime in the past. This was as visceral as the sexual urgings she had begun to feel, probably something from Jedily. It didn't make sense. She wanted to say to herself that a woman wouldn't normally want a man who had been badly hurt emotionally, but nevertheless there was something appealing about the idea of . . . what? Nurturing him? Healing an otherwise attractive man, guiding him . . .? Perhaps. She wondered about that. She remembered Damistofia well enough, especially the memories of Cliofino, which she enjoyed. Cliofino had been a rat, but as a lover he gave a lot more than he knew himself. What a dilemma! The men who were good lovers invariably either had severe character defects or obstacles to coming to one, or else they were good fellows and dull lovers. Women liked fireworks, too! *Damn!* She thought, suddenly, shaking all over. These intrusions of Jedily's were like possessions, a déjà vu experience, where it was not remembering, but feeling your whole mind slip into a well-worn groove. Whatever Jedily had been, she apparently had led an active life, with plenty of men. Yes. She had thought the thing herself . . . but the pattern had been Jedily's. Patterns but no memory. And with Damistofia, she had memory, but no patterns.

She also used the calculation to carefully sift Marisol and Clisp for any indication of plot or organized efforts to find her. Curiously, there was none, but in all the scans she ran, there was the hint of something . . . but not here. Something malevolent, full of evil will . . . but very far off. Now ineffective, unable to see *her*. Good. She had time. The Prince, Amadeo, she also found to be uninvolved. But he was weak, undisciplined, subject to considerable pressure through the number of women he entertained himself with. *Them*. Sooner or later they'd find him out. Probably already knew. And they'd . . . what? She erased the *Map,* and cast another. *Aha,* she thought as the counters fell into place on the paper, aligning into a pattern. Yes . . . they would not use him. That day had passed, but they could derive intelligence through him, without his awareness of it. They would know what he knew. Therefore he must not know. This was indeed useful information. She had room to breathe and plan, now, but not much. And it was clear that the answers she sought were not to be found in Marisol, or in all of Clisp. Clisp, for all its contemporary resurgence as a nation-state, was an incident on the periphery of the larger problem . . . which had started in Symbarupol.

As she turned her thoughts to Symbarupol, she felt a flash of momentary horror, something unimaginable, pass through her. More. Disgust, loathing, incredible horror. But not the emotion itself, or the memories that would cause such an emotion, but simply the pattern of reactions left behind by them. She, Nazarine, followed them out without understanding why. The moment passed. She shivered, shook her head, and got up from the small table and went to the window over the canal, opening it wide, breathing deeply of the midnight air alongside the canal. She inhaled the clean air, the canal scents. When she had put her thoughts directly on Symbarupol, thought of it, directed her attention to it, that was when it had occurred, probably because she had sensitized herself to Jedily's old reactions earlier by the thought-pattern about men. And Symbarupol keyed something unspeakable in the pattern Jedily had left behind. Not something . . . that happened to her. It didn't have that flavor, but happening to someone else.

Nazarine felt faint from the strength of that pattern, and that was just a fragment. Horror, disgust, outrage, they were all

there. But not done to Jedily. Nazarine knew well enough what
had been done to Jedily, and no one remembered that. Of
that—whatever they had done to induce her to *Change* into Rael,
there was absolutely no trace. She didn't need the aid of the
calculation to help her see that Jedily had once known something. In Symbarupol. But what?

She sighed. There was no avoiding it. She now realized that
that pattern had been so strong she had actually avoided thinking
about Symbarupol, and had been avoiding the inevitable trip she
would have to make there. And she would have to go. To do a
reading, she would have to have an idea of where to start, how
to aim the question, and at present she had none. She breathed
deeply. But it would start there.

She closed the window, leaving it open at the bottom, and sat
on the edge of the bed, starting to undress for bed. She was
down to her underpants when it occurred to her to ask one more
question of her system: *Was there need for haste?* Still half-
naked, she went to the table and ran one more scan, asking the
deceptively simple question, making sure to include the extra
computation at the end, the line item that gave the reason why.

The answer was a clear "yes," the clearest affirmative she
had ever seen. But the reason line read *"mu." No answer*. No
reason. It was the blank line. Data insufficient. Fill in whatever
you wanted. It was the first time she could remember the oracle
failing her, or anyone she had been. She turned out the light and
lay down, weary. *The Beamliner leaves in the morning*. She did
not sleep particularly well, waking often. But she made it to the
station on time, and left Clisp behind, with an odd sadness she
did not entirely understand. But she felt a distinct premonition, a
certainty, that she would never see Clisp again.

The entire journey back to Symbarupol had been a horror for
her and she endured it as best she could, relishing each moment
of the journey falling away in time. The journey back: that was
one thing she would never have to do again.

Once there, she found a place to stay, one of the few surviving
hostels left over and functioning from the old days, and then
went straight to work. She found there was a little trouble in
using the cartouche, but not much—rather less than she had
expected. It seemed that whatever doctrinal differences existed
between Clisp and Crule, which Symbarupol was nominally a
part of, these mutual detestations did not extend to money.

Pompeo's cartouche was good, and it was honored, if grudgingly. No one seemed to be put off that she would be poking about the ruins, either. This was adequate commentary on the fall of Symbarupol. The action had shifted somewhere else.

Much was ruinous in the city, evidence of revolution and turmoil. The Mask Factory complex, somewhat on the edges of the city, showed some damage; someone had tried to burn it, and there was considerable evidence of vandalism, but in the main, it had remained mostly whole, if deserted.

Posing as a researcher, Nazarine had gotten permission to investigate the Mask Factory, although she had been required to sign a series of hair-raising oaths and testimonials certifying that she would make no claim in case of injury, maiming, fright, impotence, or disease, any of the above being related to her voluntary entry into a prohibited ruin.

Coming up the walk to the building, she felt a curious emotional state, of at least three components: The excitement of anticipation of what she might find here; the curious abstract emotions of Rael, which did not correspond with any normal human emotion directly; and the pattern from Jedily. No doubt about it. Jedily had been deeply involved with this place, in more than one way, none of those ways positive. She looked up at the soft-cube shape, which had been preferred in mainland Lisagor for government buildings, now with cannon-fire pockmarks spotted randomly on it, and the main doors blown open and not repaired or even boarded, and recalled wryly that even with Rael's memories, she had no idea of where to begin. There was a patch of rubble off to one side. She assumed that it was what was left of the Residence. Total destruction, there. Besides, it was unlikely they would have kept records there. That was what she was looking for. Records. The Changeless State had believed in voluminous records of the most trivial events, and recorded *everything*, believing that somehow, as in faith in magic, that the simple act of perpetuation would keep Change away. *Perhaps it had helped.*

There was a guard just inside the door, but he was bored and disinterested, and made no comment at her pass. She asked, "Where did they keep the records?"

The guard glanced along the lines of her body, once, and then decided she was unreachable for any number of reasons, and said, "I don't know, except somewhere toward the back of the building, so I'm told. Not much left back there. What wasn't looted out during the troubles was hauled off by salvagers. They came from nowhere, everywhere, wanting to buy everything left.''

''What, the furniture?''

''Everything. The building's just a shell. Some idiot even hauled off all the old paperwork.''

''What about the computers? They had some. . . .''

''First thing to go. Some of that was still operable. Down and dead, of course. But they had that stuff in a separate building, out back of this one.''

Nazarine stepped back toward the entrance a little, and made an uncertain motion. ''They had records and computers both?''

The guard shook his head as if disbelieving. ''They used the computers in the lab. Computations only. The records section was all hand work. Most of the back part was storage. They tried to burn it, but there was a lot left.''

''You ever hear who bought them?''

''A Makhak trader living in Karshiyaka. It's his hobby. I've seen him myself since they put me on this post. He finished clearing out the last of it not all that long ago.''

''Whatever in the world would a Makhak want with old records?''

''You got me short, miss. You know Makhaks, or what we hear of them; every one of them has some odd thing they spend their lives on. This one wanted old records, and he didn't much care what kind, as long as there were plenty of them. He was pleased with what he got! He can spend the rest of his life on them.''

''You said you saw him. Did you speak with him?''

''Once; asked him what he wanted all that junk for, and he rolled his eyes and exclaimed, 'Statistics.' Then he left. Who knows?''

''You don't recall his name?''

''No.''

''Well . . .''

''There's almost nothing left in there. Go look.''

''Thanks. I will.'' And working her way through the piles of rubble and some broken walls, she found the place where the records had been kept, but it was as the guard had said. It had been cleaned out. You could even see scars in the floor and walls where the metal racks and cabinets had been torn out. A few scraps of paper left on the floor. Nothing. She returned to the main entry and spoke with the guard. "You were right. They even dug the screws out of the walls in there. Nothing left."

"Didn't think there would be, say, ah. . . ."

Nazarine made a polite, if cool parting, and set back out for the main city. There was nothing in Symbarupol for her, at least nothing of note in the Mask Factory. Some Makhak trader living in Karshiyaka took them for his hobby. There was perhaps one other place she might look while she was here—the old registration section. If their records were still intact, she could find out what Jedily had been before she went in the Mask Factory. If the records still existed.

They had. The same day, in the afternoon, Nazarine found the Hall of Records, and posing as a long-lost relative trying to trace her Guardian after losing her during the troubles, soon gained access to the records. But not directly. These records and files were still active, and it took a small army of clerks to keep up with them, even in these dimished days. So the clerk she spoke with averred. But after much muttering and pacing back and forth, the clerk returned from the stacks and presented Nazarine a dossier with the name Jedily Tulilly written plain along the file designation strip. The strip also had an extra notation opposite the name: RESETTLED. (File Inactive.)

Nazarine asked the clerk what this notation meant. And the clerk, a small, pale girl who gave the impression of having been sold into slavery as a child and never having known any happiness whatsoever, answered, in a peculiar, off-center manner musing off into some neutral space, "Well, it's supposed to mean that those personnel so designated were sent off somewhere else, but since those days are gone, I would venture my own private opinion that this was how they indicated invoices into the Medical Research Facility."

"In short, she was so listed as a conscript to the Mask Factory."

"Yes."

"You have been in Records a long time?"

"All my life."

"You saw a lot of this?"

"Some . . . some more. A bit. I couldn't say 'a lot.' Maybe it was. I shipped no one off. I kept records."

"You have done well . . . you survived. But did you ever see any indication of how such people were selected?" And here Nazarine felt the urge to embroider things a little: "I mean, I lived here, but I never saw anyone carted off, and no one I know saw this, either. How did they do it, never mind whether it was right or wrong?''

The clerk brightened a little. Here she could tell her story. ''Oh, that's easy enough! They picked up the loners, the self-destructive, the dissatisfied, you know, the kind of people who . . . move around a lot, play with other people, then leave them. People who had fallen to vices. Sick people with no friends. *People who had already disappeared!* Nobody missed them!''

''That doesn't sound like the Jedily Tullily I remember, or that I've heard friends speak of.''

The clerk retrieved the dossier. ''Let me see, perhaps there's a clue in here. . . .'' She opened the folder and began scanning through the entries, the forms, the singular traces left behind of a woman's life in a community. As she looked, Nazarine watched her face begin to register some emotions: first, puzzlement, then a kind of shock, and as she leafed further, finally a kind of anger.

The clerk pursed her lips, and said, in an undertone, ''There is a lot wrong with this file, and as far as I'm concerned, whoever posted it last did it badly!''

''How so?''

''Well, to begin with, they show here that she was a dischargee from a rehab center, and was employed as a sanitary technician 4th class at the Bureau of Public Roads. But there's no entry form, or when. Then there's a huge gap between her early entries, which show educational level and so forth, and this last thing. They show several associations and registered liaisons*, and there are several children shown, three, spaced out at rather large intervals, but that's all of the middle part of her life. There should be much more! I shouldn't say this, but my guess is that somebody . . . changed this file. And did a poor job of it.'' The clerk glanced back over another form, which was still in the file. ''Yes, this is odd, indeed. According to this profile, such a person would expect to lead a life of stability and considerable progress, and the few mid-life entries left bear that out,

---

*Lisagor had no social equivalent to marriage. An ''association,'' resembling an article of incorporation more than a marriage, was the nearest thing to a permanent bond. A ''registered liaison'' was nothing more than an affair which had been registered at City Hall.

and yet, there she comes out of rehab and winds up a scrubwoman. Then selected for the Mask Factory.'' The pale girl had gotten so agitated over the condition of the file that she had forgotten her official phraseology, and dropped into the argot of the street, the alley, and the Dragon gamefield.

"Well, that's curious. I left when I was young; I was not one of her natural children.'' Here, the clerk nodded knowingly. "But I recall her as being very stable, very . . . how should I say, forward-moving. She enjoyed things greatly, you know.'' Here, Nazarine favored the pale girl with a lewd wink, which the clerk acknowledged and understood, but also gave a look which suggested a degree of prim disapproval. Nazarine added, "I saw nothing which would have caused anyone to remand her to a rehab center.''

The clerk nodded sagely. "There is certainly nothing in here to indicate any reason. But there is something else missing.''

"What's that?''

"Her employment. I look here and there's no way you could tell where she worked, or what she did. I know she wasn't a scrubwoman.''

"How do you know this?''

"The children's indicators. Jedily paid for the maternity services. All three times. Not her lover, and she didn't use the public facilities. No, no. She took the best, *and paid for it out of her own pocket!* Whatever she was, she was well-set.''

Nazarine said, to hide her emotions more than anything else, "Well we never wanted for anything we really needed, I recall that.''

"Right! Then you know what she did for a living?''

"Of course . . . but it doesn't matter now. And I'd imagine you couldn't correct your file without something more than recollection. Documentation.''

The clerk shook her head, but with sympathy. "I am glad you understand. So few do. It is a thankless job.''

"Just so. So, then, there's no more to be had in this. . . .''

"I'm afraid not.''

"Well, then, I will be on my way.'' Nazarine turned away from the counter, and then turned back. The pale girl clerk was already headed into the stacks. Nazarine asked, "Would the Mask Factory have had any control over people going into rehab?''

The clerk turned and said, quite without thinking, "Generally not, as I recall, although they always had a representative in here who scanned the rehab rosters.''

''Really? Do you recall if it was anyone you knew?''

The girl blurted out, ''Who could forget that repulsive little slug, always creeping around the stacks, grabbing a feel here, a feel there, always groping. That flunky over at the Mask Factory, the errand-boy. Avaria was his name. Elegro Avaria. I can say that because he vanished in the Troubles and hasn't been seen in these parts since.''

Nazarine made a motion with her hand, indicating that she wished the clerk farewell, and turned away to go, but her real reason in turning away was to hide her face from the girl, because when she heard Avaria's name, the alarm bells in her head must have been nearly audible to passersby. Oh, yes, Nazarine as Rael-memory recalled Avaria well enough. Well enough indeed. And there was something worth finding out. She could hardly wait to get off in solitude, where she could add this datum into the oracle. On the surface, it wasn't much. But of necessity, the entering edge of the wedge is narrow and sharp. But it can widen enough to crack open the thing it's applied against.

7

> "At the impassable and irreducible core of every meaningful and deeply real thing there lies irrationality pure and undisguised: Transcendental Numbers, irreducible fractions, even,—gasp!—imaginary numbers. And that is how you tell the Real from the unreal. And those things that can be reduced to rational, fixed ends? Trash, illusion, nonsense, Maya, ghosts, the demonic. They only have power over us to the extent that we waste time worrying about them."
>
> —H. C., Atropine

Nazarine returned to her tiny rooms at the Symbarupol Traveller's hostel and stretched her long body out on the simple cot that served as a bed, watching the mellow, diffused light of the afternoon sun evolve across the wall on which it slanted. Evolve, not move. Sunlights and shadows alike moved too slowly to perceive on Oerlikon, but move they did, whether one watched them or not. Now she reviewed the facts and suggestions she possessed, reaching for the right question.

She now knew, with reasonable validity, that Jedily had been selected for the Mask Factory, by no less a person than Elegro Avaria. Pternam didn't pick his victims. They were brought to him. Also that Jedily had once, most of her life, been somebody of some success. The records had been badly stripped. Whoever did it hadn't cared if his work was noticed. Only that her former life vanish from records. Why? At the first approximation, for the simple reason that the record of her life would not justify "rehabilitation." Also that she wasn't well-known. A success, but quiet about it. But why rehab a quiet success? Jedily didn't fit the pattern. There was definitely something here that didn't fit. In one sense, the question went nowhere. But these unknowings were the life blood to the original Rael, and Nazarine had not forgotten how to work with these "unknowns." One solved equations for them!

She sat up for a moment, watching the sky beyond the window, and then went to the crude little table under the window. There was a blank pad of paper there, which she had left. Now she bent over it and began laying out the lines of Rael's oracle, concentrating on the question of what had Jedily been. One by one the outlines began filling in, an indecipherable hieroglyph to the uninitiated, barely comprehensible even to her until the very last step. But at last she had it: *Jedily Tulilly was a spy.*

Nazarine pushed the chair back and leaned back even farther. *A spy. Then she had been caught.* But that made no more sense than before. *A spy for whom? Doing what?* Nazarine knew that because of the majestic indifference of the Makhaks, and the monolithic Lisak society, there were in fact few real spies and those that were, were in a local resistance. Or were . . . offworlders, of which the Lisaks knew nothing. What had the Answer said? A spy. If she had been of the Lisak Underground, there would have been no rehab, but outright execution, summary justice on the spot. And if for the offworlders, there would have been more hue and cry. She went through rehab. They knew everything. And yet they did nothing, and in fact she knew very well as Rael that they didn't know about the offworlders. Dead end either way. Another unknown. Now how to address it:

in what direction should she approach this still-unknown? She bent to the pad again, and began concentrating. A spy for whom? And who caught her?

The sunlight faded, became more golden, and moved imperceptibly diagonally across the wall a bit before she had this answer: *Jedily was an offworlder. She was caught by the offworlders.*

Nazarine ran her slender fingers through the brown, loose curls of her hair, and pursed her full mouth in perplexity. There, too, was ambiguity. She was an offworlder, then, working for the offworld group which was actually maintaining an artificial stability on Oerlikon, for their own purposes. Presumably Jedily had also worked to those ends. Quietly, but in such a way as to lead a quiet and prosperous life, with plenty of time for three children at wide intervals, presumably with different lovers, that being the custom of Lisagor. She reached for the memory knowing it wouldn't be there, but she felt a framework it had left behind. A sense of completion, satisfaction. There had been no bitterness in it.

Very well. Then I am an offworlder myself. I am not child of Jedily, but a replication of her, in a different body, derived from the potentials latent in the orginal Jedily DNA. For a moment, the knowledge made her a bit lightheaded, dizzy. But caught by the same group she belonged to . . .? How so? Would she have gone too far native and turned against her masters? Nazarine did not think so. That didn't feel right. The offworlders were the most conservative group on the planet, and if one had turned on them, surely such an event would have left traces. No. There were no ripples of that anywhere. But somehow she opposed them, and they "caught her." Nazarine did not wish to ask another scan. She felt the presence of too many unknowns. She needed to try to find those records from the Mask Factory, and she'd have to catch the Beámliner late tonight, to start for Karshiyaka. She removed the used pages from the pad and shredded them into tiny pieces in the wastebag. Satisfied that the room looked secure, she glanced at the fading light, and nodded, leaving the room for supper at one of the few remaining operable communal dining halls.

After supper, alone in the midst of multitudes, absorbed in her own thoughts, she returned to the hostel and retrieved her few belongings, and checked out, walking slowly through the deserted streets, still guarded by the improbable monolithic government buildings, now untenanted save for a handful of squatters.

Using the cartouche, she went to the beamliner station and purchased a ticket for the end of the line, Thurso's Landing, and when the liner came in, swaying on its suspended track of I-beams, she boarded it, without looking back. But she was still wrestling with the unanswered questions and an incomplete oracle. There was something here that escaped her powers. And that could only happen in such a case that the answer could be derived by the ordinary progress of everyday reasoning. But it was maddening: She couldn't find where the discrepancy was. She was still worrying herself like a dog with a bone when she found an empty seat, and in arranging her bag, she looked up, sensing that she was the object of someone's attentions. A few seats back was a bald man of no determinable age, watching her with interest, and perhaps appreciation. She returned the look, with a slight internal grimace: *No. Not that one.* But as she started to sit, some subliminal alarm system planted long ago by Rael went off. She didn't dare look back to find out what it was, but something he'd done wasn't right, wasn't Lisak. A thrill slid upward from the small of her back, and lodged high up between her shoulder blades. Offworlder! On the liner, from parts west, perhaps Clisp. Looking for a trace of Phaedrus? She shivered. *I'm getting paranoid.* A second inner voice suggested, *Maybe not paranoid enough?* The voice of reason answered, *Maybe not looking, but he can at least find one who does.* So she sat very still for a long time, until she felt it worth risking a glance back to where the bald man sat, and to her immense relief, he was asleep, his mouth slightly open. With almost no movement, save a series of graceful flows from one position to another, she carefully gathered her bag up, and slid out of the seat, and then out of the coach. At the next stop, she got off, and it wasn't until she caught a fleeting glimpse of the bald man passing in the departing coach that she felt some measure of reassurance. The pressure had been intense. And suddenly letting down, the answer she had been looking for crystallized and emerged fully developed, complete. *Of course! It couldn't be any other way! Jedily hadn't been sent to a Lisak rehab at all: Her own people, the offworlders, did their own version first. They didn't care what Rehab got out of her then—she'd already been cleaned out like a gourd. She knew or did something, and they—*she hesitated at the word—*erased her, and dumped her back into the*

process by which the Mask Factory obtained its recruits. And
now she had a real problem for the oracle: what was Avaria's
connection? How could they be so sure she would vanish into
that hole? But as Nazarine walked tiredly through the unpaved
streets of a very minor little town, looking for a place to stay,
she thought that she would hold those questions until she had
tried to find the missing Mask Factory records. She needed one
more piece of Jedily, if possible, before *asking* again. And of
course it was also true that you couldn't push it too hard, and
depend on the answers. So for now she would let it be.

She never found a place open, but returned to the station,
where she made do on one of the wooden benches. And in the
morning, red-eyed and stiff, she wandered all over the town until
she finally located a dray-wagon headed north for Karshiyaka,
the end of the world, whose driver reluctantly agreed to take her
aboard as a passenger. She rode in the back of the wagon with
the load, apparently large burlap bags full of legumes, and
watched the rolling, empty lands pass under the indigo skies of
the north.

Karshiyaka was the place where the northern tier of hills
across Lisagor turned to the northeast, diminished to a series of
hogback hills and low rises, and vanished into the gray-green
waters of the Cold Ocean. There were no trees; the land was
covered by a low, brushy plant which gave off a bitter, aromatic
odor. The climate was damp and misty, and the houses and
towns were half-sunken into the rocky ground. The monotony of
the landscape was broken only occasionally by squat, low towers
with conical roofs, apparently the residences of hermits, for to
Nazarine's eye they seemed to have little relationship to any
activity near to them or far away. Going by what little she could
see, it was cold, and she had burrowed deep into the harsh bags
for warmth. This was the northeast, far from the sunny, light-
swept distances of Clisp, plain and mountains, or from Marula,
far away in the south. And the season, however mild, was
indeed winter. She burrowed deeper into the lumpy bags and
tried to ignore hunger and cold some more.

After the passage of several days, which had stretched into a
uniform dull blur, the power-wagon and its trailer rolled onto
hard, stony streets, closed in tightly by the lowering, half-
submerged houses and shops. The streets curved and intersected
with a sense of willful perversity, all eventually winding down

slippery cobblestones to the harbor, which surprisingly looked full and busy. The wind off the water had a bite to it, and the few people she saw about, went about their business without wasted motions or socializing. The wagon reached a section of warehouses along the docks, and Nazarine got off there, and went looking for an inn or hostel. She did not know what she would find here, in this land's-end corner of Lisagor: already it had a foreign air to it.

The town was called, unimaginatively, Karshiyaka. But whatever went on here apparently called for a lot of transients, for there were a lot of inns and taverns, not to mention the traditional Lisak hostels. Nazarine, feeling more secure now in this impossible corner of the country, and feeling acutely both hunger and fatigue, decided on one of the better inns, which included a warm tavern, and to her relief they accepted the credit of the cartouche that Pompeo had given Phaedrus without question. In fact, they accepted it willingly. She selected a large room with heavy half-timber walls, small round windows, and which had a plain but well-furnished bath attached. And the water was hot. She glanced at the blue, overcast twilight, through the windows, and ordered supper sent up to her. After supper, a bowl of herbal sea stew, accompanied by a hard-crust bread and hot beer, she filled the old iron tub full of water, and after bolting the doors, removed her clothes and settled gently into the steaming water, where she scrubbed madly, and then lay back to soak. She woke up a bit later, feeling guilty, surrounded by now-cool water. The room was cool, too, but she found enough blankets to pile on the bed, and lay down wearily and slept deeply, untroubled by dreams or problems that she could remember.

She slept through the day and the next night as well, waking only enough to roll over. But by the next morning she finally woke, and set about the things she had come to Karshiyaka to do. First came some heavier clothing, and then she went about the town making discreet inquiries about an eccentric Makhak supposed to have settled in the area. Eventually she derived directions to one of the towers on the southern side of the projecting finger of land, and set out for it, walking.

It was a bit farther than she had thought, and she could feel the cold through the heavy clothing by the time she approached it, but there was no mistaking it. The Makhak immigrant lived in an eccentric stone castle built out on the end of a low headland, an irregular structure of no particular shape, with three towers of different heights, none especially tall.

The building was enigmatic and blank-faced; Nazarine walked around it three times before she found what appeared to be an entrance, and the day, already well-gone toward evening, was nearer night before someone within finally opened the door for her. This was, apparently, a servant or bondsman. Or bondswoman; she could not tell. The person was tall and gaunt and curiously indeterminate of gender. It met her without a single word at the door, and conveyed her through a series of empty stone corridors to a large, drafty room, where another tall and cadaverous person, not a great deal different from the servant, sat before a peat fire and brooded. The servant left.

Presently the one by the fire turned and stood up. This one, at least, seemed to be male, and well-advanced in years as well. He was thin and sticklike in build, moving with an odd reserve which suggested fragility—but great strength as well. He spoke first, in a low, muttering tone, almost a whisper. He held his hands stuffed into voluminous sleeves.

"I am Yakhin Pakhad."

She said, "Nazarine Alea."

"Lisak?"

"Yes and no."

"Ah, the followers of the old ways; always ambiguity, duality."

Nazarine smiled a tremulous little half-smile to herself. "Indeed, sir, duality . . . and the half has not yet been told."

Pakhad nodded, recognizing something of a private humor he had keyed in her. He said, after a moment, "We are private people, you know, we Makhaks. And you being young and graceful and with an entire continent of stalwarts at your back, I must conjecture, I must assume. . . ."

Nazarine knew of the Makhak distase for superfluous conversation. She interrupted, "I have heard of the Makhak ways, of how each of you follows an 'excellence.' "

"Just so; we are great scholars."

"It was described to me how a certain scholar of Tartary resided in this neighborhood, one whose excellence was the study of statistics."

"I am such a person."

"I am in the service of Clisp. . . ."

"We do not require reasons."

"You obtained the records of the old Mask Factory, of Symbarupol? This was reported to me there."

He made a slight nod of agreement, leaving his face turned down.

"I am no statistician. But in those records there may be mention of a person I am trying to trace. Therefore I ask your assistance." She hoped it was short enough. One never knew with Makhaks exactly where the line was between essential speech and rudeness.

"Curious."

"Why so?"

"I would have imagined them valuable—the records. But they sold cheaply, and no one has come asking anything. A poor investment, but a treasure-trove for me. I will never finish unraveling them. And of course it will be difficult to find one person in all that. Is there haste?"

"I don't know. If I must say yes or no, I will say yes, but it is no emergency . . . yet."

Pakhad made a subtle signal with a hand, which he removed from its sleeve, to which responded the servant. Pakhad made a few more signs, and then made an easy waving motion to Nazarine. "All is arranged. Food and rest. Sleep well, rise early. Tomorrow we will see. Do you require entertainment tonight?"

"Entertainment?"

"Young men? Girls?"

Nazarine smiled openly, at last able to give something back. "Neither. I have an excellence of my own to pursue. Food and rest will suffice."

"Curious, curious. Have you considered emigration to the Free Land?"

"No, but I think I will wind up there, whether I would or not."

Pakhad raised his bushy eyebrows at that, but turned away to his peat fire and private thoughts, signifying that for the moment, conversation was over. Presently the servant reappeared with a bowl of some crushed fruit and a loaf of crusty bread, and a flagon of cold water, which had something of the flavor of the outside to it. Nazarine suspected it was rainwater. She accepted it without comment, and ate stolidly, not entirely certain when her next meal might be. And after that, the servant appeared again, and in total silence led her through the odd and disjointed corridors of the old castle to one of the towers, so she surmised

from the stairs she ascended, and to a cold room with a rude
cot, which thankfully was furnished with a number of coarse
homespun blankets. In the darkness, she climbed into the cot,
piled blankets around herself, and listened for any sounds she
might hear. She only heard a distant, soft murmuring, of an easy
surf on a narrow sandy beach.

Pakhad was as good as his word, and sent the servant for her
at dawn, or something near to it. She could see little difference
from night itself. Breakfast was half a loaf and more rainwater.
And then another passage through the dusty, random corridors,
apparently to another one of the towers, where she was conducted to a large room filled from floor to ceiling with stacks of
paper. Pakhad waited for her.

"And now we begin."

She looked at the untidy stacks of paper, seemingly in no
order whatsoever, and for a moment almost gave in to total
despair. *This bookworm couldn't find his own name in that
mess!* She drew a deep, slow breath of the cold air, and let it out
in a long, uninterrupted sigh. "I am looking for one each Jedily
Tulilly."

Pakhad looked about thoughtfully and asked, "Give me some
categories. some references. A woman, yes? That alone will not
help us."

"I know very little of exact facts; what I have is approximate,
relative. Age elderly, past maturity. I know she was in the Mask
Factory, but I do not know how long, or when she went in."

"Did she come out?"

"No. She ended there."

"More?"

"Before she went in, she was apparently well off, but I don't
know the occupation, or residence. Presumably Symbarupol,
although there I am guessing."

"But definitely in the Mask factory?"

"Yes. Immediately before that, she was a rehabilitee, working in
the Bureau of Public Roads. I think she was in the Mask factory
for a long time. What they did to her there couldn't have been
done fast." Nazarine suddenly felt a hot flash of embarrassment,
at herself. For all her powers and all she knew, what she had on
Jedily was still almost nothing.

Pakhad glanced about the random stacks of paper, scratched his
chin, paced back and forth, adjusted the lamps, and muttered to

himself, inaudibly. Finally he selected a stack of papers, and went through it, searching. Then he put the stack back in its place. He said, "I haven't yet succeeded in setting up the kind of order I want, so one has to try things out. There is no index. I was not, of course, interested in individual cases, so I have little on that. Only as one of a category will we find anything."

"Can I help?"

He shook his head. And went on searching. Pakhad tried another stack, with the same results. And another. Presently, he came to a stack which he first started going through rapidly, and then slowed down. Leafing through, he finally stopped on a single bound sheaf, which he extracted, and handed to Nazarine. "This is it. Do you want it, or will you study it here?"

"Here will do. I travel light. There may be something there, maybe not. But what I need from there . . . I don't need a copy."

"I have work here. Use the main room."

Nazarine took the papers and threaded her way through the structure, back to the sitting room, where she settled in a chair before the smoldering fire and began to read through the forgotten documents. Hesitantly at first, but with growing absorption. The nameless servant brought her some herb tea in an earthenware pot, with a matching cup, but it cooled before she thought to drink it.

Nazarine walked slowly back up the coast road, if one could call it that, back toward Karshiyaka town, her head full of unassimilated facts. Much of the file had dealt with the regimen of treatments which Jedily had been put through, at which Nazarine alternated between outrage and astonishment. Those things had been done to her herself. True, she had no memory of them, or at best, mercifully obscured horrors which even Rael had avoided and forgot as much as he could. But what was the most amazing thing of all was that the procedure they were using on Jedily was one that had been used many times before, an exercise that took place in territory which was very familiar to the people performing the . . . exercises. They had had plenty of failures, but they were working within the bounds of a known system. Something that had collected its own idioms and cross-references. *They had been trying for the Morphodite for a long time*.

They had expected more of Jedily than the usual subject that fell into their nets. There were notes jotted down along the margins of some of the sheets, to indicate that someone knew she was less than their usual prey. More than one marginal note made reference to "twice-rehab." So they had not been grabbing at random. Perhaps at first. Not with Jedily. They knew what they were getting. That could only mean that there was someone within the Mask Factory who had contact with the offworlders—the group covered by the Oerlikon Mission.

As for Pternam, who had seemingly set the process in motion, he was revealed to be a relative latecomer, only brought into things late in the game, when they began to think that they would succeed. There was their error, she thought wryly. Pternam had been ever more unprincipled than they had been, and quickly took over the whole project to his own ends. And that raised its own question, which she dared not ask, knowing that there are evils in the world and time that one would rather not know: what would they have done with Rael without Pternam? They had been reaching for the deadliest weapon in the universe, and surely somewhere someone knew what that weapon's target was to have been. It was Pternam who had turned Rael loose upon Lisagor.

The file had contained numerous reproductions of Jedily at various parts of her life. Nazarine had looked at these with disbelief, and some amusement. An odd sensation of vertigo. *After all, this was me!* Jedily had been a rounded, soft woman, with a ready smile and alert, flashing eyes, slightly taller than average. There was no resemblance at all to the thin and saturnine Rael, who resembled a half-civilized Makhak, or the petite Damistofia. Jedily had had a slight double chin which, someone had noted, suggested a sensual disposition.

They were thorough, and covered their tracks only superficially. There were two types of visual reproductions easily distinguishable: One set covered Jedily's life in Lisagor, which apparently commenced when she had been in her late twenties, standard. There was another set covering her younger days. No mention was made of where those came from, but they were equally obviously not Lisagor: Spiky stone buildings and odd vegetation with needlelike foliage in the backgrounds. Within that group, there were a few of Jedily as a child. There the backgrounds were innocuous, but there was something alien about them. Not Lisagor. Not Oerlikon.

Jedily's profession had been interesting, too. She had been a physician. Although few women practiced medicine on Oerlikon, apparently no one had questioned her, once she was established. She had worked within one of the larger clinics in Symbarupol, and specialized in the treatment of degenerative ailments of the aged. Her certifications had been managed as a case of self-education and success as passing the myriad tests of Lisak society. Once established, she promptly buried herself in one of the enormous civil service hierarchies as a supervisor of some obscure program. This was traced out with meticulous care. They seemed to think it important, as if somehow these facts were justification for something. There was one line which had been particularly interesting: it had read:

> *"Last assignment:* Certification Section, Symbarupol. Oversees induction of indigents and defectives into re-habilitation processes. Approves quotas set by Medical Experimental Station."

Indeed it was! Jedily had been the monitor of the input into the Mask Factory! The conclusion was unavoidable: she had been promoted routinely into a routine position, but there was something she saw in that for which . . . the offworlders silenced her by erasing her and dumping her into the very program she was monitoring.

Nazarine walked on, shivering in the cold wind; perhaps more than from the wind blowing off the gray-green sea, under the damp cloud cover. She felt emotions for which she had no name, but which gnawed at her vitals, at the foundations of her precarious existence. She had drained the cup of revenge upon Lisagor and the Mask Factory, but had not yet tasted that which was of the killing of Meliosme and the children. And now another draught was set, as it were, by an unseen hand, on the counter before her: she wondered if there was any bottom to this evil at all, and she was reminded of the Tale of the Chagrined Optimist, a folk tale widely circulated throughout Lisagor: The Optimist said, as disaster befell him, "Cheer up! Things could be worse!" And as he cheered up, so indeed things got worse. And for the first time, she began to wonder if the way Phaedrus had chosen hadn't been the right way, after all. *Disengage.* It was beginning to seem as if there were wrongs whose scope visibly exceeded her formidable powers as the Morphodite to right. But just when the gloom of hopelessness closed in on her, she looked around herself, at the bleak shores of Karshiyaka, and she thought, *Disengage, is it? Go back to the warmer parts of Lisagor and find an obscure place for myself, with a bit of fun with men to liven up the times . . . Yes, and no matter who I found, no matter how much it would mean, there would never be an escape for me, or those I might love, like Phaedrus. They killed Jedily, and they hunted Phaedrus, and they'll come for me, too. And whatever powers Rael developed, nursing his own plots, none of us expressions of the immortal is a god. We've got a blind side, and they'll waste enough agents to find it. No. And I've painted myself into a corner with the identity changes. The next one's to be early childhood. I could die of nothing more willfully evil than simple overexposure after Change, lying in the open and feverish. No. This has got to be seen to the end, and the definitive action carried out.* Some of the chill left her then and, rounding a headland, she saw ahead in the evening gloom the lights of Karshiyaka Town, riding lights on the ships in the harbor.

8

"When the situation has become impossible, incomprehensible, the meaning invisible, then we are wont to cry out: 'Give us the Truth! We must have it, come what may!' But it is in these very situations that the truth is in fact a horror that we could not bear to see, something far more awful than we could have imagined in our darkest hours. And then we do not change it, but it changes us. No, I think we don't want Truth, whatever we say. Facts, maybe, and not so very many of them, either."

—H.C., *Atropine*

It was evening, in Tartary. Cesar Kham imagined that he had been walking for hours, with that same rude castle bulking on the horizon like some unlovely animal, that he had ceased to move and that it was the castle drifting, enlarging, obscuring the western sky, where a tattered yellow fragment, like burnt cloth, peeked under the masses of gray and streaked clouds that covered the sky. Did they never see blue sky in this land?

He shook his head, annoyed with himself. First failure in Clisp, and then this, brought on by having to operate out of this impossible location. Two failures, not one! Failure to accomplish the mission with confirmed results, and failure to turn anything up, a trip undertaken at great risk. And now he would have to spend more time in this bleak country, arguing endlessly with Palude over what they could do next. He came into the darkness of the castle, close, now, and thought, *"Well, absence of proof is not proof of absence. Perhaps that raid did the job, anyway. Perhaps if it didn't actually get The Morphodite it scared it off. Might well be skulking along the south coast of Clisp, hiding out in that empty land. What the hell—a person neutralized by fear was the same as dead, anyway."*

When he came to the door, it was opened by Arunda Palude, at which he expressed surprise, stepping quickly over the threshold to keep the cold, windy, dry air out of the chill castle.

"Waiting up for me?"

She said, pulling a cloak closer around her, "We knew you were coming; besides, out here on the plain you can see someone coming for hours. There's not much else worth doing, you know."

"I know. You must be bored to death."

"I am."

They made their way through the castle to their own quarters and sat down before the fire. Kham said, "Well, vile as it is, I'm glad to be back."

Palude sat before the fire, trying to wheedle a bit more warmth out of it, the light casting harsh shadows along the planes and lines of her face. She looked drawn and pinched. She said nothing for a long time, but then asked, "Find anything?"

"Not a trace. Nothing. Zero. I'm almost convinced that the job got done, or else it scared it off."

"None of the agents you contacted had anything?"

"Nothing. No trace of it. I'm sure that fortune-telling must be wrong. After all, if you asked for a reading on a dead man, you'd get a present answer, which is nonsense."

"There's a convention to these things: one doesn't predict death, and one doesn't ask nonsense questions of the oracle to test it—of course, the answer would be nonsense. But however that is . . . I imagine it was after you left Clisp, but one of our agents in the palace managed to get a report out by radio. It was relayed into the port, and a messenger carried it to me."

She had said the last with some difficulty, not looking directly at Kham. Now she looked at him. "It was the custom of the old days of Clisp to allow certain agents of the House to carry a sort of medallion, something they had had from the old days. There were very few of them, all under strict controls. Amadeo doesn't believe in handing them out, and so has recalled them all, and so they reside now in the State Museum. Except one."

Kham shrugged. "Could have been lost. Agents get killed, or accidents happen, otherwise."

"Somebody is using one. It's like a credit card. The user can buy anything he wants, and bill it to Clisp. They are honored all over Oerlikon."

"Why didn't we know about them?"

"The danger has been so great their use had been rare. But they are good everywhere on the planet and, so I am told, in more civilized places off it. And somebody is using one now. The royal bursar has invoices from Marisol, and from Symbarupol. Somebody has one of the originals, and is currently using it."

Kham looked across the room, small as it was, as if seeing a great distance. "What sort of purchases?"

"Women's clothing. Food, lodging, all temporary."

"Did anybody get a description?"

"No. The agent sent what he had. Fortunately the invoice for the clothing was highly detailed, as would befit a billing to the royal house of Clisp. Sizes were included. The agent was able to derive some generalities therefrom: a rather tall woman, slender in build, rather full-breasted. She also picked up some cash, but small amounts at any one place. The second report was on a billing from Symbarupol."

Something began stirring in Kham's mind. A coincidence? He began sweating. "What kind of clothing—nice stuff or work-men's coveralls?"

"Serviceable stuff, but rather nice in cut. She didn't stint on the quality, or so he said. It was also all stuff which could be adapted to different climates by using less of it. Why?"

"How long ago the report?"

"At least a tenday. You were probably still in Lisagor."

"Fits."

"What do you mean?"

"I think I saw her. She boarded the beamliner at Symbarupol.

Something caught my eye. She looked out of place, taking the night train, and economy class, but dressed well."

"You saw her!"

"Yes. Same as the description. Young and good-looking, tall, with curly brown hair. I was going to keep an eye on her just in case, but I dozed off and she was gone. Some intermediate stop in the eastern mountains. Of course, it could be just coincidence, but I did see a woman that fits that description, who had no good reason in these times of poverty to be traveling at night, dressed that well."

"Did she see you?"

"Looked right at me, but turned away. She didn't look interested, if you know what I mean."

"How old? According to the information I have from back there, when that thing does *change*, it regresses in age."

"Definitely not adolescent, but young adult. Twenty to twenty-five standard. I wasn't close enough to see better."

The expression on Palude's face softened somewhat. "Then it couldn't be the one we're looking for. The one you saw is too old. We're looking for an adolescent, and one nearer childhood. From the predictions I have, I don't see how there could be any confusion. No matter how well-built."

Kham leaned back and rubbed his bald head thoughtfully. "Maybe. It was an odd incident, though."

"Would you recognize her again if you saw her?"

"Oh, yes. No doubt. The one I saw isn't bland or plain. Very aristocratic, good-looking, sure of herself . . . only one thing: she doesn't look like any woman I ever saw in Lisagor."

"How do you mean?"

"I can't put it into words, exactly. I don't know if it was the appearance or the mannerisms, but there was something very un-Lisak about the one I saw. More like someone back where we are from. A more sophisticated society, a different gene-pool. Not Clispish, either."

"Could be nothing more alarming than one of ours."

"They aren't bringing any more in to my knowledge, and all those from the old days had full training in Lisak mannerisms—you, for example, fit perfectly."

"A Makhak?"

"Doubtful. This one looked too soft for that."

Palude sat quietly for a long time, and then said, "All my past experience suggests strongly that this one has a high probability of being the one we look for. But it's too old. I can't figure that. The process of change is supposed to be invariable in the rate of regression. If that one we found in Clisp was the Morphodite, then his successor would have to be no older than about, say, fourteen standard.''

"No way this one was fourteen. This was an adult.''

"Blocked.''

"Maybe we are overreacting.''

Palude considered, and then said, "We can't take the chance, as I see it. The last ship in sent a message to that effect. They want results. We can't stall them much longer.''

"Hellfire and brimstone! We don't even have proof it's alive! And if worse comes to worst, I'll bite the bullet, report failure, and have the planet quarantined. We can stand it here if we can't do anything else.''

"We need to find that girl you saw.''

"Difficult. Trail's old by now. All I have is a description.''

"Possible use of a medallion. That would be sure.''

"*If* she's the one using it. We don't know that. Besides, I am not going back to Lisagor, ransacking the countryside, on a lead that small.''

Palude nodded, and said, "I see. Very well, you are basically right. The tactics are impossible. But if that movement we saw reported is that thing, it's coming this way, and it will have to get here, in Tartary, to get offworld. And if a young woman like you saw showed up in the port, with a medallion, and tried to buy passage offworld . . . we'd know it.''

"I can circulate the description down there.''

"Do so immediately . . . have you eaten?''

"In the port. Not since.''

"Let it wait. I'll have them bring food, and some hot water for a bath. Rest, relax. Go tomorrow morning.'' She stopped, and looked at the fire again, an unfathomable expression on her face.

Kham thought he understood. He hadn't thought she'd be made of nothing but mission dedication and logic. He said, "I'd imagine it was no fun here, either, waiting.''

"Impossible. We. . . .''

"Never mind. Don't speak of it. I understand. I, too. Leave it at what it is.''

Arunda looked up at Kham from the fire, and said, "I fit in Lisagor, you said.''

"So do I. We all did."

"Just so. And there are customs of that country."

"I know them well. Most of my life. No one will judge it amiss if two Lisaks spend the night together to console one another's loneliness. Certainly not two Lisaks, rather more native than the originals."

She nodded, and her face softened, and her eyes took on more life in the firelight. "I'll send for the food and the tub."

Kham thought that his appearance always convinced the women he met that he would be violent, stormy, tempestuous. For some, who seemed to expect this most, he allowed himself to be. But with others, who would allow him to be himself, he was softer, gentler, more feminine. He let Arunda create the situation, let her manifest what was deepest in her. They had both been without for a long time, they both had needs. This was no deep striking of the thunderbolt, but a truce, a sharing, a treaty. It was not really what they wanted, either of them, but it was good for a while.

Now they lay side by side in the cold dark, wrapped up in the rough homespun blankets of Tartary, hearing the wind moan and fret outside, angry at finding this stony obstruction in the midst of this empty land of boundless air and spaces.

She said softly, "In the old days, I never saw much of you; when I did, you never looked at me the way you did at others."

He: "You were too important. Not Glist, or whoever had been before him. Just a figurehead. You did the summations, the real work. No disrespect—to the contrary."

"I know. I always spent the nights with real Lisaks. None of the mission people."

"That's why they always thought you cold-blooded."

"There were many of us who did it that way. It was dangerous for associates to have affairs. Aril, who was always carrying on with our own people, she was the first one pulled in when the trouble started, and her links with others. . . .we knew it would come that way. And you?"

"Much the same. I was terrified of it, though. I always feared that I'd become entangled with some Lisak girl . . . and I'd want to give her everything. Take her offworld, the whole thing. Doubtless she'd have thought it worse than leprosy: 'I gave you diamonds, you gave me disease.' Returning to a universe of flux and change, inbred for generations to hate it."

She: "They were less like that in Clisp, in Marula."

"True about Clisp, although not as much as you might think. Remember that province is the one that retained a royal family more or less covertly—the very epitome of conservatism. As for Marula, that was only surface. They were deeply, even more extreme than the rest. You could never trust anyone in Marula, and one never forgot it, either."

Arunda sighed. "That wasn't such a bad world."

"True. I miss it already. Things seem less clear, now. I don't like this business at all. I've done my duty, very well, but it's not like before. The rightness is gone out of it."

"I, too. Well-said. The rightness is gone. But what can we do?"

"I considered vanishing back into Lisagor. The Morphodite may be worth all that trouble, but I'm not. I could disappear. So could you."

"Is this a proposal?"

"No. An alternative. We can run."

She: "Not very far. And you only saw *them* at the end, when they had already made up their minds. I saw more of it. I could not avoid the idea that this problem with The Morphodite was more important than the whole project . . . and had been for a long time."

"Did you try to extract data from these impressions? I recall in the old days you were pretty good at that."

"No. I did not want to ask. I did not want to know. I always had somebody to report to, when I knew something, someone to hand over the dirty work to, and with this, there was nowhere to turn—had I found it out. I turned away."

"No escape there. Now we're back here, worrying."

"Yes. And I feel that we'll find out, too, in the end."

He: "Perhaps."

"Did you know anything about how they made the creature?"

"No. Nothing. I knew that some funny things went on in the Mask Factory, but not making anything like that."

"I have the same lack of knowledge, and that bothers me."

"Why?"

"Because we penetrated every facet of life within Lisagor. In effect, we really were Lisagor. It couldn't have lasted without us. You know that. But I never picked up anything about them trying to make a mutable human in the Mask Factory. Nothing. And don't you think that's odd? I mean, they couldn't just jump

up and do it, could they? There would have to be some prepara-
tory time, research, experiments, trials, failures. There is no
reasonable path from point A to B. This implies. . . ." Arunda
left it dangling. She did not wish to say it.

Cesar said it for her. "That was closed to us."

"How? We penetrated everywhere else!"

Kham: "Our own people!"

"It's the only conclusion. But I don't understand why."

"Right now I don't even want to think about that."

"Exactly. All the possible implications are ill."

He: "If we follow that out, as they may well imagine that we
may do, then our lives are worthless. If they would send us here,
back, to kill the Morphodite, then if we returned we'd be walking into a trap."

She: "Possible. I'll run a computation on it tomorrow. Not
tonight."

"What do we do about *it?*"

"Report it dead, depart, run away from Heliarcos."

Kham was shocked at the candor, and more at the boundless
mistake that would be: "Foolish. We don't know the old worlds
well. We've been here, on this backwater planet."

"We may have to. I want to think about this. Weigh alterna-
tives." At the last, her voice had sounded weightless, drifting.
Kham listened for her to ask something else, but instead he heard
the deep and regular movements of the breathing of sleep. He
readjusted his position slightly, feeling the warmth of the woman
next to him, and fell asleep effortlessly, like a child. But he had
some disturbing dreams of running from a formless thing that
materialized wherever he turned. And another one, about a
sworn enemy protecting him. He remembered these dreams,
because he had few that he could remember.

In the morning, they slept late, and woke up looking guiltily at
each other; not for finding a fellow-body in bed with one, but for
becoming so lazy. Palude chided Cesar Kham: "One night with
a woman, and already you've gone to hell in a handbasket."

Kham sighed and put his hands behind his head. "Worthless,
I admit it. Absolutely worthless. And you know, there's something to that, too."

Arunda sat up, wrapping the blanket around her, and untangling the strands of her hair. Some of the strands were gray. She
yawned lazily and asked, "What?"

"I was thinking of a way to make sure that you would have a society that would be proof against change, against responsibility, against all forces. Make sure it's acceptable for everyone to have as many affairs as possible, and all the rest of the decisions will be made for them by the higher-ups. And of course cover food, housing, and a little money. Not much. None of that happened by mistake, I think."

"You mean by accident."

"Yes. By accident. I think it was designed in from the beginning. And the Changeless weren't anywhere smart enough to do that. They just wanted a place to get to where they could stop Time. They didn't have any idea why it moves."

"You mean the Regents were into this planet . . . from the beginning?"

"A long way back. Maybe before the Changeless came. But they saw the opportunity . . . and that with all those different cultures and racial types coming together, they would never, never fuse together into the monolithic whole they wanted unless one built in the sexual connection from the beginning."

Arunda leaned back, and said, "But they always said that they wanted to study this society, that it was unique in its resistance to change. . . ."

"Then how is it we had no warning about what was going on in the Mask Factory? That place should have been crawling with our people, reporting through you at Glist."

"No reports, no people."

Arunda looked at Cesar. "I never questioned that. That was just the way it was when I came to Oerlikon. I assumed that we had enough control to ignore it."

"Uh-huh," he grunted. "Just right. Me, too. We were all told we were there to . . . study it, and add a little bit of stability; but how many of us were there, really. Do you know?"

"I only knew the actives. And when we did pull out, even of those we only took the key people. There were many others. . . ."

"How many? Assume all this had been going on from the beginning. . . ."

She looked up at the dim ceiling, sooty beams, and thought. Finally she said, hushed, "Cesar, that's almost sixteen hundred years—Oerlikon years, according to that insane calendar."

"A lot of continuity, a lot of people shunted onto Oerlikon over that period."

Arunda looked away, and then back. "Why? If it went on that

long, there would have to be an iron will behind it, maintained with more severity than the Lisaks used. Transferred from generation to generation. That's hard to believe."

"You were deeper into the administration than I. How far back do you know it goes?"

She: "Well, I don't *know*. I mean, I ran into the Oerlikon project when I was in the University, on Heliarcos. It was in existence *then*. They described it as a long-term project." I never saw how long. I assumed it went back a few generations, but never how many." She stopped. "This is unreal! What could possibly be the purpose for such a long-term project?"

Kham looked off, straight ahead, eyes unfocused as if viewing some personal demonland. "Consider the possibility: if true, then the population of Lisagor would come to consist of a majority of offworlders, trained to a specific social identity, sworn to secrecy, and retiring on the planet. *There were no Lisaks!*" He stopped, and then went on, "I exaggerate. But a situation was created in which the stabilizing faction came to become a majority. And who would question it? Most of the project people either retired with a stipend on Lisagor or went back to Heliarcos to teach, or enter the Regents. We were never on Lisagor to observe. We were there to control!"

"Why?"

"To make sure that there was one place where somebody would have a long time to do something, long term effects of hormone and endocrine controls. And what did the Mask Factory do? And why was there no entry into it for our people?"

"For God's sake, Cesar! Next you'll tell me the Regents were the ones making the Morphodite."

"Well?"

"Why?"

"Who knows that? But here, they would have time, and they would also have a place where the people wouldn't ask questions. Those who did would wind up finding out first hand what went on in the Mask Factory. The planet was out of the way, and of no great interest to anyone, everyone there tied up with his own pet interests. And if they were trying to create a creature like The Morphodite, and it got loose, they would have it isolated here. Let it ravage Oerlikon! They could keep it here!"

"But your argument fails in the present. They don't want quarantine."

"Of course not! They'd have to say why. Doubtless the reason they would give would be untrue, but there's still great risk there. It contaminates the experiment.''

"Then that is why they send us back.''

"Exactly.''

"When did you . . . understand this?''

"This morning. I just thought of it. It came together in my head. Remember? They want us to use these priorities: First, to capture it and secure it; Second, to kill it. Losing Pternam was a real blow to them, but they could work from a specimen backwards. They *want* it.''

"What about Pternam? Was he one?''

"Of them? Oh, no. They'd have their controls there, but it wouldn't be the visible key people. No, Pternam was working his own game. He was a real Lisak, and now that I think of it, probably a very sick one, too. I mean, he had no relationships with anyone, and he was pathetically eager to sell out to the offworlders. I detested him after we cut Charodei out of influence, and had him thrown overboard with a great deal of pleasure.''

Palude reached out of the rough bed to the cold floor, trying to find her robe where she had thrown it out from under the covers the night before. Finding it, she slipped into it, and stood up, wrapping herself in it against the cold. She said, turned away from Kham, "I didn't feel at all good about coming back here on this mission. Here, I felt more uneasy. There was something profoundly unright about it, some concealed purpose I could sense but couldn't define. But if half of your conjecture is true. . . .''

"Oh, I'm sure the idea I have seen isn't all of it. It may be yet worse. But so much is enough, anyway.''

"Too much! And this of course makes the problem a personal one, now. And if we haven't scared it off, but awakened it, it certainly has reason to come looking for you and me.''

"It might well pursue you to the ends of the universe.''

"Perhaps. But it may also see a more pertinent target and not spend so much time on us.''

"Cesar, we set off a series of events that killed its closest relations!''

"If not us, they would have sent someone else. Oh, we are guilty enough—I do not scamp that. But the impetus comes from back *there*,'' and he gestured with his head at the invisible sky beyond the ceiling. "*There*. And if that thing is as dangerous and perceptive as they seem to think, it probably isn't going to waste a lot of time on tools. One doesn't execute guns for murder, nor does one maim hands. One goes back to the will, the heart of the matter. At least, that.''

"Will you alert the port authorities?''

"I think not. But we should move down there. If it's that girl I saw, I'll recognize her again. I want to . . . make the decision then. Anyway, we won't have another opportunity.''

9

> "*A stable and a worthy world, a quality world in the sense the Sophists used the term, a Tao world, is built, line by line, not of brilliance and technique, but simply a matter of timing, as in music. And after John Cage, sometimes the right note is silence. One measures the beat by the emptiness between. Figure and ground. This is neither old-knowledge nor that which is yet to be seen, but a transcendental that each must reaffirm.*"
> —H.C., Atropine

After she had returned to Karshiyaka, Nazarine had spent several days integrating the facts from Pakhad's files into what she already knew, and building a new base for a reading of conditions as they were. The results, in one part, did not surprise her: the impetus for the sustained work on creating the Morphodite, which they referred to as The Transformer, was wholly offworld, as had come the decision to dismind Jedily and dump her into the Mask Factory. Wholly. The minds behind those decisions were not on Oerlikon, had never been. For her there was even less reason to pursue the remnants of that group than there was to disengage. They were scattered to the four winds. When she ran a scan through the oracle for the location of Avaria, the reading was "not available." Not "died," or "in a particular place," but "not available." Unreachable. When she had tried to amplify the scan, push it a bit, it gave out the symbol for insignificance. Wherever Avaria had gone, he was both powerless and inconsequential.

And if the Change in Lisagor had caught the main body of

offworlders by surprise, it had devastated the creators of the Transformer. They were not only unprepared, they could not even conceive of such a thing happening. Nazarine did not know how far back the work went. But it was far back, and in the tumults she had set off by Rael's single act, she had managed to negate the laborious plodding and secrecies of generations. If for no other reason, they would punish the creature they had suffered so much from, that its freedom and escape not go unavenged. She could not run, she could not hide, and she could not interpose a defense between her and them. Therefore the only course remaining open was to attack. And to attack meant that she had to go offworld, back into whatever kind of society had sent them all out in the first place.

She reasoned that since there was no direct contact with Lisagor, that the contact would have to have been done from Tartary. Somewhere in Tartary. And careful listening in taverns and along the docks soon revealed that there was only one port of significance in Tartary, and that strange folk walked there yet, people neither Lisak mariners, Makhaks, nor any other Oerlikonian race. The oracle confirmed it.

Passage across the ocean to Tartary was not easy to arrange. Most of the ships and crew tied up in Karshiyaka harbor were strictly local traders who worked across the north coasts in the easy seasons, and southwards to the Pilontaries in the winter. A few venturesome souls rounded the point of Zamor to go on to Marula (where there was much destruction of porting facilities yet). A trip around the continent to Clisp seemed to evoke astonishment, and a voyage to Tartary elicited gasps of awe.

Nevertheless, she eventually turned up one, the *Rondinello*, loading fleischbaum pod, and its captain and owner-aboard sailed whenever he had a full cargo, fair sea or foul, and he rarely asked questions. He and his scanty crew made a living working the margins where others dared not go. The *Rondinello* was a rounded, ungraceful sailing ship with a central hold for cargo, a forecastle for the crew, one cabin for the Captain and the Mate, and two small cabins, hardly more than closets, for whatever passengers might wish to risk the vast unknown seas of Oerlikon. She had contacted the Captain, paid her debts off with the cartouche, and carried her small baggage aboard.

Nazarine noticed the crew paid little attention to her; they were so inured to the stark ways of the *Rondinello* that even a woman aboard did not seem to wake them up. They glanced at her once, dismissing her as totally out of reach, and then went stolidly back to work.

The navigator was a dour little man, pot-bellied and bandy-legged, and when asked about departure, growled, "Evening, night, maybe dawn. The cargo's loaded, the ship's stowed. We're waiting for the Captain now. Stay aboard. He's looking for another passenger. Bad luck to go with an odd number of them." At that, the mate vented off a muffled little chuckle, turning his mouth down to one side, as if finding another passenger in this season were the most impossible task imaginable. Nazarine went inside her tiny cabin, in the chill harbor-damp air, and wrapped herself up in blankets from a wall-cupboard, and waited. After a time, the afternoon, already late, slowly faded into evening, and lights began to come on in the ships anchored out in the harbor, and across the docks in town. She made herself comfortable, and drifted off into a dreamless light sleep, soothed by the quiet motions the *Rondinello* made at her moorings.

She awoke in darkness. She looked through the porthole and saw nothing. No lights, no ships. There were no stars. The ship was moving with a gentle, but deep rolling motion, and Nazarine understood that they were underway. The wood and cordage made quiet flexing noises, and the water made soft noises against the hull. The rest of the ship was quiet. She arranged things as best she could, made a light supper of some bread and hardcurd she had thought to bring with her, and went back to sleep.

The morning came under leaden skies, a bitter wind out of the northwest, and a loping, rolling motion of the ship. Nazarine came out onto the deck and glanced at the steersman's binnacle. Their course was northeast, edged off toward the north. Into the dim daylight of the high latitudes, regions of wind and wave that circled the watery poles of Oerlikon forever.

Tied up alongside the dock in Karshiyaka, half hidden by bales and boxes, the sails shipped, the *Rondinello* had been nothing more than a thing, an artifact, a member of a class. But now, out on the open ocean, it became individual, realized, something powerful real and unique. Nazarine, who had never seen any sort of ship except in pictures, the act of seeing, perceiving the *Rondinello*, was a luminous experience. She went to the rail over the bulwarks and steadied herself against the powerful roll and pitch, cloaked and hooded against the cold wind, surrendering to becoming part of the flow of real time, now, eternity.

Like all the ships of Oerlikon, save the powered vessels used only by Clisp, the *Rondinello* carried lateen sails on the main and mizzenmast, the mizzen considerably smaller. In addition, a stubby bowsprit protruded from under the forecastle, supporting a small artemon to steady the head. Three pieces of canvas against the immense gray ocean, the overcast sky, the wind that never stopped. The ship itself was all of wood, cloth, and cord, round and tubby at bow and stern, broad-bellied in the tradition of millennia of merchantmen on the seas of a thousand planets, about thirty meters in length, ten broad at the widest part aft of the mainmast.

The wind was steady, and few of the small crew were visible. Nazarine, while experiencing this moment as something pristine, nevertheless felt herself unconsciously adjusting to the ship. It came so easily that she forced herself to ask herself: *How do I know how to walk, to stand without motion sickness?* Jedily again, the template left behind: not a memory, but the set of actions left behind by the imprint of a memory. Jedily had sailed on this very ocean, sometime, somewhen. Long ago. Perhaps she had made this very journey to Tartary, for reporting to her superiors. There and back. And certainly she would have made the first trip, from Tartary. Maybe more than once. She shook her head, trying to banish the ghosts of ancient movements, to return to the present and the *Rondinello*. She thought, *I am now only what I am and I have a job to do.* And that worked, but as all real acts do, it raised further questions. *And what in truth is that job? To release the Apocalypse? To punish the guilty? Bullshit. The guilty punish themselves to the end of time, and the misery they cause is only a by-product of their self-torment. A billion deaths would not bring Meliosme back for a microsecond, nor would they restore the center feeling that Phaedrus once, for a little while, attained.* Then, out of nowhere, the connection invisible, came the thought, the realization, *I was created an instrument of a hostility and a rage so deep it could not be plumbed. Down the ten thousand stairs! But I have to learn to love, to give. That is all that prevents us from falling upon one another like vermin and rending one another. I have the Power to destroy; but how would I configure this Power, to create? I was Rael, the Angel of Death, I was Phaedrus, centered, desireless, at rest, neutral.* She sighed deeply, inhaling the cold *air. And now I must learn the most difficult of all the arts. And stay alive while I'm doing it.*

Returning to the present, into existential time, she saw that the other passenger had come up from the cabins and was standing by the mizzenmast, steadying himself with one hand, and looking out over the endless ocean as if he found it difficult to believe.

The outline of the passenger was hooded and cloaked against the wind and cold, and little identifiable showed. The pearly, shadowless light further obscured the figure of the passenger, flattening the relief of the shape beneath. It could be anyone, any age, any sex. The figure turned slightly, an alert, defined movement, without hesitation. Not old. Some of the face showed, but only hints. Nazarine stepped back from the rail and joined the passenger at the mizzenmast.

The passenger proved to be a young man of slightly shorter height than Nazarine, pale of skin and dark of eye and hair. He had a delicate, almost girlish face, but the finely drawn features were utterly without the harshness of Marcian or the perverse willfulness of Cliofino. It was, refreshingly, a face whose innocence was still written plain on it. She said, "You're the passenger we were waiting for?"

"Yes." He spoke hesitantly, and then added, "They found me. I had just about given up getting a passage."

She looked off at the sea, and said, "It's a strange thing that people should now pay to sail to Tartary, when not long ago they would avoid even speaking of it much."

"True. All sorts of things now happen. Why would you be going?"

She thought before answering. *Is this one they have sent? Impossible!* She looked closely at him and decided to step off blind, trusting to reflexes. "I'm going to go offworld. I hear one can do that from Tartary."

Now he looked out over the moving, tumbling waves. "I also." He shifted his position, as if uneasy, or thinking something over. Then he said, "Returning."

She leaned closer to the mast, feeling guided by something inside herself that was less than a memory and more than an instinct. "I have heard tales. . . . You were one of our visitors?"

"Yes. They say we can speak of it openly in Tartary. No one bothers with keeping it secret anymore, but all the same they don't advertise it, either. I came in the last group, just before everything fell apart.''

"Were you in danger?"

"No, not really. I was in Symbarupol for a time, acclimating, but they sent me on to Severovost. There was little action there, and what we heard was always yesterday's news. When we heard they were trying to get some people off in Crule, it was too late."

"You take considerable chance telling me this."

For an instant, something flickered across his eyes. Fear? Calculation? She did not know. He said nervously, "You are not a Lisak, whatever you are."

Nazarine smiled now, looking directly at him. "True. I am Nazarine Alea, an agent of Clisp. Tell me your name."

"Lisak or real?"

"Lisagor is gone forever and Change is upon us. We have to be ourselves, for better or worse. How do you want it?"

"Cinoe Dzholin is as it was, and will be again. On Oerlikon, I was for a time Aristido Bandirma."

"Your name is strange and foreign, but it sounds more fitting to you, even though I do not know its meaning or significance." She glanced toward the forecastle, and added, "We will still have to be discreet until we get off the ship."

"I agree. But it's also true that they don't seem to care very much, now. At first there were some incidents, but it quieted down, faster than anyone expected."

Nazarine nodded. "It's true, that. But people were used to the idea of stability, of . . . channeling energy into private pursuits, and of seeing without perceiving. That was the way of life, here. They'll learn another way, but it'll come slow. I'd imagine there aren't so many of you going back, now, are there?"

"After the pickup, most of the older ones elected to stay. They'd grown used to it. A lot of the younger ones, too."

"But you didn't."

"No."

"Could you have?"

"Yes. But there really wasn't anything here for me. In the initial tumults, I lost some close friends."

"I'm sorry. I apologize for the circumstances." She thought, *You don't know how sincere I am in that. You were clearly not one of those who ran the Mask Factory in secret, but one of the gullible supporters. And whatever, whoever you lost, it wasn't because of the random mishaps of the planet, but was caused by me. These people suffered cruelty, too.* She said, "Only tell me what you will. I do not pry. I lost much, too."

"What interest has Clisp in us?"

"In the sense of absolutes, I do not know. I have imagined that they wish to find out what really was going on, here, and why; those are reasonable questions an alert and perceptive native might ask. At any rate, so I ventured aloud, and no one corrected me. At any rate, there is little enough Clisp could do about it . . . or prevent a recurrence, since by no means does Clisp control Oerlikon."

"Could it?"

"I doubt it. If you know Oerlikon well, you know we only had one war, and Clisp lost that one; we are not, by nature, grandiose people. Events like that are far off. No, revenge is not, as far as I know, what they have in mind." She thought, *It's easier to cite a government reason than a private one, as if that alone conveys legitimacy.* She added, "Besides, the events allowed things to fall our way. And I imagine that we will rejoin the community of those peoples whom we can reach. We have forgotten much here—we know little about the stars we came from. And so here we are." She laughed a little. "You were a harmless spy, and I am about to become one."

Cinoe laughed, too, a shy little chuckle with a hint of a sly reserve, too. "Yes, I was harmless. We had all sorts of ideas about cloaks and daggers, but when we got here, it was not that way. . . ."

"Never forget that Lisagor had real powers, and did not hesitate to use them in the end. I don't know how you people live back where you came from, but Femisticleo Chugun was as evil and ruthless as anything you'd have elsewhere."

"Yes, yes, but we didn't worry about that. It was as if we were somehow more *Lisaschi* than the real Lisaks."

She answered, "And when we get back there, among all the strangers, perhaps we will be even more strange, after the same manner: poetic justice, would it not be?"

She half-thought he might take offense, but he didn't. He said, "You have a wicked wit."

"I learned it at court. That's one thing at least such governments are good for."

"We lost them long ago, in the idea we could do better. What we got in place of Kings and Princes were even more ambitious, and less principled.''

Nazarine said, ''I believe you are a covert royalist at heart. First a spy, and then royalist sympathies. That is two. Are there more?'' Nazarine felt control of events slipping away from her, felt herself saying things she herself did not wish to say, necessarily. Of course, Cinoe was attractive enough, and maybe under other circumstances, she might have taken time to explore this part of herself. But inside her deepest memory there was a pattern of a woman who had taken the Lisak way of life to heart and wrung it dry. Jedily. Presumably she had responded so to men she wished to meet. She wanted to take some control back, but at the same time she also wanted to trust the Jedily-perception inside, too.

Cinoe said, as if relaying her own mind, ''Are we going too fast, or are we just disoriented travelers seeking company?''

She looked out to sea. ''Both.'' She gestured at the forecastle. ''These are worthy men, hard-working, brave . . . but they are not mine. And I see no other women. Circumstances. . . . The Lisak way is to make do with what opportunity and fortune present, for these alignments will never happen again. They are unique. I admit, it's a lazy way, an irresponsible way, but we both know it.''

''As strangers who learned it.''

''Yes. There is more stress on legitimacy in Clisp, an obligation and mutual owing. How are things where you come from?''

Cinoe shrugged. ''The young people have some adventures more or less, according to temperament; later, they become settled and make more permanent arrangements. Being in Lisagor was like . . . never growing up, and yet never being a child either. But I learned something there.''

''What was that?''

''That it is important to share, to reach; everyone brings something of value.''

''If the other can but find it.''

He came back, ''If the one that has it can find it to give.''

''Well-met! Well-met, indeed! And now, let us go back toward the captain's cabin and find out if there is something aboard the *Rondinello* we can eat. I am starved already, and I'm sure we have many days yet ahead of us.''

* * *

There was a cook, who lived and worked somewhere below the poop, in a part of the aft hold walled off for his purposes. Moreover, there was some heat in the officers' cabins, conveyed through the bulkheads by an ingenious system of flues and pipes from the cooking fires below. Some mild complaining by Cinoe and Nazarine uncovered the fact that some of the hot air could also be diverted by the two passenger cabins, although it didn't do very much good. Nevertheless, the mate said he would try to adjust the system so they could have some heat as well. Presently he went off to see if the adjustments could be made.

They also met the cook and discovered the hours of service: four meals a day were served on the *Rondinello,* dawn, noon, dusk, and midnight. They were early for noon meal, but the cook made allowances and set up something for them. On precisely the stroke of the noon hour, the captain came in, said nothing, and ate standing up. He left immediately. The mate returned, bearing the information that only one of the cabins was heatable, ate, and then he also left, muttering something about changing course more around to the north, so they could pick up a stronger wind. Cinoe and Nazarine were left alone.

She looked around the small cabin. After a moment, she said, "I don't want to pry through his things; I'm sure he would resent it, even if he's said little or nothing about what we can or can't do."

"True. I'd feel uneasy. This is no luxury cruise. We could go and see which cabin has heat."

"Yes." She made a face. "Probably yours. I always get the bad luck."

"Maybe not."

As it turned out, it was Nazarine's cabin that had the heat, and although by no means warm, at least in that small space the warm walls took some of the edge off the sea cold. They sat side by side on the edge of the bunk. Cinoe pulled his hood back, revealing shoulder-length thick dark hair. He said, "I became accustomed to the cold in Severovost. But you, in Clisp, you had no cold there."

She said, "No. Although Clisp is never hot, neither is it very cold. I have to admit I was thinking of desperate acts."

He looked at her sidelong, from under his eyebrows. "Such as?"

"I thought that if we were agreeable to each other, we might have to agree to share what warmth we could find."

"I had thought of that. But. . . ."

She leaned back against the wall, feeling the warmth at her back. "Your cabin is still icy. And according to the mate, the Captain is taking us farther North still. It will be colder. However hardy you became in Severovost, I'll bet you had heat in the houses."

"We did." He placed his hand over hers, lightly. She did not withdraw hers. Cinoe seemed to lack the brash self-assurance of Cliofino; he hesitated, as if waiting for a clearer sign from her.

She said, "You should stay here, then."

He leaned back against the wall beside her, letting their shoulders touch. "I would like that very much."

Nazarine knew what was happening, and something in her wanted it to. She moved closer, to feel the body-warmth forming between them. The part of her that was continuous shouted *No, no, not this way*. But the template of Jedily reactions said, softly, *Lie back and enjoy this. There's little enough joy in the world: Anyone's world. Take your share, too.* She avoided Rael, Phaedrus; she remembered Damistofia, how she felt. She could smell his scent: sea-air, cordage, smoke, something pungent, faint, underneath, that communicated directly to her body. *It* knew what to do. She leaned her face over toward his, and he turned his face to hers, too, and kissed her, softly, barely touching. Their lips were dry.

She relaxed, and then drew back a little. "Go lock the door. Something's happening to us." He got up, and fastened the narrow cabin door, and came back, settling closer to her, touching her arm to arm, flank to flank, hip and thigh against hip and thigh. Nazarine felt unworldly, not of the world, and yet focused at its very center, softening, melting, flowing; her legs felt weak at the knees, disjointed. Cinoe started to say something, but before he could voice it, she shook her head. "Don't talk, now." They turned to face each other, now kissing again, mouths opening, relaxing, exploring each other. Sliding over in the narrow bunk, clumsy with the motions of the ship, the newness of this; he whispered, "Better than the words." And she whispered back, "Let them speak as they will," pulling his body close to hers, and they lay down, touching face to face along the length of their bodies. His mouth was soft, light, gentle nibbles, and the body was wiry and strong beneath the heavy clothing, which they now began to remove without losing contact; a difficult maneuvering, full of elbows and knees, a tender, patient clumsiness with which they tangled themselves together, lower bodies bare, warm flesh behind cool air. She hardly felt his weight. There was a soft, insistent pressure between her legs, and then he was inside her and they were one, and for a little time, time stopped, except for the motions they made, together. Like climbing a long hill, steepening toward the top, and there a bright plateau where her breath caught in her throat and she felt a sudden surge of heat from him, deep inside her, then, at that moment, at her center. And very slowly, then they kissed each other's faces like children as they fell back into the present, the world, ordinary time. They felt the chill air, the sea damp, the motions of the ship; the rough covers of the bunk. They could hear the water against the hull, the voices of waves, the wind, the tramp of the mate on the deck, odd and random calls to and from the crew, as if from far away. The light from the tiny porthole was bluer, dimmer, later. They shifted a little so they could lie side by side, her leg curled over him, but they did not disengage for a long time, and they did not say anything; what was there to say that was of greater truth than that which they had just told each other?

Cinoe curled close to her, his face between her breasts, and Nazarine enfolded him, twining around him, feeling both their breathing lengthening, evening out. She felt, all at once, invaded, possessed, captured, and also an emptiness filled, and something long denied now completed. She felt very good, for the first time she could remember. She thought, *There is a rightness here and now, a flow I could surrender to.* A flower was unfolding at the center of her chest, and she wanted to sing, to shout, to whisper in a hoarse voice unspeakable things. It felt so good. She relaxed, moved a little, and also thought, *For a little while, more of this. And then we'll have to choose, won't we?* She felt Cinoe relax, and knew he had drifted off, sleeping, although she knew she could wake him easily. She tried, perversely, to recall Rael: it was unreal, now, an odd fantasy. Phaedrus was hardly more substantial. *Now I have become Jedily.* And that thought reminded her, once again, that Jedily had things to do. Yes. There was no escaping that. It had to be that way. But for now, they had the world of the *Rondinello*, and the endless ocean, and time. And she knew how she would get offworld without being stopped.

10

*"Constantly, over and over again, one discovers
that the people who made the greatest virtuoso use of a
discipline, an Art, really discovered something within it
(instead of exploiting it), were most often those who
cast about courseless for years, usually gaining reputa-
tions as hopeless ne'er-do-wells. Then, one day, they
saw the light. Chance meetings, coincidences, accidents.
All this is undeniably true; equally true is the question,
what becomes of those for whom the door never opens,
the light never shines?"*

—H. C., Atropine

Nazarine understood with the wisdom of several pasts inside
her, that to love, to experience the unblended pleasure of it, one
had to lay down defenses and become vulnerable, exposed. The
nudity with which one made love was more than exposure of
skin, it was an analogue of a deeper emotional nudity. But more,
it was irrational and impractical, an utter refusal to consider
consequences, where things might lead, or what could be in this
for her. Or him. They felt timelessness. They filled the endless
shipdays with each other.

The difficulties they transcended or ignored. That was the way
it had always been. Nor did they, either one, ask why, except
now and then, as a rhetorical question that expected no answer.

But deep down, she knew that this love affair that filled her
with light *was* illusory, that the endless ocean, gray and wrinkled
and heaving with its own passions, was not endless. Somewhere
ahead was Tartary, and beyond that, another voyage across a
deeper ocean. Here, Cinoe was just another wanderer in the
no-time of Oerlikon. That was, too, illusion. He had come
from somewhere else, another life, another time. He was returning to his own past. And she was about to leave hers forever.
They were both passing through unstable zones of transition. She
thought again. Perhaps it was so good for that very reason.

Now she stood on deck by the rail and looked out over the

waters. The sea was always the same, and never the same. The waves and the patterns and motions they made changed hourly, and sometimes by the minute, and above the waves, the sky changed equally fast. She had lost count of the days, down below. She had lived in a different world. This one had become a little strange. Now the sky was more broken up, streaks and patches of open sky alternating with multiple layers of clouds. The worst of the bone-chilling cold was gone. Nevertheless she felt a chill pass through her. She knew she was, in some tormented and torturous way, Jedily, who had come *here* from *there*, but that was neat, logical, reasoned out. She only could remember back to Rael. Oerlikon was all she knew. She had been a weapon tailored to this particular world with a precision never before attempted, or attained. Her sense of the arts she knew told her that the art would work anywhere, and yet there were so many unknowns there beyond the sky. So many!

Cinoe appeared from the passageway leading down to the cook's cubby, looked about for a moment uncertainly, and then brightened when he saw her. He crossed the deck and stood beside her at the rail, content now just to stand close. "Watching the sea again?"

"Yes. It is the same, but it always changes and is never the same. Both, at once." She shrugged. "There is little else to do." She laughed warmly, "When we are together . . ."

"I know. Plenty there to do. I haven't done all, yet."

"Nor I."

"I was talking with the navigator. Ran him down in the galley. He says we look for landfall sometime tomorrow. We have made a record passage."

"How would he know? They have no idea of time here."

Cinoe chuckled to himself, showing laughlines at the corners of his eyes. "Oh, yes, on land. But navigators compute things differently. They use sidereal time. And their dayclocks, on land as well as sea, are quite accurate."

"Landfall, then. And then?"

"They'll have to see, where on the west coast of Tartary we actually are. Then we follow the coast around to the south. Might be a day or so more."

"So the voyage is ending?"

"Yes."

"And us?"

"We're both leaving Oerlikon. . . . At least for a time, we can stay together."

"True. We never spoke of that, did we?"

He said, "No. I didn't want to. It would have spoiled the magic."

"Just so."

"I don't know where you are going."

"I don't know myself. I always assumed that you would be returning to Heliarcos."

He said, "Yes. At least there, first. Then, I don't know. We have passage back there. But I don't know how things are there, what with all those who went back earlier. There may be nothing there for me to do. So I would have to find another place." He shrugged. "You are being sent out to see and observe. Certainly we could be together for a time. I don't want this to end."

"You are inviting me to Heliarcos, with you?"

"Of course."

"I will come with you. I don't want this to end, either. It has been good, what we've made between us."

He went on, "You've not been offworld. It's different, out there. The same, other ways. Humans don't change that much, but there are a lot of things you'll need to know. I'll show you."

"I won't embarrass you?"

"Definitely not!"

She mused, "You give me so much. I wish I could give you as much . . ."

"You already have. Yourself."

"Humbug. I gave you me, you gave me you; I mean something else."

"Well, maybe you'll find something. Or not. It doesn't matter."

She said, "I'll look." And for a moment, she was tempted, as she had never been tempted before, to give him at least part of the terrible secret she bore within her. The many deaths of immortality. Think of it. Forever. What every lover dreamed of. But here, a warning, a sourness, that came from the echoes of Jedily. If she tried, she could put it into words: *"Never give everything. Love is sweet, but it fades. It's a moment. And it changes. Remember that. It changes. It's the best thing in the world, never forget that, but second only to that is knowing when to leave. Love was given us to console our loneliness. But to loneliness we always return. The contrast is what makes both worthwhile.* She said, ''What kinds of things do I need to expect, where we're going?''

Cinoe looked off over the sea for a moment. ''I don't know you well enough to tell you what would be hard or easy for you; there are places, little enclaves, that are more primitive technologically compared with the whole than Oerlikon, and those people don't seem to have great difficulties adjusting. In fact, they often become themselves the foremost modernists in the use of things that are really wonders in their own right, but most people just take for granted.''

She ventured, ''I think I understand; standing in a line is much the same wherever it occurs. You do have lines to stand in?''

''Oh, yes. Lines to get a place in other lines.''

''I can manage that.''

''Some of the . . . devices you'll run into may require you to learn new forms of dexterity, coordination. A different language. But that's all basic stuff. What will be hard is something I am not sure I can describe.''

''Try. I am from Clisp, remember?''

''Compared with here, the way people relate to each other is more casual and more selfish at the same time. It is easier for strangers to meet and make love; harder to feel any lasting loyalty. It has to be that way: people move around a lot. There's little sense of permanence.''

Nazarine heard this and thought, herself, *Here is a key I need to understand what happened! This was why they could be so cruel and ruthless and casual, about matters of life, death, revenge.* She said, ''People who love don't necessarily stay together.''

''No.'' He stopped, there.

''What else?''

''You have to be alert, clear-headed, to find your own way among diversions that can trap you, prevent you from accomplishing; people are more casual about sex. You can't afford to become obsessed with it. Mind, it's not restrictive or possessive. But you won't find much like you had here, except in certain lower-order areas, ah, people there who have given up the idea of personal development.''

''You sound as if you're hinting at something.''

''That was one way they kept Change from happening here. It was set up that way and kept that way from the beginning. The energy spent on affairs would leave little energy left for more serious pursuits. There were some subtle methods involved.''

Nazarine felt as if she were being pulled, firmly, in two different directions. On the one hand, the loss of something that had been very good. Cinoe was telling her plainly that once they crossed that line that demarcated Oerlikon with its artificial environment from *there,* they'd go their own ways, sooner or later. On the other hand, lovely as he was, and as good a lover as he was, he really wasn't very alert to the power she had to extract meaningful data out of very little original material. He had already dropped two pieces, casually, completely misunderstanding the value of those bits to her. She sighed. ''I think I understand what you are trying to say kindly. Well, that's not so different as you might think from here. And of course I have things to do on my own.''

''I hoped you'd feel that way. I thought you might. There's something about you I can't see, but that makes me think you would understand and adjust. And of course, for now. . . .'' He took her hand and held it.

She returned the pressure. ''Can the cook heat us some water for a bath?''

''Salt water.''

''Enough. We should make tonight last.''

He said, ''I thought so. Tomorrow everything will get busy.'' She turned from the rail, taking him with her.

When she woke up, she was conscious of two things immediately: the small bunk she shared with Cinoe was empty, save herself. The second thing was that the motion of the ship was different: all the way across the ocean it had been mostly a pitching. She had gotten so accustomed to it she had forgotten about it. She wryly smiled to herself, and stretched her legs out into the cold parts at the foot of the bunk. *Got used to it already, did you?* It was time to start waking up, to become alert, to use the *art.*

The motion of the ship was now more a roll, with a shorter and more choppy motion. Nerving herself for the chill air, she threw back the covers and stood up quickly, feeling her bare skin prickle with the sudden cold. The deck underfoot felt odd, unlike the surface she had been walking on, for so many uncounted days. She washed quickly, shivering from the cold water, to wake herself up. She looked down along the lines of her body, which apparently had stabilized: her nipples were pinched and wrinkled. This body had high, full breasts that filled the space across her pectorals rather than out. The belly, flat, carried a hint of an opulent curve to it. She thought, *Watch that: this body will run to fat if I'm not careful.* The thighs were long and lean, the legs graceful, but filled out and solid. She smiled again, despite the cold: *I like this body.*

Nazarine dressed and went up on deck. The sky was clear, for a change, a flat, opalescent blue streaked with pearl: high ice clouds. The sea was deep blue, almost black, broken with white-caps. And to her left, a long, low brown smudge along the horizon, seemingly as flat as the ocean, but slightly higher: a brown line that faded away over the horizon to the north. She looked about uncertainly for Cinoe, and found him up on the quarterdeck, speaking with the helmsman and looking about. He saw her, and came down to meet her. Together they went to the port rail and looked long at the loom of Tartary.

She said, "Tartary, of course."

He nodded. "Tartary. They raised Cape Malheur at Dawn. Or so the watch announced. I cannot make any details out of that line on the horizon. At any rate, the landfall was somewhat farther to the south than they expected, and so the coasting will be shorter. They expect to make port sometime tonight."

She felt a sudden odd discordant emotion; as if it were one part fear and one part anticipation. The real adventure was about to begin. And perhaps another adventure was beginning to end.

She said, "We might well be here for some time, waiting for a ship out."

"Perhaps. And one might be in now. One never knows."

"Are you anxious to return?"

The wind ruffled his dark hair, stray black loose strands escaping from under his weather-hood. He looked off at the distant continent for a long time, and then said, "I was before. There was nothing for me here, in Severovost. Now? For a dare, I'd turn around and go back to Severovost, fish processing and all, if you'd go back with me."

She looked at her lover closely now, trying to see him as he was, not as she had let herself see him. The two images were only slightly different. He was a slender young man, graceful and strong, delicate and almost pretty around the face. For a minute she was tempted more strongly than she could ever remember being before. It took a terrible effort to refuse, to say no, to herself. She said, taking his hand and squeezing it, "I, too, have been tempted to just that. You will not know how much. But you know the world has no patience with people in love. We have things to do. I am to go out and see this fabulous yonder we abhorred so strongly, to see what place has Clisp in this new universe we've inherited."

He said, turning to look at her, "That's odd, you know? Usually it's the man who has to move on, for duty."

"I'm not leaving you; we're going together." She shrugged. "Besides, it's not as if we had been together for years. We really just met not so many days ago, even though it seems like longer. . . . Or maybe you do not fear me leaving, but what you'll do once you get, ah, back."

Cinoe leaned on the rail and looked down at the water. "We will both change, when we go back, that is true, Nazarine. One mask will come off. Another will take its place. But the past doesn't haunt me, anywhere there." He glanced up at the sky. "I brought my past here with me when I came, and that vanished without a trace. But it was long gone before that."

"You did not leave a girl behind; you came here with her."

"Yes, that is the way it was. No matter now. I say that to show you that in the way of lovers I am as free as you. There's nothing back there."

"Tell me. I have also known happiness and disappointments before."

He looked sidelong at her, curiously. "You are passionate and gallant. Yes, that's the word. But it was long ago."

"Say rather that it was in a different time. It seems long ago. I ended it, but it hurt as if it had been done to me. Tell me of yours." For a moment she caught an echo of Rael, and she tried to project this young man in the arms of another woman, a girl. What would she have looked like?

"I don't suppose her name matters. What it was back there isn't important. Here she was to be Aril Procand, and that was mostly how I knew her. We assumed our identities some time before we came to Oerlikon. It was all very ordinary—we were students together, and we sort of drifted into it. On the way here, she became interested in someone else. When we arrived, we found out we would be posted to different locations. Or perhaps she had gotten her new friend to arrange it. She went to Symbarupol and I went to Severovost."

Nazarine's skin prickled, and she felt a violent chill.

Cinoe asked, "You shivered. Are you cold?"

"Just a moment. It's fresh out here. I had to awake alone this morning, you remember." But something was opening up in her memory, a configuration of reality which she had once, as Rael, manipulated. Aril Procand! She asked, "Who did she have an affair with? I know some of that group—from Clisp." It was a hasty lie, but she needed confirmation.

Cinoe said, "His name, here, was Enthone Sheptun. He had somehow gotten connections with Central Coordination, and was playing an influence game. Aril fell for it."

Nazarine nodded, absorbed. Sheptun! What incredible fortune! She said, "You know, of course, that he was killed. There was a great outcry."

"Yes. They say Aril died during interrogation. Rumor. I don't know. She was never seen again. She didn't ship either. I asked."

"I'm sorry." But it wasn't the tale of love and betrayal that interested her but the information that even after the complete disruption of the operation, this very green spy had still managed to get some kind of contact with the outsiders, and probably still had enough of that contact to arrange his passage out. She wouldn't need to cast about all over the universe looking for her answer; Cinoe would take her directly to it.

He asked, "And yours?"

"Cliofino. Let it go. I put that behind me, and now I want us to go as far as we can."

He chuckled. "We've tried a little of that."

"Not enough. And now let us raid the galley once more. I haven't had anything to eat yet today, remember. I'll bet you've already been at the ship biscuit."

Amew Madraz entered the common room that served Kham and Palude as workroom, dining room, and rarely as a gathering place for various sorts of conspirators, all of whom had negative reports to tender. Madraz restrained his contempt for these gabbling offworlders who spent their entire lives worrying over time in the conditional tense. Like most Makhaks, he was tall and gaunt to the point of emaciation, but in addition to the usual traits of the race, he possessed an extra quantity of a prized trait the Makhaks called *indzhosti*, a word which did not readily translate into any single concept. Aloofness, reserve, effortless calculation and mastery of realities, great personal force released only under steely, precision control. All of his movements occurred with a measured, inevitable cadence, the effortless grace of a dance whose rules and music could only be guessed at, for the uninitiated.

Madraz looked down at his guests from under overhanging brows and said, in the same low, uninflected voice he always spoke in, "Word comes from the port that we have a visitor from space."

Kham and Palude had been laying out alternating series of probability tracks, and they were surrounded by an untidy mass of papers and curious diagrams which somewhat resembled logic flow-charts. Now Kham looked up at the austere Madraz and asked, with some surprise, "How so? According to what we heard during the last communications cycle, transport isn't due here for months yet. Should be summer, or what passes for Summer here, before we hear from them."

Palude looked up also, adding, "The *St Regis* isn't anywhere near Cerlikon, now. Did they turn and come back?"

Madraz intoned, "Not your support ship. That one still runs on schedule as far as I know. This is another. Before, such ships passed through this section without stopping, when they came at all. Now perhaps their captain hears that Oerlikon is open to visitors. This one, according to tale, is called *Kalmia*. The lighter is down now, its agents going all up and down looking for fares, cargo, trade. Our factors engage them now."

Kham looked at Palude, and she looked back. He said, "Accident. The astrogator stopped reading comic books long enough to notice where they were, and they stopped on a whim. What luck!" To Madraz he asked, "And those passengers who were waiting for the *St Regis* to come back?"

"The ones who can pay or have it billed are boarding."

Kham asked of Palude, "What now?"

"At the least, we have to go down there and see who has gotten on."

"What had your last reading of the oracle suggested?"

" 'Journey by water,' from Tarot. *I Ching* said #64, 'Almost There.' "

Kham asked Madraz, "Are there any waterships in the port?"

"Two. One yesterday morning from the Pilontaries, so they say, loaded with refugees. Another from Karshiyaka, a trader with a load of Fleischbaum, last night."

"Judas!" Kham exclaimed. "Chance sets us all astray, while

we wait and ponder! Arunda, get your things. We'll have to go, and maybe keep on going."

Palude got up, hesitantly, but stood quietly. At last she asked, "Are you not going to report? Shouldn't we wait . . .?"

"Wait for what? If that thing gets loose back there, we'll probably find out about it when the ships stop coming here at all. Come on. We've got to see if there's a young woman loose down there. Before the lighter rejoins the main ship. Once she gets on one of those things it'll be worse than trying to find it here."

"How do you mean? It's just a ship. It's got limited space; we can run it to Earth there, surely. And it's a long way to the next port of call from here."

"It's a long way between calls, yes, but if you've never spaced out commercial, you don't know. Those commercial liners are enormous, the size of cities. Cargo and people, both. That ship up there in orbit is probably larger than Marula. And we won't get any cooperation from the crew, either."

"Then if you think it's gotten aboard, you'll follow it and try to kill it."

"Find it and follow it if I can. Kill it? Not on a commercial liner. Captain's his own law aboard one of those. Traditional penalty for murder is ejection into space, *in transit.*"

"Then what could you do?"

"Identify it and follow. Are you coming?"

"I . . . yes, I will come."

"Good!" Kham set about gathering his few possessions, and said, over his shoulder, "Settle accounts with Master Madraz, in case we don't come back. I'm going ahead."

Kham disappeared into one of the back rooms, reappearing after some noisy efforts with his things crammed into a bulging travel bag. Madraz was still there, unmoved and unmoving. He seemed to view the activity with the mild disdain of a small boy who had just poked an anthill with a stick. He withdrew his hands from the folds of his robe and proffered a small package to Palude and Kham. "Our commercial representative sent this along with the word of the arrival. Well he listened to your words, and well he complied. This, he said, was for you."

Kham stopped, came across the room and took the package. It was wrapped in brown paper, the sort used in wrapping breakable goods, but it seemed unwontedly heavy for its size. Kham unwrapped it carefully. What was inside appeared to be a small metallic tablet, about the size of a small woman's hand, rectangular, with rounded corners. It bore curious pictographic signs, some line figures of animals, others heraldic symbols whose pictographic aspect had been lost. The metal was silvery, untarnished, utterly without color of its own. It was very heavy in his hand. Kham looked at it for a long time in utter silence, and then handed it to Palude without a word. She took it, and asked, "What is it?"

"Bad news. That's the missing Clispish credit card."

"Then it's aboard the lighter."

"Exactly. And that thing can buy a lot of privacy. Yes, settle things here. We're going traveling."

11

"To appreciate an art: there's a fine thing. But better to use it to express what one imagines to be truth. But at the summit of mastery, contradictorially, one submits to it and shyly allows it to speak with one's voice, borrowed, as it were. Then you get truth, that makes the rest mere vanity."

—H. C., *Atropine*

Nazarine sat back in the depths of an enormous overstuffed chair facing a window and looked out on the port from the lighter. Cinoe was close by, but busily talking with a group who had arrived just before they had. Offworlders who had filtered into Marula and were still trying to get off Oerlikon. Some of them he recalled from earlier times. She let him talk; above all, now she needed time to herself, time to integrate everything.

One thing was a streak of incredible luck, and that luck, she knew, was a fickle thing, like having a love affair. One might have it, or not, but however it went, one had to get on with one's business. *True enough!* But what was her proper business? She did not feel any sense of escape at all; to the contrary, she felt an increased sense of danger. Every minute now she moved closer to the source of danger, and she had to comprehend the nature of the environment she was in.

She was also certain that however easily she had gotten aboard the lighter, they must have set off alarms all over the planet when she had had Cinoe, under pretext of her not understanding the language of the offworlders, which was true as far as it went, exchange the cartouche of Pompeo for something more negotiable. Whoever was here looking for her would surely have a chance, because of that. Having Cinoe do it, with her close by, would confuse them, but not for long.

Tartary, from the landing-point of the lighter, didn't look like much: the land was treeless, covered with mats of dull-brown vegetation. Or else bare mud and rock. The mud was brown and apparently sticky, the rocks gray or dull black. The port had a hasty, ramshackle look to it, and also a foreign look, as if it did not belong here. There were native Makhaks in evidence, but only as the lowest sorts of laborers—she could sense that they were outcasts, and that the real Tartary lay elsewhere, somewhere off over the northern horizon.

Tartary was enigmatic, hidden, subtle. Nazarine looked out the window, sensing a powerful secret doctrine locked in the tawdry and ordinary scene she was looking at, if she could but find it. There was the weakness of her skill, carried forward from Rael, Damistofia, Phaedrus, and now herself: *She had to know what questions to ask.* Without that, she was as blind as the rest of the confused and terrified people around her, each seeking their tiny shred of the future surety, even if one of foreboding and dread. Tartary was like a bosel. They, too, were fascinating, enigmatic, full of arcane secrets, arrangements of life stranger than anything she could imagine. But bosels did not send forgotten people to the Mask Factory to become obedient lobos . . . nor did Makhaks invade one another's holds with the fire and steel of the Pallet-Dropped Heavy Troopers. Interesting, yes, but not important. Bosels were distractions; so was Tartary, however ordinary this part of it seemed—mud, stone quays, winding paths down the bluffs, sweating undermen, ramshackle taverns. Yes, that was it. One was surrounded by a million things that cried for attention, but only a precious few mattered, in some cases, only one thing. One could die of nothing more serious than simple fascination. She looked from the window to Cinoe, seeing his girl-delicate face in profile. She felt a reflex constriction in her loins, a desire-reflex that she did not deny. She had given herself over to it utterly, and felt no regret or condemnation. *It was beautiful. It is so yet. But it, too, is a*

distraction no less deadly than the rest of the things I have seen.
Phaedrus had tried to reach for oblivion, for utter ordinarity,
complete submersion, and it had failed, and in pain and terror for
those he loved most, a gentle, lustless love. She thought,
somberly, *I did not ask for it, nor did I wish it, but I was created
to a deadly purpose, and I must use that in order to . . . what?
They created more than they could imagine when they made me.
I could create a universe in which such evil could not exist,
could not be imagined, could not even be denounced as a vice.
Yes. I have that power.* And even as the strange joy of that
realization flooded through her mind, like an echo there followed
on it the converse, inseparable: *without the freedom to commit
evil unimaginable, what little good managed to get done by
accident would be meaningless!* Even more clearly, she saw this
simultaneously: an image of herself and Cinoe joined in love,
climaxing together, (how different his face was then from now.
Her own, too, she supposed), knowing that sex was not an end
in itself but a way to reach for a deeper sweetness that was
ultimately unreachable, that essence of loneliness one could
never share. All that, a meaningless procreative rite, conducted
in boredom, without those other losses, those other never-was,
never-could-be's. Figure and background. Signal and noise. *And
I'm in terrible danger of being swamped by noise.*

She stood up and laid her hand on his shoulder affectionately.
When he looked up, away from those others with whom he
shared something she would never know, she said, "I'm going
to the cabin and wait. I feel too exposed here."

In that instant, she glimpsed something flicker across his face,
a slight annoyance. When they stepped across the threshold of
the bursar's office down below, she had become a burden,
someone who would have to be shown everything. He nodded.
"You're still worried about being followed?"

"You get an instinct for these things."

"I'm not one to disagree; I've known that feeling myself.
Well, then—go ahead. Tell you what you could do, while you're
waiting; there's a self-paced language-assimilation set in there.
Drugs, RNA, hypnotic learning programs. If you strap yourself
into that, you should have the basics down by the time we join
the main ship. They have them because you never know where
one of these ships is going to stop. It will make things a lot
easier for you, on the ship and back in the real world, so to
speak. You can pick up the fine points as you go."

"I wondered how I was going to get through that."

"It won't change you at all—just give you the means to communicate."

"Do they really have the language of Oerlikon stored in there?"

"Oerlikonian? I doubt it. No, you'll talk to the machine, and it will learn from you, enough to start you off. I'll stay here—don't worry about being in the way."

"You're sure it's all right?"

"Certainly. I'm just catching up on things, swapping horror stories. I'll stay here, and meet you upside when we link up. And then you can begin to experience the real world."

"You're sure it's safe."

"Absolutely. Just lock the doorseal and engage the wall set. No one can hear you. Let it do its program on you—it won't change you, so don't fight it."

"When do we leave here?"

"According to what I hear, it will probably be night, and then at least a couple of hours getting docked with the mother ship."

"How will you get in?"

"Once you lock it, I can't. Come and get me when you're finished." He glanced at the others. "We'll be here, just telling yarns. No worry, we won't run out of them before takeoff. Go on and do it and get it over with, and come speak to me in my own speech."

She turned, saying, "Just so." Then Nazarine made her way through the eddying crowds in the lounges and passageways back to the small cabin they had taken. She opened the door, entered without looking back, and turned and locked it. Then she looked around. The bed was high up and partly enclosed. The cabin was spare and functional. Some pop-out seats along the wall, a bath cubicle in the rear. No windows. She nodded to herself, and began methodically taking her clothes off. *First, a hot bath. Then, the machine.* She only had one concern, and that was about possible side effects of the accelerated learning she was going to take. She remembered that the particular arts she practiced as the Morphodite could not be expressed in the language of Oerlikon—that whole system was both illogical and impossible in that language. What effect would Cinoe's language have on the oracular powers of the Morphodite? She tried to reason it out by analogy, but lacking any knowledge about how the offworlders' speech was structured, she could only guess.

While showering, she tried to run a short-scan mentally, without using the hand symbols she had developed, and she actually did get a very blurred and indistinct reading. The question she formulated was: *Will learning another language degrade my abilities to compute in the oracular system?* The answer seemed to be negative, but it was a curious negative, with all sorts of side-features and eddies growing out of it. Still, it was a negative. She reluctantly rinsed off, dried in a warm air blast, and climbed into the bed, still naked. There, in the wall, she found a pull-out fixture whose operation seemed to be self-evident and failsafe even for one like herself. She feared this more than anything she had done yet, but after one deep breath, she activated the device, catching herself thinking that it was, after all, a shame that Cinoe would not be here with her. She smiled wryly at that. *This place was the first thing we had done together, in concert. Ours. And not really ours at all. Well.* And as the operating light illuminated on the viewscreen of the device, she said to it, in her own speech, "Very well, bucket of bolts. Do your worst!"

At the foot of the entryway to the lighter, Kham and Arunda Palude found a temporary office which had been erected for the convenience of the bursar. The lighter was itself a large construction of curiously irregular shape, as if it had been constructed with no aim for dynamic flow whatsoever. It stood on the flats before the water on many metal legs, a flattish, angular thing like a small city, casting a cold and windy shadow underneath.

The "office" was made of timbers lashed together, scraps, pieces of plastic sheeting that bowed and fluttered in the wind. Inside was a very modern communicator, presumably linked with the mainship *Kalmia* topside, and perhaps through it to other places. The bursar had thoughtfully brought down a portable heater which labored mightily to fill the tent with heat, but much of its output leaked out through flaps and rents in the plastic. Still, the outside noises faded. Kham felt an odd prickling about his ears and thought he could sense a sonic deadener. Speaking, he confirmed it. Their voices had, in this place, a flatness, a loss of timbre.

They had no difficulty identifying themselves and booking passage. But there seemed to be some problem about finding the person they were looking for, whom they identified as an associate long lost in the tumults of the revolution in Lisagor.

The bursar rubbed his chin, scratched his temples, and ruminated, "Well, yes, in fact, er, ah, I was the one who handled the transaction with that metallic slab. Well, myself and the local factor, who vouched for its authenticity. That was no problem. We've had some of these Clispians before and knew where to set up the billing to. But it very definitely was not a woman who traded it in, but a young man. Odd, that. He knew our procedures fairly well, but seemed, ah, a bit unsure of himself about the tablet itself. But no matter. It's a bearer-security, and the account has been an honorable one. They pay their bills."

Kham asked, "You are sure it was a young man? After all, identities can be disguised."

"The person who came to me . . . Wait, I'll describe him to you. Then you can see if this is your friend. He was not tall, but slender, a little nervous. A straight nose, large eyes, a well-formed mouth. Delicate, like a girl in a way, but he didn't move like a woman, if you understand my meaning. No beard or mustache; as a fact, I couldn't see any trace of one. Didn't look depilated. Rather long hair, shoulder length, loose and wavy, very dark, almost black. He had no special mannerisms, except for a slight nervousness."

Palude asked, "What language did he speak?"

"Same one we speak now: Universal Semantic Reference System. Spoke it like a native, too."

Kham: "Voice?"

"Definitely male, although I thought rather young, or someone from a late-maturing stock. That seemed to fit the beardlessness. Oh, yes, he looked green and inexperienced, but he also had something of the air of a small-time bravo with a woman stashed somewhere."

Kham sat back, puzzled. He glanced over at Arunda, and in her eyes he read the same perplexity. He had given her a full description of the woman he had seen on the Beamliner, and in the descriptive system they used, she would have almost as good an image in her mind as his, which was memory, and a trained one at that. He remembered the girl well. And in no way did this person the bursar was describing resemble that girl. Especially the nervousness. Kham remembered that particularly vividly. The girl on the train had possessed an almost supernatural, reptilian calm. And from what they knew about the Morphodite, there was no possible way it could have *changed* and retained its age. Unless: unless the girl he had seen was just an ordinary person. Possible? Still, what had happened to the one living in Clisp? He felt a powerful surge of indecision, of the sense of an impending mistake of judgment so vast that it could never be corrected from. He fought a panicky urge to throw his passage vouchers down on the desk and bolt from the tent. They had been wrong from the beginning! Then he went back over the ground he and Arunda had covered and recovered a thousand times, waiting up in that castle, speaking with furtive men who came by night, and spoke in whispers. He said, to the bursar, "Well, it seems like we've missed something somewhere, but we're reasonably certain that our friend is aboard."

"Could be. This one bought an open-group ticket. You know, like a family plan. He could have had friends with him. We were encouraging that procedure to make the workload lighter."

"Yes, of course. Well, we will go on and board, and see if we can find our friend."

"I wish you good fortune."

Kham motioned to Palude to follow him, and left the tent. Outside, in the windy, dusty open spaces under the bulk of the lighter, he said, "The only thing I can figure is that our target *is* here. But somehow she's managed to pick up a decoy."

Palude sniffed, "Hm. Fine piece of work, to catch someone and then trust him enough to handle that financial transaction. The value of that cartouche is immense! It's pure platinum as well as I can tell, and in itself worth a fortune."

"Maybe he didn't understand that. Whoever he is, he seems to be a bit young."

"It's possible. I have the image you painted for me, and I admit she must be rather attractive, tall and good-looking, sure of herself, enough not to skulk. She could do it."

Kham gestured upward with his head, motioning to the metal bulk above them. "She's up there, sure as the sea's salt. And I don't think we can hope to find her before this thing lifts off and docks with the main ship. That will hold a lot of people."

Arunda nodded. "True. We've got less than a day to go through the lighter, and it doesn't look feasible with just the two of us. But remember that the voyage back to more settled space is a long one, even in a liner like *Kalmia*. Not impossible. Just hard."

"You know what bothers me?"

"No. Speak of it."

"That thing has an uncanny ability to move unnoticed right out in the open."

Arunda: "Yes, that especially. A sneak I could deal with. But this open invisibility . . . that's scary. You know, if she's as attractive as you say, that in itself could be a screen, too. And then of course she's got the *Art*."

"True. But we don't know how much she's using it. I think it's difficult and time-consuming for her to perform one of those divinations, and she's using it very little. I think that *was* her on the Beamliner, and I think further that I surprised her."

"But you said she disappeared."

"That can be explained by nothing more than a little fashionable paranoia, or extra care, however you want it. From what we have managed to put together of that thing's abilities, I feel reasonably certain that if she had known what I was, I would never have seen her, and never returned from Lisagor on that last trip, and. . . ."

"And?"

"And we have one advantage."

"Tell me."

"She doesn't know you. And I don't think she's sure of me, yet. But we know what she looks like."

Arunda reminded him, "We know what the one we *think* it is looks like."

"Very well."

"But your argument has weight. I think she's in there, too."

"Has to be. Her mission has been long done here. And because the assassination squad failed, she knows Oerlikon's not safe. She may just be moving for those reasons alone."

Arunda said, reflectively, "I follow it well enough. But mark, Cesar; she's got time now to start asking questions and use her *art*. We have to be more careful now than we ever were before. And we won't have the freedom of movement we had here."

"Oh yes, a fine merry mess. But never you fear. We've still got a chance, and it may be the best thing yet, having that thing locked up in a ship with us. At least that narrows the range of the hunt."

"How are you going to handle it? You know you can't kill it aboard and get away clean."

"We'll identify it, and then transmit ahead for help. Sooner or later we can surround it in a space small enough to control it." And as he said that, something flickered through his mind about

not killing the Morphodite, but capturing it and harnessing its
vast incomprehensible powers. That was very tempting. And, as
Cesar Kham saw it, within the realm of possibility. Only they
had to be careful; they walked on eggshells and razors, and
below that lay the descent into hell unimaginable. He shook his
head. Yes, tempting, but the price of failure. *Consider the price
of failure.*

Nazarine had not slept, but she awakened. She could remember every moment, every hour, every motion of the lighter, but
distantly, as if the reality had been the dream. The instruction
program was completed. She now possessed a foreigner's gram-
mar, rudiments of rhetoric, and a basic vocabulary from which
she could build. She sat up in the bed, conscious suddenly of a
backwash of fatigue. And of other things, too; the passage of
time.

She knew more than language; she knew certain basic machine
skills, how to speak to machines. She reached, stroked a touchplate,
absentmindedly, as if she had done it all her life. She thought,
And so I did, once, in another age, another life. The questions
she asked were simple: how much time has elapsed, and, where
are we now? The machine voice answered. She translated the
unfamiliar time system into Oerlikon divisions of the day, and
was surprised at the length of time she had been under. And the
lighter had been late taking off, and was having to chase the
main ship around the planet, instead of going directly there. But
they were in initial approach already—the lighter pilot had mainship
in sight. She commanded, "Show surface of planet."

The screen flickered, jumped, and then steadied as the proper
sensor was selected. The screen showed a watery, deep-blue
world slowly turning beneath, a land mass visible, curious and
spiky in shape, the main body illuminated in soft morning slants,
and a spine of mountains cast in sharp relief far to the west.
Dawn among the peaks of The Serpentine. Clisp was yet in
darkness. Swirls of cloud shrouded the north country, and fish
scales and curdled masses covered the southeastern extension of
the land, Zamor and the Pilontary Islands. Simultaneous thoughts
and emotions collided in her mind, making her eyes burn: *I am
leaving a place where I was tormented and mutated into a thing.
and. . . .I am leaving the only home I can remember. In any
event, never to return. Never.* She commanded the image to
terminate. The screen went blank.

Nazarine climbed down out of the bed and went to her luggage to find some better clothing than the traveling clothes she had been living in aboard the *Rondinello*. She selected a light knit gown, boots; the gown was a soft gray and followed the lines of her body, moving with her. The bottom of it was loose and fell to mid-calf. Over it she put on a darker gray felt half-tunic, very loose, a sleeveless strip almost as long as the gown. She moved about, experimentally. It had been an extravagance, hopelessly exotic for Oerlikon, but here, among all these strange people. . . . She leaned over the bed and touched the commplate again, commanding the screen to show her typical female clothing of the times. The screen illuminated and displayed a series of images of women, of all ages, shapes, races, and occupations. The variety bewildered her, but also reassured her. There was here a variegated pattern she could hide within. She asked the machine what was the suitability of what she wore. The machine flashed STAND BY FOR HUMAN OPERATOR. And the scene shifted to an unidentified space. A woman was there, older, thin, intense. Bushy gray hair, coveralls and a loose jacket. Crew? The woman said brusquely, "Passenger. You need assistance?"

Nazarine said, "I'm a stranger to your ways. What is my clothing suitable for?"

The woman looked hard, offscreen, as if at another monitor, and said, after a moment, "Tasteful day clothes for a rich man's mistress going on a long cruise. Are you?"

Nazarine laughed. "No, to the first; maybe, to the second."

The woman made a wry face. "Whatever. What do you want to do?"

"Feel comfortable and not be particularly noticed."

"That does it, although with your body you'll have a time being invisible. But a nice choice. Nice stuff. Get it downworld?"

"Yes."

"Local?"

"Oh, yes. They don't have full trade yet."

"Hmf. Go on and wear it. It'll be all right." For a moment, the woman stopped, as if she were finished. But hesitated, and then added, "You're a local, from downworld?"

"Yes."

"On your own?"

"More or less."

"I understand; stop there. Look me up after we secure, I'm on the crew roster: Faren Kiricky, Structeering Section. I'll show you. Clothing is messages and meaning. Going to stay with us?''

''I think so.''

''To find a place? Fine. Look me up. I can at least keep you from making statements about yourself that you may not want to be true.''

''I'll do it. I need that.''

''Super. Call me then.'' And the screen blanked. And Nazarine stood back on the floor feeling very risky and foolishly pleased with herself. What were the woman's motives for offering her help? Charity? Simple? Complex? It didn't matter. She had dealt directly with an offworld stranger, someone with no connection at all with the hidden manipulators of her world. That one, Kiricky, was not hunting her. The encounter had been totally ordinary. It was such a relief she laughed out loud.

She climbed down out of the bed and stood for a moment, uncertainly. Something was incomplete, but what was it? There was something she was supposed to do. What? She shook her head, sending her hair flying. Something was wrong. She stopped herself dead, centering. Where was she? On the lighter, moving to docking with the starship *Kalmia*. She had spoken with a woman of the crew, Faren Kiricky. There was where the wrongness was. But what about it was wrong? She cocked her head, disturbed. *Gods, I'm slow!* She had spoken with Faren, in Faren's language. That was what was wrong. She had felt the idea and spoke it. Simple basic everyday language, but it had come without thinking. She was thinking in it now. She could see the holes in its continuum where there were words and concepts she didn't know.

Nazarine pulled down one of the little foldout seats and sat wearily on it, putting her head in her hands. A fit of dread and fear washed over her, icy cold along her back, which was suddenly damp with sweat. Her hands were wet, too. She suppressed a sudden nervous urge to urinate. She looked up, at the blank and silent walls of the machine she was riding, to an unknown destination. She remembered Oerlikon.

What did that goddam machine do to me?! She felt tears of anger flush her eyes. *I gave myself to that incredible unknown mechanism, and the damn thing even gave me words to curse with. What else did it give me, and what has it taken away? Yes, gave myself, guessing, just like I gave myself to Cinoe. Unknowns there, too.*

She got up and went to her baggage, from which she extracted a common paper tablet and a pen, and she began working furiously, sketching in the outlines of a reading of the oracle, finding that it somehow went differently. Harder some ways, easier, others. It was subtle, but the way she handled it was different. She was doing a general reading of the environment around herself, with herself and two knowns, Cinoe and Faren, and an unquantified unknown who was the one, or group, who had sent terrorists against Phaedrus. Some of the operations she had to stop and reach for, hard, wincing at the memory that in some ways this was harder than when she had first tried *reading* as Damistofia. But it came to her. She remembered, and the operations began to flow smoothly, building to their conclusion. Nazarine sat back and looked at the diagram she had made, which she understood now resembled an ideogram of an ancient language, Chinese, only fantastically more detailed. Where in the Chinese, there had been a single line, in this there were scores of finger lines. It was as if the Chinese characters were blurred-out and overprinted blotches of her oracular answers. And of course, her ideograms were complete sequences, not just single word units.

This oracle said: *Protective coloration. Change guides; your old one has lost the way. You will have to lead him. Danger is present, but ineffective, as long as you move in shadow. Remain firm in course. On the way. Attempt no attack—this line is now too fragile. You cannot change it without affecting yourself.*

She looked up and sighed deeply. She had been completely oblivious of time, and wondered how much time had elapsed while she had been *reading*. But she knew one thing about her system that this exercise had taught her: it was a great deal more sensitive to subtleties. The finer focusing came a lot easier. She could still sense the upper range of it, but now she saw that as just the beginnings of the whole system. She could now ask for and do a lot more finely focused things. She breathed deeply, relieved. Her hands were dry.

Nazarine looked up at the bed, absently, and felt a short, small, sharp motion in the lighter. There was a distant, muffled, mechanical bumping, which did not alarm her. The lighter was docked. She was a part of the world of *Kalmia* now.

12

"Power is always relative—appropriate. In the conventional sense, one who is a power in one environment loses that power in changing to a different surround. Few change willingly; they are usually changed by others who arrange shifts to make this lessening possible. Is it any wonder change is a fearsome thing?"
—H. C., Atropine

During the wait after boarding, and during the trip upworld From Oerlikon to *Kalmia,* Kham and Palude had separated and circulated quietly among the passengers and open spaces of the lighter, hoping to catch a glimpse of a tall girl-woman whose image they both carried in their heads. Kham himself saw a couple who might have been, but on discreet closer inspection proved to be different from the one sighting he had had of the girl on the train. One in particular had her height and general bearing, color hair, and smoothness of face, but when he saw her from the front, any resemblance vanished; this girl had a long, equine face and a nose that was distinctive in that there was no indention of the brow line. His target had a rounder face, and a rather small nose. The other lacked the body, although she was graceful and willowy. Too slender.

As agreed, he met Arunda Palude by the exit ramp as they were nearing docking. He said, without gesture, "I had no luck. You?"

"Nothing. Although there's no shortage of smallish men with delicate features, girlish."

"Spacers of the commercial variety. Travelers. Bad fortune, that we never saw him and only had a fragmentary description to go on. Could be anyone."

"Why so many like that?"

"Agility, precision, fine-detail work. That's the sort you see in this kind of travel. Not like what we're used to."

144

"She couldn't possibly know what she was doing when she picked him."

"Couldn't she? What if she's recovered Jedily Tulilly? What if she's used her *art* to see beyond Oerlikon?"

Arunda looked off at the wall for a moment. "You're assuming the worst, which is good tactical thinking, but which may not be true. I have another explanation, which will do almost as well: the attack that failed alerted it enough so that it knows it has to get offworld. It's moving blind. Cautious, sighted in part through its oracle, but nothing more. And some luck on its side. That won't run forever, and it's in our world now, not us in its world. Sooner or later it will have to move, and it will become visible. Then we can deal with it."

"Possible. Either way. But we'll get one more shot here in the lighter, here, by the exit ramp. After that, we've got a larger environment to search."

Palude did not seem worried. "And more time to look for it in. Here, it could hide somewhere, but there it will have to move eventually."

"It's seen me. If it sees me again. . . ."

"I know. That means I do most of the looking."

"Not the way you think. You'll do the close work. But I'll be working, too."

"We don't have people on *Kalmia*?"

"Doubt it. Almost surely not."

There was a small movement of the lighter, followed by a short vibration, and then silence. Far off down the corridor they could hear announcements being made through the PA system, and while they were waiting, a crewmember, wearing a plain gray coverall marked only by a horizontal color strip above the left breast, approached them. He looked them over, and then made a visual inspection of the telltales, before unsealing. Apparently everything was in order, for he reached into a recessed panel and operated the switches that would activate the door. Behind him, the corridor was filling with people, none walking hurriedly, more drifting along in the general direction, most of them carrying bundles, some larger, some smaller.

For a time, they were able to wait by the door, but eventually the movement of the people created a small bottleneck, and one of the crew asked them politely but firmly to move along, and at a glance from Kham, Arunda complied. They entered the *Kalmia*, which at least by the entry seemed not greatly different from the lighter that serviced it. A long, dim corridor, unbroken and gently curving, unrelieved by side openings, windows, vents, or wickets.

They walked slowly along the corridor, and Kham said, "We only had one shot at it back there. Best to move on. We don't want to attract any attention. Not until I've had a chance to feel out the security officer."

"Where do you think it is?"

Kham gestured over his shoulder. "Back there. It'll be one of the last out. If this runway was straight and we could stop and look, we could probably see it now."

"Why don't we wait here?"

"Under observation."

"Then we've got the whole ship to go through."

"Right."

"Then we'd better get settled and get on with it."

Kham nodded, dolefully. He had an idea how difficult it was going to be, aboard a ship the size of *Kalmia*. "Right. Soon as we do get settled, I want you to relax, concentrate, and do a reading, see what you get."

Nazarine knew they were docked, but she composed herself and waited. She knew Cinoe had to come back here before he went on to the main ship, and she thought it would be better to wait for him, although she knew very well now, from her session with the teaching machine, that she could very well go on alone. *No. Let this develop as it will*.

It seemed a long time after they docked, but eventually he knocked at the door, and then tried it. He said, "I thought you might have gone on."

Now he spoke in the language of the offworlders, which to Nazarine's ear, although sensible and comprehensible, sounded harsh and clipped, congested with consonants. She answered him in the same speech, "No. I waited."

"Do you still want to share a room?"

"I don't know. I realized from the machine how little I know. I will have to have a lot more. I suppose they have such devices aboard."

"Yes. That one, like on this lighter, is just the rudiments. You can tie into the mainship's computer to get the rest of it."

"I feel like a Fleischbaum Gatherer in the city for the first time."

Cinoe stood back and looked at Nazarine carefully. "You certainly don't look like one."

She almost told him of her conversation with the crewmember, but she didn't. She said, "What do I seem like to you? I bought some clothes to travel in, but I don't know how these people present themselves."

Cinoe laughed, but there was a slight uneasiness in it. "What you have is fine. Very good taste."

"We are by no means bumpkins in Clisp."

"Yes, just so. Well, you will have to excuse me; the way I must go involves no frills. I get three meals a day and a place to sleep, and the good fortune to have a ride back to civilization. Otherwise, it's much the same as on the *Rondinello*. Except, of course, the heat. We won't be cold again."

She smiled. "Yes, the heat. I thought I would never get warm again."

"No I. But we seem to recover fast."

"Yes."

He hesitated, and then ventured, "You understand that if you remain with me, we'll go into the steerage dormitory, with the rest of us refugees."

She said, thoughtfully, "I'm not a refugee. I'm a spy, remember?"

"Yes. With an unlimited expense account underwritten by the Prince of Clisp. Well, down there it's pretty plain and not a lot of privacy. . . ."

"You could come with me. . . ."

For a long moment, she saw indecision reflected in Cinoe's face, in his body movements. Then she saw the change in him: he decided. "Might be better for us both if I didn't. Of course, we're not prisoners down there—we have the run of the ship. There's a lot here; has to be. This kind of ship does some pretty long runs. Months, sometimes years. So everything is here. . . ."

She sensed that he was looking for a graceful way to leave her. Why? She said, "I suppose you'll want to spend a lot of time with people you haven't seen in years."

"I've already met several I knew before. All have amazing tales to tell. There were some events in Marula!"

"Yes. I have heard some, from our side."

"And you will need to move around, learn, study. And do whatever things you must do."

"Yes. But we could still meet."

"I'd like that."

"I would also." She picked up her bags. "Come on. They'll lock us out here in the lighter."

Cinoe laughed, "Already you're learning to be civilized and be in a hurry."

Nazarine flashed him a quick, sharp glance, and let it go. It angered her that he would toss that off so easily. Uncivilized, was she? She had felt a dull pain in her chest at the thought of losing someone with whom she had been in love, with whom she had made love, yielded up everything, held nothing back, but that revelation from him blunted it a great deal, and restored some of the simmering anger she had almost forgotten. Of course, it didn't make up all the difference, but she thought she could live with what she had to live with. And she caught herself smiling, and thinking with some of the corrosive cynicism of Rael, from long ago, *You aren't here to rub bellies with prettymens, you're here to visit some of these people with fire and sword and worse. Like microsurgery*. She tossed her head, sending the gold-brown curls flying. "Come on." And she set off out of the room, into the corridor toward the gate, walking with a confidence she did not really feel, but she knew that would come in its own time. Cinoe followed, not saying anything, as if he knew he had already said too much.

When they had traversed the long corridor into the ship proper, they came at last to a long counter where accommodations were assigned. Cinoe went first, identified himself, and was assigned a place in steerage with a minimum of comment. The officer handling the assignments motioned him toward a group waiting toward the end of the counter. When Nazarine's turn came, she presented her credit voucher and asked what was available. It turned out that the *Kalmia* was somewhat crowded, more so than usual, but some places were still left, and so she settled eventually for a single room, with its own entertainment connection and a separate recreation room. The cost of it caused her to swallow hard, but she signed the voucher and the officer handed her a packet containing a chart of the ship and where she could find various things, including her rooms.

She approached the group Cinoe had joined. They were all silent now, not chattering as they had on the lighter. She said, "I will tell you my room number."

He shrugged. "No need. You can query through the shipmind. It'll tell you, unless you pay extra for unlisted registry."

She shook her head. "Too much already. No, I am listed as myself. Nazarine Florissante Alea, native of Oerlikon."

"I am listed as Cinoe Dzholin, as you know."

"I'll call you."

"Please do. I'll wait."

At that moment, a porter appeared from a side passage, and picked up her bags. This one wore a crew uniform, and asked her what her number was. The porter was a girl, stocky and solid, but graceful and smoothly economical of movement. She didn't even acknowledge the presence of the group of refugees. "What apartment, Serra?"

Nazarine hesitated a moment, looking uncertainly at Cinoe, who had turned his attention to a girl in the group and was talking with her. "Four-Q-two."

The portress nodded. "Right along. Up the lift and along the slide. Good choice. Come along. Won't be but a minute." She hefted the bags and set off down an adjoining passageway, not looking back. Nazarine looked back once, and then followed the girl, who strode along purposefully, looking neither left nor right.

Up to this point, everything she had seen had been more or less like things on Oerlikon. Now was when she began to feel the strangeness of the environment she had launched herself into. The portress went a short way along the passageway, and turned at a set of double doors in the wall. The girl said, to the doors, "Open," and they did. On nothing. A shaft, full of a curdled milky radiance. The girl waited for Nazarine to catch up with her, and then stepped off into the nothingness of the shaft, calling out, "Q." She fell upward. Nazarine followed her, stepping off into the lights. Nothing happened. She hung in space, supported somehow although she didn't feel that she was standing on anything. After a moment, she said, "Q," with a resolve she didn't feel at that moment. Then she began moving upward. Eventually she stopped at an open door, where the girl was waiting for her with a bored expression on her face.

She stepped out of the lift, not aware of having traversed any great distance. The girl said, "A short walk now, and we'll transition to section four. That's a slideway, but it's a fast one."

"Do I need to pay attention to how we are going?"

The girl looked around, and said, over her shoulder, "Good question, Serra, for a newcomer."

"Do I look it?"

She shrugged. "They all do. Look scared to death. Never worry. Ship doesn't bite."

"How do you find your way?"

"Oh, that. These are service runs. You'll never see these again, likely. They gave you a map?"

"Yes."

"Spend the next day shiptime studying it. If you get lost, in the passenger section there are commpoints all along the walls. Just use one. Say, 'where in the bloody hell am I?' and it'll tell you straight off, it will. Then venture out as much as you can, get a feel for it. It's a long run to next halt."

"Is this that isolated?"

"You wouldn't believe. . . . The Jefe-Maximo heard there'd been trouble here and diverted for it. Plenty of money in those rescue billings, he says. Otherwise we'd have transited straight across. Stop in the middle like this and the time's quadrupled. Passengers don't care—they don't pay by the light, but by mapcoords."

"Explain."

"The space the ship moves in is like a diagram of realspace, except that the distances in transspace don't always match. What's a light in real might be a cent, trans. And vice versa. This place is in the middle of a hole. Nothing there. Long in real, long in trans, both. Funny place, that way."

The girl now shifted through an oval opening onto a tubular passage whose floor seemed unstable, not-there. She stepped onto the "floor" and was whisked off. Nazarine followed.

After several more arcane routes and traverses along floors that weren't floors, and passageways that seemed to go nowhere, they emerged through an ordinary push-door onto a balcony, overlooking an enormous open space which Nazarine first failed to grasp. She had to stop and get her bearings.

She was on a balcony or walkway, floored with ceramic tile in subtle geometric patterns, with a rail, which overlooked an immense atrium or park or vivarium. She couldn't tell. Down there, somewhere far below, was a forest, or a park, or a city. She couldn't tell. She saw what looked like trees, interspersed with low buildings and parklands. She could tell there was another side, somewhere far off, but she couldn't make out details. It was dim. All she could make out were strings of lights.

They passed one door, stopped at the second. The girl said,

"Put your hand flat, palm down on the plate." Nazarine did so. The door opened, swinging inward silently.

The room was modest, quiet, low-ceilinged. There was a single large bed, a sunken area with a lot of cushions, and another door leading off to the side. The girl followed her eyes, and said, "Bath there." She went in, and saw another door on the other side. "Study cubicle." The portress set the bags down, and paused.

Nazarine handed the girl some of the money she'd changed down below, with Cinoe's help. The girl looked at it for a moment, and then fished in a pocket and handed Nazarine some change back, "Too much the first time. I'm honest."

"May I ask your name? I may have to ask for you again. I Don't know many people here, and there are some things I need to do. . . ."

"Esme Szilishch. But you probably won't see me anymore."

"But could I ask, if I need to ask something? This is my first trip."

"Um. You grow up down there?"

"Yes."

"Call if you like. Got someone?"

Nazarine stopped, unsure of herself, and of offworld manners. She said, uncertainly, "I had. Not sure so much now."

Esme nodded, as if thinking to herself. She looked up, spoke with an odd directness. "Plenty of time to find someone. But I'll help if you like." She made a short little curtsey, which caught Nazarine a little off guard, and left. Now she was alone, in her own place. *First, I need to sleep,* she thought, and began pulling clothes off, all the time looking at the large bed, which looked more inviting by the second.

Sometime much later, she woke up, and for the first time in what seemed like months, her mind was clear. She turned on the lights and began looking. She didn't move from the bed. The room was surprisingly large, larger than the rooms of most houses she had seen, and larger than some of the rooms in the palace she had seen when she had been Phaedrus. But low-ceilinged. She guessed she could stand and stretch and touch the ceiling with palms flattened. There were no windows, real or imitation, nor were there any sort of decorations on the walls. Bath *there*, on her left, Study cubicle *there*, on her right. She nodded. All seemed correct. Now to explore.

After dressing in the same clothes she had worn before, she went through the information packet carefully. Her fare included room service, which was handled by an automatic dumbwaiter, and so she ordered breakfast. All of it was slightly odd, but there were fruits and cereals and something like meat, and so she ate it. They had no hagdrupe, which she recalled Rael being fond of, but they had coffee, which was a bit better, and she ordered a pot of it. Then she began reading in earnest, puzzling over odd phrases which made no sense to her. That was the most curious, puzzling aspect of the robolearning she had taken: when she came to a word she didn't know, her mind refused to recognize it. It looked meaningless. She had to stare at it a long time. But time she had, and she worked at it until most of them did make sense. She found out this class of room also had a complement of clothing for the convenience of travelers, who might have to spend months aboard. Already sized from holograms taken of her during entry. Standard stuff in basic cuts, but it would certainly do. She thought back to the price of the fare and smiled to herself. Perhaps it would be worth it after all.

Then she began unraveling the map of the ship, which was rendered in a highly abstract manner that revealed nothing of the shape of the ship or its size. But it made considerable sense, once she began to understand it, and was able to locate her own quarters, which she felt was a real accomplishment. The one thing that puzzled her was that she couldn't find the accessways Esme had taken her through. Well, natural enough. They wouldn't want mere passengers wandering around, but she bet that the ship was riddled with them, and she made herself a promise to look further into that. She might have to use them.

She also found out how to use the comm facilities in the room, and with some anticipation, she touched the commpoint, querying the ship.

A short buzz from the speaker beside the bed, and a neutral male voice said, "Ready."

She said, "Reference Passenger Cinoe Dzholin, location and call-code."

The speaker produced a time marker, a soft repeating bass pulse, and then said, "Passenger Cinoe Dzholin ten Sub D barracks five bay sixteen zero delta zero five one six." Then the tone ended. She punched this number through a small touch keyboard and waited for someone to answer. It seemed a long time, but finally someone did answer.

"Sixteen."

"Cinoe Dzholin, please."

"Wait . . . not here."

"Did he leave a message?"

"No."

"Thank you." She wrote the number down, but sat back now, pondering. *Well. I couldn't expect that he'd always be there. It must be a dreary place, down there, with the whole ship to wander around in.* She touched the query button again.

Buzz, then, "Ready."

"Contact reference, Crew Faren Kiricky."

"Crew freetime now, Two alpha Delta five one six."

Nazarine coded in the number, and presently a woman's voice answered, "Kiricky." The voice was neutral, efficient. No more.

She said, "Nazarine Alea. I'm the girl who got contact with you on the lighter."

"I remember." It was short, but the voice warmed, became more personable.

"Are you free? If it's not a bother, I'd like to ask to meet you."

"Free? Yes, a couple of shipdays, and after that a tenday of standbys, where I'm free, but on call, you know?"

"I'd like to ask some . . . ah, guidance, if I may."

"Are you afraid of somebody?"

"Is this line secure?"

"Reasonably."

"I think somebody followed me aboard. I need to learn to fade."

"I understand. Yes, I think so. Where are you?"

"Four Q Two."

"Well! Who's paying the rent?"

"My employers, so to speak."

"Well, I don't suppose they have any other way to learn. Very well. Go to your left, to the lift, and then to level A. That will put you on the section-four concourse. Follow the walk straight out into the concourse from the lift, until you come to a diamond-shaped intersection. There's a small park there, and I'll see you."

"When?"

"Start now. I'll be along." She broke the connection from the other end.

* * *

From above, it had seemed vague and blurred, but from what Nazarine kept thinking was the ground level, the concourse resembled nothing in her experience. It was in part a public park, and in part a commercial district of small shops, some offering everyday things, others extremely exclusive. There were restaurants, bars, every sort of entertainment. She had to admit she was impressed.

She had waited for some time, and was thinking of giving up when Kiricky approached the bench she was sitting on. Nazarine got up and greeted the woman. Faren Kiricky in person looked different from the image on the screen. For one thing, her hair was not gray, but a tightly curled mass of mixed black and silver. She was slight in build, shorter than Nazarine, but not petite or small. The face was sharp-featured, crisp and a little foxy, and there were laugh lines at the corners of her eyes and fainter ones at the corners of her mouth. She wore pants which were tight at the hip and loose and flowing at the bottoms, tan, and a black turtleneck sweater.

They touched hands briefly, and Nazarine said, "You don't look like I expected."

"What did you expect?"

"Crew."

"And so I am, when I'm on duty. Now I'm off, and I can be as much me as the rest of the idle passengers."

The voice was slightly roughened. Kiricky was not a young woman, but Nazarine could not accurately guess her age. She said, "You've been in space some time."

Kiricky nodded. "Most of my life, so it seems sometimes. Backwater planet, ran away from home, stowed away, got caught, choice of prison or navy, much the same. Took Navy. Then the merchant service, and finally liners, like this. This isn't the best pay, but it's probably the closest most of us will get to the good life. All in all not bad. And I get to meet people sometimes who have interesting stories to tell."

Nazarine admired the brevity of the story. This woman had compressed her life into a few scant sentences, and yet she sensed no hint of failure or regret. It sounded rough, and she said so.

Faren agreed, without resentment. "Truth there. I've seen some hard times, and some scary ones, too. But some good ones, and those I enjoyed when I had them."

"I had some scary times, too."

"We heard you had some kind of revolution downworld."

"Something of that sort. I took employment with one of the surviving states, and so was sent here. Now I find that I'm more at sea than I thought. I need to know what kind of world I've walked into."

"You mentioned someone following you."

"That, too. I don't know who, but I'm sure someone is."

"Where from? Downworld?"

"No. Offworld."

"They were there? What was going on down there?"

"Rightly, I don't know. Something was going on, and it went all to pieces. I've been shadowed since Clisp—the place I came from. I don't know where they come from."

Kiricky thought for a moment and then said, "Since you ask, I'll do what I can. You were not as I expected, either. You look younger in person. But at least you have enough sense to ask. Yes. I love a little intrigue."

"I need to know values." This was not curiosity about manners, solely. From the data she could get from the value system of these people, she could work that into her system. Nazarine *knew* that the same idea that built and staffed this spaceship and filled it with passengers also produced the sequence of events that led to Oerlikon and the Morphodite.

Faren said, "Come along. I'll show you some sights. We can talk along the way. I'll tell you some things, and you can tell me a few as well. And if you've got an enemy, maybe we can lose him or her." Faren glanced around and her face shifted into an expression of sly but triumphant wickedness. Her eyes flashed and she smiled easily. "When I was a bit more reckless than I am now, I did a bit of smuggling, and if I may say so, did rather well at it. But I knew then when to quit; I enjoyed the chase as much as I did the money. That's time to quit."

Nazarine raised her eyebrows in mock surprise, glancing upward and rolling her eyes as if it had been more than she could stand, but she set off with Faren in the direction the woman had indicated.

Faren asked, "You're not offended?"

"Why should I be?"

"I just admitted a criminal habit, and a most demanding vice."

"I saw some things down there, where I'm from, that make

what you call vices seem to be almost admirable virtues. Offended? I'm relieved."

Kiricky nodded. "Just so. So now I'll risk offense one more time and tell you something: you look young and empty-headed, but I sense something behind you with depth. No, not a disguise. You're who you seem to be, all right, a scared and mostly proper young lady with looks that would be stunning in the right clothing. . . ."

Nazarine interrupted Faren, "Or lack?"

"Strategic lack," Faren corrected. "And a wit, too. But you're hiding something."

For a second, Nazarine's heart stopped dead. A wave of fear washed over her, falling down from her shoulders through her legs. She actually felt faint. *What had Kiricky seen? How far?*

Faren took her arm gently, and continued on, walking through the concourse as if nothing had happened. She leaned slightly toward Nazarine, and whispered conspiratorially, "I don't see it, and I won't ask. Tell me what you will. But you're not one of us yet, and you don't look like one of us, and if you really want to fade, then there's some things we need to do. It's like swimming. You jumped, fell, or were thrown in, and don't swim well or at all. I'll show you how. Simple."

Nazarine recovered, and said, "That would be fine. Why would you do that?"

"Curiosity. Boredom is the ever-present enemy. But more important, a sense of relaxation and being able to be myself without watching too closely. I *know* you mean me no harm. No one, no matter how polished, would have been so direct. And so here we are, a couple of girls idling our break away, strolling around the gardens, just as if we were looking for a couple of pleasant and assertive fellows to have an adventure with." Her eyes flashed and sparkled, and the mischievous enthusiasm was so convincing that Nazarine actually thought Faren might do just that. But Faren looked suddenly thoughtful, and said, in a lower tone, "But we aren't, are we?"

Nazarine shook her head. She said, "No. And we aren't really looking for those assertive fellows, either, are we?"

Faren looked off into the green distances, and said, barely audibly, "No. Not that now. Maybe later. Maybe not. We'll gamble with the cards we have dealt to us."

13

"People fear war; people fear violence and threat and economic ruin and disease. Also loss of status. They fear change, and lack of change. But most of all, they fear each other. All our loneliness is self made."
— H. C., *Atropine*

Cesar Kham sat in the side street of a cafe, watching people passing by. This one was in the lower decks, a concourse much like others placed throughout the ship. He imagined that the others would be more tastefully arranged, larger, cleaner. But this one was acceptable. He had seen much worse in Marula, although he had to admit that public places in Clisp had more style. But they served their purpose—to give people something to do while passing the long voyage times.

Kham was too experienced to go rushing off to the upper decks, checking passing faces. Brute force. Number crunching. Mass. He had a better idea than his quarry how big this ship was. If he tried to look at random, with the procedures he could use he could easily spend the whole voyage to the next port of call and never once see her. He could easily move about; passengers were not generally restricted. But for the present, he waited, felt out his environment, and waited. Now, he had a little time. He wanted to think it through very carefully.

The girl's name. That was key. If she used her own, or the one she traveled with. He couldn't have asked the bursar for it, down below, because he wouldn't have given it anyway. And besides, they'd have had him thrown out of the office. Ship Security Sections were notorious for keeping incidents from happening. They could deny passage to anyone they didn't want, and above all, they didn't want trouble. More than one starship had been overrun by crazed passengers whose hysteria had been ignited by a vendetta, or even an overzealous Enforcement member. The large ships recognized no sovereignty save what their captain and his troops could enforce at gunpoint: a legacy of the

Times of Trouble. He smiled faintly to himself. It was a notable problem.

Palude was working another area, like this one a few decks up, casting a loose net to catch rumors, just like him. He finished the coffee, left a charge chit on the table, and got up to leave. He had already decided that contacting Ship Security was not a feasible course. They'd laugh, whatever he thought up, and say, "Your sectarian differences have no bearing on a Captain's Bond—to ship passengers in safety." And if he told them the truth, they'd lock him up in the brig and put him off at first port of call. He understood this was delicate and probably foolish, but it was, after all, their last chance.

As he walked along, through the crowds and the massed hum of conversations, he thought, *There's got to be a way. Aside from his/her abilities, she's had incredible luck and coincidence all along the line, from Clisp on.* Cesar Kham did not believe in luck, and he never relied on it. *More likely extreme caution on her part. And even more so, now. She's vulnerable to identification, now, because she's too young to run another identity/sex switch. But we know one valuable piece about her: somewhere along the way she picked up a young buck, and he's here, too. And the probability is high he doesn't know enough to keep silent. And so we cast a net of ears. Only two pair, but might be enough.* Kham was looking for a young man with fine features, in with the refugees, hence, somewhere here or nearby, who might recount something of what happened to him. Kham smiled wickedly to himself. *She trusted him with incredible value, to do a transaction for her, knowing he would do it. She had had a hold on him. What?* He thought he could guess. And he wondered at that, how it would be to see the most ancient human problem from either pole, both. And according to their information, it had been sexually active: testimony on Rael, testimony on Damistofia, and their own conclusions about Phaedrus. An irreverent thought crossed his mind and he chuckled almost out loud over it: *She must be an incredible lay. Make a man call out for God.* Trouble was, they had no direct testimony, no witnesses. He added ruefully, *Or else we made sure with our bumbling that there weren't any.*

There was an open space nearby, a kind of park, in which some kind of entertainment was taking place, and Kham allowed his walk to drift over that way. He couldn't quite see what it was because a fair crowd had collected. Moving subtly through the crowd, he managed to see what was happening; a troupe of tumblers was performing. Presumably something put on by the ship, a diversion. Such things were known on the larger ships, that made the really long runs between major terminal areas. This was a small group, three men and three woman, slender and agile, working through graceful routines without music; they didn't seem to need it. Kham admired their agility and timing, and in particular the supple grace of the women, who moved effortlessly, sometimes seeming almost to float in the air. A gravity grid? Possible, but he didn't think so. all wore pastel skintights that concealed very little, but at the same time did not reveal anything. As he watched the act, he also listened about him, to the noises of the watchers, and to their random conversations. Most of it was about the tumblers or related topics, or perhaps the attractiveness of the members of the troupe. Kham agreed; they were all singularly attractive, if a bit exotic for his tastes, although with their faces heavily made up in mime makeup, it was nearly impossible to determine what stock they were.

The act concluded, and after a discreet pause, those watching began applauding, restrained in good taste, but with genuine enthusiasm. The members of the troupe performed a little bow, repeated several times to different sides, and then the group broke up, like little birds scattering, and they ran into the audience, to mingle with the people who had been watching. Kham thought he understood. Ship's whores, every one of them. For some who had watched, there would now come an unforgettable experience—perhaps nothing more serious than an innocent thrill of meeting one of these exotic creatures, and for others, as dictated by circumstances, there would be something more serious, but equally entrancing. He still listened carefully; the crowd was beginning to drift now, the center of attention gone, except now for seeing who would meet whom.

". . . Heard of this before, but never saw it."

". . . Tumas came down to Marula with us, but he didn't show up one day and we never heard any more."

". . . I heard they come from a place called Pintang; put on these shows all the time. Every community has at least one troupe . . ."

". . . Girl in blue . . ."

". . . Bunch of crap, stopping off at that planet. No damn good—take forever . . ."

". . . Bring any locals out with you?"

"Not in our bunch."

"Ours neither. Some tried, but we couldn't get any to leave."

"I guess they heard about the awful offworlders, poor devils."

"Guy in my cubicle had one, but she went off on her own. I never saw her, but Franko saw them down below, said she was really nice."

Kham had almost missed it, but now he listened more closely, straining with every ounce of skill he knew to be invisible, just another unknown part of a random crowd.

The conversation continued:

". . . had her own income, and went to a better section. He wanted to get loose of her anyway, didn't want to be a tour guide to the known universe."

"That rascal. He was like that, though."

"Right. Get the sugar off before the bloom fades."

"Good old Cinoe. Never changed. I guess he liked it down there."

"I would have thought so, but he told me that they put too much into it for his taste, got too involved. But you know it was the national pastime—having affairs. Nothing like a light little one-nighter, you know, recreational sex, something to make you sleep better."

"Better than sleeping pills!"

"And as habit-forming!"

"What's that fellow doing? I haven't seen him since school."

"Didn't you see him? He was across the way. Girl in dusty-orange was headed that way."

Number two looked about. "I don't see him now."

"Oh, Mona. Did you know him then?"

"Oh, yah. Never forget Cinoe Dzholin. I always wanted to have his skill at catching them, but I guess I always wanted to keep them too long. Maybe it shows, or something."

"Well, if he's that way, he's right on top of it, you know. You heard that old song, 'Ya gotta get out before you get got out on.'"

Number two laughed. "Hadn't heard that one in a long time. 'Good old days' says it all. Wonder how things have changed back there."

"Not much, judging by the crew. Going back to Heliarcos?"

"Not me. I'm going home and find a quiet place. I signed on

for adventure, and I had one. Shit, a revolution! Who'd have thought it!''

Then the two who had been talking drifted on their separate ways, making small waves. Kham allowed his steps to continue, but he really wasn't paying much attention to where he was going at the moment. He tried to evaluate what he had overheard. A false lead? He had heard a tale of a young man who brought a local girl on with him, a girl with money of her own, and none of the others had managed to bring locals with them from Oerlikon. The girl was allegedly attractive, and this bunch was from Marula. And he had a name. Cinoe Dzholin. Across the park with a harlequin. For a moment he hesitated, as if to strike out over there. Find a slim girl in dusty-orange, and there he would be. But he thought better of it. *No. Not now.* He could find out where Cinoe resided, and catch him there, and then he'd find out what name the Morphodite was using, and then find her through the ship's computer. *If that was the one.* Well, he still had to follow it up, either way.

But before he left the area entirely, he did turn back and circled back across the park, slowly, inconspicuously, just to see if he could perhaps catch sight of something. Nothing appeared to be out of order, nor did he catch sight of a girl in dusty-orange. So Kham continued along that way, heading for an eventual meeting with Arunda at one of their agreed-to places. He was early, but that didn't matter.

Kham stopped off at a kiosk and purchased a small brochure which told about the tumblers. He read the text and looked at the pictures, confirming his suspicions. He smiled to himself. It was part of the local religion, an honored role in that society. In fact, so popular was the practice that they had too many of them and many went to space, where they were welcomed on the ships. Dance and pick up strangers; who knew why they did it? Who knew why anyone did anything? Kham chuckled at that cynical reference to anthropology, and caught sight of one of the tumblers walking alone by herself. In dusty-orange. She looked downcast, disappointed and walked slowly.

On an impulse, Kham got up and approached the girl. When he neared her she noticed him and smiled, but weakly, and said, ''Thank you, but of course it's too late now. It has to be the one whose eyes catch yours during the exercises.''

Kham nodded politely. ''Let me extend my appreciation anyway. Your people put on a fascinating display.''

The girl bowed slightly. "I understand."

He said, "Perhaps we might meet again."

"Or others. It is to be hoped."

"Indeed. Forgive a stranger to your customs, but how do you know who to go to?"

"It is part of the rite, a long process. We know what to look for, but of course these things are not exact, and so you can't always judge. I made wrong choice just now. I understand and obey the will of 'Rizheong in this. By being refused I know I have fault, and must correct myself. I go now to purify my thoughts."

"You were refused? A girl as lovely as you are, as graceful as a dancer?"

She looked down submissively. "To value the self too much, that is a great error. But it must be true, because when I went to him, his thoughts were not of me, but of a girl he had left on her own. I sensed it, because we are trained in these things, and the aim of desire. I asked him, because I must, and he told me. And now I must go, and become corrected. The person of Cinoe Dzholin was surely motivated by 'Rizheong in this."

Kham asked, masking his excitement, "May I ask for you?"

She looked thoughtful, and then shook her head. "I think not. That would go against the rite. We seek to eradicate the idea that one human can possess another, and if you asked for me, or I hoped to see you . . . I'm sure you understand."

Kham nodded and made a little bow. "I wish you the success of your rite, then. Perhaps someday."

"Or another. May the magic visit you, ser."

Kham watched her walk away. And went back to the bench, to await Palude. But he felt an irrational sense of fortune riding with him now, of a thread growing into a rope, a cable, a hawser, that would lead him straight to the Morphodite. *Now, now,* he thought, hoping that his excitement didn't show.

But the time came and went for Arunda to show up, and there was no sign of her. Kham reasoned that she had gotten farther afield than she thought to, and was late. In a way, that suited him well enough. Now was as good a time as any to check things out. He got up, and began looking for a public comm terminal.

Nazarine and Faren walked through the concourse aimlessly for a time, saying little of substance, watching each other covertly, making small talk, mostly Faren pointing out the real value of

some of the things offered for sale in the little shops worked
tastefully into the landscaping of the parklike interior space.
Large as it was, it was carefully arranged to seem larger than it
was; the distant enclosing walls of the ship were kept in dim
light, while the concourse itself seemed bright and sunny; looking up or toward the horizon one expected, one only saw a dim
suggestion of shape. Or, during the nocturnal periods, banks of
lights that seemed to shimmer like distant city lights. The illusion was very strong that one was not *inside* anything, but
outside, under the stars or in ordinary daylight.

They stopped beside a wooded glade, which had an upper
level of gracefully contorted trees with smooth, gray fluted
trunks and small, delicate leaves. There was an intermediate
level of smaller trees or shrubs with broad, glossy leaves and
brown, fibrous trunks, slender and twisted, almost like vines.
The ground was covered with several different kinds of mosslike
plants. It was fenced off by what looked like an ornamental iron
fence, but along which were the telltale probes of a repellent
field.

Nazarine asked, "What's in here?"

"An enclosure for Lenosz. The landscaping, I am told, is Old
Earth Authentic; those are real trees and moss."

Nazarine peered into the shade, the denser parts. For the
moment, she saw nothing. "What's Lenosz?"

Faren smiled archly. "It's just an animal. I don't know where
they came from originally."

"Dangerous?"

"Yes and no. Mostly not. At least, in the conventional sense
that we understand danger from animals—nature red in tooth and
claw, as it were. No, they are quite gentle. Omnivores most of
the time, not at all aggressive."

Something gray moved in the forest and Nazarine looked that
way, certain that nothing had been there before. It moved again,
tentatively and stood out more in the open, and she saw it
clearly: a Lenosz. It had four legs and a tail and gray fur, and
looked ordinary at first glance. Something doglike, perhaps.
Everyone learned the animals of early man. Except this was
subtly different.

There are, it had been said, certain outlines and shapes of
things which terrify, or disgust. These are ancient archetypes of
ideas that never reach the verbal level—childhood engrams shaped
into resonance by thousands of generations, of subtle reactions

shared. Were that true, then the other pole would be true also, that there would be shapes and outlines that stimulated other emotions, longing, desire, admiration, affection. This was such a creature. On the second look, it ceased to look doglike at all, but became something supernatural. It ambled over toward the fence, approaching until it wrinkled its nose in distaste at the sensations the field transmitted, and there it sat back on its haunches, looking elegant and idle, glancing first at Nazarine and Faren, and then out of its cage into the concourse.

The Lenosz had a long, tapered muzzle, delicate flap ears that drooped like a hound's, a rather long neck. It was furred, the fur being so short and dense and soft it looked like a second layer of skin. It was a living embodiment of the idea of dogness raised to the tenth power of aesthetics and form. It made an ordinary dog seem like a child's drawing by comparison, honest in form and function but crude in execution. Nazarine said, "It's beautiful."

Faren nodded. "That's the problem. They are very affectionate, and also either intelligent or gifted mimics. And of course they are indeed beautiful. That's the danger. They seem to form a symbiotic attachment with sapient life forms, and eventually become parasitic. In short, people become too attached to them."

"You mean pets."

"The practice was outlawed, and severe penalties were set out for possessing one. The ones that were pets were gathered up, one by one, and put in enclosures like this one. No one had the heart to kill any of them."

"Why?"

"You own one, you fall in love with it. Unlike other animals, it doesn't grow fat or ugly on pampering, but becomes even more beautiful."

Nazarine looked at the gray-furred creature across the fence, and it seemed to respond to her attention. It looked back at her out of fathomless liquid brown eyes. The soft fur seemed to be made expressly for touching. Sleek, gray, streamlined. Nazarine looked away from the animal with an effort.

Faren said, "On the planet where they were discovered, they found evidence of a high sentient culture: houses, roads, some remains of machines, writing. Not much, but enough to know something had been there. Native to that planet. All gone. No war, no craters, no nothing. Just gone. And these creatures."

"Their descendants."

She shook her head. "No. These didn't originate on that

planet. Their chemistry is different, their DNA is different. Not that planet. Close enough so that they can eat our food, and presumably their food, on that planet. They have a special chemistry that enables them to ingest and use many different substances. The explorers . . . the Lenosz were glad to see them, when they came. It was much later that they understood what they had done on that world. Somewhere a spacefaring people found them, and took them in, and they became part of that people, and so much so that these people dwindled and died out. Keeping Lenosz. Or so they think. There are all sorts of dangers.''

"You showed me this for a reason.''

Faren looked down at the ground for a moment, and then directly at Nazarine. "Yes. The message is obvious enough, I think.''

Nazarine shook her head. "I don't need reminding.''

"You need learning that there are things out here you haven't even dreamed of, and that some things can only be enjoyed at a distance, and then you must go on about the things you must do. *Those* are our values. We'll start from that. That thing's not dangerous: there's no record anywhere of one ever attacking a human without extreme provocation, without clear and obvious reason. You get one of those and take it home. It's clean, it learns and adapts easily, it needs nothing of its own, and it responds to you. It's even a comfortable size—about that of an adult human of small stature. You feed it, breed it, take care of it.''

"What happens if you mistreat one?''

"They make fast animals look like slow-motion. And it will protect you, too. But now tell me of your danger.''

"Someone, I am sure, followed me on the ship.''

"No great problem. You simply lose yourself. Does it know your name?''

"No, I don't think so, yet. But I became involved with someone on the way here.'' And in much abbreviated form, Nazarine sketched in an outline of her adventure, and the present curious limbo it had gone into once on the ship. Faren did not seem to be surprised.

After a moment, she asked, "He never tried to call you?''

"No. I tried to call him, but he wasn't there. Still no answer.''

"So. Wait here.'' Faren left the Lenosz enclosure and walked away a short distance to a small, inconspicuous post set into the ground near some shrubbery. She opened the upper part, and removed a device which expanded into a headset, through which she spoke with someone or something. Then she put it back, and returned to Nazarine. "That does that."

"What?"

"Now you are carried on the ship's roll as an unlisted number. I hope it's not too late. That will slow them down."

"What about him?"

"Were he going to come to you, he would have done so directly, or called you immediately after boarding. You can follow that up, if you wish."

"I know—never mind how—that he is not part of any operation against me."

"Doesn't matter. You've got to cut the possible others off."

She gave Faren the number she had for Cinoe's area. "Could he be in trouble?"

Faren said, "If someone saw you with him, or tied you to him, they can get to you through him. May be doing so now."

"How do we know they haven't already?"

"Ship's registry says no calls to your place, no queries logged. Are you certain they are real?"

"They tried to kill me once. They missed and I went into hiding. They will keep trying."

"Why are you such an important item?"

Nazarine shook her head. "I know something . . . or they think I know something. It doesn't matter which way it really is."

Faren leaned closer. "What do you know?"

The intensity of her eyes was terrific. Nazarine could see nothing else. Faren's eyes were a pale blue-green, almost gray. She came to a dead stop inside, and then said, "Not all of it. I'm still working on it." She felt control coming back. And she added, "What would you do if you knew? Sell me to them?"

Faren laughed, exposing even, perfect teeth. And the expression on her face softened noticeably. "No, no. I might use it for myself, but I won't sell you to anyone. That I promise. We are thieves and deceivers one and all, but we still have some honor, we star-folk, whatever you think of us."

Nazarine looked back directly at Faren, and said, "You may but these people don't. They kill children even when they miss."

Faren thought a moment, and then said, "All right. Come

along. We need to collect your friend and get him out of the way for a while.''

"How? What are you going to do?"

"We'll get him in a part of the ship where he isn't so easy to find. Won't hurt him at all. And we'll also find out if he's been contacted. Then we'll know more what to do."

"We're going in the open?"

"Why not? Don't worry, I know a few tricks of my own. But one way or the other, we've got to get him out. And the way we're going will be just as fast. And fast we need." She stopped a moment, and looked back at Nazarine. "You're getting more complicated all the time."

She smiled in spite of herself. "You don't seem to mind."

Faren raised her eyebrows and glanced at the invisible ceiling. Flick. Nazarine sensed it was a standard gesture. Faren said, "Not yet, anyway."

Between the concourses of the ship, the public areas, ran narrower public areas which were something more than access tubes and something less than actual concourses. Illuminated signs hung from the ceiling indicating routes to various areas, and various diversions alternated with blank passages to make passage through them diversions in themselves. In the first part of a flight, the new passengers walked around a lot, finding various areas of interest, so now the number of passersby was steady. By no means crowded, the ways were still reasonably full, and Arunda Palude had spent a very tiring morning searching out faces. To no good result. She hadn't even had the exercise of making a close match.

She stopped for a time at a health-foods shop and purchased a sack of salted nuts and a flask of mineral water which had a faint sulfurous odor and left a metallic aftertaste of iron. She winced at the taste, and thought, *Why is it that everything good for you tastes so bad, and the stuff that tastes good is bad for you or actually harmful? Now there's a mystery*. She took the flask outside into the hallway and settled on a bench, glancing idly up and down, seeing a few people, none of any particular interest. She had looked over the shipmaps carefully and picked this area out as the goal of her first line of search; it was near a junction of several other cross-lines, and one might expect to see more here than just any place picked at random. But this hadn't seemed to work, either. The density of people was not a great deal greater here than anywhere else. But she was persevering and long-suffering, and so decided to stay for a bit and watch before turning back. Rest in the afternoon, and then try again in the night-cycle.

To pass the time, she tried to fit professions to the people she watched passing; this was all the harder because some were wearing the pastel shades and neutral styling of shipwear, which conferred a certain anonymity to the wearer. These she watched closely. Others wore what Arunda imagined to be approved local costume appropriate to their station. Still others strode along with a jaunty familiarity and an arrogance that suggested Crew, some in various uniforms, others in their own clothing. Yes. Far down the corridor she saw two women walking along, not in a hurry, but not idling either. They were Crew, for sure. She looked away. She felt the hair on the nape of her neck prickle, a hot flash across the shoulders, and a tingling along her back. She looked again. The pair were much closer now and she could see them better. One was average height, rather slender in build, and although attractive, bore some evidence of aging and a hardened disposition on her face. *That one's been rode hard and put up wet*. The other was taller and walked with a looser striding motion. The taller one was barely a woman, more a girl. *But God, she's tall*. Arunda looked very close at the tall girl. Long in the legs, well-filled-out at bust and hip, but also trim. The face: small straight nose, large eyes, pale tan coloration, loose curly brown hair. She walked along with the smaller woman, holding back her natural stride to match her companion's. She wore a knit gray dress, a darker gray vestlike overgarment, and soft gray boots. *I see how I almost missed her. An older Crew and a younger, out on an adventure, that's precisely what they look like*. The older woman wore smooth tan pants and a black turtleneck sweater, but despite the difference in type, they both cast the same impression. *How does she, it, do it? She can't have known that woman more than a day, and yet they look part of the same environment, and knew each other well. That thing's got abilities we don't know anything about*. She found the thought chilling; they knew from briefings and various reports some of the abilities of the Morphodite, and as they were, they were bad enough. But to have a chameleon's gift of background mimicry, that bothered her more. *That thing's damn near invisible*. She had guessed about clothing and come up right.

Palude did not rise and follow them, but watched them carefully out of the corner of her eye as they passed her, and turned off onto an access ramp leading downward to Concourse Area One. She evaluated what she could see of the two and decided she did not want to risk identification. Even though the Morphodite was reported to be rare to use violence, it certainly had the abilities, and the other woman, the Crew, looked capable enough on her own. They could be formidable if confronted. She reasoned correctly that at least she needed to inform Cesar and get confirmation of identity before going farther. Yes. That tall girl matched the ID coordinates Cesar had given her.

Palude noted that they had gone into the express access tube, and she knew there was no faster way she could use, but she got up and set off purposefully, getting into full stride and pushing it, going back the way she had come. She thought, *The girl doesn't know Cesar yet. She's only seen him once, and knew nothing then. But if she sees him again, she'll know. And then it'll hit the fan for sure. I know they're not looking for him or me, yet. Yet.* She repeated that word to herself. She had already decided, she realized, that she did not want to have the Morphodite looking for her. Oh, no. No way at all. And then she thought, *But they're going down there for some purpose. What?* She increased her pace until it began to hurt very slightly in her thighs.

14

"*A crisis is the definition of a situation in which you know what you have to do, but you hesitated to do it and so lost control of events. One takes sensible and reasonable precautions, but if action is needed to head off negative patterns, that's the best cure for it. Because no matter how much talk you hear about good intentions and positive attitudes, some still do cruel evils, and nowhere, in no law or philosophy, does it state that one is required to be a victim.*"

—H. C., Atropine

Kham got the listing for Cinoe Dzholin easily enough. As a
fact, it was close by his own, and easy enough to check. He
didn't expect to find the fellow in, but he could wait for him. He
didn't have a clear idea of who he was looking for, just a general
and vague description, but he trusted enough in his reflexes to
pull it off. *Trust to proven tactics!* First, meet him, then attain
temporary confidence, and then, in a quiet place, some discreet
questions, with persuasion as required. Here, Kham felt back in
an environment, a situation, in which he could trust his own
reflexes. His quarry now was no changeling Morphodite, with
the ability to see him coming, or suggested skills in defense. Oh,
no. Lisak or operative, Kham felt certain of himself. He flexed
his fingers as he walked, moving swiftly and covering distance
without seeming to do so.

It didn't take Kham long to arrive in the section he wanted.
This section had what they called bays, which housed ten men or
women each, all connected by a staggered hallway, strung along
like peas on a pod. Ahead, he saw a young man using one of the
public comm terminals, or more correctly, finishing using one.
The young man turned away from the commpoint and started
toward the room Kham was headed for. This one matched the
description from downside. On an impulse, Kham approached,
cutting him off before he went in. He said, ''Cinoe Dzholin?''

The young man answered, ''Yes.'' Guarded, but not suspicious. Kham felt good. This one knew little.

Kham said, ''I am Cesar Kham. Does that name mean anything to you?''

He hesitated. Then, ''Yes. Oerlikon. I've heard of you.''

He looked now both impressed and a little apprehensive. Yes,
it was certain he'd heard of Cesar Kham. After a moment, the
young man added, ''I thought you had gone back.''

''I did. But there was some unfinished business on Oerlikon, and
so I had to come back. And now there is another matter I must
follow up, and I ask to speak with you for a bit.''

''Go ahead.''

''Not here. A more private place.''

Cinoe looked around, as if getting his bearings. ''There's a
cohab lounge down the hall. Place where strangers can meet and
. . . you know. We find an empty one, lock it, and it's pretty
private, so the ship's brochure claims.''

''Lead the way, then.'' They went onward along the passageway, plain gray, unrelieved by decoration or suggestion of func-

tional shipform. At the end of the passage were several doors, all closed, with a red and a green light over each. One showed green. The remainder were red. Cinoe laughed a little nervously. "I didn't expect they'd be so full this time of day." He pushed open the green-marked doorway, and went in, Kham following. Inside, there was a spartan little room, with some soft chairs, a severely efficient bath, and a fold-down bed, still in its wall cubby. Cinoe locked the door. He turned around. "Very well. Private. Ask on."

Before speaking, Kham observed the young man closely. Dark, loose hair, almost black, worn long. A thin, straight nose, small mouth, a little slack and sensual. Deepset eyes. He looked girlishly delicate, slender in build. Kham decided to come to the point. "You came on board with a woman. I need to know her name. We need to ask her some questions."

A shadow passed over Dzholin's face, something too short to be an expression. Just the shadow of one. He said, "What for? She's not one of us."

Kham thought, *Aha, he wants to fence a little. Very well*. "Then you acknowledge my allegation?"

"Yes . . . To my knowledge, she is not one of us, but a native. I tested her."

"How?"

"Speech. She didn't react at all to our speech."

"Well, that's true enough. She's definitely not one of us."

For a time, there was silence, which Cinoe felt as a pressure to say something. "What do you want her for?"

"You don't need to know, but I'll tell you part of it. She possesses some very dangerous knowledge, and we need to find out how she got it."

"She said she was a spy for Clisp."

"We know that she is that, in part. She is something much more. Her Name!"

"Oerlikon is finished. The project is over. I don't see what use this is."

"Let me tell you something. I came back here for the sole purpose of tracking her down, and you are the only thing that stands between me and her now. But excuse my manners. Let me advise you that you protect something dangerous to a degree you cannot imagine."

Kham knew as soon as he'd said it that it had been the wrong move. Cinoe's face registered disbelief, confidence. *Amazing!*

The fool actually thought he could talk his way out of this. He might even take a poke at me.

Cinoe said, after a moment, "She's not dangerous. She's just a woman, no, a girl. You've got the wrong one."

"How do you know that?"

He said, defiantly, "I slept with her, that's what."

Kham barked out, derisively, "Are you fool enough to think you can understand a woman from between her legs?"

"It's not like that. She's not the one you're looking for. This girl is green as grass. I know the difference."

Kham shook his head. "There's a lot more I could tell you, but it's just not the best thing. Let me contact her. I'll decide. I know what I'm looking for."

"What are you looking for, Ser Kham?"

"A destroyer of worlds who is on the way right now to turn loose the apocalypse in our own system of worlds."

Cinoe turned a little, tense, but he shrugged. "Wouldn't do you any good to know it. I tried to contact her. She's unlisted herself."

Boseldung!, Kham thought. *Already alerted somehow! How does the bitch do it?* He said patiently, "I can take care of that problem. But I need a name."

Cinoe said, "I know the law and custom. Your authority doesn't pass between worlds. Only back there, and that's finished. Go Captain's-Mast with me, and I'll tell you."

More delays, and even now she's somehow gotten alerted. Dammit! And this moonstruck smartass wants to play legal games. He said, "I don't have time anymore for games. Give me her name and let's put an end to this. What passed between you and her, that's your business. This is mine."

Kham saw him tense and began his motion countering by reflex, before the blow actually started. Cinoe aimed a quick, hard jab at Kham's head, but it never connected. Kham was already moving backwards, thinking, *Fool again! Punching to hurt or warn off!* He hadn't been in position to disable or kill, and that was, to Kham's mind, the only possible motivation for violence. He fell back, grasping the fist that had come at him and pulling toward him. A simplistic maneuver, but it worked like a textbook exercise. Cinoe, off-balance from throwing the blow, fell forward onto Kham and before he could grasp the older man, Kham threw him neatly into the corner, where he landed with the sound of meat against something solid. Kham recovered his balance and faced Cinoe, partly crouching, arms wide, hands loose, betraying no identifiable skill save readiness.

But the stance was unnecessary, for Cinoe wasn't moving very well. His face was twisted with pain, gray, perspiring, mouth working. The boy's arm was at an odd angle, and his shoulder looked lumpy, distorted. Kham looked incredulously. *Dislocated shoulder, maybe a compound fracture with it*. Kham shook his head at what he must do now.

He approached Cinoe slowly, measuring his steps. When he was a the proper distance and angle, he reached forward in a blur of motion and, grasped Cinoe before he could resist, and made a series of curious motions about the shoulder. He felt the ball reset in its socket, but the boy had fainted. Kham revived him. "Now, the name!"

The boy reached with his good arm and began throttling Kham, a move so unexpected that Kham actually was taken off guard and felt the hot surge of panic. But only for a split second. Then he broke the choke, and straddled Cinoe, performing certain motions in a careful, quick sequence. He worked on certain nerve systems, junctions, ganglia. His operations made no sound, and Cinoe made only throaty, gargling noises of no great volume, and after a time, even those stopped. At last, himself perspiring from the effort, Kham leaned back and looked at the boy. The face was almost unrecognizable. Blank, utterly vacant. Kham leaned close again and whispered, "The Name. You want more of that?"

Cinoe muttered, in a low monotone, uninflected, "Nazarine Alea."

Kham got up off the boy. He said, "There's no fixing what's been done here. It's irreversible. I didn't want this, but it can't be helped. And I can't wait through explanations. So I'll leave, and after I release this hold, you'll sink and go to sleep. No more pain. And I'll lock the door going out, so you'll be left alone for a long time."

Cinoe said nothing. He looked off at some noplace, eyes unfocused. Kham thoughtfully added, "You shouldn't have tried to resist. She isn't worth it. And she left you anyway. No nothing all around." He shook his head regretfully. Then he released the last hold. Cinoe seemed to shrink and fold into himself, although his actual position only shifted a little. The change was more in attitude than anything else. Kham turned away.

Then he made a quick inspection of the room, looking around, making sure he hadn't touched anything. At the door, he set it to lock, and left, pulling it shut behind him. There was no one in the corridor, and the other cohab lounge door lights were all still red. He nodded to himself, and set off back down the corridor, headed for the level Concourse again. He moved with decisive speed, because he had to get clear of this area as fast as possible. Now for two reasons. One, to run the girl to earth, and the other to escape association with this area. He was well out in the Concourse, sitting on a bench, sorting out things in his mind, when he realized the situation he might have precipitated. He thought, edging carefully around the idea, as if he didn't want to touch it, *Now I've got two enemies, Her, and Shipsecurity*. He understood. Cesar Kham knew how to hide, and how to move invisibly. Had he not done so for years on Oerlikon? Had he not been the chief field operative of Lisagor? The exertion had left him a little lightheaded, and he let it flow, moving with it. He set priorities in his mind, and identified Shipsecurity as a distant nuisance. The real problem was Nazarine Alea. Unlisted call-number. *Well. There are ways around that, too*.

Nazarine noticed that Faren picked up the pace after she turned off to enter the express passage, but did not stop or say anything until they were secured in the small *pneumatique* and moving. She said then, "Just before the turnoff, as we came down the openway, there was a woman sitting on a bench. Seen her before?"

"No. I noticed her then, but never before."

"She had a backwater-planet look to her, but also something else: a spotter."

"You're sure?"

"Yes. We'll not see her again. She's gone to report, and bring up a field operative who will doubtless try to get in closer. That'll be a man."

Nazarine asked, "How do you know that?" She was astounded at the quick responses of Faren. To spot things that fast she must have done some things in which observation and responses had to be honed to a fine degree of perception and unquestioning reaction.

"When they use a woman as a no-contact spotter, it's always a man who does the dirty work. Sometimes you'll find a man spotter in some tricky, sneaky situations, and then expect a woman, and a bad one at that, to close in." She shivered. "Brr,

Worst scapes I ever had were reverses. But pay attention: she noted me, but spotted on you. That means description. What do you make of that?"

"They couldn't have a description of me, I. . . ."

"You what?"

"Never mind. I've been careful." But she thought about the facts as Faren presented them, and it had to be that way. The woman knew who to look for. How? Suddenly she felt very foolish. She had moved openly, trusting to her new identity to protect her. But she had been in the open, and used the cartouche of Pompeo. Bought clothing. But that would give such a general description that you couldn't react on it. That she didn't believe. No, it was something else. Who? When? Not Cinoe, surely. She said as much to Faren.

Faren nodded. "No, not Cinoe. I agree with that. He had his chance on the ship coming across the ocean, as you told me. This is not youngman work. But somewhere, somebody saw enough of you to derive a transmittable image. Wasn't that woman. Her reactions were too obvious, and *slow*."

Nazarine thought, hard, trying to remember the past months, looking for something. The guard at Symbarupol? The Makhak in the castle? The one had been too ordinary, the other too Makhak in his detachment. They wouldn't even chase a Lisak for pay.

She remembered there had been one occasion, on the Beamliner from Symbarupol, when she had felt uncomfortable about a man, and changed, just to be sure. The bald one. Him?

"A man watched me too closely on . . . a train, something like that. I thought it would be prudent to lose him, and so I did. But he didn't follow me. There was only a moment."

"If he was trained well, and experienced, that would be enough. There exists a standard set of descriptive tags so that he could transmit a passable image of you to one similarly trained. What did that one look like?"

Nazarine recalled what she could. "Bald, stocky, heavy torso, like a wrestler. An intense, disturbing stare."

"Can you fight?"

"Yes."

"You don't look it."

"Trust me. Call it one of my secrets."

Faren did not look convinced, but she assented reluctantly. "All right. A bald, stocky man. It will be sneaky, so we had better stick close for a while. Two pair of eyes is better. And seeing me with you, they've got an item on me, too, and will assume partnership. So I have to depend on you."

Nazarine said, "I can contribute something to this, but I have to have some time to do it. Quiet."

"What?"

"Get me five minutes, maybe ten. I'll show you."

"Now we get Cinoe out if we can find him. Stash him somewhere and you forget him; we can cure that."

"What about the woman? Are we walking into a trap?"

"Not likely. Possible, but probably not so. We'll get to Cinoe's area before she can: we are on the fastest route to that area.

The express *Pneumatique* ran level for a short space and then slanted down sharply, sounding into the belly of the ship *Kalmia*. Then it stopped, and they emerged into another accessway similar to the one they had left. This one, however, showed less care than the upper: there were faint smudges on the walls, marks left unfinished from patching. Faren commented, "These are the haunts of the sloggers, the proles, and the riffraff. Traditionally it is called steerage." She spoke in an even, conversational tone, but her eyes betrayed her anxiety: they shifted in a regular pattern from side to side, sweeping, calculating. She added, "Come along smartly, now, and be alert, if you know how. We want to be bold marauders, coming boldly and leaving silently as ghosts."

Shortly they came to another of the vast, cavernous concourses, this one being much more plain and functional than the upper one. They skirted around the edge of it, avoiding the more densely populated center. Each person they passed they watched carefully, but neither one observed anything suspicious, and they traversed it without incident. As they entered the residence areas, Faren turned and said, "We won't come back this way. Wouldn't have done it this way from the beginning if I had known." She stopped, and then went on, rather more thoughtfully, "If I had known, might not have come at all."

Nazarine said, "Regrets?"

"No. I'm being cynical—another of our vices, which you must learn."

Faren knew the quarters number she was looking for and led them directly to it, walking along the passageways with an easy familiarity which Nazarine followed closely and soon fell into. When they came to the door, it was open, and three young men, ostensible Lisaks by their clothing and shoulder-length curls, invited them in, speaking in the language of Oerlikon. Faren shook her head and insisted, in her own speech, inquiring after one Cinoe Dzholin, and eventually, one of the young men said, stumbling a little, that Dzholin had gone out much earlier and not returned.

Refusing invitations to come in and party, Faren and Nazarine stepped back into the hall. Faren said shortly, "Not impossible, of course, but it's a fine mess having to go look for him. I could have him paged, but that would attract a great deal of attention, the kind we don't want. And things being as they are, I don't favor the idea of milling around out in that concourse, either. It's not a trap, but it's too easy for us to be seen. Do you have any ideas?"

Nazarine looked at the room, the hall, and the light of the concourse beyond, flooding down the passage behind them. Reluctantly, she guessed, and concluded she would have to expose something. "I have another way. I do not display it before observers, but it seems there is no other way." She hesitated. Then, "Is there a place where we can go where we can get privacy for a time? This takes time, and I can't be interrupted."

Faren put her hand up alongside her nose and rubbed the side of her nose, looking off and thinking. "Yes. For each one of these sections they have an adjoining suite of cohabs—rooms where people can go and be alone. The usual reasons. We can use one of those, if we can find one unlocked. Randy lot down here."

"Show me," Nazarine said, and Faren nodded and set off, going deeper into the section, following the passageway as it began to turn and twist. At last, the passageway narrowed down into a corridor, which terminated in a cluster of small doors, each with a red and green lamp above it. All the lit lamps were red.

Faren looked disgusted and said, "Just our luck. Everybody decides in this section they all want love in the afternoon at the same time." She looked disgustedly at the closed doors, and then looked again. One of them wasn't quite closed.

She indicated this to Nazarine. Then she knocked at the door, and stood back, listening. She whispered, "Could be just care-

lessness, haste." But no sound came forth from the room. She
said, "Come on. We'll see." Faren pushed the door open,
looking into the room, seeing no one, and stepped up and inside.
"Nothing here. Hm. Wonder why they left the red light on. It
looks like nobody's been here."

Nazarine followed her, but just inside, Faren, slightly ahead of
her, motioned her to stop. She said, very quietly, "Nazarine,
close and lock the door."

"Why?"

"Do it." Nazarine complied. When she turned around, she
saw Faren move stealthily across the room, around the corner, to
where a body lay, sprawled in an odd and grotesque contortion.
Faren muttered, "No wonder it was left like that. Good-looking
kid, too. Was. Doesn't cut much of a figure now." Nazarine
came forward and looked more closely. She said, "We're too
late."

She looked at the curious still figure in the corner. Unques-
tionably dead. She felt nothing, oddly. This did not resemble the
Cinoe in life that she knew. The feeling of it would come later.
She knew now they had little time, and she had to act fast. She
did not need Jedily, or Damistofia, or Nazarine, now. She
needed Rael, and from deep in the most buried part of her
memory, she summoned Tiresio Rael, the callous, the merciless.
She felt Rael's lanky, awkward figure fit uncomfortably into
her own supple limbs. She felt odd, ill-fitted, in her own body,
that she'd spent so much of herself to really become. When she
spoke, it was in a harsher, colder voice. "That was Cinoe. The
conclusion is that the one hunting me killed him, either to
prevent him from getting to me, or to derive information from
him. Probably my name, so he can trace me through the ship. If
so, now he knows how I call myself, and he knows what I look
like."

Faren looked back at Nazarine sharply, sensing some change
in the girl. After a moment, she said softly, "You take the death
of your lover lightly."

Nazarine did not look at her, but said, "I take it as I must. I
will feel later. But know that this is not the first. They tried for
me once before, and missed. And before that, they sent an
assassin against me. I killed him."

Faren observed, "It seems I place myself in immediate peril
by associating with you."

Nazarine nodded. "Just so. You may leave if you wish. I am

grateful for the help you have given me. Go. I understand. I do not ask you to stay. I will do what I have to do. I can find him on my own. We will end this forever."

"You actually think you can find the person who did this, on this ship, and punish him?"

"I will hunt this swine to the end of the universe." It came unbidden. Cliofino, Krikorio, Emerna, Meliosme, Cinoe, persons in her past came flooding into her mind. And with them came an emotion for which she had no name: it was icy, cold, calculating, implacable. It made hatred seem like mild displeasure by comparison. She added, "I can. I will. But first I have to do something."

Faren turned to her and held her shoulders. "Listen. I believe you. I believe that you believe you can do this thing. But alone? No, that's not the way. I will stay. I do not know why they hunt you like this," here she glanced over her shoulder at the still figure in the corner, "But you must have allies, and I will have them for you. This is an evil thing, and I think if we look closer at him, we will see something else."

Nazarine relaxed a little. "Show me. I know something of these things. We may call them different things, but if a pattern is there, it should show to both of us."

They approached the body carefully, not touching it. Faren squatted down on her haunches and examined the body, searching it completely. Nazarine, beside her, got down on her knees and also examined it, in time touching it, feeling certain parts. After some time, they both finished and looked at each other.

Nazarine said, "This work was done by someone very knowledgeable of the uses of pain. Slow. There are almost no impact marks."

Faren nodded. Her voice was now cold also. "The shoulder was dislocated, and then reset. The other things. . . . There are several forms of this kind of art, and I will not bore you with terminology. I know some things, but of this, I know only enough to recognize the marks of a master craftsman. This man hunting you is dangerous. If he would do this just for a name. . . ."

Nazarine stood up. "We have seen enough here. Are we still secure?"

"Yes. No one will pass the door."

"Should we report it?"

"I think it would be a good idea. It will distract him."

Nazarine said, "Do it discreetly. I want no outcry, no hounds-and-hunt. This one I reserve for myself."

Faren assented, "There's such a way. I have friends, and some of them will help me. They owe me, so to speak. I will call on those obligations."

"Press the case, but let him run loose. I want him alive."

"We'll do as much as we can. But mind, if he stands and fights, it'll go as it must."

She agreed, reluctantly. But agreed. "If it comes, then. Now I need some paper."

"Paper?"

"Paper and something to write with. And some time."

Faren looked around uncertainly. "May be something here, but . . . can it wait?"

Nazarine's face was set in grim determination. "This has to go before we leave this room, and I will let no one see it save you. And ask me no questions."

Faren said, "Very well. I will see." And she began looking through the room for something to write on. Eventually, she did find some notepaper and an electric pen, which she handed to Nazarine without comment. And she felt curious about the other girl, too. When they had met, Faren had assumed a certain position of superiority. It had to be. She was older, more sophisticated, experienced, and Nazarine had been . . . over her head. Now she wasn't so sure about those identifications. She neither feared nor disliked the girl; but she felt almost as if it was she who was the inferior, and it was more than a little uncomfortable. Still she asked herself: Who was Nazarine Alea. More importantly, What was Nazarine Alea? She watched Nazarine sit in a chair and begin writing, as if drawing something, and she shrugged. *Well,* she thought. *I did ask for an adventure.*

Nazarine took up the pad and pen and sat on the bed, for a moment looking off into space, eyes unfocused and not tracking, and then she looked down at the pad, and, hesitantly at first, began sketching in what seemed to Faren to be an odd, abstract diagram. She would work like that for a time, and then tear a sheet off, and transfer part of the figure, leaving much of it behind, and seemingly start the process over again. On the discarded sheets she did something that looked like math—it was symbols and simple operational signs—but in no known number system, and what Faren could see of it followed no logical system which she could recall. The results of these computations would affect the developing figure.

After a time, Faren could not sit still any longer, and she asked, "What are you doing?" Nazarine did not answer, but cast her a glance of such intense malignity that she turned away.

The girl became oblivious to her surroundings, and made small subvocal noises under her breath. Some seemed to express a grim satisfaction, or exultation, such as at the fall of an especially hated enemy. Other times, they approximated groans of woe, or gasps of horror. Gradually, the noises slowed and stopped, and it seemed that Nazarine reviewed the steps she had progressed through, nodding at some places, glaring at others as if *they* were her enemy. Then she put the papers aside, and hung her head down, wearily. After a moment, she began speaking softly, in a breathy, low voice that was barely audible, even in the silences of the cohab suite.

She said, "His name is Cesar Kham. At least, such is how it was on Oerlikon. I knew of him, very distantly, almost solely by rumor. He did this, he also sent terrorists against me in Clisp. These things are not important to him. And yet this is not decided by him, but by someone behind him. The same people that fixed events on Oerlikon to their own purpose. I can get echoes of them, but I can't locate them—either my system is too ill-defined to work well in space or they are well-concealed. I see here that he was sent to kill me, but now he leans more toward capture—hah. His motives are unclear; sometimes he wants to use me to his own benefit, other times, he would take me somewhere."

Faren interrupted, "Do you fear that?"

She answered, "I fear nothing. They have me to fear." Then she went on: "That much is clear. What is difficult to see into is what we can do about it. We can run and conceal ourselves, but for a period of time—less than the voyage time of this ship, but not much less—we cannot attack him."

Faren said, "When attacked, you can move, screen or counter-attack."

Nazarine nodded. "Exactly. Also do nothing: that's also an option. But access to all the lines going to him directly is blocked, and even if you can get through them, the consequences are all of negative value. I have done this before, but I have never seen a snarl like this. We will have to wait. There's a place where it clears, I can see that, but I can't see through it now. It must have been learning your speech that changes it this way—I see now in much greater detail.''

''What were you doing? Are you a . . . what? I don't have the words. A Witch?''

She shook her head. ''Nothing like that.'' She looked down at the floor. ''What I do looks miraculous to you, but to me it's ordinary, everyday. It is difficult to do, certainly, but still ordinary. To me.''

''Could I learn it?''

''Not as you are. You could not remain Faren Kiricky and do this. You have to start with a clean slate, a blank. . . . You know, it is the everyday world that looks peculiar to me. I have spent all the life I can remember trying to become a part of it, to be free of what I am. Yes. Really. There is much, much more to it than that.'' She sighed deeply and looked up, directly into Faren's eyes. ''I want you to understand something. Everyone in your world works for power of some kind. The exchange varies, the payoff, but all the same: power. Cratotropic. And I, who have it, want nothing in the world so much as to throw what I do have away. And I can't. Somebody is hunting me, something that does not stop no matter what I do or where I go.'' Her eyes now were very bright. ''And this was why Cinoe . . . I almost thought that I could do it through him. I sensed the failure of it even as we did it, the impossibility, but that never matters, when we reach so hard—it is the reaching that distinguishes us, not our failures. He was selfish and shallow, but he did not know what he gave me, which was greater than anything he took. And now this. I know this does not make sense to you.''

Faren said, ''I understand better than you think about wanting, and seeing those dreams fail. That much I know well. And fighting back as you can against . . . the smug, the self-satisfied, the idiots who get a little edge and step on everybody else's fingers.''

''Do you fear me?''

''No. I think I should, but I don't. I am not one for causes. I mind my own affairs. But I think you need someone to help you, and I will offer it. With some misgivings, but nonetheless. . . .''

''Why? You know little enough of me.''

''Because I think that you can do the things I cannot but always wanted to. You are driven by your own . . . oracle, but it's mine too. Don't misunderstand me, but it's like falling in love—you know it, when to reach, very soon. Not instantly, but very shortly. Will work, won't work.''

Nazarine nodded, agreeing. "Yes, like that."

"So I've seen some things, done others, liked some, and feared some. So, you looked clumsy, worse than a tourist, but you had a light in you. In fact, what I want you to do is learn to conceal that, to become a little more like us, adept at concealing, able to rationalize away our own best interests in favor of trash. . . . Then you can really be invisible. Those are not all my motives, be so advised. And now we have some practical things to attend to. I have a friend in Shipsecurity who can handle this with no fuss."

Nazarine looked blankly at the still figure lying in the corner. "Yes, I understand. Can you keep this discreet?"

"How discreet? There'll be questions. Never mind us being suspects—neither you nor I could do this kind of work. But still they will want to know something. Anyone can see it's no accident."

"Can we say we don't know who did this?"

"We could. . . ."

"It's important that Kham run loose. I can't see why yet, but it must be, for anyone to have an open course to him later. I mean, if anyone catches or stops him now, I lose my only link to what I came here to do, and also, I lose the ability to do anything about it. Things are balanced on razors right now."

"All right. If you think so. Is that from the oracle?"

Nazarine looked up sharply. "Not an oracle, not fortune-telling. Not occult. *Science*. A method of organizing, objectively, what you know, but more importantly, what you don't realize you know, and projecting from it. And what I have to do is let Kham lead me to the people he comes from. Once I have that, then I can set a balance with him."

"In other words, we follow this maniac, as he hunts us."

Nazarine laughed, shakily, but a laugh despite everything. "Essentially, yes."

Faren stepped close to Nazarine, and placed an arm lightly on her shoulders. "I am sincerely sorry about this. No one earns deeds of this sort. What of it that was good—remember that. Believe someone older and wiser—there'll be others."

She answered, "Being what I have been, you lose faith that a final answer exists, for this."

Now Faren laughed out loud. "You don't have to be you to understand that. I gave up long ago. Now. Let's get out of here—another way. I'll see to the reporting."

15

"Not seldom, passersby glance my way and marvel, smiling: 'Who is that village idiot, that fool, that wild man?' What they miss is a deeper truth that madcap antics, appreciation of irony, and zany remarks bordering perilously close to bad taste are all, considered together, the best defense possible against cruelties and disappointments. I never heard a blues song with these words but one might well be written: 'Laugh or cry, there ain't no in-between.'"

—*H. C., Atropine*

Arunda Palude returned to the section she and Kham had been assigned to, and she carefully checked places that they had previously agreed would be good sighting-places, but he was not in evidence. A quick run by the room he had been in also revealed nothing. She returned to the center concourse for their level and sat on a park bench, disconsolately. That was just like the way everything had gone since they had been on this terrible mission. Everything went wrong, constantly. Now she had valuable information, and she couldn't find Kham.

Someone stepped from behind the bench; she hadn't heard him approach, and say, passing, "Follow me at a distance." She glanced up and saw it was Kham, who seemed to stroll along no differently from the rest of the passengers, now wandering off through the aimlessly milling crowds. She got up from the bench and started out, and then fell back, barely keeping him in sight. Something was wrong, something had gone badly wrong for him to drop into a defensive mode of behavior like that.

Kham led her along roundabout, wandering courses that seemed to have no destination or purpose, but after a very long and tiring walk she saw him duck into a darkened drinking place. She waited for a time, but he did not come out, so she followed, as if she had had the greatest difficulty making up her mind. Inside the bar, which bore a softly illuminated wall plaque calling itself the "Nile Green Potationary," complete with illustrative pyramids, camels, palm trees and other equally improbable flourishes, the dimness and dark furnishings made it impossible to make anything out clearly, but after some uncertain motions, she finally saw Kham and joined him in a booth. He had already ordered a drink for her, something in a plain glass. She picked the drink up and looked at it skeptically. "What is it?"

Kham said, "House specialty: Lillie Mae's Reliable Vermifuge. It's supposed to cure warts, etc. It's also rather strong, so don't bolt it down."

Palude sipped at the drink, made a face, and then sat back with a foolish grin on her face. "Tastes awful going in, but the aftertaste is spectacular! A few of those and you'd bay at the moon, even if there wasn't one."

Kham glanced at one of the florid, arabesqued decorations arranged along the walls. It would have been a crime to call them paintings. He indicated she should also look and reflect. "True; the management has thoughtfully provided one for those who require such an orbital object to bay at." The moon bore, in subtle shadings, the suggestion of a theatrically overdone princess in the headdress of the ancient Egyptians.

She said, "You have the oddest tastes in meeting places."

"This is a good one. It's never crowded. It's done up so low-class people will think it high-class. Naturally, only serious drinkers visit."

"I have information for you."

"I likewise. Perhaps you should say yours first."

"Very well. I saw the girl, according to the coordinates you gave me. She has a helper, or comrade, or something I don't know." Here she gave Kham a set of coordinates for the recognition of the older woman she had seen with the girl. Kham nodded when he had a fair grasp of the image in his mind's eye. She continued, "I did not follow; they seemed alert and poised. The older woman looks street-wise and partly reformed. They were headed this way, and probably got into this area ahead of me—took the express passage down here."

"I've seen neither. But we now have another problem . . . ." And here he related, in sparse, tactical language, the events encompassing the death of Cinoe Dzholin." He finished, "The girl's name is Nazarine Alea. I tried the listings. She's unlisted."

Palude placed both hands on the glass and held it, on the table, but at arm's length, for a long time, saying nothing.

Finally, she ventured, carefully, "I have no specific comments on that, of course. You already understand the error."

Kham nodded.

"No need for me to add to what you already know. This could put some serious complications into things."

Kham said, "There were no witnesses. It is possible nothing might happen at all."

Palude looked directly at Kham. "Yes, maybe. *Maybe*. And *maybe* we might wind up being the hunted instead of the hunter. Somebody's going to find that body, eventually, and then the fun and games starts. How good is Shipsecurity?"

"Thorough and professional. Slow and steady, and bound by few or no laws. It won't take them long to link him with her."

"And so she'll know, and she also will have an alibi."

"Presumably. You are sure the girl you saw matched the coordinates I gave you."

"Yes. A Class-one match. No doubt. The girl you saw in Symbarupol, on the beamliner, is on this ship."

"Your evaluation?"

"Her appearance works against her, and she seems . . . what's the right word? Clumsy isn't it, maybe inept. And yet there's an order back of her, too. If she was inept as she seems she couldn't have made contact so fast. And I have a suspicion the older woman made me. Maybe not. But she looked directly at me. Not casually. For strategy, assume she did, and warned the girl."

Kham reflected, "So what they warned us of has occurred?"

"What? Oh, yes, that it would be alerted. Well, certainly that, by now."

Kham said, with wry fatalism, "Then we may expect the worst."

"I don't know . . . There is something very strange about all this, if you think about it. I keep having this suspicion about all this case that she's not really looking for you or me. That with the ability that thing has to read the present and determine courses of action, if she were after you she would have come long before. Or she could have set something in motion."

"Yes, I have thought that, too. Odd, that. By any ordinary standard, she would certainly have reason to bear a grudge."

"Exactly. But against whom? There's the question. Face it this way: assume she knows you are the root of the events that have happened to her. Two attacks. And assume she's still using the original system, the one whose parameters I was briefed on: and yet she doesn't attack.''

Kham added sardonically, "Not yet."

"You are the field tactician. Isn't there a circumstance in which you would allow a lesser figure to run loose, even though you had a clear case against that person?"

"Oh, yes. Common practice."

"In such a circumstance, you'd wait, and go for the higher-ups. . . .''

"Where you had the feel of reasonable expectation you could get at them through your obvious target."

"Yes."

"Then there's your answer. She's going to let us lead her to her real enemies."

"In a way, that's worse than being the target. Do you have any clear idea of her range?"

"I don't even believe in what they say about it. Range doesn't seem to enter into it at all. Spatial distance. . . . Using that system she's got, apparently she ignores it."

Kham looked into the darkness, focusing on nothing. "Then it becomes vital we get to her before she gets the range of her target. To our knowledge, she hasn't done it yet. This means she either can't see it yet, or she can't act yet. Either way, her powers are neutralized, and we've got time and opportunity. There is sense in what you suggest."

"We have comm through the ship. The committee should be notified."

"I suppose so, although we will pay a price for that, you know. Have you considered it? They'll say, 'you let that animal *loose!*' No matter what we do, it's no-win if we call them."

Palude stopped and reflected for a long time. Then, "So you'll try again."

"Have to. Hold your report for a bit. This is, after all, a closed environment. That thing can't breathe space, or transit-continuum. It's here, on a very small, closed world. And listen."

"Yes?"

"This world it doesn't know. We do."

Palude looked back at the mad Egyptian moon on the bar mirror. It seemed to communicate moonly wisdom, impalpable and subverbal, but something wise nonetheless. She said, "Maybe. But don't be too sure." She added, after a moment, "I'm sure you've heard the phrase, 'Crisis management is a contradiction of terms.' Remember it. What do you have in mind now?''

Kham was ready. ''We should stop off at those rooms and see if the work has been discovered. I was unseen. We can of course pose as a couple seeking privacy. If necessary, we can report the heinous crime ourselves. It might be a good touch.''

She asked, ''Why not from here, now?''

''Would be a bad move if it's already been reported. Things would get warm fast.''

Palude slid out of the slick leather seats and stood, now somewhat uncertainly. ''Very well . . . my!''

Kham smiled. ''Yes, indeed. Strong, isn't it?''

''One would never know.''

''Come along, then. Then we'll know something. And know things we must, now, all of it.''

On the ship, the illusion of day and night alternation was maintained as rigorously as that of gravity. When Kham and Palude emerged from the dim interior of the bar, the faraway overhead illumination seemed softer, dimmer than when they had entered. It now seemed like early twilight, under a high overcast. Kham glanced instinctively upwards, as if to judge the impending weather by the sky. Arunda chuckled when she noted this gesture. ''Ha! Looking for the sky, are you?''

Kham shook his head ruefully. ''The illusion is strong, true enough. One spends a lifetime outside, one looks at the sky, whatever the world.''

Arunda took Kham's elbow and said, ''No fault there. But it's not a world, this ship, and it doesn't have weather.''

Kham nodded. ''I understand your meaning. Very perceptive. Our usual reactions, even good ones, won't be good enough.'' He made a grimace. ''They weren't good enough, on Oerlikon.''

Palude pursed her lips thoughtfully, and suggested, ''I have spent many long nights thinking about that. If it were just one thing, one incident, perhaps it would be meaningless. But it begins to form a pattern. It does not emanate from us—you are not making mistakes. You are going about it with uncommon skill. And yet at the crucial instant, the actions don't work, or misfire. Do you know what I think?''

''That the Morphodite has luck? If so, I would agree.''

''No, something like that, but stated differently, and the difference is crucial. I begin to think that that thing . . . disrupts probabilities. There is an expected range of coincidence operant in the universe. For some reason, that thing, by existing, somehow de-coincidizes space around it, or trains of probabilities that lead to it. I don't think it's conscious, or even an ability, but a condition its existence imposes on the fabric of the universe. I'm not sure, of course, but there is a funny pattern to all the events leading up to now."

Kham walked along, silently, thinking. He said, "Perhaps. That would explain much. And yet it raises questions, too."

"Yes. Exactly what I thought. They told me, back on Heliarcos, that it changed the world, at least Lisagor, to a different configuration, a different idea-world. Things shifted. Kham, that thing created a world somewhere along the line, knowingly or unknowingly, that protects it, somehow. Shields it."

Kham was skeptical. "Lisagor, maybe. But here?"

"I don't think it knows it; how far it reaches, at least yet."

They had now left the lower-class concourse and were passing along one of the dim hallways leading to the residence areas. Kham said, "That would be in our favor."

"But think! Every time we have moved with violence against it, it has become more . . . enhanced, so to speak. We may have to rethink our options on what we must do with it."

"I think I see. The more we attack, the stronger it gets. And where before its effective range was limited to a single continent, now it can reach farther."

"Much farther. I say again, I believe it doesn't understand how far it can reach, or how far into the basic fabric its effects go. I do not want the basic probabilities of the universe tampered with. They're in a certain range, that makes things possible."

Kham walked along, turning into a side-corridor. "Perhaps. And yet what are our options? No matter what the cause, it's moving now, and it's in our world, motivated by our own acts. We don't know what it knows, what it doesn't know, of what it wasn't supposed to see. Do you imagine we should try to negotiate with it? Can you imagine the price? Even if we could find it and deal directly, there's no assurance it would stop with us. Its actions suggest it knows there is something behind you and me; so it would take us and just keep on going."

"I want to suggest we try to make some kind of contact with it."

"It's difficult to even see. I only saw her once, and you once. So far it's evaded every snare we've set for it."

"You agree we would have to find it on the ship before we take any further action?"

"Oh, yes, without doubt."

Now they had arrived at the section given over to cohabs for this residence area. The corridor light was dim, dimmer than the normal corridor lighting. Ahead, the rooms were closed, with the small witchlights above them indicating occupancy. Three were open, one of which was the room in which Kham had dispatched Cinoe into the darkness. "Last house on the left." Kham said, "Come on."

They stepped up to the doorsill and pushed the door open. Arunda held her breath. This was a crucial instant of time. Also, she found, looking at herself, that she really did not wish to be in this room with a dead man. There was a sense of profound wrongness about it. But inside, she looked around, forced herself to look, and there was nothing in the room. It was as if nothing had happened. The covers were neatly arranged on the bed, the lights were turned down low, everything was in order. She turned to Kham, who was looking around uncertainly. "Are you sure this is the right cohab?"

Kham nodded. "Assuredly. Indeed, this is the very room. No mistake."

"There's no body."

"Just so. I verified the room. So it's been discovered. Lock the door. We'll stay about half an hour, and then leave. We should return to our own quarters. I'll meet you tomorrow, on the concourse. It should be safe."

Arunda observed, "We should go somewhere and eat. I'm starved and I can't recall the last meal I had. That drink just set it off. And on the way out, we ought to nose around a little, to see if anybody around here knows anything."

Kham agreed. "Aye, that. Both. To hell with the half-hour— we'll go now."

With a last glance around the undisturbed room, they turned and left it, pulling the door shut behind them. Inside, its sensors picked up the door closing, and turned the lights out. And high up on the wall, in a dim corner, something infinitesimally small glittered for a second, and then also became as dark as the rest of the room.

Cesar Kham and Arunda walked back along the corridor, Kham looking along the plain gray walls for the room number he had derived for Cinoe Dzholin. He found it, and was on the verge of knocking, when a group, apparently bound for the furtive nighttime activity of the lower concourse, opened the door and came out. Kham started back for a moment, and then recovered, and like the good tactician he was, asked, of the group in general, "Excuse me, is this the room where a Cinoe Dzholin is billeted?"

One of the party turned back momentarily and said, "He's 'signed here, sure enough, but nobody's seen him all day. Popular fellow, that Dzholin!"

Kham asked, "How so?"

The other said, "Two women came looking for him awhile back."

Arunda, sensing the flow of things, asked, "What did they look like? They may have come from the party we came to fetch him to."

The other fellow pondered for a moment, and then said, "Young girl and an older woman. They didn't say who they were. The younger one was tall, very nice." The others agreed, smirking. He added, "The other one was average size, a little hard-looking. Looked like, the pair of them, one from the upper decks and a crew on off-time. Must be some party."

Arunda nodded and said to Kham, "They already came for him, and they didn't tell us."

Kham made a polite gesture to the party, who responded and started off. Kham added, so they would hear, "Probably dragged him off for awhile first. Hmf." He thought his voice carried just enough disapproval, tinged with a bit of envy. They remained by the door, as if uncertain what to do next, and as they waited, the others passed up the corridor and turned a corner.

Kham said, "All right. Now we know."

Arunda said, "They came down here to get him, probably, and found him. Doubtless we may assume it was reported, and the body removed."

Kham nodded.

"What do you have in mind now?"

Kham rubbed his bald cranium thoughtfully. "I don't think they have anything yet. You are clearly not in danger—they have no way to connect you. So what I recommend is that you move to better quarters, a room of your own. But stay on this level."

Palude shook her head. "They aren't on this level. And they probably won't come back, unless it's on the hunt. And we should not be separated, now."

Kham was insistent. "If they came soon enough, they will have picked up traces of whoever was in that room, and they could possibly make me. You don't know. There is a possibility I could be captured. In that eventuality, you must carry on, and do what you must. But however it would have to be, someone would have to stay behind, here, to see if they have started. How else would you know? So you see it's all clear."

She nodded. "Now, for some food. I see your argument, but I am not convinced yet. Let us talk it over, over a meal."

"Agreed! Most assuredly agreed!"

They returned to the concourse, now darkened into its night cycle. Kham had not been conscious of the place being crowded before, during daycycle, but now it seemed busy, full of people, all strolling along, looking for something to see, something to do. He and Palude selected a place without ceremony, an open-air restaurant serving plain and simple fare, and sat down to eat. Both of them were hungry, and so they spoke little for some time, nor did they pay much attention to what was going on around them. He was surprised when Arunda pushed at his leg under the table with her foot. He glanced up, caught her expression, and suddenly became alert, without visibly seeming to do so.

He listened. At first, there was only a confused blur of sound from the nearby diners, and the nearer members of the passing crowds. Then a pattern began to emerge:

". . . told Corlean that she could take it and shove. . . ."

". . . and after that, let me tell you, we. . . ."

". . . not any new ones out tonight. Same stuff. . . ."

". . . haven't seen them once this trip, and now out in force."

"When did you ever see two, and in uniform?"

"Carrying Tracker-Lenosz, too."

"Never mind, they're probably looking for a purse-snatcher."

Kham let his eyes wander, as if aimlessly looking over the crowd. For a second, he saw nothing significant, but then he registered the image. Two men, rather thin, wearing one-piece gray coveralls, walking now away from the restaurant, accompanied by two sleek, gray animals who loped along beside them without visible connection, but who also moved as if they were part of the two men. Their passage seemed aimless, but the agent part of Cesar Kham noted the subtle movements of their heads, men and animals, which indicated a careful scanning pattern, even though he could not see their faces from this angle. Shipsecurity agents, patrolling, of course. But looking for what? They had passed, certainly, within hailing distance of himself and Arunda, and yet passed on. He breathed deeply, and turned again to his meal, as if he had seen nothing. The murmur of voices around them continued, against a background susurrus from which it was impossible to extract anything.

" . . . saw them carry a body-bag out of. . . ."

" . . . go upstairs and harass the swells in. . . ."

" . . . wouldn't mess with. . . ."

" . . . and when we got to Havaerque, we ran slap out. . . ."

" . . . Nedro is nothing but a hoage. . . ."

" . . . onliest way I know to. . . ."

" . . . and she was so fat that if you told her to haul-arse, she'd have to make two trips. . . ."

" . . . routine patrol, likely. On the *Banastre Tarleton* they patrolled steerage almost hourly. And we were glad to have it, I can tell you, all those crazy religious colonists . . ."

" . . . on the *Pedro Francisco,* they'd turn Lenosz loose in a heartbeat."

Kham looked up at Arunda. "Shipsecurity. Seems to be a routine patrol. Somewhat out of ordinary, but within tolerance. Why worry? Had they been coming for us, they'd have had us now."

"All the same, it gave me a fright. When did they start using Lenosz?"

"I wasn't aware they were being used. It's news to me. Still, we've been out of touch. Heliarcos, then Oerlikon, Heliarcos, and back here. Who knows?"

Arunda ruffled her fingers through her hair, shaking her head slowly. "There is much we don't seem to know, ourselves. I have to vote for us staying close together."

Kham leaned forward, massaged his eyebrows. "Yes, of course. Tonight. But here's the way we arrange it: you get yourself shifted to one level up, a double. Then I'll follow."

"Why not come with me?"

"I've got to find out how much of an alarm is out. Some fine work. I can't do it with a partner. We have to know some of this—how bad it is. Then we can decide what we need to do."

"Very well. How long will it take?"

"About a day, should be. Stay put."

"How will you know where to find me?"

"Re-register openly. I'll call."

Arunda nodded. "Tonight."

"Oh, yes. Tonight, for a fact."

"And what about the girl? Are you going to press on with that, too?"

"For the moment, the girl will have to wait." Kham picked up the bill, studied it for a moment, critically, and then signed it, citing a particular alphanumeric code group. Then he said to Arunda, who had already gotten up to leave, "Do what you can to try to trace the girl. We'll take that up again directly."

16

"For the hard choices that define you there are no preset priorities, no magic answer; you place value and choose. But the proof lies in the obverse—when we start explaining away things by saying 'it just happened,' or some such similar nonsense, we admit that we did not choose anything, save to drift away into oblivion on a current of vagrant passions and miscellaneous lusts. No one can deny the beauty and ecstasy, but those moments were also balanced by equivalent amounts of terror, heartbreak, self-doubts of truly industrial strength. And in the end, surrounded by ruins, we ask why, and blame a cruel god."

—*H. C., Atropine*

A soft, almost-inaudible chime of exquisite high pitch sounded, having no perceptible source. Nazarine had been lying back across the bed, not asleep, nor yet awake, but when she heard the chime she looked across the room immediately, to where Faren had been dozing in a soft chair. Faren left the chair and stood by the bed, touching the commset. "Who calls?"

"Ngellathy here."

Faren said, to Nazarine, "My contact in Shipsecurity. That one is safe."

"Let him in."

Faren released the door, and into the dimmed room stepped a slender man in one of the ubiquitous shipgray uniform coveralls. Slipped into the room might be better. Or even better, flowed. He locked the door behind him and joined the two by the bed. To Nazarine's sharpened senses, it seemed something brief passed between Faren and the man, who seemed a curious blend of irreconcilable opposites: tense, yet also internally totally relaxed.

Faren glanced at him once more, and then to Nazarine. "Here we have Dorje Ngellathy, a Securityman who most of the time is a hopeless attitude case, but who, in a tight spot, is the only one I can depend on." And to Ngellathy she added, "This is Nazarine Alea, lately of Oerlikon, our unscheduled stop."

Ngellathy nodded, impatiently, curtly. Satisfied at last that the preliminaries were done with, he sat in the chair Faren had just vacated. He said, "Here is how things stand now. The body has been picked up. Faren, you were right in your suspicion of the pattern of trauma. Medical is going over it before ejection to see if they can derive a pattern. Some of these hand-assassins follow discrete schools. As for the killer, we used Alea's description of the probable, and presently he reappeared at the room. We had a viscoder installed. Had a woman with him, matches your description. They came aboard at Oerlikon, but are not, apparently, using Oerlikonian names. He lists as Czermak Pentrel'k, she as Morelat Eikarinst."

Nazarine said, "You haven't done anything!"

"No. We are holding, partly on your request, partly because we want to find out exactly what we are dealing with. Sec/Chief doesn't care for that pattern of injuries and wants to know."

"How?"

"We have an intermediate stop on Teragon. It's not in the route, and you can't buy a ticket for it, but *Kalmia* always drops in for a while."

Nazarine looked across the space between them. Ngellathy was difficult to see, to realize, to describe. Shadowy, subtle, even sneaky, there was strangeness writ hard all over him, but even so, she could see no particular evil in him. At the least, he was no more disreputable than Faren. She said, "What's Teragon?"

"Once was a small planet on a small system. That was long ago. Turned out it's near the center of our planetary communications system, so there they built a city. And more city. The whole planet is now city. They even figured out a way to make their own food. You can read about it. But there, we can tie in and get the proper patches to link up and dig deep before we move. And never fear—Pentrel'k isn't getting off this ship alive.''

Faren asked, ''Dorje, you don't know where they come from?''

''No. They claim to be from that planet we stopped at, but we have eliminated that right away. No, we've got him where we want him, and he'll stay there.''

Nazarine said, in a low voice, almost a mutter, ''I need him alive.''

Ngellathy turned now directly toward her, and said, ''I hear, but I can't understand why.''

''He has been hunting me, and I need to find out where he comes from. Not where he was born.''

He laughed, softly. ''Why not ask him?''

Nazarine folded her arms under her breasts. ''Perhaps. But consider: the woman with him—would she not be from the same place?''

''High probability.''

''Are you watching her?''

''Certainly.''

Nazarine looked away from Ngellathy, lest he read what was in her face. He saw the motion, and added, ''Shipmatter now, of course. I know you understand how that must be. No vendettas, revanches, loitering with intent to suborn mayhem, and so forth. I'm no stickler for forms for their own sake—there are more people involved in this than just you, now.''

''No, nothing like that. I was thinking that it might be possible for your people to separate them, and we would . . . have a short chat with her. All under supervision, naturally.''

Again, that small, assured chuckle. ''Naturally.''

''What do you think?''

He looked off into the shadows of the darker parts of the room. Then back, abruptly fixing her with a strong gaze. ''It could be arranged. And what afterward? Confinement?''

''I was thinking you could simply turn her loose. She'll tell her partner what I asked, and what I said. . . .'' She let it hang.

''Maybe not so good. We don't want him too highly motivated to excellence.''

''Could you just put her off, say, at the planet we'll stop over at? Teragon?''

''Hmf. Now there's a rich one. You're full of them. They have cross-world comms there, and doubtless she'd report back to their bosses. Might stir up forty kinds of hellation. We don't know yet who they work for. Some of the more obvious things we have already eliminated, but that doesn't mean they don't have connections, in fact, that they are not obvious argues for excellent connections. We don't want to arrive at the first scheduled port of call and have *Kalmia* impounded."

"I see." Nazarine stood up. "Take me to her. No recordings, nobody but me. And arrest me if she's harmed."

Faren now interjected, "Are you sure you want to do this?"

"Yes."

Faren now stood up and said, to Ngellathy, "Take her."

He shook his head, but stood anyway, still shaking his head. "Come on. We'll cook something up on the way. I will probably have her confined afterward."

Nazarine added emphatically, "I don't want them dead or harmed. They're worth nothing to me dead."

"Let's go," said Ngellathy, and the three of them stepped out of Nazarine's room, into the balcony-passage high over the middle-level concourse. It was nightcycle now out in the immense inside space, and the overheads that illuminated it and lent the appearance of daylight were now out and the space was dark. But far below, there were piercingly bright lights under the trees and awnings, and across the concourse, watchlights by another wall of rooms and suites glimmered like distant city lights. Nazarine walked with energy and anticipation, but looking out over that space, and understanding that she was riding, a passive passenger inside an enormous artifact, she caught herself holding a fugitive memory from Phaedrus, of the open, empty spaces and starry nights of Zolotane.

Down on the floor of the concourse, it was now the ship's analogue of night, and nighttime gaiety was well advanced: well-behaved crowds sat to their tipple in taverns, while in other places, the throb and wail of music wafted out into the illuminated squares and plazas, and in the dim interiors they sensed rather than saw directly the pulse and motion of dancers. Outside, small groups and solitary individuals strolled, leered, followed one another, or gathered in small groups to watch troupes of acrobats, or musicians, or wonderworking prestidigitators who plucked flowers from ears, removed gold rings from pockets, or perhaps colored handkerchiefs would be made to appear from the most unlikely, and slightly vulgar places.

As they walked through the plazas, Nazarine covertly watched

Faren and Dorje Ngellathy out of the corner of her eyes. They
both seemed perfectly in their element, not so much as partici-
pants in the merrymaking, but more, perhaps, as lifeguards on a
beach, who might take a short stroll from time to time. She also
saw that they seemed to lose concern, and concentrate more on
each other, at least in short, fleeting fragments of time. For a
time they held hands lightly, almost absentmindedly, and by
some change in inner state Nazarine saw an expression of innocent girlishness flicker into life on Faren's face. Dorje, who was
more visible in the plain light of the concourse streetlights, now
became something less mysterious and more human. The face
was basically that of some hardened mercenary, or veteran of
obscure border actions; high, prominent cheekbones, a hawk
nose, a wide slash mouth whose upper lip was fuller than the
lower, and epicanthic folds at the corners of long, drooping
eyelids. He wore his hair cropped off unfashionably short. In
build, he was slender, but wide at the shoulders, as tall as
Nazarine herself. He moved easily, loosely, but wary. And he,
too, changed in short little instants, managing in those times to
shed the hardness and seem something from another time, another place. A young hunter; a successful candidate from the
tribe's Rite of Passage, one who had undertaken the long quest and
who had seen the Holy Man.

They stopped briefly at one of the communications-points, and
Ngellathy spoke for a time. When he had finished, he said,
"She's taken a couple of rooms down here on the floor, in a
small pension above a jeweler's shop. Now she is alone. It's not
far from here."

Nazarine asked, "How will we do it?"

"We'll go in and talk with her a bit, and then you can go in."

Nazarine nodded assent, and they continued. Their walk now
took them into a part of the concourse arranged to appear as if it
were some small shopping quarter of a fashionable resort: small
buildings of light-colored stone or soapstone tiles alternated with
discreet little shops of stucco and stained wood. In between were
carefully arranged plots that seemed like vacant lots until one
noted the careful, almost over-tidy landscaping, the fussy attention to details.

They arrived at the shop, which had an upper floor devoted to
apartments, as seemed common in this district. It was situated on
an alley, with more of the same sort of structures behind it, most

connected to the street level by a series of rambling staircases of old-fashioned and quaint construction.

The second floor of the jeweler's shop was reached by one of these stairs, and they went up the narrow way in a line, Nazarine last. At the landing at the top, Dorje and Faren knocked on the door. After a time, it was opened cautiously, and a brief conversation ensued, after which the door opened farther and they went in. The door closed. Nazarine held her place on the stairs, waiting, occasionally glancing around. A few people passed by out on the main thoroughfare, but none seemed to look up or notice her; they were preoccupied with their own concerns. And while she waited, she slowly let herself move into a greater awareness, listening, sensing everything she could. As she did so, the illusion of a city on a surface faded, and the concourse seemed shadowy, insubstantial. She could hear a very soft but persistent ultrabass vibration, which was of course the ship. Sounds also had an echoing ring to them, unnatural in a true open space. The smells were too clean, too mechanical, technological. Somewhere, someone should have been frying onions. There was no woodsmoke, no sweat, no pungent scent of some domesticated animal.

Above, on the landing, the door opened, and Faren came out, followed by Dorje, who motioned to her. She mounted the remaining stairs and turned at the top, while Dorje said, in passing, "Remember. No action."

She nodded, and went through the door Dorje held open for her. Inside was a small room, rather like a parlor, connected with others on the far side. There was a simple sofa, facing wooden chairs. On the sofa sat a woman who stood when Nazarine came in. The woman was well-proportioned with no fat, but she was clearly past her prime, retaining as her most striking feature a long cascade of rich, dark brown hair. Her features were regular and clear, unremarkable save for a mouth that was slightly too large for the face, which gave her a slightly childish look. But one other thing distinguished the woman's features as Nazarine saw them: the woman was holding herself under rigid control, and was clearly terrified.

Nazarine did not know how to begin. The woman was so tense, almost anything could happen. She decided to keep it simple, and retain the advantage of fear that she held. She reached for Rael, and found that selfness waiting. As that came into her awareness, her perception of the woman shifted slightly, subtly: she seemed less vulnerable, and more contemptible, rather like a child caught doing something dangerous about which it has been repeatedly warned. She said, softly, "You recognize me." Statement, not question.

The woman hesitated, then said, "Yes, I know you from ID Mindset."

"My name is now Nazarine Alea. You also know what I am and who else I have been."

"Yes."

"Please sit down. I arranged this, not to attack you, but to try to understand some things. As you know, a securityman waits outside on the stoop; had it been my method to use violence, I would not have asked him to announce me, or to wait."

She sat gingerly, watching Nazarine all the time. Nazarine sat on one of the wooden chairs. After a few uneasy moments, the woman said, "You seem to have thought of everything."

Nazarine said, "Neither you nor your partner have any meaning for me dead."

The woman said, "I fear you, but what I fear worse than that is knowing the probable consequences of your remaining alive, and finding your way back. We seem to have lost initiative in the latter case, and so await the former with the usual dread. What else?"

Nazarine observed tautly, "When I was Phaedrus, you sent commandos against unarmed children to get me. Your agents killed what little family I had. I lived with a plain woman who could see forever and was one with the earth; she was one in that house who died. And in my present embodiment, your partner killed my lover. True, I understand he was selfish and had his faults, but such as he was, he was mine. Someone sent a man to seduce me and then kill me when I was Damistofia Azart. Who are you to inflict such terror, and in whose name?"

Palude said, "I will tell you nothing."

Nazarine said, "How would you prefer it? I can do what I need to do from where I stand with what I know, or can determine without you. But the focus is ill-defined, smeared-out. It will be like on Oerlikon, in Lisagor. Or you can cooperate, and what I have to do will then be clean, surgical. No innocent need feel the blow."

"But you'd do something, all the same."

"I'd do something. I'm not sure yet exactly what. But I know that when I'm finished, you'll make no more Morphodites. And there won't be any more Oerlikons."

Palude shook her head. "There will always be Oerlikons. Fools hide from the inevitable, and exploiters come and ransack them, without their ever knowing it."

Nazarine digested the cynical remark, which Palude had said easily, as if the thought had been an integral part of her selfness. She thought, *That's a widespread view in her world, and interesting for that reason.* She formulated that in the peculiar symbology of reading she used. A statement of belief. She said, "Don't you understand that when victims come easy, anyone can become one—even you. Whoever your bosses are, they exploit you as callously as they exploited Oerlikon, and to no better purpose. Is this the meaning of your life, that you travel unimaginable light-years to suborn the killing of children?"

Palude looked down, unwilling to meet Nazarine's eyes. But she said, "You're no better than they are; you would end up destroying our whole way of life, an honorable mode that has existed for thousands of years. And you don't know as much as you think you do; if you knew where we came from, you wouldn't be here talking to me."

Nazarine again let the remarks settle. A picture was forming in her mind, but it wasn't yet clear exactly what it was. She thought a moment, and then said, "Have it your way. But you've failed in your mission: You haven't gotten me."

"Yet."

"Knowing where your enemy is, that's the best defense there is. We have Cesar Kham bottled up in this ship. We have you. This ship will stop at Teragon. They have proper facilities there. What I need to know, I'll find out. Security is checking the account number you billed your passage to."

Palude said, "The transit isn't over yet."

Nazarine shrugged. "It's as long for you as it is for me. Maybe longer."

"What are you going to do with me?"

"You? Nothing. You're free to wander as you will. I imagine you'll tell Kham I spoke to you. That's exactly what I want you to do. It will stimulate him to take certain actions."

"You've seen the consequences of this?"

"Of course." Nazarine lied, deliberately now, relying on the woman's resistance and fear of losing something for this failure. Not her life. Not drugs. But they had some kind of hold on her, and it was long-term and powerful. She added, "And of course there's the option of doing nothing at all. I really want to be free of you people—that's what I want. I could disappear again."

Palude smiled now, an eerie expression in the context. She said, "Oh, we know enough about you to know you can't do that again. You lose age in Change, we know that. And you should be a lot younger than you are, so we know that you've found a way to slow that—but not eliminate it. So you're stuck now as Nazarine, for a while, at least. And as long as you're one person, you can be traced, no matter what."

"You've been briefed very well. That information could only come from the Mask Factory, from Pternam, or three of the leaders of the Heraclitan Society. So now I know that there's a connection between you-now and them-then. And it's reasonable to assume that you were sent back because you knew Oerlikon well, hence were there before."

"I'll say no more to you."

"Think about what I've said." Nazarine stood up and turned to go. She looked back, over her shoulder, and added, "Since you know so much about me, consider what you must know about how far Rael can see. I am still Rael, you know. Tulilly, too. I want the ones who gave the orders."

Palude said, "The ones who gave the original orders are long dead. They have escaped you."

Nazarine reached for the door. "The ones who gave you *your* orders are alive and prosperous somewhere: I will change both circumstances. Have a pleasant evening." And she went out, to where Faren and Dorje awaited her on the landing. Dorje looked inside to assure himself that Palude was unharmed, and then rejoined them.

He said, "Did you accomplish anything?"

Nazarine shook her head. "No. Or very little. She is defiant and uncooperative." They went down the stairs to the street, where they let their footsteps guide them back into the main open areas of the concourse. After a long time, Nazarine said, "She fears her own people more than she fears me, or Shipsecurity."

Dorje looked off, and said, "That might tell you something about what kind of organization she comes from. But let me ask you, what are you that they would hunt you so thoroughly?"

She answered, "I am someone who escaped something no one was supposed to escape from. They fear what I know. What they don't know is that I don't know what they think I do. If they had left it alone, I would never have come this far."

He said, "You should move to a more secure room."

She shook her head. "No. That one is not an operative. I could see that. And you have Kham under surveillance. He will doubtless become aware of that. No, I can protect myself adequately."

Out in the concourse, they passed one of the small uprights containing a communications terminal, and Dorje checked in on the net now covering the movements of Cesar Kham. After a moment, he told Faren and Nazarine, "He doesn't seem to be aware he's being covered, but nonetheless he seems to have retired for the night. Curious, that: it's early yet. But in essence they have him covered. I think we can relax for a little bit. I would like to stop working for a bit and sit down to a fine dinner—or at the least a glass of cold beer. Yes?"

Faren immediately agreed. Nazarine first demurred, but as she did so she became conscious of the undeniable fact that she couldn't recall when she had eaten last. Then she agreed.

Dorje said, "There's a fine place not very far from here that serves an excellent braised fowl, accompanied by pilaf and green peppers, ranging from interesting to excruciating. And they serve cold beer," he added, raising one finger vertically, demonstratively. "I believe it's called The Bel Canto. And suiting action to intent, he set off across a wooded glade of drooping shaggybark trees to emerge on the far side almost in front of the very place he was seeking.

Nazarine looked at the place and exclaimed, "It looks like a waterfront tavern, and disreputable at that!" She laughed, and added, "Do they include drunken sailors as part of the decor?"

Dorje pretended to look aloof, and said, in a mock-haughty tone, "No aspect of the illusion of reality is too good for our guests. We even furnish brawls for a fee."

Nazarine nodded. "I'm sure." The establishment bore the façade of stucco arches, washed a stained pink, with globular lanterns hanging from metal rods bridging them. Through this arcade crowds eddied and flowed, around flimsy metal tables at which customers sat, reading newspapers, books, or drinking various beverages: espresso, clear ouzo which turned milky when one added water to it, slender, crude glasses filled with an oily green liquid—absinthe, and crocks of brew. Inside, as they passed through the foyer, was even more detailed: here people were eating, drinking, conversing, devouring various grilled, spitted, and smoked foods, gesticulating with their hands to emphasize various points. The din of their voices and the rattle of crockery was deafening.

They found a winding path through the chaos, ducked down a low hallway, and emerged, after a short, cramped stairwell, back into the night, and the matchless quiet of an arbor covered with grapevines growing along rustic rough-hewn poles. This part was almost empty, and they could choose their table, rude planks covered by a checkered tablecloth. A girl came to take their order, wearing a linen peasant blouse, a loose cotton skirt, and barefooted.

Dorje ordered, including a round of beer for each of them, and sat back in his chair. "And now, for a small carouse."

Nazarine looked off across the arbor, under the grapevines, and said, "It will have to be small. The events of the day are catching up with me."

He said, "To be sure. We have a cure for that, too. You are our guest."

Faren added, "Whether they have a handle on Kham or not, I would hold your room to be less than safe. We should watch over you for a time."

The girl returned, bringing a tray of frosted mugs and a pitcher of beer. Nazarine said, taking a mug for herself, "I don't refuse, but I need to be alone for a bit."

Faren answered, "No, it's the other way. You shouldn't be. Now is when you need company, forgetfulness. And," she added, "there is still much you should learn about us. The best way is to experience it."

Nazarine sensed a subtle pressure behind the statements, almost an invitation, but she wasn't sure yet to what. She shrugged the feeling off. *What of it? No matter what they have in mind, it certainly won't be hunting me as I have been. I could almost welcome that.*

After what seemed a short time, the barefoot peasant girl returned with a larger tray, containing, as Dorje had claimed, platters of braised fowl, pilaf, and a plate of several sorts of peppers, some of which looked suspicious indeed. Dorje stirred from his reclining posture and indicated a round, pale pepper which seemed inoffensive. "Appearances are deceiving with these if you have no experience with them. This one, for example, is not for the unprepared, while this deadly looking little purple number has nothing but fine taste to recommend it." He rolled his eyes, popped the round pepper in his mouth, and immediately followed it with a bite of fowl, an expression of alarm growing across his face.

After the meal, which all three attacked with singleminded determination with little conversation in between, the serving girl brought another round of the icy beer, pungent with hops, and they settled back. Nazarine had, more than once, caught herself smiling at Dorje's adventures with the peppers, which had been heroic, epic, and wildly comical all at once. Now, his face perspiring from his exertions, he sat back and sipped guiltily at the beer, looking around from time to time to see if anyone had noticed them. Faren had been more restrained, less volatile, but she also had attacked the peppers and beer. Now her eyes were alight, dancing, alert. She thought, *How could I have ever thought her dull and businesslike?*

But there was an element common to both of them, presumably both members of this strange transtellar civilization, which she could not recall seeing on Oerlikon; an ability to let go, to become a magnified version of themselves, to express a unique strangeness which lay at the heart of every individual. This was part of the whole she was seeking, too.

She ventured, "I am now full, also of beer, and wonder, why of all you could choose to ask, why you have not asked why these people follow me with such dedicated persistence, causing so much ruin along the way."

Faren volunteered, "You were clearly being harried by tramps and thieves! It didn't take me long to understand that! And since you were as green as you were, it would engage me to oppose whatever was going on."

Dorje's answer was more complex, and much of the merriment left him gradually while he composed it. "Inhabited space is large, larger than one person can encompass in a lifetime. Crime and vice exist, never doubt it! Enforcement remains limited. One cannot correct all evils. Therefore we try, as an ideal, to attain an overlapping consensus on agreeable points. We agree to differ, so to speak. Also consider that some things remain relatively stable. This ship, for example. Many factors shape this vessel, and only a minority are within the realm of science and technology. Some forces are economic, others are human constants, others still constants of other sapient creatures with which we have traffic through a series of mutual accommodations. You can't enforce ways of thinking—only behavior. So here, for me, this: your pursuers, for one reason or another, do not choose to invite us to help capture you. Either that pursuit is clearly criminal in itself, or else we have a spillover from one sphere into another. This life Faren and I inhabit is one sphere, with clear limits. Suppose you were a religious refugee, fleeing the grim derogators of infallible doctrine. So long as you behave reasonably *here*, your differences *there* must not enter into it. You came to us, asked us what *our* rules were; they set to work breaking them without stint, and they show signs of knowing them better than you, perhaps better than I.''

"Surely you have curiosity."

"Of course! And yet we are each in part dreams and fluff and projections of what we would wish to be. This is how we come to terms with all the interesting things we will never have a chance to be. In order that I have the ability to project, I must allow you that same latitude. I see before me someone who is driven by purpose—whatever that is—and I also see an attractive girl who wishes very much to be accepted as what she seems to be. What you were before—therefore—must be your own. I will not spoil your illusion. Besides, you did not ask us what we were beforetimes, or why we spend our lives in this cargo-pallet between worlds, why I reside in the Securityman barracks and Faren keeps to the Technicians' cubicles. It is in part a germ of truth in what the Acrobats of Pintang suggest in their rites, that the magic is accidental, aleatory, and we must take it as we may. Let the higher-ups scheme and plot: we will take what is ours, the fleeting luminous moment."

Faren said, "Well said! I had not heard you declaim so before. But true! Antinomy lies everywhere, therefore we do not inquire into ultimates too closely. It would fracture what little coherence we have. We accept you as you are, yes. Be what you wish to be. Conduct no inquisitions, attack no innocents, and. . . .''

Dorje added, nonsensically, "Rotate your tires." He had become slightly tipsy.

Faren stood up and stretched, catlike, and suggested, "We will fall into terrible habits if we stay here."

Dorje agreed, and also stood. "Exactly! There are more sights to be seen, things we will show you. You fear forgetting what was good and will be no more. We do not ask you to forget, but to understand. It all has its place.''

Nazarine smiled despite herself. ''Where to now?''

Dorje said, ''First a longer stroll, to clear the fumes away, and then, I think, to the baths.''

''The baths?''

''You are new to us, but you will become us. We will initiate you. You must become.''

''Become what?''

''Yourself.''

Arunda Palude sat where she had been for a long time after Nazarine had left, thinking, reflecting, considering. She could not, try as she would, find an alternative to the situation as it appeared to her. She thought she had done well enough in meeting with the girl. She thought, *It's impossible, but that thing actually is a complete, genuine woman. No imitation! And sure of herself, too.* Yes, she had done well enough, but of course it wasn't good enough; merely a sop to the little sense of honor she had left, the old loyalties. Their efforts and long mission had come to nothing, outmaneuvered at every turn and juncture by this creature, who seemed to distort the very laws of probability. She had cut them apart like a surgeon, isolated them with an instinct which was terrifying, like a magic, or some fantastic superability. *We have failed. Moreover, our acts may have, probably did, activate it against the very thing we feared.* It seemed to her in one way that this arrangement of things had just happened, but another way, she could see a thread of causality stretching back and back, past herself and Kham, into a time she could not imagine. She caught herself almost, but not quite, asking the fatal question—what had the regents been doing on Oerlikon, anyway?

But she rejected that line of thinking. *That way leads me into impossible, totally untenable paths.* She thought of the long years on Oerlikon, a lifetime committed to a specific sense of identity, purpose, goals. *I cannot throw it away.* But the conclusions of this evening's work could not be escaped, either: *We have failed. What was to have been mine cannot now be. We cannot return, we cannot go forward. For a time Kham may proceed, but his progress is an illusion. Zeno's paradox! The closer he comes, the slower he goes. He will never catch her while she dismembers Heliarcos like a witless cretin dismember-*

ing some insect. And Kham, she saw, would dredge up every skill he knew, long after it had become hopeless. It was already past that point. And he would blunder onward like a berserk machine out of control, steadily increasing the casualty rate of bystanders, innocents. She saw it!

For a second, the possibility flickered before her of going the other way, of giving Nazarine the pieces of the puzzle she needed. That would be a relief. Perhaps the girl was correct, right, and their pattern wrong. Tempting, but unthinkable. She could not go against every decision she had participated in. It was a sorry pass to be in.

The awful sense of depression deepened as she thought of one more horror: they could not communicate with Heliarcos, either. Not until they stopped at some place which had planetary mass. The old way, when the project had been on, they had relays good to a certain distance. But here, now, they were bound to the routines of the everyday universe. *We can't even tell them that the thunderbolt is loosed, and falling on them, through the negation of Transitspace.*

She arose, and went to the windows, to look out on the street below the apartment over the jeweler's. It was late, and passersby were few, or else congregating in the parks and plazas of the concourse proper, not in this isolated little byway. The shops were all closed now, anyway.

She turned away from the window, and walked slowly, carefully blanking her mind, into the small bedroom. There it was dark, the shades drawn against the streetlights outside. She felt the edge of the bed, and lay out full-length on it, feeling a sense of purpose coming back to her. She thought clearly, *I do not wish to witness any more of this*. And, *There is one way left*.

She felt back in her mouth for a false tooth, implanted against the necessity that one day she might have had to face the redoubtable Femisticleo Chugun in the interrogation rooms of Lisagor. Arunda clamped her jaw down hard, feeling the material give a little, and then snap. A sudden flavor, as if of cardamom, or oil of eucalyptus, filled her mouth and nostrils. She swallowed, nervously, and waited, fearing, and yet relieved. *I have control in this. The bottom line*. There was no pain, or discomfort. She felt sleepy, and her mind wandered, daydreaming. For a moment, she seemed to sink slowly. Never had she felt so tired. Drifting on the edge, circling a whirlpool that led down into a cool darkness, dreaming. She felt her self draw closer, and the acceleration began.

17

> *"Looking at a collection of old photographs, it came to me that those events, now so quaint and meaningless to me/now, once meant something terribly important to them/then; now all for the most part vanished back into the earth they sprung from, leaving only these small artifacts behind no one understands the significance of today. But for them the sky displayed its infinite permutations, the seasons changed, wheel in the sky. For them, the men were handsome, stalwart, full of visions, and the women lovely, immediate, supple . . . the vine-covered sun-drenched summer afternoons of a thousand watermelon yesterdays. That/then was as real as is this/now, to us: terribly significant, filled with meaning and mystery, by turns warm and comforting, or else dire and full of unspeakable menace. Each of us would like to think that our own view is the brightest, but it was always bright to each of us, bittersweet and fading even as we reached for it. Perhaps a commonplace, still it needs resaying, maybe several times over, that we don't denigrate them, and that we don't enlarge ourselves too much."*
>
> —H. C., Atropine

In his long career as an agent, fixer of mistakes, instiller of renewed zeal, and supervisor of various clandestine operations, actions, and deeds by night and day, Cesar Kham had always operated well within the bounds of the elementary tactical theory he had learned when he had been selected to enter the Oerlikon project. He had grown used to that theory, at home in it, sensitive to degrees of concepts within it. He knew, sometimes to fine detail, exactly to what degree he was being followed, if indeed he was. The problem was that on Oerlikon, within Lisagor, one only saw a certain range of these activities, and for the rest of possible techniques, one either forgot them from disuse or came in time to ignore them. He understood now, aboard *Kalmia,* that this was a failing that could be fatal, and so he spent his first few hours away from Palude recalling his lessons, some of them rusty indeed, trying once again to bring up the skills that had enabled him—and others—to move about Lisagor undetected and unsuspected.

Back in the multiple-occupant quarters he had been assigned to, too big to be called a room, and too small to be called a barracks or dormitory, Kham lay back on his bunk and meditated on what he had seen so far, and what inferences he could possibly draw from it. *This kind of accommodation they called a "bay,"* he thought irrelevantly. But he recalled in full clarity and high contrast the fact that he had sighted another group of strolling, apparently aimless Security Shipmen, near the entrance to his bay section. *They've got a random grid on me.*

This was a refined pattern designed to keep a loose tether on a subject, and to narrow the search range should they wish to move in. So soon! But a glaring anomaly persisted. That they reacted so swiftly, that argued for the solution of a crime; but that in turn brought with it the idea that apprehension would shortly follow. And it hadn't. Instead, this zone-defense operation. Kham had carefully pruned his psyche of paranoid tendencies, but even with that, he knew with virtual certainty that the net he had seen was clearly aimed at him. And he could reasonably assume that they'd know within minutes if he tried to escape the confines of this bay, for some other part of the ship. Openly. There had to be a way. One could evade a zone defense of men. There were simple exercises to accomplish that. And that was why the Securitymen were accompanied by Lenosz. You could make a play on the human nervous system by sleight of hand, but the olfactory sense of the Lenosz would render the usual range of disguises useless. The conclusion was not difficult: he had to find some point of access into the ship's own internal passageway system. Use of the public corridors and areas would alert them immediately. Thus invisible, he could accomplish many things, before they could locate him again. Kham had no doubts what the conclusion of this would be, no illusions. He knew that if he could reach the peak of his powers, he could probably survive for some time aboard *Kalmia*—he had heard tales of that very thing. But he'd never get off it anywhere or within any time that would do him any good.

Ironic, that: The name of the ship was the name of a lovely, delicate flower, quite scentless, which grew on a quaint, gnarled, fibrous-barked tree of Earth. Whose sap and foliage were deadly poisonous. Yes. One moved warily among the evergreen shiny leaves of Kalmia Latifolia.

Kham tried to recall what he knew about the interior arrangement of the large, deep-space liners. They were irregular, bulky structures, utterly unstreamlined. Inside, they were chains of open areas, the concourses, which were joined by trunk corridors, often deliberately designed to be rambling, indirect, partly to give the passengers something to do, and partly to discourage mass movements from one area to another. Between areas there were more direct routes, not really restricted, but plain and intended primarily for crew use. Besides these accessible volumes, there were the crew areas, generally insulated from the passenger areas by blind pockets and mazes. But there was also a maintenance access system, a way technicians could follow and repair the miles of piping, HVAC ductwork from Environmental, electro-pneumatic lines. There were also waveguides and optical channels for inship communications and cybernetic systems. Kham reasoned that access into the maintways would have to be simple and available at many points. But of course the entries would be hidden, or locked, or subtly disguised. After all, it wouldn't do to make it easy. A person could hide in one of these ships, assuming he had food and water, for years.

He knew from the orientation of the corridor outside, that the bays were separated from their neighbors only by a simple bulkhead. He doubted if the maintways ran as far as between rooms and bays. But there was the floor, the ceiling, and the back wall opposite the door. He was alone, so his task was a bit easier: he carefully went over the floor, looking for almost invisible seam lines, recessed DZUS fasteners, slight mismatches of tilings that would betray an access point. There were none. The floor was tiled in a curious irregular pentagonal tiling that was difficult to follow with the eye, which suggested camouflage, but there was no break in it. The ceiling was featureless and seamless. The light fixtures were clearly only that, and besides, were far too small. That left the back wall.

There was a row of small vents along the juncture with the ceiling, small, unobtrusive. He looked along the floor line; another set of the small vents there. Inlet below, outlet above. He looked harder at the wall. It was divided into vertical bands, broken at odd intervals by horizontal mouldings. Yes. It had to be somewhere on that wall. The vertical bands were separated by different widths of paneling; some narrow, some broad. He went to one side and began testing the wider ones.

Kham finished at the far end of the back wall. None of the panels seemed to have any give, either way. Moreover, they sounded solid when rapped.

Part of the wall was interrupted by a small table or shelf, partly built-in, part supported by struts from the floor. He looked under the table. There was a single square panel there, not quite the same color as the rest of the room. As if it had been replaced. Yes. He felt along the edge, pushed, at first to no purpose, but by pushing in and up in the center, the panel gave first inward, and then swung up. Kham crawled into the space without hesitation, reached back, and swung the panel shut, taking one last look back into the room as he did so. There was no one there. The panel clicked faintly.

He breathed deeply, looked around. This was a different universe. There was lighting here but it was very dim, just enough to make out general outlines. This was at the end of the maintways, and was close. Piping, cable trays, ductwork joining into larger assemblies. He recognized a microwave waveguide. He was in a small pocket, joined to a corridor, a little wider, in which he could stand. He looked carefully. To the left, that was the way to the cohab rooms. The sound down there was flat, deadened. The ductwork got smaller down that way as it passed bay junctions. That had to be dead-ended. The other way, then, to the right. He stepped onto a metal grating, roughened for sure tread and set off along the corridor. At first, his footsteps sounded on the grating, but he forced himself to step lightly, almost glide along, using an irregular rhythm; there were faint sounds in the maintway, clicks, hollow, distant thuds, fragments of sounds, logoi of an unknown language. At intervals small lights illuminated the dark tangle, which grew more dense to the sides as he went farther. The corridor turned and twisted, running in short, straight jogs. Finally he reached stairs going down through several turns. There was slightly more light down there, but no sense of presence. Kham carefully negotiated the stairs, guessing that he had made it out to the main trunk corridor leading out onto the lower concourse.

At the bottom, he was disappointed for a moment. This was a small junction with no frills, no hint of going anywhere. But as he looked around, he felt a surge of anticipation. There was a map. It was mounted on a board, behind scarred and dented plastic, difficult to see in the weak light, but it was a map. Kham forced himself to relax, and then began making a series of stretching motions to limber himself up. A map. Now he could move. He had known that there would have to be one, somewhere.

The orthography of the system map was simple and direct, and presented the ship, as seen from the point of view of its functioning systems; to the end of simplifying the system aspect, some distortion could not be avoided, and the particular distortion was in the area of scale. What was a straight line on the map might not be, and usually was not, a straight line upon which a human being could walk. But Cesar Kham was not daunted by these difficulties: he plotted the courses he would have to take, and began following them out, doggedly and persistently, passing along the dim catwalks and runs, sometimes in near-darkness. In many ways, it was a strange and surrealistic journey he was making, a passage through the underworld. Sometimes he could catch faint echoes of voices, or of distant work going on, a dropped wrench, a profane or scatological exclamation. Then he stopped, and became very silent, and listened. More often than not, he heard nothing. Had he heard anything? He could not be sure.

Apparently the maintways were not popular places. It was easy to understand that: they were ill-lit, where lit at all, and their routes seemed convenient to no passage. This was the slow way. A labyrinth. But when he came to relatively broad thoroughfares, straight bores running directly through the bowels of the ship, he fairly raced along, exulting that if it was troublesome to him, it would be doubly so to anyone interested in following him. They would have to take the ship apart a section at a time.

For a time, he caught himself almost enjoying the experience, the thrill, the subterranean ecstasy of slinking unseen through the hidden ways. They even thoughtfully provided ration stations at certain points along the way, presumably for the workers who might be engaged in these passages for extended times. The food wasn't fancy: basic nutriment cakes and distilled water. Kham thought more than once that if worse came to worst, he could just remain here. Become a ghost, living from moment to moment, while outside the years passed, and uncounted parsecs between stars, sectors, crossings run over and over again.

In no way could the shape of the ship be discerned from the

arrangement of the maintway access lines. Neither the outside nor the open, public interior parts. Indeed, from what he could see of it, he could not recognize any part; he might have been near a concourse or far away from one. All he knew were the piping, the ductwork, the careful geometry of waveguides, the odd angularity of water and reclamation lines.

Once he caught sight of a party of people. They didn't see him, he thought. At first, he thought they might be a maintenance crew, but as he watched, they seemed to accomplish no activity, nor did they seem prepared to work. Far off, across a tangle of piping, the group sat in an unused open section with a cleated floor. They spoke to one another in low, whispery voices that seemed to float, disembodied, in the damp and the cool darkness. Stowaways, escapees? He did not know; he could not discern their conversation, which seemed to go on interminably. And if they were hiding down here, then what would they talk about? The world they left behind, now virtually imaginary, legendary, the "real world," where people succeeded, built bright, shining cities, walked proudly among the shining towers with their healthy, prosperous families. Here they were safe, more or less, at least as safe as the crew and passengers, fed. Somehow they found a way to make some sort of order among themselves. But they were prisoners, too. Safe here, in the guts and nerve linkages, they could never reenter the other world.

The journey went on, interminably. He reached an area, which according to the diagrams and schematics, was close by concourse level four, where he was going. He knew he had to start looking for a way out. In this section, there were a lot of water lines, and underneath, holding tanks, heaters, all sorts of accessory equipment. Overhead there was a tremendous flat construction, condensation dripping randomly from the bottom. From the main section, which seemed to have no visible end from his viewpoint, smaller lines seemed to connect to satellite enclosures which had both power and air connections, as well as the extensive water lines, pumps, and filtration associated with the larger mass. A hydroponic unit? Possible. But why the side tanks? And, more significantly, there seemed to be no entry from the maintway system, which he would have thought would have been a necessity. Also, there was heavy structural bracing and supporting structure associated with this area, much more than usual.

Kham consulted the chart, at the next major junction.

Deciphering the small print and symbols in the dim light, he discovered he was under an area called The Baths, which was in fact an enormous swimming pool. Presumably the satellite tanks were smaller cubicles which could only be reached underwater, by swimming. He looked upward again, tracing out the outlines. Yes. There were different levels, and the thing was mostly flat-bottomed. He went back to the schematic, now tracing out the water lines, the conventions of architectural symbols. Circulation, heating, and here (tracing the pathways out with his finger), he could follow the main fill lines, as well as an emergency dump system, with simply huge pipes, which seemed to lead to a sealed reservoir. How did they keep the people from going down the drains when they dumped? Sirens, early warnings, waterphones? That they would have such a construction aboard a ship argued an ability to anticipate emergencies in time to act on them which amazed him.

And a pool, too. That implied something about the long-term stability of the ship, too. One would never think twice about a pool on the surface of a planet, but in a spaceship? The idea gave him a subtle sense of distortion, a nightmarish world-gone-negative quality. He was crawling about on the wrong side, of an interface between two unrealities. The real universe had ceased to matter, and of course, once that, had ceased to exist. What moved? Ship or passing universe? He shook his head violently and muttered a Clispish oath under his breath, an incestuous obscenity.

Kham looked back at the map. Here would certainly be a number of access-points into the other world of the passengers' ship. He oriented himself according to the chart, and, glancing upward from time to time, studied the configuration of the massive tanks overhead. Finally, he saw there was an access point, not too far away, up an elevated catwalk, into a warm-air ductwork system, and out through a grille. Looking about once more to get his bearings fixed, he started off, away from the chart junction.

He found the catwalk, which rapidly ascended into the maze of lines either serving the baths or detouring around it. It was just like the chart symbolized, easy to follow from memory; Kham climbed ascending ramps, ladders, short traverses, presently finding himself passing directly beside the bulging flank of the main tank. He felt the material, gently, so as not to make any noise. It was not metal, but a composite material, covered with a layer of a softer mass, perhaps insulation. Here and there the covering had been disturbed—torn or abraded, and the inner material showed through. It seemed glassy, transparent.

Ahead was one of the side-tanks. His pathway passed over the tube that connected it with the main tank, over a short ladder. At the top something caught his eye in the darkness, a streak of light from the satellite tank. He looked closer. Here a patch of the insulating material had been carefully peeled back. Kham stopped and looked. The material on the tanks was semi-transparent, and here one could see through it, somewhat indistinctly, but nevertheless one could see. He suppressed an inane chuckle. Was that entertainment for the maintcrews? To climb up in here and peer into a side chamber? He looked into the tank. Whatever the material was, it did not transmit sound well, or at all, and it only transmitted light along a narrow path. You could not see the far edges of the chamber.

In this one there were three people, a man and two women, sitting on a ledge built into the tank. All three were nude, but at the moment seemed to be doing nothing of particular interest. The view was slightly blurred, but he tried to make them out. The man was slim, wiry, well-muscled. One woman was pale, with a rather long body and short legs, slightly built, not particularly young. The other was . . . hard to see, because of the angle. Something familiar, something just beyond perception. Yes. Long legs, full breasts. Younger than the other two, more smoothly curved. She sat, clasping her knees. The other woman moved out of the field of view momentarily, and returned, and began rubbing the girl's back. She lifted her face up from her knees, and almost looked directly at him. However, she was not looking at anything. Her eyes were unfocused. But he recognized the face immediately. It was Nazarine. The slender woman moved closer, on her knees, and began working the girl's shoulders, the back of her neck. He could see movement of their faces; they were talking. The man gestured to her with a hand, and extended it to her, and she reached, hesitantly, and took it.

Kham looked away, back into the underways, the dimness, the half-light. The piping, the ductwork. He put the insulating material back the way he had found it, and violently rubbed his face to massage the tension out of it.

Right there! Not three meters away! Playing threesomes while I crawl through the sewers for my very life. And there's no way to get through that stuff, we don't even know how thick it is. And even if I can actually get out, up farther, there's no way I could find that particular chamber before they left it. Crap and diarrhea!

He thought of what he was actually doing, trying to reach Palude secretly, and the thought sobered him. Kham looked about him, regrouped his bearings, and climbed down, to the next catwalk. After a passage through a narrowing series of rising accesses, Kham found his way blocked by a large, smooth tube, with an oval airlock protruding from it. The way ended here. This was the ductwork. He looked back along the way he had come: the view was no different than what he had been looking at before: pipes, tubes, grids of narrow walkways, bulk-heads. Dim, distant lights. A maze, a labyrinth. He opened the outer door and crawled into a mini-airlock, pulling the door shut behind him before opening the other door, immediately in front of him. Not to have a pressure leak—that would set alarms off all over this ship.

Opening the inner lock, he found himself in a tubular passage, the air moving slowly, warm and humid. This would be the exit air line from the baths, and to his left, facing the airflow, there would be a removable grille. Kham stooped over, half-crouched, and began walking forward, feeling his muscles protest at the unnatural posture, grimacing in the dark. Not quite completely dark. Light was leaking into the air duct from somewhere ahead.

The line ended at a locker room, which seemed to be empty. There was no motion, no sound. Far off, he could hear splashing, voices, but it was far away. *Now.* He pressed at the grille, and for a moment felt a cold wash of pure panic when it didn't give. He sat back, trying to think it out. He reached, caught the grille, and pulled, felt it move, and release, and then it swung up, back into the locker room. Kham stepped out, and replaced the grille.

He wasn't certain which way to go from here, but toward the sounds seemed the only way; he set off and traversed the room, finding that it ended at a blind passage that led one way, left, to the baths, and right, apparently, to the concourse. Kham went right, and began walking in what he imagined was an ordinary manner after the stooping and ducking under pipes he had been doing. This passageway joined others, flowed into a lobby, and into a courtyard of ornamental paving, overhung by the graceful shapes of Benjamin Figs, here grown to unheard-of sizes. The courtyard apparently was down. One had to go up. The lights of the concourse seemed far away, across enormous spaces. Here, small footlights followed the pathways. But there was a sense of open space, and darkness far, far overhead. Much more so than the area he had left behind. Other folk passed, parties of several men and women, couples, some family groups, all busy, chattering, oblivious. Kham wanted to run but could think of no reasonable excuse to do so.

At the top, where the sunken courtyard merged with the general level of the concourse, he located a bank of public communicators, and used one to call for the location of one passenger Morelat Eikarinst. The operator read out the address, and on the accompanying vid display, caused a simple map to be traced, showing him where it was in relation to where he was. He broke the connection and set off. At another comm-point, he called the number that went with the rooms, but there was no answer. Now Kham looked about him carefully, eyes scanning the crowds, now thinning as night became very late indeed. He sensed no pattern. He thought that curious, inasmuch as he had almost given them his position, if they were covering him closely as he thought they might. He thought about that as he walked, and of all of it, that made the least sense. Or perhaps he had truly done something unexpected, and actually gotten away from the watch on him, momentarily. They would still be looking, back down in steerage, area-covering, waiting for him to move. If so, he had to make the most of it. He couldn't keep on going up, into higher classes; even here, he would be out of place, but higher—he'd stand out like a polecat at a picnic.

Kham found the area, rather sooner than he imagined it would be, and located the store easily. The rooms above were dark. He went up the stairs, and knocked at the door. No one answered. He hesitated, listening, feeling. There was no presence, no sense of tension. He tried the door, and it was unlocked. Inside, light came from the streetlights outside, and the faraway concourse lights. It was a simple arrangement: a sitting room, with a small kitchen unit toward the rear. A hallway with doors—there would be closets and the bathroom. And double doors beyond. Two bedrooms.

There was a peculiar air to the place, a suspense he couldn't quite identify. Someone had been here, he could tell that. Small things were out of place. A glass by the sink. Palude's wrap was laid across the sofa. She had been here. He went quickly to one of the rooms, pushed open the door. Nothing. The room was empty. He pushed the other door, and saw Palude asleep on the bed, completely relaxed, mouth open slightly. But it bothered him that she would lie down to sleep and leave the door unlocked, or that she would sleep with her clothes on. And then it dawned on him that she was very still, and that her chest did not move with breathing. He approached the bed slowly, reached to Palude hesitantly, and touched her forearm. Cold. It was cold. Arunda was dead.

Kham's first thought was, *Dead, and not a mark on her! Now Nazarine repays me for the things I have inflicted on her.* He turned away, and stepped back out into the hallway. There was still no sound, no sign of pursuit, or of a trap closing. Then he thought, *There is nothing I can do here. Best I leave quickly. I've got things to do yet before they close the net on me.* Kham looked back, once, and then turned back to the apartment. He left, closing the door behind him, and walked down the stairs to the alley and the street, not thinking anything. He let his steps guide him aimlessly back into the concourse, now noticeably thinning out and almost empty, save for a few night owls and small groups of tipsy revelers, who ignored him. It seemed that he thought nothing as he walked, but when he reached a secluded spot and sat on a bench to think it over, he understood that in some strange subterranean manner, he had already made up his mind. Oh, yes, it was all clear now. He knew what he had to do with a clarity he had seldom known in his life. And from here on it would be for himself, not for Oerlikon, not for Heliarcos. He assayed the difficulties, the odds, the forces now arraying against him. It would be difficult, yes. But it could be done.

18

"The real evil in the world (never never never doubt for an instant that it exists) does not reside in the dark towers of sorcerers nor in the black hearts of thaumaturges, nor yet in the schemes of dictators, kings, or chairmen, but simply in the petty crimes, evasions, petit-betrayals, arrogances and insults we all take on the hubris to practice on one another, imagining that

*each of us is the center of the universe, that it was
created expressly for us. Ha! Don't expect you can cure
this by law or logic; the counter simply doesn't exist in
those quarters."*

—*H. C., Atropine*

Nazarine woke up in a strange room, to the sounds of someone apparently pottering around in a kitchen. These quarters
were not passenger spaces, she could see that; a long, narrow
room, with an oddly high ceiling. A cubicle behind the head of
the bed, and across the room, the other wall was taken up with
bookshelves, electronic devices, a desk, whose sole ornament
was an abstract sculpture in some lustrous gray metal, all
flowing curves. Everything was done in apparently industrial
fabrics, in soft, muted colors, neutral gray, dove-blue, accents
in rust and plum. It conveyed a subtle sense of ownership, and of
opposites carefully balanced: discipline, countered by slight lux-
uries: the bed was soft to the touch, but firm in support. She
called out, "Where did I wind up?"

Faren Kiricky looked around the corner, the black and silver
curls making a contrast with the hard gray lines of the room. "It
seems I entertained guests last night in my modest suite." She
vanished back into the kitchen unit, an alcove off to the right.
Presently she reappeared, wearing a loose caftan of a soft,
flowing charcoal-colored stuff. "After the baths, we went to
Harry's for a nightcap. You were much taken with the potations,
and, Dorje and I, thinking you would be better off with us,
brought you here and tucked you in. Simple."

"True, I was very relaxed. We. . . ."

"A little magic, that's all. May not have the chance again.
Not to worry."

"I felt good."

"Of course. So did I. They are rare occasions: something
extra."

"I feel as if I'd stolen something from you."

"Wouldn't be here if you had."

"What is your relationship with Dorje?"

"We are something more than simple friends, and something
less than owning each other. We do not seek to imprison the
other by reaching for what permanently can't be had."

"Is this unusual?"

"Not in the circumstances, no. People like us, living as we do . . . it couldn't be much of any other way. We form loose groups because no one can take them away from us, and yet we also leave the door open for chance encounters, a little magic. You are new to this, I can see, so have a care. Take it and learn and go free."

"Where is Dorje, back at work?"

"In part. He is out looking into the whereabouts of our friend. As a fact, he's overdue, now. He was supposed to come back here for something to eat."

Nazarine sat up and slid out of the bed gingerly, expecting a sudden headache, but there wasn't one. The cubicle behind the bed proved to be a bath cabinet, which she used after some hesitation over the controls. And after she had gotten it started, she hadn't wanted to come out. But eventually she did. Her clothes were folded neatly on the bed, freshly cleaned. As she dressed, Faren told her, "We didn't want to go all the way back to your room to get fresh clothes, so. . . ."

"You went to no trouble."

"No. It's automatic. A processor in the closet."

There was a soft rapping at the door. Faren opened it from the kitchen, and Dorje entered Faren's room, with his usual loose alertness and dancer's grace overlaid with some tension. Nazarine saw it immediately. She said, "Something's wrong?"

He nodded. "Very wrong. Two wrongs. The woman, who is listed as Morelat Eikarinst, killed herself last night after we left her. Had a false tooth, complete with poison."

Faren came out of the kitchen unit and asked, "Do they know what kind? Different groups have their preferences. . . ."

"Ship's surgeon says the main ingredient was a buffered andrometoxin. It primarily lowers blood pressure. The buffering apparently is to mask its intense bitter flavor and subdue the side effects. Interesting stuff: $C_{31}H_{50}O_{10}$."

Faren asked, "Why interesting?"

"It's not common at all. As a fact, it comes from plants originally found on Earth, the laurel group."

"Then she was from Earth?"

"Definitely not. Body chemistry indicates two places, neither on Earth. One is recent, the other traces. Where she lived and where she came from. Where she lived, they can't identify."

Nazarine said, "That would be Oerlikon. She was there."

Dorje nodded. "Reasonable enough. Then you'd show the

same trace elements, as would Pentrel'k, or Kham. But the other part, that's a rich one. Heliarcos.'' He looked at Faren, meaningfully.

Nazarine asked, "What's Heliarcos?"

Dorje answered, "A strange sort of place. It's in part a university, in part a research center, maybe some other things. But it happens to be a place where the early settlers brought the laurel group, and they apparently thrived. It's fairly well known for that; most Earth plants don't do well on other planets. But andrometoxin's associated with a history of, shall we say, very odd incidents.''

Nazarine asked, "What sort?"

"Different places. . . . The deaths are always suicides, and the victims are always ultimately associated with Heliarcos. But beyond that, they don't follow it up: the circumstances don't seem to threaten anyone.''

"What are the circumstances?"

"People working in medical research areas."

Nazarine could almost see the answer coming. But she asked anyway, "Do you know what kind of medical research?"

"Odd that you'd ask. The surgeon knew and told me. Hormone system work. Anything from the way the body makes specific message units up from a cholesterol precursor, to organ responses. I mean, it's open scientific work, so why have a spy in it in the first place. But he said it's odd enough to have been cited in the literature.''

"Why do they elect to kill themselves?"

"No one has ever found that out. Oh, there are suspicions, but nothing that can be confirmed. And remember, it's not very common. There are a lot of worlds, and people die every day. Andrometoxin's had its day, and now it's something else in the poisoner's handbook. Yesterday, Andrometoxins; tomorrow, Phalloidins.''

"How so, 'had its day'?"

"Most of the cases noted are several generations back, in fact, some are far enough to be called, properly, history.''

Faren interrupted, "You said two wrongs. What's the other one?''

"Survey lost Kham-Pentrel'k."

"Lost him?"

"He was in a cul-de-sac, couldn't get out without being tracked. But he vanished.''

Faren nodded, and said, "Then he's gone into the maintways."

"That seems to be the case. Comm reports a call was made for the woman, data given, and not much later, someone tried to call her. Both calls were from the level four concourse. It's a fair bet it was him. So what we think is that he used the maintways to go to level four, emerged briefly, and then went back underground. Lenosz confirmed he was in her rooms, but they lost the scent."

Nazarine asked, "Can they catch him there?"

Dorje shook his head slowly, indicating not a negative, but that he didn't know the answer. "Hard to say. Down there, it would take years to go through every part of the system. We already know we have stowaways down in there—some of them have been there for years."

"Could he do any damage to the ship? He might do so, thinking he could get me that way and be sure."

Faren said, "He could make a nuisance in specific areas. But the ship-critical areas are sealed off. There's no way he could get into those. No, I'm not worried about that. But I am worried about you; he shows unusual persistence."

Nazarine looked at them thoughtfully. "Yes. I see what I will have to do."

Dorje said, "Ah, never worry. We can handle the likes of that, or at least keep him on the move. When you leave us, he'll remain behind. I mean, whatever he might have been working to save, that's useless to him now. He's truly trapped down there."

Nazarine said, "No offense, but I need more than defense, however good it might be."

Dorje looked at her sidelong. "You can't take action against him. That would endanger you. Then you would have to hide, or Shipsec would come after you. We don't want that. As you are, you are worth holding on to."

Nazarine said, "No, I don't want to attack him. But I do want to find him and ask him some things. I need to know why he pursued me so far and with such force."

Dorje took her arm gently. "All right. Assuming this is true, understand that you would be dealing with a skilled and alert killer, who has risked everything and now apparently has nothing to lose. He would be hard to find, harder to attack, because of possible side effects. We'd have to subdue him mano-a-mano, so to speak. Hand to hand. He won't do much talking."

"I can handle that part. Just help me find him."

"I can't. We don't have enough surveillance systems to close off areas and eliminate them, the way we could in the public parts of the ship. There's food and water down there, and as long as he keeps moving and disturbs nothing, then he could avoid us indefinitely. We know there are some down there, already. And he can't locate you by using shiprecords. You were already on limited-access. Now we've isolated you completely. Whatever he wanted to do, that's over now. He's got a defense, but the price of that is his goal. So we'll keep you until we make planetfall by Teragon, and there you can transship. Think about it. Carefully."

Faren interrupted, "While you think, eat. Breakfast is ready."

Kham now sat back in the comfortable darkness, or more precisely, dim semi-darkness, of the maintways, munching on meal-cake, washing the dry stuff down with a flask of distilled water. He congratulated himself on having acted with such boldness and verve. True, he was back underground, as he chose to think of it, although to the best of his sense of spatial orientation he was not actually "under" but somewhere over the section-four concourse. They hadn't expected him to suspect the interface which allowed him to escape into the maintways, and they were certainly laggards with regards to responding to his call. Curious, that, indeed. He reflected that their response seemed lax, even uncaring. He finished the meal-cake and the last of the water, and looked about himself observantly. From where he sat, on an enormous section of ductwork, he could see only more of the same: ducts of various sizes and shapes in cross-section, some plain and covered only with a protective anticorrosive, others painted in bright primary colors and further identified with cubist tiles of color patches, which doubtless revealed more information. There were also cable trays, catwalks, inspection ladders, piping of a hundred sorts, waveguides, all coded or lettered. The letters, of an obscure blocky style, conveyed no more information to him than the color patches, although he assumed he could eventually locate a manual which would render the system intelligible.

So far, in his inspections, he had found very few places where he could have attempted any control of the channels he saw all about him. At some junctions there were various switch cabinets, circuit-breaker boxes, monitor units. Some enigmatic blank units, marked only with a pattern of colored lights, he suspected of being slave computer monitors. All these devices were carefully secured, not with the primitive locks and plates and chains of Oerlikon, but with more sophisticated modern methods. Many of the cabinets were monolithic, to fission and open only under a careful sequence of magnetic commands. Some, he did not doubt, could only be opened with the cooperation of a remote unit, complete with passwords and authentications. These he did not have, and could not reasonably expect to get. Comm-points were fairly common, but of course he would have to be extremely careful in using them. He would plan lines of retreat, make his tests of the system, very small tests, one at a time, always leaving the area immediately. In that manner he could eventually build up the requisite knowledge, and finish the Morphodite off.

This area was clearly an area of no great significance. He stood up, forgetting to duck, and bumped his head against a cable tray, causing him to make an exclamation. He stopped, rubbing his head gingerly, and listened carefully. No sound. Good. He had to be careful. With all the metallic and hard surfaces around, sound seemed to carry in unexpected fashions; many times already he had thought to hear sounds of movement, or work, or conversation, only to find that the source was either very far away, or invisible, hidden behind the tangles of piping. Yes, quiet. He climbed back onto the catwalk he had been moving on and set off the same way he had been going. There was nothing in this immediate area he could use.

The expanded-metal walk went forward a few meters, and then made a remarkable detour around a mass of junctions. Beyond the junctions, the way ended in a metal spiral with cleated metal steps, leading down. There was a nearby light, dim, of course, but in this light, the steps seemed to be worn with much traffic, and the way suggested somewhere important, down below. Kham set out without delay.

He had a picture in his mind's eye of his approximate location, relative to the level-four concourse. But as he went down, flexing his knees at the steepness of the spiral, he noted only an occasional landing or access-point, and his legs began to tire. Still, he followed the spiral down. Sooner or later it had to terminate at the ceiling of the concourse. He tried to estimate how far he had come, but found that he could not with any accuracy. In addition, the spiral did not run straight, but shifted orientation every so often, so that one could not look up or down and see any great distance along its length. Impossible to estimate. He stopped, and paused, and then set forth again, still down. No point in going back up: he already knew there was nothing up there. Apparently the environment was controlled at various points, too, in here as well as out there in the main part of the ship. But now he began counting the steps he took down. The scenery, as it were, seemed not to change appreciably. Still pipes, waveguides, cable trays, ducts of various cross-section.

When he had counted a thousand steps, he got off the spiral at the first landing, his legs aching. And the spiral continued, after a slight radial jog, even farther down! Here there was a certain dankness to the air, and some odors seemed magnified. He touched a pipe passing overhead. It was cool, and his hand came away wet. He looked again: beads of condensation covered the pipe. It bore no legend save an arrow indicating direction of flow. And the landing was even more enigmatic: The only object here was a small fuse-panel, an adjoining panel of switches, with indicator lights, all a dull green now, and a comm-point transceiver.

Kham looked about uncertainly. He was sure he had started his descent from a point over the concourse, and that being true, long before now he should have reached the ceiling. He looked into the dim confusions of the piping, ending in darkness only a score of feet away. Nowhere did he sense a wall or border. Just the darkness, and the piping. He listened. There were faint sounds of things moving in the pipes, distant drippings, a soft hum of an induction pump running somewhere. Another sound, even softer, more percussive. And something else. Like singing, or chanting, in time with the pump:

> "Ai mft- tu Jai-nmf dum,
> dumdum duh eh fumdum,
> Wuh bah n o hun kun,
> N duh u hunh dusung:
> Tai-samóhkambú dai-yéi!
> Tai-samóh Kambú!"

Kham could hear the repetitive choruses, but the verses were muffled and distorted, and the words made no sense in any language he knew or had heard of. Some sort of folk chant by the nearly invisible denizens of the maintways, stowaways and renegades? He did not know, and at the moment did not wish to find out. It sounded vaguely menacing, in an alien way that made his skin crawl. He decided to go, for a time, along a catwalk, very narrow, that seemed to lead away from the chanting.

Kham followed the catwalk for a time, not paying much attention to whether it went right or left, up or down, or in what order. The catwalk, assisted by metal stairs and short ladders, made all four changes in vector, and after a time, Kham could no longer hear the chanting. He tried to see through the piping to determine where the spiral was, but he could not locate it. He stopped for a moment and looked around himself, suddenly realizing that he was hungry. And that he was quite lost. He had no idea where he was in relation to anywhere. And this section seemed to be narrowing, closing in. He looked again. The ways were narrow here, very close, but he could not make out a wall or termination to any of the lines. He thought back, and all he could recall clearly was that he had come a long way down from where he had started. Now there was something more important to attend to. Finding another junction, with a map, and a food-store cabinet. The Morphodite could wait. At least for a while. It wouldn't do to starve down here.

After she had finished breakfasting with Dorje and Faren, Nazarine told them that she wanted to return to her own room for a time, in part to sort things out, and to make some queries of the ship's computer.

She was halfway out the door when she realized she didn't know where she was. "Hey!"

Faren looked up. "Did you forget something?"

"I don't remember how we got here from section four."

Faren looked curiously at nothing for a second, and then said, "That's right. You start off down the passage until it forks to the right, and then you take the first lift to the left . . . Wait a minute. Let me get dressed, and I'll show you."

"Where are we?"

Faren's voice was muffled by the closet, which she was halfway into, pulling clothing out. "Section one: Crew. Besides, we took some shortcuts, you know, crew only, last night. Would be better if I went along, at least until you get back into public space." She pulled out several things, but in the end settled on a crew coverall, not greatly different from what Dorje was wearing. As she stepped into it, and then pulled it up the rest of the way over her shoulders, she added, "I'm on standby anyway, and if they called me, I'd have to come back here and change. Party's over, at least until next break.''

Faren finished zipping the coverall up and hung a communicator on a loop by her waist. "Can't go anywhere without my trusty bitch-box.'' And to Dorje she said, hurriedly, over her shoulder, "Lock it up when you leave, will you?''

"Right." Dorje was still in the kitchen, drinking coffee, smoking a cigar, and stuffing dishes in the cleaner. He called out, as they went out the door, "Don't worry about Pentrel'k-Kham. Ship's computer is set now to alarm whenever he tries to use any comm device. We register voiceprints on boarding. And major access points are also keyed. He may be loose, but he can't do anything.''

As they walked, for a long time they said nothing, save directions, and some small talk about places they passed. But as they neared Section Four, a silence fell between them which did not end until they were actually in it, and Faren had shown Nazarine the correct corridor.

"This one. Just follow it straight on, and wind up at the base of your block of suites.''

"Do you have anything else to do?''

"No. Not really. I've got the box, if they want me. Why?''

"I've got an idea that you know those maintways better than you'd like to talk about openly.''

Faren blinked, and then smiled, a wicked, knowing smile. A delinquent smile, perhaps even a peccant smile. "I thought you'd never ask; yes, I know my way around down there. But have a caution: only *somewhat*. Nobody knows everything there is in the maintways. Not even the ship's computer. We've had maintechs get lost there, too.''

"Is that why Dorje doesn't want to press it in there?''

"In part. He knows how difficult it is. And he puts limits on things—he has to. As far as he goes, the problem with this Kham is solved: if he shows or tries to communicate, they'll have him, and then it'll be Captain's-Mast, and doubtless, *outside* with him. Or else he'll dig in deeper and stay there.''

"But they're strict about ship security! What about the maintways?''

"No-man's land. A jungle. Weapons are damn near useless: you'd hit or cut something that didn't need cutting. As far as that goes, there is considerable risk in going into the system. Not for crew—they leave us alone. But it's said they prey on each other.''

Nazarine looked at Faren sharply. "For what?"

"Not money; they don't use it. Nor basic foodstuff—there are ration boxes throughout. But one gets tired of meal-cake and distilled water, so they combine the thrill of the hunt with a bit of fresh meat."

"So that's why Dorje's not concerned about Kham."

"More or less, that. He stands a good chance of being caught and eaten. Dorje didn't want you going in there after Kham, for that reason, and he thought you might have that in mind. I thought so, too . . . so I thought I'd go along a little bit. We're maybe more casual than you're used to, but we care, too."

Nazarine looked away momentarily, and then said, "I wasn't sure I'd do it. There's some things I have to do first."

"Another reading?"

"Yes. But also I need more facts to put in it. I'm still missing pieces; I can't reach for the answer I need yet. And I'm glad you came; I will push it harder this time. And to know what I must do, Kham is essential. I don't want to kill him; I only want to talk to him."

"The woman gave you nothing."

"That's true, in a sense . . . but she also added a valuable piece. I'm waiting to use it. Come on."

When Nazarine pressed her palm to the door latch, and it opened for her, she half-expected to see the room in disorder, totally ransacked. It wasn't; the lights came on, and everything was in place. It looked exactly like the first time she had seen it. First she went to the closet and quickly flipped the clothing through, selecting a loose pullover of a soft, deep-brown velour, and a pair of pants. While she changed, she explained, "What I had on, that's fine for protective camouflage, strolling along the concourses, and being inconspicuous in a genteel atmosphere, but we will be climbing around, and may need to be freer in movement."

"Those will do fine."

She went to the study cubicle, slid the port aside, and motioned to Faren. "Please show me how to work this thing."

Faren joined Nazarine in the cubicle and touched a small green rectangle. "You're on. What do you want to know?"

"Dorje said the poison she used was associated with a place

called Heliarcos. We have to start with some assumption; I will assume they came from there."

Faren nodded, saying, "I would suspect as much . . . here, we'll insert the code for Gazeteer, yes, and here, Heliarcos, and initiate scan, and go. Read.

On the screen of the console, writing began flowing into view, beginning at the bottom of the screen and moving upward as more lines filled in below:

HELIARCOS (Orig. "HEMIARCTOS"), Second planet of Theta Palinuri system, which consists of. . . .

Faren pressed in PASS. The screen cleared, and started printing again:

History: Discovered 1366 Lerone Tuzjuoglu, it was rated marginal-habitable and initially surveyed by mining interests who located suitable grounds of Lanthanide-series rare earths, (assays which see), and exploited under charter of Hector-Grovius Metals Ltd. . . .

Faren pressed PASS again, but this time only for a little. She said, "Doubt mine poobahs would go to so much trouble. They are a direct sort, dispensing with poisons and plots at the first. Prospectors, likewise. Let's see who else is there. We can always come back."

The St. Aristides Society established a scholarly retreat, soon followed by other bodies. Their successes soon encouraged other groups to do likewise, and several faculties were founded, these bodies gradually asserting greater degrees of autonomy from their parent bodies, and eventaully becoming independent *de facto* if not, in all cases, *de jure*. Notable among contemporary institutions are (see under separate cover, Higher Education) Hudson-Brunner Institute, Hubbard College, Velikovsky Foundation, Hammer School of the Arts, Graham Theological Seminary, Wu Wang Society, Zed Aleph Tav Group (Setzer Memorial Division), as well as numerous smaller units treating with restricted technological areas, such as . . .

*   *   *

Faren pressed in PAUSE. She said, "This looks awfully dry. What are we looking for?"

Nazarine leaned back for a moment, thinking. Then, "Hormone research. Also something in the psychology-sociology-anthropology area."

"Why those?"

"The people I am looking for work in those areas, and have been for a long time. Find an organization that does both, in some depth."

"Hmm . . . let's see. We will want to list them all, according to known specialties, which would show up in notable publications. Also. . . . Wait a moment, this will be a little tricky, and will take up a lot of print space. I'll have it print a hard copy. So. . . ." She rapidly pressed in a series of commands, and shortly, a strip of paper began unrolling from the printer slot.

It seemed that the researchers and students of Heliarcos had been both numerous and busy. Some of the institutions which produced the most intense efforts were hardly notable as major institutions, while others seemed to scatter area studies all over the academic subject list. Most of the major ones had active psychology and anthropology departments, with sociology running a poor third. One medical school, The Reich School, was especially strong in endocrinology and related topics but seemed to have no other areas of interest.

The list that confronted them was both long and highly detailed, and they had to read through it, noting likely candidates. But in the end, they found one. Pompitus Hall. Faren went back to the console and requested a detailed description, to be printed on hard copy. The printer began rolling.

19

"There is no such creature as a realist: that is only another pose, another fantasy, for all are dreamers and fantasists. We do not opt to dream or not to dream, but rather select from a catalogue of fictions. Some of these are more worthy than others, doubtless, in the sense of being productive or the opposite, to be destructive to

self or others, but this utilitarianism has no bearing on the reality of the projection. This one pursues Business— that one, political action and social goals; this one seeks sensual gratification and strews broken hearts behind like fallen leaves, that one cultivates a voice that would worm a dog; this one tinkers with automobiles and that one writes novels—it doesn't matter which, Fords or Chevrolets, or romances or science fiction. We are all on the endless sea and the only thing that matters is the skill of our sailing. Therefore identify the dream and you have identified the person and their aims. Outer reflects inner, as electrons match the number of protons in the nucleus. Ionizations are special exceptions. Some people live in very strange worlds indeed, and often the most bizarre of them all are those who seem the most ordinary at first glance. Or as the mad poet avers, 'secure behind the masks of their automobiles, I have seen their mad faces gleaming in the twilight, the spittle flying in the throes of their rage.' ''

Faren finished reading the print the terminal had provided and handed it back to Nazarine. ''That would seem to be the one you are looking for. Hormones, biochemistry, and related disciplines, and then, oddly, an extremely heavy social sciences concentration.''

''It's the only one that displays that particular mix.''

''Well, yes, that; but the clincher was 'Conducts unspecified field research under Beneficial Grant 377Y.' And when we ran that one down, turns out to be a charitable grant of The Alytra Foundation, which in turn is owned wholly by Bogatyr Mining, whose stockholders are the Regents of Pompitus Hall. I should say a nice setup, if one wished to do questionable things.''

''Questionable things indeed.''

''What was going on, back there on that world you came from? And what are you, that they should single you out?''

''They were conducting some of that unspecified field research on that world. All on the quiet, hidden by a very clever double-blind system that gave them a place to work on something without anyone asking questions. I don't doubt they stumbled on Oerlikon by accident, in the beginning. But they took it over, and used it both as a place to obtain raw human material for their experiments, and as an overflow point for their own personnel, who wished to retire, or who were relieved of duty.''

Faren looked at the print again. ''What were they working for?''

Nazarine shook her head. ''I don't know for certain. I have had some suspicions, but ultimately, none seems to fit. What I think they were originally trying to do was find a way to fuse the nervous system and the hormone system under one conscious mind. But they were caught by a revolution, which wasn't even directed at them, and even after the old order had been overturned, they were more or less ignored. How ironic. Where I fit in this is a longer story than I can tell you, because there are some missing pieces I don't have yet. I think I have the basic outline of it, but I'm still working on the details. Suffice it to say that I was originally one of them. Who found out what the real purpose of the Oerlikon Operation was, and made some waves about it. And was disposed of into their research station, there. They called it 'The Mask Factory,' on the streets, because inside it one underwent changes.''

Faren said, softly, ''You were changed. . . .''

''To a degree you may not be able to manage to believe. But yes; So indeed I was. I was not supposed to have survived, and I was not supposed to have remembered. I did both. And so they sent those two after me, to finish the job. Apparently, in my original identity, I knew a lot about their procedures, and could have damaged their program.''

''You haven't recovered it; I know people. You have a strangeness about you, a fey quality, but not that kind of purpose.''

''I recovered *that* it was; not *what* it was the original knew. That is gone forever, lost. All I have left of that is sometimes a rightness about the way things feel—or a wrongness. The barest shreds of the echoes of a personality. What you see and feel is me, not some stranger.''

Faren straightened, standing away from the console. ''Well, so be it. You are fine, as you are. Nor do I blame you for being desirous of a revenge: indeed an excellent idea! But also consider: These are people who, whatever their origins, stepped over the line, saying then, 'the rules don't apply to us.' That's not an idle pleasure-seeker or fun-seeker speaking at that point, but a criminal, and they are not reticent about using criminal methods— spies and assassins. They have a certain measure of power and will not happily suffer threats. How much damage can you do them, one person, against, in essence, a University, a sophisticated Financial Management Company, and a mining Trust?"

Nazarine said calmly, "For now, you must take it on faith, but I have the ability to end them. All. My problem is that I do not wish the blow to fall on innocents, too."

"Most wouldn't care one way or the other."

"I know what happens when you don't. I have used it before, without worrying overmuch about the consequences to the innocent."

"All right. What if you can't get a clear shot at them?"

"I suppose I'll have to give it up."

"Are you serious?"

"Yes. Absolute limits. We have to have them."

"What would you do—I mean, for a living?"

"File reports to Clisp, I suppose, about the strangeness of the rest of the universe. I don't have an income, but they pay my expenses—at least for now. That was my last arrangement with the only home I can remember."

"You mentioned a little of that in passing a couple of times. But what are you going to do now?"

Nazarine looked upward at the blank walls and thought for a moment. Eventually she sighed and said, "I want to try to make some kind of contact with Kham. And I want to do a reading before we try it. A hard one, a deep one."

"You want me to leave you alone for a while?"

"A little while. But come back. Please."

Faren nodded. "I understand—leave it to me. I can run an errand while you are working on it."

"What sort of errand?"

"I'll go collect a small assistant."

"What sort of assistant?"

"A surprise. Leave a few of them for me, will you? And don't push it too hard while I'm gone—where you are going next, you are going to need all the alertness you can manage."

Faren turned and left. For a moment, Nazarine sat very still at the console and stared at the keyboard. She thought, *I could use this thing to do some of the routine steps in the reading I am about to do. But that is the deadly way, isn't it? I can always shut it off, but once you create this kind of logic in a machine, there's no way to turn it off. That's the analogue of what they ran into when they created me—Rael. The Monster's out of control*. Nazarine managed a wintry smile, which she could see a little of in the reflections on the console screen. But no. *This monster's under deeper controls than they ever imagined*. There was some blank paper by the machine. Nazarine took the sheaf of it and began carefully laying out the questions she wanted to ask of it, this time the full divination, if one could call it that. She knew she wouldn't be finished by the time Kiricky got back, but hopefully, she would have the hardest parts of it done with by then, with just the routine fill-ins left. It was a shame, having to force it this way, without the data she wanted to put in it, but she felt the subterranean pressure of time passing working on her. Even without actually doing the exercise, she could sense that Kham was fading, fading. She could sense it directly without going through the formal procedure. Yes, that, and she was beginning to sense how she affected events around her, too. *It's not a gift*, she thought. *It's an unbearable weight. I will work harder to suppress it than an ordinary person would labor to attain it*.

She settled on the first question, and even as she began to assemble it within the symbolic formulae she used, she could see that the three questions she was to ask were in reality phases on the same question. In their parts, they asked: What is the method to reach Pompitus Hall? What is to be done with Kham? And what am I to do with myself? She changed a line here, adjusted a symbol there. Yes. All one unity, one question.

Nazarine finished the final strokes of the ideogram, this one intricate beyond anything she had ever done before, but for all its baroque richness of detail, there was no partitioning of it: it was One Answer. She drew back a little and looked at it as a whole. She shook her head, slowly, and then released her breath slowly. She had been holding it for so long she couldn't remember when she had last drawn a breath. Yes. The way was clear, absolute, no doubt, and there could be no hesitation. It followed the outlines Rael had discovered and put into such ruthless practice: All the time since Rael, and even with him, even then, she had looked for a way to negate the limits and demands required by this form of . . . what? Knowing? Divination? Operation on living societies, a form of vivisection? Here, knowing and doing were one, and the observer intruded upon the observed, and affected it, powerfully. She could do it. She had enough to act on. The moment was now. The focus was soft, but not especially blurred. Another shot at it wouldn't come for a long time . . . maybe never. Yes, it would work, and yes, there would be minimal effect on bystanders. It worked just as it had in Lisagor. But of course there was a price. She took another deep breath. *Very well.*

The door chimed, and Nazarine reached around and touched the release switch inside the console cubicle. Faren Kiricky came into the room, followed by one of the lithe gray shapes of the doglike Lenosz.

She stood and said, "This was your surprise."

Faren smiled. "Yes. I borrowed one from the patrol that was out in a pattern for Kham. This one has the scent."

"You know how to handle one?"

"Of course. Don't worry—they are not naturally vicious, but they are extremely good trackers, and we do use them now and then for that. We have made formal agreement, after the manner of Lenosz."

Nazarine looked closely at the sleek, limber animal, now resting on its hindquarters and looking up at Faren with its soft chocolate eyes. This one was large, despite its sleekness and svelte lines, which made it seem smaller. On closer inspection it seemed less doglike. That shape and the recollection it suggested in the human mind was an accident and an illusion. The paws were more handlike than any dog's could have been, and instead of a dewclaw there was a small, but fully opposable thumb, and although it did walk digitigrade, the paws, or hands, more properly, seemed deft enough to grasp and to handle.

Faren followed her eyes, and said, "Yes, it can climb. Will you need a weapon?"

"No. I have what I need."

"Ready?"

"Yes."

"Did you find what you were looking for?"

"Yes."

"You will do it."

"Yes. Everything is clear."

"Well . . . let's go."

Sometimes he thought he was in immense spaces which were almost filled with the systems that kept the ship a living and moving object. There was no solid wall ending this interior support system labyrinth at all. It was all support. The world the passengers thought they moved through was nothing but a carefully prepared illusion, miniature living environments controlled and ministered to by miles of feed lines, rec sumps, HVAC flow lines and ducts, breeder vats for bacteria which had in turn viral controls. He could not remember seeing a ship from the outside, nor could he remember seeing a diagram of one. Sometimes he laughed to himself, and whispered that the reality was that the whole universe was in fact a support network, in which were imbedded small and limited little spaces in which people (and possibly other sorts of creatures) moved and imagined that what they saw was all there was.

And sometimes, in his travels, the surrounding free space compressed into tiny crawlways so narrow one had to slip through them sideways, or else so low one had to get down on one's belly and crawl like a reptile. There was something on the other sides of the bulkheads, but he could not determine what those somethings were.

And alternately, sometimes he came close to the passenger spaces of one class or another, or perhaps portions of the crew space. A long gray corridor, which he observed through a floor level vent grille. He had watched for a long time, but no one had passed along that corridor. Nor had there been any sound. (He had thought himself safe, and allowed himself a short catnap.) A large, communal dining room, more like a mess hall than anything else. Rows of plain metal tables, casual diners coming and going, a loose camaraderie in effect. Crew? Something even lower than steerage? Higher than the highest he could imagine? An arcade, where people stood in tight ranks and pitted their skill against electronic and mechanical games, but the most popular of all the games was a simple mechanical one in which one fired a ball-bearing to the top of an obstacle course of little pins and wheels. Vertical. The cascading balls made a bright and tinkly sound and the patrons stood enraptured, putting their all into the release of the spring, hoping for the correct collection pocket at the bottom, exulting when they won, groaning when they lost.

Walking onto the ship from the lighter, he believed that it had been arranged in actual levels, one atop the other, or maybe one in front of the other, like soldiers in a line ('Tighten that line up, soldier, until the man in front of you *smiles*!'). Yes, levels. That was the word. Levels. But seen from this side, air, warmth, coolness, water, sewage, power, communications, structure, there seemed to be no order whatsoever: the levels were all mixed together, and the differences were actually only in the minds of the passengers.

For some time, he had followed the route indicators which he sometimes found at major junctions, but these proved not to be uniformly dependable. And as he had burrowed deeper and deeper into the real workings of the ship, he had gradually lost his conception of reference. Kham could neither remember meaningfully where he had been, nor conceive meaningfully where he wished to go. Therefore the schematics and route designations were totally meaningless. The ship was a sphere, including within its volume an unspecified number of smaller spheres or ovoidal areas. Once, he had found a dim and scratched transparent panel, of some sort of polycarbonate material which did not give when he pressed on it. Inside, poorly visible, had been people working at some kind of controls, a large console completely filled with meters, readouts, graphics, switches, keyboards, touchplates. They all seemed at ease, but also intent on their work, engaged in it, not just passing time. Something to do with the ship, he thought, but he also thought that the actions didn't look terribly different from those people playing games in the arcade. Maybe the rules were different.

But those were secondary problems now. He had, in his travels, noted a major junction, and threaded his way to a catwalk leading to it. Approaching, he had seen a number of people, and had gone forward with anticipation, knowing that here, at least, he would be able to find something out. But the light had been poor, and as he had drawn nearer, he had seen that they were dressed either in rags or borrowed things which fit them poorly, when at all. There had been six of them. They ignored his emergence into the junction, which Kham thought curious until it dawned on him that they probably had heard him coming a long time. He had gone to the food locker, but it was empty. They moved aside to let him go to it. And closed behind him.

Kham had tried to speak, his voice strangely loud and raspy after long disuse. They had not answered, but made quick, flickering and lambent glances at each other, and rarely at him. He remembered their words, which made no sense whatsoever:

—Pisha boot?

—Da-la dum-li totchel 'orosha.

—Da pisha, Seich' Zakwat im!

And the six of them had all stepped forward, and their attitudes had not been those of friends, but of animals closing on prey. Kham remembered his training, and slipped into a relaxed slump, from which he could move easily, by relaxing. He had a wall behind him, man's best friend. The first one to come forward had been kicked in the crotch, the body rebounding to lay on the grating, where it emitted an odd series of multilingual cries, a strange, borrowed half-language, half jargon, half animal subvocalizations. *"O ti malalacula! Bolezin! Bomogi, beysti!"* it had cried.

The others had drawn back a little, eyes glittering like those of feral insects. They were impressed, but not daunted. Two others had moved as one, from opposite sides. Kham pulled them to him and cracked their heads together. Both fell. One lay on the grating, making swimming motions and twitching his feet, while the other one lay still with blood oozing from his ears. The rest stepped back, eyes alive, darting, their bodies moving slowly, deliberately, the stuff of nightmares. And gradually they moved back, out of the light of the single dim bulb and a few illuminated panels.

Since then, he had moved quietly, making certain he made as little noise as possible, but he never lost the crawling sensation that somewhere off in the jungle of pipes and ducts someone—or someones—was watching him, following him, at a distance.

Now he approached groups he saw warily. He would catch glimpses of people, ghostly shadows by a lighted junction point, but when he got there, they would all be gone. Vanished, as if they had never been. He allowed himself short little catnaps, after finding places he felt more secure in than along the open catwalks where one could be seen from above, below, and also from the sides. But never long. He would catch himself nodding, and set his head upright with a jerk. He sometimes saw lights when there were none. Odd clusters of moving lights. They were waiting for him, out there in the well-lighted open spaces through which the passengers and crew moved so easily, so unconsciously. And in here, they were waiting for him, too. There was not too much difference, subjectively, in the final result in either case, save that one would transpire with solemn ceremony and judicial pronouncements, while the other would be with grunts and howls and the smacking of unclean lips.

But Kham reasoned that if he could survive long enough, down here, he might in time come to gain a measure of security.

For one thing seemed certain: those above did not pursue those
who went below, nor did they seem to harass those few who
stayed below. There, it was surrender. Here, he had a chance.
But then he remembered to ask himself: why didn't they follow
people below?

Faren led Nazarine and the Lenosz, first along some passageways which seemed innocuous enough, although they seemed to
lead nowhere; these soon became both narrow and empty, and
after a short walk, terminated in a heavy metal door which
operated from a single handwheel set in its center.

"Here we are. Can you read the graffito scratched in above
the door, on the lintel, as it were?"

Nazarine moved closer, stretched, stood on tiptoe. She read,
" 'Abandon all hope, ye who enter here.' "

Faren chuckled. "A wit among the crew at some time. That
was supposed to be the inscription over the gates of hell. This is
one of the legitimate entrances. Work the wheel and go. But
from the other side—now that's different. It's a procedure even
for someone with a pass, like me. No pass—ah, well, one
creates a problem. All the legitimate accesses have traps built
into them; you have to walk into the trap to operate the identification system. Blow it, and they come and collect you. So we
don't have unwanted visitors."

"There are other places they could come out, I'm sure."

"They don't. There are very few of them in there, and the
ones who survive don't want to come back. That's probably a
crucial reason why they survive."

"How many are in there, do you think?"

"No more than thirty, probably less than twenty. Somewhere
in that range. Might be as high as fifty—but I doubt that."

"How do you know?"

"Rate of ration turnover. There are drop points throughout the
system where ration packets are dropped off—the system refills
itself automatically. Shipcomputer estimates how many are probably alive based on the rate of turnover."

"What's the food for?"

"For us, when we get in a job we can't stop. You get a
problem down in the system, you don't stop until it's fixed."

"So you've been in here before."

"Several times too many."

"And you know it reasonably well?"

"There are some that know it better but they wouldn't take you in."

Faren turned the wheel and the door swung open. Inside was a bare little chamber, lit by a single panel, which gave off a dim light compared with the corridor lights. They went inside, and the outer door closed behind them, latched itself, and locked. "Now we're in." She turned to a panel, laid her hand on it, and spoke rapidly into a small dull spot on the wall, a string of numbers and letters. On the other side, a panel simply swung open, and there was a deeper darkness beyond. They stepped out onto a metal grating platform. Stairs led down in two directions.

Faren looked around and then indicated the left stairwell. "We'll start this way. There's a connection down below where we can move along fairly rapidly, and farther on, we'll see if this overfed pooch can pick up a scent. A long way."

Nazarine said nothing. Faren led the way, and the Lenosz followed behind, several paces back, at first moving along easily, as if on some errand of its own, but gradually it became wary, its nostrils flared delicately, and its ears swivelled and turned, searching for sounds. As they descended into the guts of the ship, the open space closed in and began to fill with piping and machinery. Most of the machinery was incomprehensible to Nazarine, but it appeared as if this particular area was a sort of node where the different support flows were collected and re-routed. Some of the larger devices made noises. Others made none. They passed many indicator panels, covered with readouts, meters, generated graphs on CRTs, and simple colored lights; amber, green, red, violet, blue, orange, yellow. Then they were at the bottom, at least as far down as they were going now. There was a ladder off to the side descending still farther.

This was a broad walkway, solid underfoot, with a cleated surface, wider than Nazarine could reach. Here they set out at a hard walk. The lighting was very poor, consisting of single glow-tubes set inside thick covers, about every fifty meters. On the left was a wall of welded metal, almost covered by layers of piping and the square-section shapes of waveguides. It looked to Nazarine like a wall of the outside world of a surface, overgrown by a dense mosaic of vines, but set into a rigid, surrealistic pattern. To the right was open space, but mostly filled with larger ducting, or platforms on which sat junction boxes, machines of enigmatic function, pumps, repeaters. Then she concentrated on walking, and they walked hard for a very long time. The scenery, if one could call it that, did not change.

It seemed to Nazarine they had been walking for about an hour, more or less, some of which had been through relatively long, straight sections, similar to that which they had passed through after entering. Other sections had been ramps, elevators, drop-shafts and spirals descending, ascending. Faren strode along with the quiet authority of one who knew her way well, and along the way she had made little or no comment. Nazarine had no idea where they were in relation to any other part of the ship, and said so.

Faren stopped, and said quietly, "We've been descending along the main tracks. Sooner or later the fugitives always do this. It's easier. The various passenger areas are near the outside layer, crew deeper, control still deeper. As you go deeper, there are more control zones, more security. That is why we don't worry so much about stowaways roaming about. We are now beneath the economy section where Kham first operated from."

"Why here?"

"Good a place as any to pick up a trail. Hst! Note the Lenosz!"

Nazarine looked about, but in the subterranean gloom she failed to catch sight of the creature, which had sidled around them and now quested and ranged nervously back and forth, nostrils flared and held high. Faren nodded, approvingly. "Got a scent, it did." She made a peculiar motion with her left arm and hand, and the Lenosz came to her, making undulating motions with its slender body, as if trying to swim, nodding its head abruptly upward. Faren said, "Not old, not fresh. Passed along here, crossing. He has fear, now." She made another motion, pressing her palms together and counter-rotating them, briskly. "I told it to follow. Slow, so we can be close. Come on, and be alert, now."

The Lenosz loped off, following an air-scent for the most part, only occasionally inspecting the side walls or the deck, almost as if it felt such a crude method of scent-following was distasteful. Presently it paused at a landing, which led to a metal openwork stairs leading down into a deeper darkness. Faren made a short, sweeping motion with her hand, and the Lenosz stepped out on the openwork gingerly, placing its delicate feet gently and purposefully, so as to avoid stepping through the open spaces. Faren and Nazarine followed.

For the next stage of their journey, Nazarine opened her own senses to the strange environment listening, watching, smelling. The odors were mostly slightly stale, suggestive of damp, and overlaid by an oily reek suggestive of machinery. They passed by several landings with hardly a pause; but at one, where there was one of the ration-cabinets, they stopped, while the Lenosz carefully investigated the landing and junction with meticulous attention to every point along the walls and floor. Faren commented, in a quiet, breathy voice barely above a whisper, "Stopped here, rested, then left in a hurry. Recently."

The Lenosz continued quartering about, but Nazarine caught a shred of movement out of the corner of her eye. She looked at the place, and then away, remembering peripheral vision was better at catching motion in such uncertain half-light. She kept her eyes slightly averted, and said, in a whisper, "We have company. There, to the right, beyond that row of orange pipes."

Faren looked. When she did, the visitors, understanding that they had been sighted, made no further attempt to conceal themselves, and stood out in the open. They could see four clearly, and to Nazarine, it seemed as if they made small, betraying motions that suggested more, somewhere beyond, out of sight.

Faren seemed not to notice. She said, "They'll come to us, to parley. I see four. We can handle that." The four made their way soundlessly toward them, climbing, sometimes walking normally, sometimes clambering over and through obstructions, as if they had had long practice. And though soundless, they moved so as to remain in view constantly. Faren watched them closely, as did the Lenosz, but Nazarine felt a wrongness, a pressure. It was too obvious, too open. She turned her face toward the newcomers, but continued to scan all around, above, below, listening behind, letting an animal sort of fear drive her, but not master her. The four finally emerged from behind a massive vertical girder and stood in a group.

They were clothed in rags and scraps that might once have been clothing. A woman and three men, judging by the shaggy beards on three of them. They were wary as animals. Faren, continuing to observe them, said, "These are long-timers. Be wary." She removed a slim baton from her coverall, where she had concealed it. Flexible and limber, it became rigid when she grasped the handle. She then spoke rapidly, using an argot

Nazarine could not follow. It was no language she could remember or recall, but whatever it was, it was full of hesitations, pauses, odd reduplications of certain sound-groups. It suggested a pidgin form of a speech that had once had a full and an elegant repertoire, now reduced to a minimal set.

The members of the group replied, in an offhand, disorganized manner, as if time had no meaning for them. Languid, affected, although speaking the same, oddly broken speech. She also saw extremely brief eye-flickers darting back and forth among them, independent of the words they uttered, and she tuned herself to an even higher pitch. *There*, she thought, feeling habits she associated with Rael come back easily. *Above, in the piping. Very well. Let it be.* She looked hard at the group.

Nazarine sensed a soft, barely audible motion from above, and felt a puff of air, and then pressure about her arms, pinning her. She was ready, had inhaled deeply and held her arms rigid. Now she exhaled, pulled her arms tight, and fell out of the grasp. She grasped the arms with her hands and pulled, hard, and the attacker, already off-balance began toppling forward, trying to regain balance and break their arms free. Nazarine slammed its face down onto the metal floor, levered it aside, gained her feet and stamped its windpipe flat. There was no time to see further to it, for two had grappled Faren, one turning toward her, as if in slow motion. Baring a long knife, obviously ground down from some scrap. With a motion she stepped close, almost dancing, brushing the knife-arm aside and striking with the heel of her free hand, directly onto its sternum, which shattered under the impact. The other, struggling with Faren, swung around, and Nazarine leaped up, reaching for the pipes she knew were there, finding them, getting leverage, and kicking while pivoting her hips. The other one's neck broke with an audible snap.

Still thinking as Rael, she took a quick inventory of those left. The four they had first seen had stepped closer, to be in on the spoil, but now they turned, were turning to vanish off into the night, the darkness. Nazarine swung, hand over hand, and dropped in the midst of them, felling two with simultaneous forearm blows. In one, she felt a collarbone snap, and in the other, the tendons holding the head up tore. She seized the woman of the group by her long, greasy hair and pulled her off her feet, feeling about half the hair give way. This one she swung to the deck and she quickly performed a series of manipulations to vital nerve centers, during which the woman emitted a series of surprised subvocalized grunts and sudden plangent cries of agony. At last, she lay on the floor, eyes vacant and glassy, but still breathing. Nazarine said, in a harsh voice, "Ask her what you will!" She drew a deep breath, held it, and cleared her lungs. Seven had become two, and one of those was a captive.

Faren shook her head, and bent over the woman. She looked at Nazarine. "What did you do to her?"

"Made her more cooperative. Now speak with her. She won't live long!"

Faren bent over the woman, looked at the glassy eyes, and whispered something in the strange, broken pidgin speech. The woman replied, like an automaton, tonelessly, at some length, and then expired, rolling her eyes back into their sockets in a ghastly fashion. Faren breathed deeply, and said, "They were hunting Kham, or so I think one who fits his eidolon. Down and not far ahead. They herd them with a small advance group, and the main party closes in. This was the main group. They thought we would make a small diversion before they took Kham. They feared him—he was held to be a great fighter, having already bested Aquarius Beasley the Bandit."

She stood up and added, "And this was an old band, one of the oldest and most adept. And you destroyed them within seconds. What in Hellviter are you?"

Nazarine shook her head, wiped her hands on her pants. "Less than successful. One got away. I have allowed myself to go slack; of old, I could have had them all and caught at least three for conversation."

The two she had injured were still where they had fallen. The one with a broken collarbone was trying to crawl away, but the other one was dead. Apparently she had also broken its neck. They turned to the single survivor. When it sensed that they were coming for him, it squirmed to the edge of the walkway, and rolled over the side without hesitating. In silence it fell, and they heard it strike objects on the way down, a series of hard, ringing, metallic blows, accompanied only by grunts, at first, and then by only silence, as it continued falling. At last, the sodden sounds stopped, far below. The echoes died away.

Nazarine said, "You see? Not that one either."

Faren stepped back a little, and asked her again, "What are you, that you could do that?"

Nazarine looked away, and said reluctantly, "Long ago, I was made to bring misery into the world. I did not desire it, but I had no other way to be free of those who held me. I did my one crime, and I have been trying to escape them since, and trying to become an ordinary person who might live her life out in peace, to know the direct pleasures and pains. Kham was somehow related to those who set me on this path. . . ." She allowed the sentence to trail off, with no definite ending.

"You're not telling everything."

"No, but I will. Soon. But first, we have to find Kham before they do. We may be reduced to the disgusting expedient of saving him from these cannibals."

"What will you do when you've talked to him?"

"Let him go."

"I don't understand."

"I said I knew what I had to do. I *read* what must be, for the pattern I want to fulfill itself. In that, for everything to work, I must permit Kham to follow his own destiny out to the end. You understand? For what I want to come true, I have to let him go. And there is one other thing I have to do."

"What is that?"

"Not yet, Faren. You and I will do one more thing, and you, who have given me so much, will give me one more thing."

20

"If you stop planting trees because you think you won't be around to see them grow up, then you are already dead."

—H. C., Atropine

They found Kham without too much difficulty, letting the Lenosz lead them by scent: along a narrow way off the junction, down a ramp, along a slanted catwalk, and down a spiral to another junction, this one a plain one on a grating deck without food or water. Here the advance party of the stowaway tribe had closed in on Kham and pinned him down. They had all the exits covered, save one, and along that one they had expected to see their own people coming along that way. Perhaps it had become too easy. This one they had cornered at last had seemed to give up wanting to go on farther. Still, it was dangerous. It half-stood, half-slumped against a circuit box, with heavy eyes that did not look directly up, but glanced off sideways, downwards. And so they waited. Patiently. This one knew what was coming, and had chosen this place—as good as any other—to meet his last engagement. No point in rushing things; they had seen this condition before. They would all come, and wait for the moment.

Nazarine and Faren and the Lenosz walked openly, no longer muffling their footsteps, and came down the final slant into the junction unhesitatingly. Faren glanced around, into the shadows, away from this chamber, and spoke quickly in the pidgin language of the underworld. For a long moment, there was no sound or movement, so she repeated some of what she had said. And one by one, silently, eerily as ghosts, the shadows became empty. The band departed.

Kham looked at them dully, almost as if he did not recognize them, although certainly he did. Faren and the Lenosz made a careful circuit of the chamber, and then retired to the entrance to one of the walkways. She said, "Here he is: cornered like a rat. Do as you must."

Kham looked up, now, and focused his eyes directly on Nazarine.

She said, "I am the one you have been working so hard to find."

Kham nodded, slowly. He said, after a moment, in a soft voice full of resignation, "You differ somewhat from how I imagined you, even though I saw you on the Beamliner. You are something that does not confine within an identity-imago."

Nazarine stepped closer. "That's what multiple personalities in sequence does to one. Different people animate my face, make motions with my body. I imagine you know about that well enough."

"Rael we had reports on; Damistofia less. Phaedrus hardly at all—he was difficult to track down. You have proven impossible. You distort probabilities just by existing."

"I know."

"How much control have you been using?"

"I have been trying to escape it. That started way back, in Marula. I would have disengaged, then. You people wouldn't let me. The early ones I came to understand. But you people wouldn't stop. There was only one answer for it—it did not really require *the art* to find it. But I still don't have it confirmed why."

Kham sighed deeply, and ended it with a chuckle, which turned into a sudden racking cough. Then, "You know who you were?"

"Yes. I tracked it down. Jedily Tulilly, one of your own people."

He said, shrewdly, "You haven't recovered all of it, or you wouldn't risk the pits to ask me."

"I have recovered enough; I know where you come from, and I know their real product. I can guess easily enough—Jedily saw the true purpose of Oerlikon and Lisagor, and tried to report it—to whoever she thought might stop it. But that world your people had victimized, exploited, parasitized for untold cycles, you had become as dependent on it as it on you. So Jedily was erased, and dumped in the Mask Factory for Pternam to dispose of, or wear out. I suppose I could say I owed you for that one, too, but it wouldn't change anything I would now do."

Kham agreed. "I wasn't there, but you have me here, handy enough."

"Do you know what happened to Jedily?"

"In truth, no. I was told that if we succeeded, we would find out in the course of time, by the time we became regents of the faculty."

"So you went forth, solely on orders from those who did know?"

"I suppose that would cover it. You realize, there never was anything personal in it—it was just part of the job."

Nazarine nodded. "I understand. That is what makes this whole thing so vile—that it was just a job. To get personal— that's where realities are—love and hate alike. When you get personal, you limit. It's when you say, 'It's just a job,' that the real devil enters into it. So you understand that it's personal with me, not just a job."

"So you'll go on and do it, then?"

"Do what?"

"Take your revenge on me and go on to turn the furies loose on Heliarcos."

"As for you, I intend doing nothing. When I leave this place, you are free. And as for them, I have already set that in motion. I don't need to go *there* to end their criminal tenure. I didn't need to leave Oerlikon to do that; I can reach as far as I need. I left Oerlikon to make sure I could get away from you people. And others like you.''

Kham said coldly, ''You will never escape people like me; we are everywhere—we make things run. And there are others dispatched, as well, I am sure. And we know something of how you make it work.''

''You say there'll be others, other efforts.''

''Of course.''

''Well, you won't die, so you can go back and tell them you failed.''

Kham smiled, but the facial configuration he made was a rictus that had absolutely nothing to do with humor in any ordinary sense. ''All so well for you to say. Charity: Caritas, to speak the ancient word. Generous, doubtless. All you do is leave me down here. Up there, they are waiting for me. A fine freedom.''

Nazarine looked slightly to the side, as if bemused. ''No, it won't be like that. You will go back topside, and by the time you get there, you'll be free. To report, to return to Heliarcos, or to run to the end of the universe—whatever suits you.''

''How will you arrange that?''

''You don't need to worry about that. Or you can stay down here, if you like.''

''Not much choice there. Hobson would be ecstatic.''

''The ones you forced on me were no better.''

''Going back . . . now there's a real barbed gift. But you know that.''

''Of course. I've put you, alive and fully cognizant, into a place you can't escape from, and you'll know it every moment. This is a lot more satisfactory. And understand this, Kham: any way you move—any way whatsoever, including the choice of not to move at all, will set in motion the chain of events I need to validate Jedily. But only if I leave you this way. And so I bid you good-bye. Enjoy your freedom.'' And then, without pausing, she turned and left the junction point, motioning to Faren to follow her.

Nazarine set out at a hard walk, going back the way they had come, and she did not look back. Faren remained in place for a moment, and then turned and followed Nazarine. It was some time before she caught up with her, and when she did, Nazarine put a finger to her lips, indicating silence. She whispered, ''Show me a way away from here, as far as possible, someplace where he can't follow.''

Faren nodded, and motioned to her, saying, "Follow me."

Faren led them, as she had indicated, along a series of paths through the maintways, using pass-doors, which she knew Kham would not follow, not returning to the upper parts of the ship, but moving across, and slightly downward, even deeper into the bowels of the ship. At length, they arrived at a security door, which Faren opened without difficulty, and they passed through, into a small, spartan cubicle.

Faren let the Lenosz in, and closed the door. She gestured with her hand about the small room, a complete habitation in miniature. "Is this secure enough?"

"This is secure?"

"It's a refuge-point—where we can go to escape harassment. There's a direct line back. Now you tell me: what was all that you told him? He can't go back. There's a warrant out for him, and it won't be cancelled until he's out.''

Nazarine smiled. "But if you had it solved, and reported a confession, then Kham would be free.''

"Maybe. But I have no such confession.''

"We can make one up.''

"Would you please explain what you are trying to do? I thought you wanted to hunt him down!''

"He's an arrow that I'll launch into flight—an arrow that will strike precisely at the point where it's needed most. But for that to work, there has to be a . . . giving-up. You understand? The kinds of things I can do require a life to energize them. That is why I kept seeing in my readings that I couldn't touch Kham; he was to be my weapon. And I was to be the energy. I couldn't face that, and so I wrote it off as an unknown I couldn't understand. But it was there all along. It is true that I have a power to change things, an absolute power such as no one has ever wielded before. But by using it to achieve ends, I cannot continue as I am and realize those ends. I can create a new universe, but the act of creation locks me-as-I-am out of it.''

Faren shook her head, and sat on the edge of one of the plain bunks in the refuge-room. She said, "I would have claimed you were deranged, had you said this earlier. But I have seen you read, and I saw you fight, and I never saw anything like that before. So you may be as you say. But what do you require of me?''

"You will clear Kham of charges by reporting that I confessed to a crime of passion and then exited the ship into transitspace."

"What is going to happen to you?"

"That's the rest of it. In one sense, I will vanish; in another sense, you will have me longer than you've had anyone else in your life. And that is what I have to ask you if you'll do, and to do that, I have to tell you the truth about who and what I am."

Faren nodded thoughtfully. "Go on. I'm listening."

"It's like this: Kham spoke of other names, you heard him. Jedily, Rael, Damistofia, Phaedrus. I was all those people."

"You wore a disguise. . . ."

"No disguise. I *was* them, in every way. And who I am now, this was the best of all and I give it up with great pain. But here is how it happened, and why you must do this . . ." And she began at the beginning, retelling the story, not as it had grudgingly revealed itself, but as she had reconstructed it, in sequence, beginning far back, before Jedily Tulilly, even, explaining, clarifying. Faren leaned back on the bunk and closed her eyes, to better visualize the things Nazarine told her, and the Lenosz curled up on the floor and placed its head on its paws.

". . . and that's how it fits together. I've told you all of it."

Faren opened her eyes, shook her head slightly, and said, "All right. Let's say I accept this tale, and everything that will result from this. Let's say it. So, then—why me?"

"In part, it's something I have read you would do. It's there, in the fabric, for anyone who has the skill or the curse I do to see; you never told me, but what you did tell me of your life, along the ways we have gone, weaves a fabric whose pattern extends into that area. You know the truth of that even as I say it—see this in your face by the most ordinary means."

Faren accepted this with neither surprise nor refusal. She nodded coolly, and said, "So, then: why else?"

Nazarine pressed her lips together until all the color went out of them, collecting her thoughts. "It's like this: this is what we would do—an essentially irrational act. By the standards this universe operates by. Irrational. I will entrust my life and the powers they buried in me to a stranger. But consider this—that by following this course, completing the sequence I started with following and confronting Kham and letting him go free, I have engaged in an act of faith alone."

"Ha! I should say so, even for openers!"

"But balance that against Oerlikon and Heliarcos—reason extended without hindrance, and measure the strength of it against what I did to Lisagor. This is the theorem of Operation extended much further. To kill the lowest changes the whole—and on to this. If you choose to look at what I do as a kind of magic—it isn't, but it helps to see it that way—then I tell you this is the most complicated operation I ever attempted, and its resultants will change the entire human community. There will be no more Mask Factories, no more Morphodites, no more Pompitus Halls."

"First you. And then me."

"And then Dorje. You will tell him the truth, come one day, and him, too."

"But you'll be gone!"

"I won't. You'll always have me—all your life."

"But you won't be you anymore, just like you're not Rael, or Damistofia. I liked those things we all did together—it had a rightness, for once—all of it."

"You know what was right about it—then pass that on. I give you a vehicle to do that to, to continue it, to spread it. You'll never see it take root—that's centuries away. So you walk into a faith as great as mine."

Faren looked down, hiding her eyes beneath her eyebrows. She muttered, "I don't have enough of what you want."

"Yes, you do. You answered me when I called on you, and you gave more than I asked."

Faren looked up, her eyes bright. "You argue all too well. But you knew it would be this way . . ."

"I don't know any more about the next instant, the very next microsecond, than you do. I read NOWS. The Present is forever, a wave. What we do changes the wave if we so wish it. Just by wishing, by believing, by dreams. To seek only the rational to the exclusion of all else makes us prisoner of the underlying patterns that lie accidentally about and so scatter the wave into entropic fragments. Life itself stores energy against the grain; life-continuity reverses the entropy gradient. But through will and idea, faith and dream."

Faren shifted her position. "Well, all else aside, you have certainly changed me."

Nazarine said, "You changed me; I could not have found this course without you. And Dorje."

"What would you have done, elsewise?"

"Tracked Kham's source down to its roots, and destroyed it,

utterly, with misery on a much vaster scale than was done in Lisagor. But this is better.''

"I can understand that. Revenge is a poor source of inspiration for artists, so they say, and even more so to others.''

"We are all artists—it's just that we don't understand that yet.''

"You understand you are going to cause me all sorts of problems with the personnel section. . . . They may even offer me the option of paying off my profit-sharing, my lays, and putting me off at next port of call, which is Teragon.''

"I understand that. But you are skilled, in metallurgy and structures, joining and separating constructions, welding and cutting—those are the prime operations of alchemy—*solve et coagula*, or so the ship's computer tells me.''

"Yes.''

"They have need of you there. And Dorje . . . what would he miss there, and what more could he do?''

"No matter; we can survive well enough on Teragon. Probably better than aboard ship.''

"You never landed anywhere.''

"There was nothing to land for.''

"Now there is. Take it.''

"I will. What must we do?''

"Call in and isolate yourself for several days. Notify Dorje, but tell him nothing. This can't be sent over any comm link. Then be quiet and let me concentrate. After that, we'll have a few minutes, and then it's up to you. You know what's going to happen to me. The sequence will keep me alive while it's running, while I'm changing, but afterward I'll be helpless. I distorted it badly to get Nazarine, but dammit, I needed an adult body, not a subteen's. Now I've got to pay that debt back. I read I'll finish up slightly premature. Keep me warm, and get me to an infant life-support system.''

"How will I know?''

"I'll cry normally.''

"And you'll forget everything. . . .''

"According to what I know about the process, yes. And if you don't tell me about it, I'll never look for it. It will all be there, of course; as a fact, going through Change makes it stronger, but I'll lose conscious continuity with how to do it. The terrible secret ends in this chamber. And in a sense, those who wished me terminated gained their wish. Their enemy will have ended.

And they will ruin themselves, thinking that they succeeded in protecting their secret, but they'll overstep, and by their own arrogance be ground to a powder. And you'll have a child, and I'll have my innocence back.''

"You never lost it. That was why. . . .''

"I know. Now quiet.''

Nazarine had long thought about this moment, for a long time thinking it would come after many long years and adventures, or else dreading what she would have to do. And in either case, she imagined that it would be difficult to reach for that particular trance state of consciousness necessary to set Change off. But it wasn't. She felt no fear and sank easily down through the layers of imagination, of dream, of hallucination, of atavistic visions, to the central ground of the inner vision.

To Faren, who hadn't known what to expect, it looked like nothing: the girl seemed to relax, sink into herself, breathing deeply but quietly, almost as if she were sleeping, and then she looked up, with a face that was suddenly clear of all doubts that had colored it before. Whatever she might have seen in the lines and planes of that face before, coquetry or innocence, or open concern, that was nothing to what she saw now.

Nazarine said, "It's done, and coming fast. Are you ready?''

"I can handle it; I helped clean up after the Onswud riots in '83 on Kopal.''

"There's not enough time to say the words I want to, to imagine all the things that might have been.''

"Never mind. I know them, too. We'd just be repeating each other. I saw the possibilities, too.''

"Teach me, next time aro . . .'' She stopped in mid-word, and her eyes glazed over, losing their lucid translucency and becoming blank as china eyes painted on a doll. Faren got up and reached for Nazarine, touching her face. It was burning hot, damp, feverish, and beneath the skin she could feel the muscles of her face rigid, working against each other. She moved the girl's body, carefully, like a bomb preparing to go off, and gently slid her off the bunk onto the floor, where she laid her down on her side. She bent close and looked at those terrible blind eyes. "Nazarine? Can you hear me?'' The girl made no sign she had heard, but continued to stare sightlessly ahead of herself onto an imaginary point under the other bunk.

Faren straightened, kneeling on the floor beside Nazarine, and pulled the pocket communicator out of her coveralls. She made two calls in rapid succession, one to Central Maintenance Scheduling, and one to Dorje, and then she replaced the unit, and bent forward once more. She brushed the loose brown curls back from Nazarine's forehead, and kissed the girl's hot cheek, gently, as one might kiss a child goodnight. And she said, in a soft voice no one heard save herself, "Go without fear. You knew us rightly and we'll do it right. You're safe." Then she sat back on her haunches and waited for the transformations Nazarine had told her would come, a series of controlled destructive changes that would reduce her to an infant. It would be several days, possibly as long as a week. She did not worry; there was food in the emergency locker. Not without fear, but with a sense of engagement she had never known before, Faren Kiricky sat back, still gently stroking the soft curls, and waited.

"Some say the evil of our days is love of machines over people, or of money; others speak of drugs, or of debauchery, but I disagree: it is nothing more than love of authority without responsibility. There is a remedy, but few choose it even for themselves, and fewer still for all."

—H. C., Atropine

A GALAXY OF SCIENCE FICTION STARS!